KISS MARRY KILL

Iron-Clad Security

Sidney Halston

SMP Swerve

AN IMPRINT OF ST. MARTIN'S PRESS

KISS MARRY KILL. Copyright © 2017 by Sidney Halston. All rights reserved. Printed in the United States of America. For information address St. Martin's Press, 175 Fifth Avenue, New York, N.Y. 10010.

www.stmartins.com

Cover design © Okay Creations
Cover photographs: man running © Hubskyi Mark / Shutterstock

ISBN 978-1-250-13242-0 (e-book)
ISBN 978-1-250-14498-0 (trade paperback)

First Edition: March 2017

Chapter 1

"Promise me, you'll be happy," he sang from the other side of the door. "Promise me, you'll always sing. Promise me you'll never settle...." He jiggled the door handle. "Meggy? Where are you, my little mouse?" he said in a singsong voice, sounding nice enough. Soft enough. Safe enough. But Megan Cruz knew better. The man trying to lure her out of her enormous walk-in closet was deranged.

Megan huddled in a corner behind all of her cocktail dresses, her knees pushed up and a butcher knife in one of her trembling hands. Just waiting. Waiting for the cops to show up, or for Ryan to finally find her. If she could stop breathing, she would. Trying to stay perfectly still and utterly quiet was an impossible feat with her hands shaking so violently. Surely he could hear her fear from where he stood on the other side of the door. If he walked deep enough into the closet, the dresses that served as a barrier between them would not be sufficient to shield her. And the fact that he'd broken into her house in the middle of the night was a good indication that he did want to hurt her.

Twenty minutes earlier she had been sitting on her bed, completely immersed in writing some lyrics in her notebook, when she heard the sound of a window shattering downstairs. Her house may have been huge, but it wouldn't take long for whoever had broken in to find her, especially since her room was the first one up the grand staircase, even more obvious because of its huge double doors. Not about to sit and wait to find out if it was her stalker or a robber who had broken in, she immediately sent a text to her parents who lived close by, praying they'd understand the message: Break in. 911. Help! Then she silenced her phone and tucked it into her bra. She had also grabbed the enormous butcher knife she'd hid under mattress six months ago when Ryan had started sending her disturbing emails and letters. At that time she'd thought he was just an overzealous fan and had worried she was being overly cautious, but now, as she cowered in fear, she realized how wrong she'd been.

Megan actually held her breath when she heard the squeaky noise of the hinges of her closet door. He was inside now. Sweat dripped down her back and her heart pounded so loudly it seemed he had to have heard it. It felt as if it was going to physically come out of her chest, together with the sandwich she'd eaten a few hours ago. Peering under the hanging clothes she could see green

Converse sneakers moving closer to where she sat curled into a small ball, her arms around her knees.

"Oh, Meggy, where are you? Sing for me, my naughty little mouse. Just one song. Just 'Promise Me,' that's my favorite." As he stepped closer, she tightened her grip on the knife. "You're supposed to make your fans happy." His voice was louder and more agitated this time.

She could hear the fabric running through his fingers as he caressed her clothes, shifting the fragile curtain of dresses and shirts she was hiding behind.

"Oh, this is what you wore to the Grammys last month!" He pulled the dress out, and Megan tensed when a sliver of light cut through her hiding place. The small gap where the dress had hung made her more visible, and if he happened to look down he'd undoubtedly see her on the floor behind the rest of the clothes. She shut her eyes.

"This is perfect. You can wear this when you sing for me at my house. Does anyone else know how much you love the chase, Meggy? Am I the only one that knows your secret? I have your new room all ready for you. We can play and sing all the time. . . . It'll be so fun, Meggy." His feet were moving slowly, as if he had all the time in the world.

She could tell he was directly in front of her now by how close the sound of his heavy breathing was and by the way the rubber soles of his sneakers skidded against the wood floor.

She shut her eyes harder and braced herself.

She didn't need her eyes open to see him—the memory was burned into her brain. His face was unassuming and his body unimposing. White skin, rounded cheeks, kind-looking face, maybe even cute, if he wasn't a complete sociopath. He wasn't too thin or too large, not too tall, not too short. Just an ordinary-looking guy. One you would smile at in line for coffee or at the grocery store. The nonthreatening Good Samaritan who helped you with your flat tire. Completely harmless, completely average, except for his eyes, gray eyes that were a bit too large and had a slight tilt upward, reminding her of a cat. Gray eyes that could be considered attractive if it weren't for the coldness behind them.

Megan didn't want to die looking into that coldness. She didn't want to die hiding in her closet, with the creepy man asking her to sing the song that was about the best four days of her entire life. The four days that also changed the course of her life. Ironic, she would potentially die thinking of those memories.

"Come on, Meggy, where are you hiding? Don't make me get upset at you. I don't think I want to play anymore." She opened her eyes and the green Converses turned as if he was going to leave, but stopped. The tips of his shoes were mere inches from her bare feet, which were tight against her body. She pressed her heel even closer to her butt. Oh, how she wished she was more flexible or had been consistent with her Pilates classes. Because right now, she had no place to go. She was cornered, and she couldn't make herself any smaller than she already was. All that separated her from the nightmare was the clothing hanging between them. His rank smell of perspiration filled her nostrils and made her want to gag, causing her to breathe through her mouth instead of her nose. She was afraid to look up and find him staring back at her with those deranged gray eyes. Fear bubbled up in her throat, and holding back a terrified scream was nearly choking her.

A sudden banging from downstairs made her jerk, and she saw his feet move quickly out of the closet. There was another bang and then another loud noise, like her front door being rammed open, followed by voices. She had her hands over her ears and her face tucked into her knees. Then it was quiet.

Jackson "Jax" Irons sat in the situation room of Iron-Clad Security watching two of his best recruits get ambushed in the middle of the Syrian Desert.

"Fucking hell, Josef!" Jax barked, standing up and leaning forward, his eyes monitoring the dots in motion on the multiple screens. It was pitch-black in the desert at this time and even with the infrared satellite imaging it was impossible to see more than colored dots, each of which represented one of the insurgents—colored dots that were getting closer and closer to their team. It was like a shit version of an eighties Atari video game, but in this game the loser always got dead.

"Damn intel!" Josef, Jax's best friend and the co-owner of Iron-Clad Security, threw down his headset. "This shit happens with Fed jobs every fucking time!" He typed something into the computer that brought up a wider aerial view of the location on one of the monitors. Mountains ringed their men from the back and to the west. Essentially, they were trapped.

"They just need to stay alive for two more goddamn minutes, Joey," Jax shouted—as if Josef had any control over the FUBAR scene playing out in front of them. Leaning into the conference call system in the middle of the table, Jax pressed the speaker button that connected him to his team abroad. "Hang tight. Cavalry is ninety seconds out." Jesus, he was getting too damn old for this shit. Sweat trailed down his back and his heart beat rapidly against his chest as he stared at the screens in front of the room. ICS hadn't lost a man yet, and today wouldn't be the day.

Joey stood by the table, looking at the dots come closer and closer to their men as the insurgents neared.

Where the fuck was backup? Jax ran a hand down his face and gripped his beard. These guys had families, wives, kids. The in-and-out mission was supposed to be simple, easy, meant to get the new recruits' feet wet. He'd practically guaranteed his team's safety when he'd recruited them for the job.

But nothing about this damn op had gone according to plan. He should've been there with them. He'd taken on and planned the mission, and he normally went himself. Except that his leg had been acting up and like a pussy, he'd heeded Joey's advice and sent Brian and Jason instead.

They never went on a mission blind, but here he was, blind as a fucking bat.

"ETA?" Joey barked into the phone. Then the sound coming from the speaker changed and his pulse calmed at hearing the familiar *whop whop* sound of helicopter blades cutting through the air. "Jesus, they're finally there," Joey sighed, turning back to the speaker. "Heads up, boys. Bird incoming to your east."

Jax tensed when the sound of a firefight erupted through the coms. "Fuck!" he roared, pressing the speaker button. "Heads down. Asses on the chopper.

Don't get fucking shot!"

"Goddamn clusterfuck," Joey said, typing into the screen to zoom closer to the scene unfolding.

Instead of the voices of the crew assuring them of their safety, a jumbled cacophony of noises—gunshots, men cursing, and the blades from the approaching helicopter—came in through the com.

Joey and Jax looked at the screen with bated breath, red flares indicating firing, either from guns or from explosives. The muffled voices of their men and now the crew in the sky made it difficult to ascertain who was under attack. After agonizing minutes, the noise cleared.

"We're on," Brian's voice called out from the speaker. "Target in hand, minor injuries, nothing serious. All men accounted for."

Joey slammed his palm on the table and slid down into his chair. "I just aged ten years. It was too close this time. A few more minutes and they'd have come back in body bags."

Jax pressed the button on the speaker. "Good job. Get some rest. We'll touch base when you get back." Then he too slid down into the nearest chair. Normally, they had other members of the team at the ready but this was supposed to be an easy mission. No muss no fuss. Mister X had a USB drive with info from a high-level Syrian official that he was willing to sell to Uncle Sam by way of ICS for the right price. The fucker was being paid millions by the US of A. The team had been assured he was trustworthy and had been vetted carefully. ICS was hired merely to connect up with Mister X and retrieve and extract the USB drive. Simple enough.

An ambush two miles out of the city had not been part of the motherfucking plan.

"I've been here for twenty fucking hours. I'm out. Need a drink," Jax said, slapping Joey's shoulder before leaving his best friend and partner to handle the debrief.

———————

Ten minutes later, Jax sat in a corner of Yellowstreet, a dive bar a block from his apartment in Miami, nursing a beer. It was the bar he always went to after long hours at work—it reminded him of the shitholes he'd frequented with his unit years ago when they were on pass for the weekend. The stale beer, old nuts, sticky floor, and smell of cigarettes were comforting. It was the first time in weeks he'd been able to have a moment to himself, and downing a beer at Yellowstreet was how he wanted to spend it.

His leg had been acting up for a while, but today the metal plates felt like razor blades rubbing against his muscles. Why did he always do this to himself? He must be some sort of masochist, because between the bullshit mission earlier today and the pain in this leg, Yellowstreet would do nothing but serve as a reminder of all that he'd lost. And damn it, he'd lost a lot.

His second tour in Iraq had been cut short fourteen months ago due to an ambush at base that killed five of his seven guys. He himself had suffered extensive injuries to the right side of his body, injuries that had led to half a year in a German hospital. Eight months ago he was honorably discharged and came back home to Miami with a slight limp, recurring hip pain, and a shitload of survivor's guilt. The only souvenir he'd gotten in return was all the metal used to fuse together his femur. And Miami's humidity made it probably the worst possible place to live with all that metal. But Miami was home, so now, together with his best friend and US Marine brother Joey Clad, he co-owned Iron-Clad Security.

ICS had been his unit's dream—their exit plan once they left the military and the godforsaken heat of the Middle East behind. A dream of opening a security firm stateside that would utilize each of their specific skill sets, from overseeing the security plans for a new company, to an unusual hacking request from a spurned wife, to corporate espionage or bodyguard work for a dignitary or a movie star. But then most of his men—his friends—hadn't made it back alive and so the eight-man security firm became a two-man team. And since Jax was six foot two and excelled in hand-to-hand combat, he was the muscle behind ICS while Joey was the brains. When there was a request for a bodyguard or security detail, Jax did it. When there was a cyber-security issue or a need for surveillance or infiltration, Joey was the man for the job.

Stretching his hurt leg, Jax leaned back in his booth to watch the Miami Marlins play the Red Sox, something that always brought him joy. Just last month he'd gone to the home opener, like he did every year except for the few times he'd been abroad. But lately even baseball made him nostalgic, bringing up too many memories. Memories of times that could never be recreated.

Feeling melancholic, Jax had a beer mug up to his lips when the baseball game on the flatscreen was interrupted by the local news.

We are just getting reports that local celebrity Megan Cruz, lead singer of TNT, was assaulted in her home on Star Island about an hour ago. It is uncertain whether Cruz is hurt. Cruz has previously reported two incidents involving a stalker. It is unclear whether those two incidents are connected to this one. What is known, however, is that the per-

petrator was able to escape through a window before being apprehended by the authorities. Stay tuned for more information on the eleven o'clock news. If you have information you are urged to call . . .

Jax almost dropped his beer. A stock photo of Megan was staring back at him on the television.

Megan Cruz? *My Megan Cruz?*

Stalker?

Lead singer?

When he'd known Megan, she was an ultraconservative, sheltered twenty-two-year-old about to start law school. He wasn't sure which of the two statements—stalker or singer—shocked him most, but the stalking was definitely what had him immediately on the move.

His heart faltered. What if she was hurt? Even though it had been too many years since he'd last seen her, knowing she was out there somewhere had helped get him through some rough days. She was an idealized memory of a perfect time and place. Always, he pictured her in a house with a white picket fence and children surrounding her. In his vivid imagination, she was always content. And even if it hurt him somewhere deep and hollow that her imagined happy life did not include him, it was okay because he'd always wanted the best for her.

But a world where there was no Megan Cruz? That

was a world he wanted no part of. And of all the things he imagined she was up to, all these years later, her being hurt—or worse, dead—was never even in the realm of possibility.

The news hit him like a two-by-four to the head.

Without a second thought, he tossed some money on the table and jogged out of the bar, a surge of anxiety hitting him all at once. Not bothering to put on his helmet, he hopped onto his Harley Fat Boy and took off for Star Island, which was just a few miles away. His heart was beating so rapidly he had to literally close his eyes and count to ten at a stoplight, just like he'd learned in therapy.

What was he even doing? Barging in on Megan because of a report he'd seen on the television? It had been too many years. She probably didn't even know who he was. Was he insane?

Fuck yeah he was.

When it came to Megan, he'd always been off his game. But he was going to go see with his own two eyes what the hell was happening. If nothing else, he could offer her his services: ICS was, after all, the best security firm in Miami.

Yeah, that's why he was hightailing it to Star Island, because he wanted to work for her. Who was he kidding?

On his way, Jax used his Bluetooth to call Joey and

tell him to put together all the information possible on Megan. Joey was, after all, the best damn hacker the military had ever honorably discharged. He needed to know everything he'd missed in order to help her, assuming she needed help. But he couldn't do that if he had absolutely no clue who she was anymore.

It had been five years since he'd seen Megan, and fuck, all the memories he'd kept locked up in the back crevices of his mind began to seep in just from seeing her for a couple of seconds on that damn news report. Which meant he needed to get his shit together before he got to her house and came face to face with her. Even if they'd only known each other for a brief moment in time years ago, he didn't think he could recover if something were to happen to her.

He drove all the way to Star Island doing something he hadn't done in years—praying.

Chapter 2

Star Island, population ninety-eight, was a small man-made island right off the coast of South Beach, where only the filthiest of the rich and famous resided. There was only one way in or out, and Jax instructed Joey to make sure he'd have full access onto the heavily secured island.

With little patience left, Jax almost yelled when he saw security guards forcing reporters and visitors off the island. He was ready to fight his way in if he had to. Fortunately, Joey had seen this obstacle coming, and had cleared a way for Jax to ride straight in as soon as the guard saw him pull up. Joey had always been this way—detailed, thorough, and analytical, where Jax was mostly a hothead who reacted first and apologized later. Or at least that's what his commanding officers had said about him when he was awarded a Purple Heart. Sometimes action needed to be taken without time to plan and analyze, and Jax was a man of action and passion—fear rarely factored in.

A cluster of police cars was all the evidence he needed to discover which house was Megan's. As he parked his bike, his phone signaled an incoming text from Joey. Apparently Megan had been busy since the last time he saw her. The brief dossier Joey had quickly compiled said she was now the lead singer of a very successful band called TNT. Pride soared through Jax's body when he saw her net worth and all her accolades, including a recent Grammy win.

This was a far cry from the picket fence life he'd imagined.

His Megan was living in a huge house on an exclusive island, and she was a damn rock star.

House.

That was an understatement if there ever was one.

It was a white Spanish-style mansion with red barrel tiles lining the roof and intricate iron work over the windows, complete with a very elaborate tropical garden and rows of palm trees lining the long walkway up to the regal double keystone stairway. It was hard to say which was more astounding: the mansion or the garden. Between the palm trees and the fuchsia bougainvilleas, there were rows of well-groomed ficus and topiaries, making it look like something you'd find hidden in a Caribbean island secluded from the rest of the world. And because of the heavy security and the small number of residents on Star Island, this was as close to a tropical paradise as one could find in Miami.

His first thought was that protecting a house of this magnitude was going to be a bitch, especially with all the trees and extravagant landscaping.

"Excuse me, sir." A police officer stopped him as he ascended the staircase.

Luckily, with the jobs he'd done in the last few months, he'd become all too familiar with local law enforcement. Being that this was a high-profile case, Marco Martinez, the chief of police, was nearby shouting orders when he saw Jax.

"Irons. What're you doing here?"

"Friend of the victim, and possible new client. Bring me up to speed."

Marco tipped his chin and Jax followed. "Not sure yet. Here's what we know. Victim has previously reported two prior incidents with a male named Ryan, last name unknown, six-foot, approximately two hundred pounds, Caucasian, gray eyes. Looks like the perp climbed the gates by the east side of the house, came in through the window by the atrium." Marco pointed to the other side of the house. "And—"

"Security didn't go off?"

"Seems she didn't have it on. We haven't been able to speak with the victim yet, which is another reason we haven't confirmed whether it is, in fact, Ryan." Irritated, Jax shook his head. Why have a security system and not use it? In his line of work he saw these kinds of things all the time and it always drove him absolutely insane.

"Why not? Why haven't you confirmed it yet?" He was anxious to get to the point: where was Megan and was she safe? Knowing he was pushing his luck by questioning Marco so disrespectfully, he waited for a response before he went apeshit on everyone for not getting answers. For not apprehending the suspect. For not doing their goddamn jobs.

"Waiting for family to arrive. She won't leave the closet."

"What?" Jax pushed Marco aside, not waiting to finish the debriefing. "Where?" He barked, his nerves at a level ten.

Marco pointed up the long marble staircase inside the house. "Up the stairs, last room down the hall." Jax took two steps at a time. Still charged from the earlier mission, adrenaline coursed through his body. Two cops stood by the door of the bedroom while one female officer hunched down in the closet, apparently trying to gently coax Megan out. There was also a cop gathering prints by the window.

"Out!" Jax snarled. Everyone looked at him suspiciously but he didn't leave any room for discussion as he herded everyone out, and closed the door behind them. Even knowing he didn't have a claim to be there, to feel this protective over her, or this irrational concern, he still felt that she needed a familiar face. The face of someone who'd treat her with care and concern. Not someone who looked at her as just another victim or witness, or worse, a celebrity they could exploit in the media.

Cautiously, he stepped into the closet. He could see Megan's toes peeking out from underneath some hanging dresses. Crouching down, he moved the dresses aside and then his heart shattered into so many pieces. He was left breathless.

Looking like a tiny ball in the corner, Megan rocked back and forth, her hands covering her ears, her eyes tightly shut. She was humming. Roughly sliding the group of dresses to the side, knocking a few of them off the hangers, he sat in front of her.

"Hey, Meg," he said softly, careful not to startle her further. "Megan, sweetheart." He wanted to kill whoever did this to her. She looked broken. "Megan?" He tried to gently pry her hands away from her ears as he spoke. Finally, she looked up at him, those big brown eyes he remembered all too clearly. At first her face was void of any recognition, as if she was looking through him instead of at him. But then—then—they widened. "Hey you, remember me?" And if his heart hadn't shattered a moment ago, her face crumbling as recognition set in completely tore him apart.

"Don't cry," he soothed, keeping his voice soft and easy as he lifted her up and carried her out of the closet.

"Is that you? Am I dreaming this?" she asked, touching all the lines and contours on his face, cataloging the changes, her eyes wide and filled with both fear and amazement. He wondered if he looked the same to her. To him, she looked different, but good different. Fucking fantastic different. And this was just at a cursory glimpse. He couldn't wait to really *really* look at her. But right now, he needed to focus, it wasn't the time to get lost in those big brown eyes of hers.

"I wish you were. I wish this had all been just a bad dream."

She tucked her face into his neck, wiping the last of her tears against his shirt. "It's a nightmare, all of it." Seeing her this way made him physically ache to make everything all right for her.

"Hey, it's okay," he said, carefully depositing her onto the bed. He went to stand up but she whimpered and grabbed hold of his shirt, her hands trembling and her eyes wide and panicked. "No. No. Don't go!" She looked petrified, so he sat down with her and held her until the crying subsided. The rush of memories and emotions was almost too much. His grip around her was maybe too tight, but he needed to hold her again, tight against his chest. Maybe this would be the last time he got the opportunity and he wasn't going to squander it. His heart raced and . . . Jesus Christ were those goddamn butterflies in his stomach? This was the only woman who could do that to him in a matter of seconds. It's as if something inside him, inside his soul, was finally whole again. He'd been missing her for far too long, even if he tried so hard never to think about her. And goddamn it, he was thinking in fucking poetry now.

How many times had he held her in the few short days they'd stayed holed up together all those years back? She was soft and warm back then. Now, she was curvier but stronger, and shivering from fear. Would it be appropriate to take off the rubber band from the knot on top of her head and run his fingers through all that thick brown silk? He could pretend it was for her well-being, to comfort her. Women loved for their hair to be touched, their scalp massaged, right? It wouldn't be for his own need or naughty memories—it would be all for her. *Bullshit. Get it together, Jax!*

"Did he hurt you?" he finally asked, almost scared to know. "Are you hurt?"

"No. He wanted me to sing. He was only inches away, but he didn't see me. He was going to hurt me. I know he was. Oh God, please tell me they got him?"

"Shhh," He stroked her back and rocked gently back and forth. "Calm down. He's not here. You're safe."

"But they didn't catch him, did they?"

He shook his head and she took a deep breath. "Wh-what are you even doing here, Jax?"

"You know, just in the neighborhood. Came by to say hi," he teased, trying to lighten the mood. She looked up and gave him a watery smile in return. "I saw it on television and came right over."

Sitting up, Megan blew out a breath. "God, I was so scared." Her voice shook when she spoke and her nails dug into his forearms, but he didn't say anything because if clawing him made her feel even a little bit better, she could keep doing it and he would never ever complain.

And that's when he realized: *What kind of asshole fantasized about hair or the way she felt against him when the beautiful woman shaking with fear needed him?*

Shifting slightly, he pushed down his feelings and tried to take control of the situation. In war, he never thought of the injured or dead bodies around him or the pain he felt when a bullet hit—those were thoughts you dealt with *after* the threat was gone. A soldier didn't break when the shit was going down. If they were going to break down, they did it after—during the calm, not in the middle of the fucking storm. During the storm, they were the ones that people counted on to get them through. Right now, he was still in the battlefield and bullets were flying. It was time to put his shit on lockdown.

"Do you think you can answer some questions? The police are waiting downstairs." Holding her like this, it was difficult to let her go, but cuddling her wasn't going to keep her safe, and in that moment Jax vowed he would do whatever it took to keep this woman safe.

"Shoot. Yeah, I guess I can talk." She wiped her face with the back of her hand and shifted to stand up, but he stopped her.

"Wait, do you have a robe?" He had been so preoc-cupied he hadn't noticed that she was wearing just a T-shirt, and that body he remembered so vividly was still there, maybe a little curvier, a little more enticing. Look-ing down at her bare legs, she gasped softly and avoided his eyes. She pulled the shirt lower and pointed to the bathroom, and he retrieved it. "Don't be embarrassed," he said when he got back. He lifted her chin so she would look at him. "With me you can walk around naked if you want, it's just with all the other men around, I want you covered up." He knew his tone was not at all light, and he didn't have the right to be possessive, but if he had any say, he would not allow any other men to look at her barely clothed.

With a shy smile, still holding her shirt down, she said, "I don't remember you being so caveman-ish."

"You have a terrible memory, then."

Rolling her eyes, but actually smiling in earnest now,

she snatched the robe out of his hands and slipped it on.

"Joking aside, Megan. Are you okay?"

"No. Not really. I just want to get this over with. Talk to whomever is waiting and forget this night ever happened."

Forget this night ever happened? He knew she was talking about the nightmare of the break-in, but he'd be lying if he said he wanted to forget one second of seeing Megan again. Even if the situation sucked, it did serve to bring them together again. But the truth was, every moment that passed without her giving a statement was an extra leg up they were giving the perp.

"Come on, let's go talk to the cops. You're right, we need to get this over with."

As she finished tying the robe, the door swung open and two women rushed in, an older woman who looked a lot like Megan and a blond in her early thirties.

"Megan!" The older woman said, embracing her as everyone talked at once. There was no way any of them knew what the other was saying. As they hugged and cried, he couldn't take his eyes off of Megan. Not just because she was gorgeous, but because he wanted—no, needed—to make sure she was really okay.

"Are you hurt? I knew this would happen. I knew it. This music thing is—"

"Mom, not now." Megan mumbled, sounding irritated.

"Meg—"

"No. I don't need a lecture right now, Mother."

God, she was stunning, all the emotions showing brightly through her expressive eyes. She was even more beautiful then he'd remembered, and he'd remembered a lot. Now, though, her eyes showed fear and annoyance and he was as anxious as she was for the police to take her statement. Experience dictated that the longer it took to get her statement the longer it would take to find the perp.

"It's not a lecture, Megan. It's the truth. These kinds of things don't happen to lawyers. It's ridiculous—"

Watching Megan get beat down was enough to send his temper flaring. She'd had a horrible day, probably the worst of her entire life, and this woman—her mother—was giving her grief instead of comfort? Jax was doing everything he could to keep his temper and agitation at bay but he wasn't there on a social visit and neither was her mother. They were all there for one reason—because Megan's house had been broken into. She'd been in danger and there was a guy on the loose who could come back at any time.

Focus. Purpose. Action.

The Marines had trained him to be a quick, quiet, and effective machine. They didn't teach about heart and feelings. He'd already spent too much time calming her down and reminiscing about shit he had no reason to be thinking about—like her hair and her body. There was no time to waste with tears and affection. Those things didn't mean shit when survival was at stake.

———————

Jackson Irons was in her bedroom.

Megan could barely believe it.

If she hadn't been so preoccupied with the events of the night, she'd have thought it was a hallucination, her terrified mind conjuring up the one memory that always made her feel happy and safe. Except it was real—he was there. Touching her, comforting her, even taking control. And she needed that. God, did she ever. She was so shaken up, she didn't even know where to start or what to do.

Ironically, though, while he'd been holding her, she'd almost—almost—forgotten about the stalker, so consumed she was with the familiar smell and feel of the man she hadn't seen in so damn long. It had taken her a moment to even realize it was him, he was so wide and intimidating now, and those once-soft green eyes looked hardened and threatening—even if he was trying to keep it under control for her sake. The lean, clean-shaven, all-American guy she'd once known had transformed into a scruffy man with a full mountain-man blondish beard, hair down to his shoulders, twenty pounds of new muscles, and a twitch in his jaw.

He was treating her as if she was the most fragile thing in the world. As if her fear shook *him* to *his* core. But then he'd noticed she was only wearing a shirt and she thought she'd die of mortification. Even if her feminine pride soared with the look of desire and possessiveness that had helped lighten the mood just enough for her to get through the next few hours of reliving the horrible experience.

But all of that had changed again in a second when her mother had opened her big fat Cuban mouth. The woman, who Megan had to constantly remind herself she loved, was like a damn needle pricking the metaphorical balloon and letting all the happiness seep right out. You could practically hear the hissing. All the air left the room, and Jax's jaw tightened and his fists clenched at his side as her mom began to give her uninvited opinions.

A minute ago he'd held her until she had run out of tears, being her anchor in a storm. He had been protective and consoling, but now? Now he looked murderous. She had so many questions to ask him she didn't even know where to start, not with everything else that had happened in the last two hours.

"Well, can you at least tell me if you're okay?" Her

mother Rose asked, holding her at arm's length, checking for injuries. Sometimes it was hard to tell whether her mother loved her. Megan knew that deep down she did. But she had a strange way of showing it. Her concern normally came masked in criticism and she was the queen of backhanded compliments. Even though she loved her mother, she could only take her in measured doses.

"Did he hurt you?" Nelly Leon, the drummer of TNT and one of her best friends, asked, her hand over her mouth and tears in her eyes. Nelly, TNT's mother hen and worrywart, had a soft and sweet look to her that made you want to comfort her, even if you were the one in need of comforting. Except when she was on stage. On stage she was a beast on the drums. She had an intensity in her eyes and a strength in her skills that made her one of the fiercest drummers of her generation.

"I think I'm okay. Just shaken up—" Megan began. She was cut off when Jax pulled her away.

"Of course she's shaken up. There was a murder—" Jesus Christ. Her mother had zero comforting skills.

"Sorry to break this up but you need to get moving. The cops are waiting. Tears later." His voice was harsh, but his touch on her wrist was soft as he glared at Rose. He didn't seem like the guy who stole her heart five years ago. The carefree dude who liked to hang out and fish, the guy who'd tested all her boundaries and made her question all her decisions within hours of meeting him. This man standing in front of her was hardened. If not for the fact that he'd held her tenderly just minutes earlier, she would have called him robotic and cold.

Rose and Nelly eyed Jax but he didn't notice. Or if he did, he didn't care. Instead he pulled Megan out of the room and began to snap at the nearby men, Megan too consumed by a myriad of emotions to react. "Martinez, she's ready. In the kitchen. One man, tops. I want a full brief of the situation as soon as she's done."

"We can discuss while she gives her statement." Martinez said.

"No. I stay with her." Jax's voice was firm, no-nonsense, and he turned to Megan. "Kitchen?"

Was that a question?

Megan shook her head in confusion. "Uh . . . downstairs to the right." He laced his fingers with hers and pulled her down the stairs. Back then, he'd held her hand a lot, it was one of the things that she loved about him. He had been so affectionate, and that was something that had always been missing in her life. Right now, his touch helped clear some of the chaos from her mind. The new Jax was clearly rougher around the edges, but there was no denying that his touch still soothed her, gave her strength and confidence when she was feeling scared and defeated. The circumstances back then may have been different, but the feelings he drew out of her were the same. She'd felt helpless back then, but by the time he'd walked out of her life she felt secure and confident.

"Wait," her mother called from behind her. "I'll stay with her. I'm an attorney."

Jax squared his shoulders, his grip tightening on Megan's hand when he faced her mother and his face set in a calm mask that didn't invite questions. "She doesn't need an attorney. She needs to tell the officers what happened and she needs to do so right now." And then added, so faint only Megan could hear. "Some motherly compassion would've been nice too."

"I'm her moth—"

"Mother, it's okay. Please just let me get this over with." Megan turned to Nelly. "Nell, can you and my mom please go check on the officers in my room. All my dresses are scattered all over my closet, and I'd like them *not* to get ruined."

"Oh, the Gucci," Nell said, seemingly heartbroken. If it wasn't for the dire situation at hand, Nelly's distraught reaction to the dresses, which Megan couldn't care less about, would have been comical. "Come on, Rose, let's go help upstairs."

"Fine," Rose huffed, knowing full well Megan was trying to get rid of her, and followed Nelly back upstairs while Megan and Jax headed to the kitchen.

Jax pulled out a chair for her. After she sat, he crossed his arms over his chest and stayed beside her, standing there like an aggravated and on-edge wall of muscles. Anger, frustration, and impatience oozed off him, and she missed his touch almost immediately.

Everything was a blur, things happening too fast. Her mind had yet to catch up—still trying to process the fact that one second she was almost killed and the next Jax was there. Jax, who seemed to have materialized from nowhere after so long. It was all too much. She was trying to compose herself, closing her eyes and counting to ten, when a police officer walked into the room. All she wanted was that strength back, that anchor, and if he wasn't so closed-off right now, she'd reach up and grab Jax's hand. Now she felt alone and scared all over again. She wasn't the kind of woman who needed a man, but Jax wasn't just any man. He was *the* man. The one she'd always compared other men to.

"Megan," Jax prompted her, nudging her shoulder lightly. She looked up at him, his face expressionless, and the beard did nothing to soothe things. In fact, it made him seem that much more impassive.

"Oh, uh, sorry, what did you say?" she asked the officer, embarrassment causing her to blush. She'd been caught staring at Jax and wondering what she could do to shake some emotion out of him. Something less soldier, and something more . . . she almost thought "boyfriend." But he had never been her boyfriend. And this time was no different. She needed to rid herself of her unrealistic fantasies and focus on the current crappy situation she was in. She needed to remember he was only there because she'd been in danger—otherwise, she would never have seen him again.

And that thought was sobering.

Sitting up straighter, her hands laced together in her lap, she turned her attention to the cop.

"I said I'm sorry to meet you under these circumstances, Ms. Cruz. My name is Officer Kline. I need to ask you a few questions, okay?" She nodded and he continued. "First off, how are you hanging in there? You okay?"

"I'm shaken up, but I'm otherwise okay." She could hear her own voice shake when she spoke. Clearing her throat, she continued. "I just want to get this over with." It was true. She was okay, or at least she would be. The last five years had hardened her a bit, taught her independence, and she wasn't going to let a crazy fan screw with all the progress she'd made. Meek, do-whatever-everyone-wants, people-pleasing Megan was long gone, and she was going to stay gone. Megan liked who'd she'd become and she wasn't going to let anyone or anything change that.

"Good. Can you tell me your full name, please?"

"Megan Marie Cruz."

"Ms. Cruz—"

"Please call me Megan."

"Okay, Megan, can you tell me what happened?"

Chewing on her thumbnail, she began. "I was sitting on my bed writing some music. It was probably around ten when I heard a window break. I grabbed my phone, sent my parents a quick text to call 911, and ran to hide in the closet, which is where you guys found me. From the closet, I could hear the sounds of someone in the house, walking around the kitchen, coming up the stars. He talked to me, asking me to come out, and then he came into the closet." Her voice broke in a soft sob before she could continue. "He told me he had a room ready for me at his home." The officer scribbled notes on his pad and she took the opportunity to look up, finding Jax's eyes narrowed on her trembling hands. Quickly, she sat on them and faced the officer again.

"Did you see the suspect?"

God, why was she so damn nervous? The threat was gone. She was safe. So why was her leg uncontrollably bobbing up and down? "I didn't see his face. I only saw his shoes."

"Any idea who it could be, or a motive of some sort?"

"I—I am pretty sure it's this guy named Ryan. I don't

know his last name, he was someone I met a year and a half ago after a concert."

"Pretty sure?"

"No, no, I'm sure," she said, confidently. It was the first time tonight she'd said anything confidently. But she knew, without any hesitation, it was Ryan who was in her house tonight. Just thinking of him made her break out in goose bumps.

Two warm hands pressed against her shoulder, startling her. She was so damn wound up. Jax leaned down. "You okay?" he whispered by her ear. It was soft and thoughtful, like he'd been earlier today, and his beard tickled her cheek slightly. Now she wasn't sure if the goose bumps were from fear or from his mouth so close to her ear.

"I—I'm fine."

He stood back up, eyeing her warily before returning to his bodyguard stance.

"How can you be so sure, Ms. Cruz? You said you didn't see him." Megan's head whipped back to the officer, surprised by his accusatory tone.

Jax picked up on the tone immediately, and spoke first, his voice hard with warning. "She's the victim here, not a suspect. Do I need to call Chief Martinez to handle this?"

The officer seemed taken aback by Jax's interruption and turned his attention back to Megan. She was so thankful Jax was there. She needed someone on her side. Someone she trusted, someone who would want to see her safe. At that moment she realized that no matter how much time they'd been apart, there was still a friendship between them, some kind of unbreakable bond. They cared about each other, that much was obvious.

"I'm not accusing you of anything, ma'am. What you went through is horrible, and you're clearly shaken, as is expected. I'm just trying to get all the facts so we can find whoever was here and gather enough evidence to make an arrest."

"I don't appreciate the way you're speaking to me, quite honestly." She was still shaken, but it didn't matter. This line of questioning was unacceptable. The night had sucked, and he was adding to it, and she was done. This night needed to end. "A man broke into my house, walked into my closet, asked me to sing a song. He's deranged. I know it was Ryan. I'm sure of it." She felt Jax's hand squeeze her shoulder, nudging her on, proudly.

She cleared her throat before continuing. "I've reported two separate instances where a fan named Ryan communicated with me. First with a letter and then with a text to my private cell phone, both alluding to some sort of twisted cat-and-mouse game. The letter and email called me his 'little Mouse,' always *his* little Mouse." She paused and looked back at Jax. For some reason, even his scowl was reassuring. "Both were . . . threatening, more so than the normal fan mail, so I reported them. But there was no way of tracing them back to Ryan. The email and letter were a dead end, and because I don't know his last name, where he lives . . . nothing happened."

Thinking about the letter, the intimate way the creep had written about her, the way he had said he'd been watching her all night and how it made him hard, made her want to run back upstairs and hide away in her closet again. Shut out the world and curl into herself. He was singing her song, he wanted her to go to his home with him. . . .

"Megan." Jax's hand brushed lightly over her hair before she'd even realized he'd moved from his post behind her. "What about tonight? What did you notice about the intruder?"

"I know it was Ryan, I heard him," she repeated almost petulantly. Her fists clenched shut in frustration. Jax kneeled, his large frame right next to her, and took her hand in his. Eye to eye, he spoke softly to her. "I believe you. I'm not questioning you because I don't believe you. I just need you to think real hard, Megan. What did he say? What did you hear? Tell the officer as much as you can remember so they can catch the asshole."

She pressed the heels of her palms against her eyes, trying to calm down. "As I said, even if I couldn't see him I recognized Ryan by his voice, by the things he was saying. He was talking to me the whole time, signing my songs back to me. He kept calling me Meggy, his little Mouse, saying he wanted to play, asking me if I liked the chase. Ryan is the only person to ever call me Meggy."

"Good girl." Jax patted her knee before standing up and looking back at the officer, pinning him to his seat with his gaze.

The officer diverted his eyes quickly from Jax back to Megan. "Did you see anything about him? Anything at all? Any identifying information? A tattoo, a birthmark, anything?"

"He had on green Converse sneakers and dark jeans. That's all I could see."

"Anything unusual about his voice?"

"Not really, no. Except that he acted like he *knew* me, like we had a relationship. And like I said, he calls me his little Mouse."

"Why little Mouse?" Jax's voice was sharp, cutting in before Officer Kline could continue.

She wished he would touch her. Her shoulder, her hand, her knee . . . any contact at all felt comforting, and she needed that right now. "When I met Ryan, it was brief but I remember his eyes. He has really unusual eyes, gray and almond-shaped. I told him his eyes reminded me of a cat, which is I'm pretty sure why he calls me a mouse and thinks we're playing some twisted game. I wasn't giving him a pet name, I was just commenting on the way they looked, but he must've taken it as some sort of invitation."

"The officers who found you said you had a knife. How did you have time to come down to the kitchen and grab a knife?" Office Kline asked.

"I didn't. I keep it under my bed."

"Pardon?" The officer asked, at the same time that Jax said, "What?"

Looking up at Jax, she answered. "Since the email six months ago, which is one of the incidents I reported, I started keeping a knife under my bed. Makes me feel better." She shrugged and looked back at the officer. "Maybe I need to get a gun." Her eyes slid to Jax.

"You ever handle a gun, Megan?" Jax asked.

"No."

"Then we'll discuss guns later."

"I'm going to be honest with you, Ms. Cruz, there's not much of a case here. We'll do everything we can to find this guy, but since you didn't actually see him, it'll be tough to prove that this Ryan is the perp who broke in tonight. Without a visual confirmation or physical evidence, and going on just his voice, it's going to be hard for a conviction to stick once we find him. *If* we find him. We don't even have a last name. Or a real place to start." Officer Kline said. This was the third time she'd been told this same exact thing by a police officer. It was such a defeating statement.

"What was I supposed to do? Ask him for identification? I was hiding. I was scared. You can't just tell me there's nothing that can be done! How many times does he have to come back for you guys to help me?" Her palms were on the table and she was leaning toward the officer, her voice trembling.

Jax stood next to her and it felt like some sort of solidarity was happening when he spoke. "That's bullshit and you know it. The shit he's saying? The other incidents? There's an MO, an MO is something to go off of." Jax had his fist on the table and was leaning closer to the officer too.

"Yes, but that's not enough and you, Mr. Irons, know that." The officer stood up and extended his hand, shutting down the conversation. "We'll have a patrol stay in the neighborhood for the next forty-eight hours. You should strongly consider using your security system and advising the island's security," he said, handing her his card and then shaking her hand good-bye.

He stopped and turned before he left the room. "I know you're scared and upset. You have every right to be.

And I'm sorry things feel helpless right now. All I can tell you is to keep your eyes and ears open, and to call us if you remember anything else. I really do want to help if I can."

Her chin quivered and she took a deep breath before nodding in understanding.

"Be right back, Meg. Sit tight," Jax said, following Officer Kline out.

With shaky hands, Megan reached for the secret stash of Nutella she kept in the pantry behind the sugar, which was rarely used since her label hired her a professional chef who believed all white foods were the work of the devil. Today, she needed Nutella.

"Oh my god, you've got the Nutella out. Rose, it's worse than we thought," Nelly shrieked as they walked into the kitchen, pulling a chair out to sit.

"What happened, Megan? What did the police say?" Her no-nonsense mother asked.

With a mouthful of hazelnut, Megan answered. "They can't even confirm it's Ryan because I didn't see him. Not that they know who Ryan even is."

"But it's him," Nelly cried. "He's crazy."

"I know, but they need proof. I think they'll arrest him if they find him, but they can't leave him in jail or go to trial or anything if my only evidence is green Chucks and the things he said to me that sounded familiar. It's the same thing they told me when I reported the letter and the email."

"They'll run prints, too." A familiar voice, one that sent tingles up her spine, said from the kitchen door.

Nelly extended her hand. "We haven't been properly introduced. I'm Nelly, Megan's best friend and TNT's drummer." Megan had never thought her best friends would meet Jax. It felt surreal to watch it happen.

"And I'm Rose, Megan's mom."

He extended his hand to both ladies and said, "Jax Irons."

"Jax as in *the* Jax?" Rose asked.

"Um . . ."

"Wait! I thought you were one of the cops. What are you . . . how did you . . . ? I'm confused," Nelly confessed. Megan took a huge spoonful of Nutella and stuck it in her mouth, the hazelnut sticking to the roof of her mouth. She would have stuck her entire head inside the container if it fit. She was *that* embarrassed and would have done anything to avoid looking his way.

"I saw it play out on television and came right over." Jax explained, then looked over at Megan. "You talked about me?" The cocky grin on his face made her embarrassment that much greater and she felt her face redden.

Nelly clapped excitedly. "Oh, how cute!"

"Shut it, girlfriend." Megan glared at Nelly, who just

continued smiling in return.

"Oh, you just came here to stir things up some more?" Her mother hissed. Luckily, her mother cut right through the awkwardness and once again made things unintentionally harder for Megan.

Megan shoved the spoon into the container and pushed it aside. "Mom, stop. That was a long time ago."

Her mother, tiny thing that she was, stood and walked over to Jax, transforming into the cutthroat intimidating attorney who annihilated her opponents in court. Except Jax wasn't intimidated, and may have been incapable of it.

"I blame you for this mess," she said, jabbing a finger into his shoulder.

"Pardon?" Jax said, eyes on her finger.

"Mother!" Megan shrieked. This night just kept getting worse and worse. The debacle in her closet was one thing, the embarrassing string of events afterward was another.

"I've been waiting five years to meet the man who caused my daughter to stop speaking to her father and me for three years. The man who derailed my daughter's life. This wouldn't have happened to her if she were living a normal life outside of the media. This is all your fault."

"Mother!" Megan didn't want to relive those years again, nor rehash all the reasons why she didn't want a "normal life outside of the media." No, right now an argument with her mother was the last thing she needed. She looked at Jax apologetically and then back at her mother. "This isn't the time for this conversation. Actually I take that back, this conversation never has a time or place because we've done this already and you know I'm not changing careers. You have to deal with it, Mom."

"With all due respect, Ms. Cruz, I don't know what you're talking about but I don't like that you're upsetting Megan."

Oh. My. God.

Her heart fluttered so fiercely she had to literally put her hand over her chest. It felt like it would come right out of her body. He was standing up for her, in the middle of her kitchen, against her bullheaded mother. Protecting her. Caring whether she was upset. She wasn't the kind that needed protecting, not anymore at least, but damn . . . it felt good.

"Excuse me? I'm her mother."

Still as a statue, he replied, "Don't care."

Rose stood with her arms crossed glaring at Jax, but Jax just glared right back. Nelly's head bounced from Jax to Rose like a ping-pong ball, unable to look away from the trainwreck happening in her kitchen.

Even though Megan appreciated Jax having her back, he needed to cool it. It wouldn't do anyone any good to start a big argument with her mother right after the night she'd had.

"Jax . . ." She reached for his forearm, trying to get him to focus on her. But he didn't. "Just let it go. It's fine."

"It's not fine. You're upset."

"It's none of your concern what she is or isn't," her mother said.

Megan pushed her chair back, causing it to screech against the marble floor. "I can't deal with this right now. Both of you, just stop it!"

Her mother's shoulders relaxed a little as she narrowed her stare one final time at Jax. "Come on, Megan, grab a bag and come stay with me for a little while until this is all sorted. Your father took a late flight back from New York and should be here soon. He cancelled his depositions for the next few days." Even though her relationship with her father had improved in the last year and a half, Megan was still surprised to see him worried to the point of putting her ahead of his work.

"That's not happening," Jax replied before Megan had a chance to respond.

Living with her parents was not a great idea, Megan agreed, even if only for a few days. She loved how they'd recently grown close, but being in the same space for a prolonged period of time would surely jeopardize whatever progress they'd made. But still, it wasn't Jax's call to make.

"Excuse me?" Megan turned to Jax.

"You're not staying anywhere that I haven't had a chance to secure." His jaw twitched with every word.

"So what do you propose I do?" Megan asked, incredulously.

"You'll stay with me for a few days until I feel this house is safe."

Megan's eyes widened in disbelief, and all her irritability morphed into shock.

"Hey, Rose, let's go see what's going on up front. There's a cute cop I'd like to get your opinion on," Nelly, God bless her, suggested.

"You do know I'm not stupid, right? Just tell me to get out, if you want me out," Rose huffed on her way out of the kitchen.

Tonight Megan had gone through the full spectrum of emotions. She was drained and even though she was happy to see Jax and was hopeful they could become reacquainted, right now all she wanted was to crawl into her bed, maybe cry a little in private, and ultimately sleep for the next twelve hours. "I'm not staying with you, Jax. I haven't seen you in five years, I don't really even know you, and I'm exhausted."

"You know me well enough. I have a spare room. And my house is safe." He had on his impassive face again. The one that wasn't warm and welcoming. The one that reminded her of how little she knew this new Jax.

"I'd have stayed anywhere with you, no questions asked, five years ago. Now, no. I'm scared, I'm tired, you're intense—and to be honest, a little scary. But most important, I knew you for four days five years ago. You could be as crazy as Ryan for all I know."

"You know that's not true. You know I wouldn't let anything hurt you, not then and not now." She let her shoulders sag a little because she did know he wouldn't hurt her—but that didn't mean she was going to go home with him. That would be foolish and irresponsible and . . . too tempting.

He pulled out a chair and gestured for her to sit, which she did. "I'm sorry, Megan." He sat on the chair across from her and took her hands in his, unconsciously rubbing the tops of her hands with his calloused thumb. "Sometimes I forget what civilian life is like. I don't mean to be so harsh, but it's coming from a good place, Meg. I didn't like hearing about your stalker on TV, much less finding you terrified and hiding in a closet."

Meg.

Wow, that brought back so many good memories. That's all she could focus on. *Meg.* How he had quickly become so integral in her life back then. No one having ever called her anything other than Megan. No one caring enough to really get to know her—the real her. The girl who wanted to sing, to be free, and wild . . . and be Meg. Not Megan, the rich proper girl who couldn't do something as lowly as singing. He'd changed her to her core in just a few days. *That's not true.* He didn't change her. He helped her see herself for the first time in her life. The change was all on her, he just brought it out of her. Of course she trusted him. It was irrational and maybe a little crazy, but she did.

"You've changed," she said, seizing the chance to talk about something other than the Ryan situation.

"So have you."

"I guess that's true."

"But I'm still the same person inside. I'd never hurt you, you have to know that."

"I do." And it was true, she believed that from the depth of her soul. But the fact that he was so brooding, even when he was being protective and sweet, standing vigil while the cops questioned her, taking her side with her mother—he was still a little scary and a lot intense.

"Please, come home with me. Just for tonight." God, another time, another place, she'd have jumped all over a proposition like that from Jax.

"I'm having déjà vu," she admitted. He had made the same request five years ago. And saying yes had been the best decision of her life.

He smiled. "It's late. You're exhausted. My house is safe, safer than anywhere else you could possibly go, and I have an extra room." It didn't go unnoticed that he repeated that second part and she wasn't sure if he was saying it for her benefit or for his own. He was still so attractive. More so, even. But with the night she'd had, all she wanted was sleep. And even though there was some affection in the way he looked at her, too many years had passed. The time they had spent together had been so short-lived that whatever he had felt for her had likely fizzled away. "Please," he begged, almost a whisper.

With a yawn, she finally relented. "Okay. I'll go tell Nelly and my mom."

Chapter 3

It was supposed to be a fun Thursday afternoon.

Jax sat in seat L213 just like he had every year since he was a little boy. When his dad had been alive, he'd sat in L214. Coming to the baseball game without his father was still difficult, and the loud douchebag yapping into his phone two seats to his right wasn't helping matters. The only thing keeping him from losing his cool was the brown-eyed beauty he'd taken notice of the two times she'd jumped up to cheer and accidentally brushed her plump ass against his shoulder. She was in seat L214, his dad's seat, between himself and the douche. With a foam finger, terrible taste in beer, and a teal Florida Marlins T-shirt, she knew when to cheer, when to boo, and when to curse at the ump's bad calls. Her brown hair was in a thick ponytail under her cap and she had bangs sweeping across her forehead that bounced around when she moved. Her thick lips glistened with some sort of gloss and her cheeks were pink from the exertion of cheering and yelling as well as from the sun beating down on them. But the best part of her—aside from her delicious jean shorts–covered ass—was those big brown expressive eyes. Not that he'd noticed much about her.

Being so close to her, mere inches away, when she put down her foam finger and took off her baseball cap to smooth out her hair meant the flowery smell of her shampoo assaulted his senses.

These last few years, coming to the baseball games had been a somber event. He remembered how his father had cheered louder than anyone else every time the Marlins got a run. He'd openly slap Jax's back and then hug him as if Jax had been the one scoring. Not an avid drinker, his dad had terrible taste in beer, much like the beauty sitting next to him. He'd wear top to bottom teal and give Jax a hard time for not doing the same. He never felt closer to his father than he did at the stadium.

But now surreptitiously watching the woman next to him had brought joy back into the game, even if only for today.

———————

"Can't that wait until after the game? They're about to start." Megan begged Richard Knight, her boyfriend of two years, to put his phone down and watch the baseball game. "Come on, it's my last fun day before school starts next week."

He looked up at her with an annoyed expression. "I had fun in law school. You will too. This is just a game, Megan. I have work to do."

"But you promised." She mentally cringed at the slight whine in her voice. She shouldn't have to beg her boyfriend to be present at the game with her.

"I promised I'd come with you, and here I am. You know how important making partner is for me. Not all of us have parents to pull strings for us."

This wasn't the first time he'd thrown that in her face. Sitting back down in a huff, Megan turned her attention to the game.

"Oh my god! Did you see that home run?" She asked a few minutes later, tugging on his shirt.

"Yeah, yeah." But he was looking down at his phone and pulling his arm away from her grip. She glared at him, even if he wasn't looking back at her. Sometimes she couldn't help but wonder why they were together.

Richard was tall, lean, with ink-black hair meticulously brushed in a side part and a beautiful clean-shaven face that showcased his impressive cheekbones and strong jaw. But he looked so out of place at the ballpark, with his jeans and polo shirt, looking like he wished he was wearing a suit. Megan, on the other hand, was a T-shirt and jeans kind of girl, to her mother's dismay. She wasn't normally the life of the party, preferring to hang back and listen instead. But Richard was the kind of man that took control of a room by his mere presence. Women unabashedly stared at him and men kissed his ass wanting to befriend him. Even here at the ball game she saw the flirty glances from the women they'd walked past. Megan routinely felt pushed aside and forgotten. But when he was present, really present, he was the embodiment of a perfect boyfriend: sweet and attentive. Lately, however, those moments were few and far between. Sometimes she felt like a wallflower and she was coming to understand that maybe she'd been made to feel that way by being constantly pushed aside by her parents and by Richard. But maybe she didn't want to be a wallflower. She loathed that she craved his affection so profoundly—the little morsels he threw her way, she'd store and relish and feel grateful for. And that made her unhappy with herself. Somewhere deep inside, she knew she was stronger than that.

The realization hit her hard and fast. She was young, successful, and attractive. She shouldn't have to plead for him to be with her. Richard wasn't better than her. No, she was too damn good for him.

Feeling annoyed and suddenly determined, she stood up. "I'm going to grab a drink."

"I'm good," he said without bothering to look up or even notice that she didn't offer to get him anything.

Balancing nachos, popcorn, and a soda, Megan awkwardly made her way back to her seat, deciding she was going to enjoy the day even if she had to do so alone. The poor guy in the seat next to her shifted his legs to the side to give her room as she sat back down and began to stuff popcorn in her mouth. Funny how she had more physical contact with that guy, whose leg bobbed up and down, brushing along her own, then she did with her own boyfriend.

When the guy stood up to cheer, Megan glanced up at him. He was also tall and lean, but unlike Richard, this guy had an all-American look to him with his blondish shaggy hair, jeans, and sweet smile. Where Richard was handsome in a "spends a lot of time in front of the mirror styling his hair" sort of way, the guy next to her looked like he woke up, threw on an old pair of jeans and a T-shirt, and headed out. He looked perfectly comfortable in his casual clothes. Catching herself staring at the way his jeans hugged his impressive thighs, she quickly looked down at her popcorn. She found herself wondering why he was there alone.

It was a close game and everyone cheered and hollered—everyone except Richard, which was making it harder for her to keep to her resolve to have a good day.

Right now, she was *this* close to pouring the entire untouched cup of beer on his head. He'd bought her beer earlier, which was probably the moment her anger began. She didn't like beer. How did he not know this? Did he know her at all?

"Oh my god! Look!" She pulled on Richard's arm and pointed up to the screen. "We're on the jumbotron! You have to kiss me. It's the kiss cam, Richard!"

She leaned over but he swatted her away and the crowd booed.

"Richard!" she yelled again, again pointing to the screen, hating herself for having to beg.

When he continued to ignore her, she hunched over and looked around, embarrassed. Once the camera was off them she leaned closer and asked, "Why did you bother coming if you weren't even going to watch?" Normally, she was quiet and reserved and internalized her emotions because Cruzes didn't show emotions. But right now she wasn't sad. She was pissed.

"I did it for you because you kept saying you wanted to come. I hate baseball. You know that."

"Actually I did not know that." *What else didn't she know about him?* He didn't know she hated beer and she didn't know he hated baseball. A day at the ballpark seemed silly now, what they needed was freakin' counseling!

Her parents had been putting pressure on them to marry and Richard seemed completely on board with the plan, although he hadn't proposed. These days, they barely saw each other. She was sick of it. She understood he had goals, but she wanted to be important in his life. How delusional had she been in thinking maybe they could have fun today, re-spark their relationship before their lives started to get even more hectic. But instead of connected, she felt even more distant.

How many times had she watched some boring political documentary because he wanted to watch it? She'd done it for him without a peep, and the man couldn't be bothered to at least pretend he wanted to be here.

She sat with her arms crossed over her chest, the game effectively ruined by his sour mood. The bobbing leg of the guy on her left was getting annoying, too. Even though he smelled wonderful—some sort of manly cologne she'd never smelled before. A scent very different from Richard's exorbitantly priced Dior Sauvage that he liked to douse himself with whenever he left his house. Lately she had been feeling things change between them. It was an overwhelming sense of loneliness that she couldn't shake off. She felt silly and guilty for feeling this way with a boyfriend at her side, so she'd shut the emotion off, ignoring it and trying to make the best of things. But even sitting there with him, it was as if she was alone.

When everyone began to cheer, she forced herself to look up at the jumbotron again. "Richard! Look!" She pointed up, wiping the scowl off her face, suddenly desperate to prove to herself and the world that there was some spark in their relationship, some romance. "It's the kiss cam again. Come on, please, it'll take two seconds."

Again he brushed her off, and she fought back tears. *What an asshole!*

People were whispering and pointing all around the stadium. She groaned to herself, *Oh, God, my humiliation is being televised for the entire nation to witness.*

She slid lower in her chair and tilted the bill of her cap down. It was a harsh reality to face in front of thousands of people, but one that struck her hard and fast like a bucket of cold water.

This was the end.

Richard was not only a selfish bastard, he was a selfish bastard who didn't want her. But the real sobering surprise was that she didn't even care because she didn't want him either.

For the second time, the asshole rejected her.

Again they were on display and again her obtuse guy refused to kiss her. She'd elbowed him, but he was too busy typing into his phone to pay her any mind. She looked downright crestfallen and embarrassed in front of a maxed-out stadium, slouched down hiding her eyes with her baseball cap.

Jax didn't know what came over him in the moment but something definitely did. It was probably his fly-by-the-seat-of-his-pants character or maybe the fact that she didn't deserve to be humiliated. No girl did. Especially not this girl.

He tapped her on the shoulder.

She turned, her eyes full of unshed tears.

From his peripheral vision he could see she was still spotlighted on the jumbotron.

He was moments away from doing something bold and inappropriate. And those big sad brown eyes, glossy downturned lips, and pink cheeks fueled him.

Without hesitation he cupped her face and moved in for a kiss.

It was supposed to be an attempt to piss off her boyfriend, or perhaps a way to counteract her humiliation. Spin things around and make her look like a desirable woman instead of some sort of scorned victim.

But something else happened.

Fuck.

Was that strawberry lip gloss or did the woman taste like fucking strawberries?

Jax brushed his lips over hers softly before deepening the daring peck into something more.

More intimate.

More meaningful.

And so very sensual.

She gasped, her breath a soft hitch in the back of her throat, which quickly turned into some sort of needy moan that made him instantly harden. She could've pulled away, she should've slapped him. But she didn't do any of those things. Instead, as the crowd cheered them on and her boyfriend yelled at them, her hand fisted his shirt and she pulled him to her, her nails digging into his skin.

And if the entire scene wasn't erotic enough, this woman, the woman who'd just been rejected on national television, slipped her tongue into his mouth. Somewhere in the back of his mind, he'd thought she wouldn't reciprocate but that wasn't the case. Not at all. She was the one taking control now. It shocked him so much that he pulled away slightly, searched her face before going in for more.

Because he needed more.

He needed everything.

In reality it was probably only thirty seconds, but it felt as if they were suspended in time. The entire crowd disappeared and it was just two people having the best first kiss in the history of kisses.

"Want to get out of here?" he whispered in her ear when they finally pulled away. He could hear the way his own hoarse voice shook. If she had said no ... he was likely to have carried her out of the stadium caveman style. Because he had just had a tiny taste and he needed more. But she looked into his eyes, then up at the stadium for a brief moment before smiling, confidently.

That was all the assurance he needed.

Lacing his fingers with hers, and without looking back, they ran out of the packed arena laughing and breathless, faintly hearing the boyfriend yelling for her. Once they were out of the stadium she let go of his hand and bent over, hands on her knees to catch her breath. "I can't believe that just happened," she said, still giggling.

"Which part? The asshole ignoring you or running out of there?"

"The kissing you part, mostly," she said, still a little breathless, the hot summer sun beaming down on them and the hum from the cheering crowd behind them. "But all of it. That's not like me. At all. Oh God, it felt so good."

He smiled, feeling ten feet tall. "It's not? You don't go around kissing random strangers at a baseball game? And my kisses usually feel good. You're welcome," he winked.

"I was talking more about the fact that I did something so crazy. But the kiss was good too. Oh, and I go around kissing random guys all the time. Especially next to my boyfriend of two years. How'd you know?" She was beaming and extended her hands and spun around while laughing. "This is so wild!"

She was so damn cute. Her baseball cap falling off mid-spin but that didn't stop her. The kiss was phenomenal and so was the "great escape," but the way she was acting . . . it made him think there was something deeper than what had just happened. And he wanted to know what that something was. But he especially wanted to know why she'd stayed with that dickhead for so long. Jax had kind of imagined they were on their first and last date, not in a long-term relationship.

"Two years." He scrunched his face. "Don't really know you, but seems like that's two years too long to be with a guy who doesn't want to kiss you all the time. Because I gotta say, I've just had a small taste and I want to kiss some more. A lot more."

Her face turned a sweet shade of pink and she looked down at the foam finger she held. Yep, she was just getting cuter by the minute. But he preferred her happy and spinning around to shy and embarrassed. He'd seen her shy and embarrassed already. Hell, the entire stadium had seen that. He wanted to wipe that image out of his brain—and hers.

"By the way, I'm Jackson Irons," he said, holding his hand out to her. "But everyone calls me Jax."

Bending down to pick up her hat, she smoothed out her ponytail and then put the cap back on. "I'm Megan Cruz," she said, shaking his hand. She smiled, still a little on the shy side. He needed to coax the giddiness and the confidence out of her again.

"Well, Megan Cruz, as far as I can tell you've got two choices," he said, still holding her hand in the air midshake. It was so small and soft compared to his. "You can go back in there and deal with an undoubtedly angry boyfriend—who, honestly, seems like a dick—or we can go have lunch."

"I don't even know you."

"We've kissed. Not exactly strangers anymore," he teased and rubbed his thumb over her hand, not letting go. He couldn't help it, he liked the feeling and the way her eyes widened and her lips turned up with every contact. It was as if she'd been deprived of affection. Damn, he could fix that. No problem. He'd love to start that job immediately, actually. "And I feel like I owe you a meal or something after that kiss."

Please say yes. Please say yes.

She pulled her hand away and fumbled nervously with the foam finger, about to tear a chunk out of it when her cell phone rang. Looking at the screen, she ignored the call and slid it back into the pocket of her jean shorts.

"It's the douchebag?" Jax asked.

"His name is Richard."

Looking disgusted, he shook his head. "Seriously? Richard? The name says it all. He's a dick—literally," he said, making her laugh loudly. "Jax is a way cooler name."

She looked over his shoulder as if trying to decide what she was going to do, or maybe it was to see if Dick would show up and fight for her. That's what he would've done if he was Dick but then again, no guy at a baseball game would be kissing his girl, especially while he sat next to her. He reached down and took the foam finger she was destroying. "I'm just going to hold on to this while you make your decision. Poor finger doesn't deserve your torture."

She laughed again. "I uh . . . I don't . . ." She shook her head side to side. "Richard's going to be so mad at me, not that I necessarily care, but he's my boyfriend. It feels wrong that I kissed you."

"Does it? I thought it felt spec-fucking-tacular," he said, and then added, in a serious tone, "If I was your man, I'd question what the fuck I did wrong to make my girl want to kiss another man. Then I'd kick that other's man's ass for touching my girl. We've been out here for about ten minutes, I don't see Dick running out to find you."

"He wouldn't run after me and risk making a scene."

"Like I said, he's a dick. Look, there's a little Cuban café down the street. Stranger danger, I get it. But I promise, I'm a good guy. We can just walk. You have your phone in case you feel uncomfortable. Plus, it's broad daylight."

Her phone rang again and again she ignored the call, but this time she let out a deep breath, slid the phone back in her pocket, and finally said, "yeah, okay. Lunch sounds good."

He wanted to pump his fist in the air triumphantly, right there in the middle of the street. But, he was trying to impress this woman, not make her think he was an immature idiot . . . like her boyfriend. So instead he smiled brightly, because she deserved to know it felt like a privilege that she wanted to spend time with him.

———————

Oh God. What did I just do? And why is this man so happy to be going to a café with me? He doesn't even know me. I'm not that fun.

"You like baseball, huh?" he asked, causing her to whip her head to the side to look at him. Her mind was a jumbled mess of questions and worry. Accidentally, his hand brushed hers, which made her heart skip but also made her fear bubble up. Her parents were going to have a fit. Richard was surely on the phone with them right now telling them what had happened.

"Megan? Baseball?" he repeated.

"Oh . . . uh . . . yeah. Love it. I try to catch at least one game every season."

"If you love it, why don't you come more often?"

"Richard never has time to come with me. I used to come to the games with my grandfather before he passed away."

"Like I said, Dick's a dick."

She laughed—she'd been doing a lot of that in the few minutes she'd known Jax. She really liked that he said exactly what was on his mind—consequences be damned. He wasn't the reserved kind of man she was accustomed to. "He's just really busy, is all." As soon as she said it, she felt like an idiot making excuses for the asshole.

"Too busy to take you to a game? Too busy to kiss you?"

"He's about to make partner at Cruz, Cruz, and Castle. Damn it, I don't know why I'm making excuses for him."

"Isn't your last name Cruz?"

"Yeah, it's my parents' firm. That's how we met." Megan saw Jax roll his eyes, and she knew exactly what he was thinking. It's the same thing that had been swirling through her mind lately.

Richard was only with her because he needed her parents' support to make partner.

"Stop thinking," he said, as he opened the door of the

café for her. "He's not here. It's just us right now. Let that shit go, at least for now."

He was so easy. Surely, there was more to this man. But right now, all he'd shown her was simple fun. And she needed that. Hell, that's what today was supposed to be about. One thing that she noted almost immediately was that Jax had not taken out his phone once—he was completely present, which was refreshing and unexpected.

This wasn't the kind of place that had a hostess, so they just found a booth by a window and sat down. And being born and raised in Miami, she knew what she wanted; menus weren't needed when there was a Cuban café on every corner in Miami, all serving the same thing. She wondered if he was also from Miami and if he spoke Spanish.

He was looking at her, his hands folded on the table, waiting patiently for the server. "Are you from Miami?" she asked him.

"Yep. Born and raised. You?"

"Yes. My parents were both born in Cuba. My dad moved here when he was fourteen and my mom when she was only four years old. So my Spanish isn't great because they spoke mostly English around the house. My grandfather used to get so mad about that." She smiled, but she knew it didn't quite reach her eyes. She missed her grandfather, the only grandparent she'd had the opportunity to get to know. He was down to earth and hard-working, and he'd taught her all about baseball. "Do you speak Spanish?"

"*Un poquito.*" He held his index finger and thumb a few inches apart. "I took some Spanish in high school, and living here, things tend to stick. I can't hold a conversation, though."

"But you like the food, right? I mean who doesn't like all the bread and fried goodness."

"Damn straight I do." He smiled from across the booth just as the waitress came by holding two menus in her hand.

"Do you need menus, or are you ready to order?" The waitress asked.

"I know what I want. How about you, Megan?" He said it in a soft, almost sultry voice, while looking straight into her eyes. Definitely, there was innuendo in the way he asked it that made her have to look away from him and to the waitress.

"Yes, let me have a *pan con bistec* and a coke, please."

"I'll have the same," Jax said, and when the waitress left he continued. "So before we walked in you were telling me how Dick wants a job at your parents' firm?"

"He has a job there already. He's been there for a few years. He's just working very hard to make partner."

"And you? What do you do?"

"I start law school on Monday." Groaning, she covered her eyes with her hands and slumped her shoulders as she said it. *Why did I do that,* she wondered. It was as if she could relax with this stranger, which made all her real feelings pour out. Walking out on Richard was the catalyst. So many things in her life were tied to Richard and the law firm, that if he wasn't in the picture everything would be different. She needed to get so much off her chest, and if the poor man sitting across from her kept asking questions, he was about to get an earful. It was easy to open up when the person wasn't there to judge or even to give an opinion—and she'd never see him again after today.

"Wow, you look so excited about that. I don't think I'd do anything that made me feel the way you just looked."

Sighing loudly, she began. "It's a means to an end. In three years I'll be an attorney and school will be behind me. It's not exactly exciting, but it is what it is, and anyway, it's too late to change things now." The busser came to the table to drop off their drinks, and she busied herself opening up the soda can and pouring it in the glass. "And you? What exciting thing do you do, Jax Irons?"

"You mean aside from sweeping women off their feet at baseball games?" He smiled, and she couldn't help but giggle. Giggle! She never ever giggled. "I'm in the Marines. I deploy on Monday."

Her mouth hung open and all humor vanished instantly "Are you serious?"

"Yep."

"Where?"

"Can't say."

"You don't look like a Marine."

Now it was his turn to laugh as he ran his fingers through his hair "What does a Marine look like?"

She pointed to his shaggy blonde hair, part of it falling down his eyes. "I don't know . . . serious. Maybe shorter hair. Don't they make you shave it or something?"

"They'll shave it. Probably chop off an ear too." He shrugged, surprisingly not caring. God, the man was ultra-relaxed; it was disconcerting. She didn't know anyone like that.

"So why don't you just get a haircut before you leave?"

"Lots of other things to do. Not a priority."

"You have four days. How many things do you still have to do?"

"All of it." He laughed and shrugged, unfazed and unstressed. "A buddy of mine is having a farewell barbeque for me tonight, wanna come?"

"I'm still dealing with lunch." She brought her glass up and took a big slurp through her straw. And if you have a bunch of things to do on your list, should you be going to a party?"

"It'll get done."

"When?"

"The anxiety you have on my behalf is palpable." He chuckled, finally opening his can of soda and pouring himself a drink. He'd been listening, giving her his full attention—no fidgeting, no interruptions, looking her straight in the eye. He was totally and completely sure of himself, not needing to fill the void with inane conversation or move around distractedly. He asked questions he wanted to know answers to, and listened carefully, asking more questions when more questions needed to be asked.

"Don't leave for tomorrow what you can do for today."

He quickly came back with, "Carpe Diem."

"Don't out-quote me, Irons." She narrowed her eyes, but she couldn't wipe the smile off of her face.

"So? Barbeque tonight?" he asked again just as the waitress brought them their steak sandwiches, made with soft toasted Cuban bread.

"I don't know." She hesitated. He was fun and charming and hot, but . . .

"Come on. You have four days 'til you start law school, after that it'll be all work and no play." He smiled—well, he never seemed to stop smiling, but this time she kept her eyes on his. And she noticed for the first time how the corners of his eyes crinkled. And was that a dimple?

She hadn't noticed before, either. Maybe because, even though his eyes never left hers, she would avert her eyes every time things got a little too serious, a little too flirty, or a little too deep.

Instead of answering, she took a big bite of her food and took an eternity chewing and *not* answering him. Mostly because she wasn't sure what to say.

On one hand, spending more time with him seemed exciting and fun. A much needed diversion. On the other hand, she didn't know him—and she had a boyfriend to deal with.

She was still chewing when he reached across the table, startling her, and wiped a crumb from her face with his thumb, cupping the side of her face in the process. It took all of her effort not to close her eyes and lean in to his big warm hand. An almost inaudible groan escaped his mouth and her heart started beating roughly against her chest.

And her decision was made. "You don't even know me. Are you sure you wouldn't prefer hanging out with your friends before you leave?"

"Yes, that's why I'm going to the party. If I bring you along that's me hanging out with my new friend, too," he said, finally grabbing his sandwich and taking a bite. "How old are you, Megan?"

"Twenty-two."

"A twenty-two-year-old woman about to start school should have a wild last hurrah. The kind of hurrah she thinks about when she's fifty years old, settled in a boring marriage with a dick named Dick and two point five kids. You need a memory that'll make you blush when you're old and everything's sagging and you can't find your teeth. And a twenty-three-year-old Marine about to deploy for his second tour overseas deserves the same thing, but with a twenty-two-year-old woman who has a greedy tongue and sweet lips made for kissing said Marine."

Her face pinked again. "Seems like the Marine in question is avoiding his to-do list."

"You seem more preoccupied with my to-do list than you are with the tongue and lips situation. And the tongue situation, Megan? That's something that should be repeated . . . soon." And he took another bite, and her eyes moved to his lips and to the way his tongue slipped out to catch some of the crumbs. "Come on, Megan. You look like you need some fun in your life."

"And you look like you need some order in yours," she replied. "How about we do five things on your to-do list and I'll go to the barbeque with you."

"Fuck yeah!"

"Wow, that was easy."

"Of course it was." He stuffed the last bite of food into

his mouth. "You know what this means, right?"

"What?"

"We have to do five fun things for you while we do five boring things for me."

"I don't remember agreeing to that."

"So you don't want to do five fun things?"

Megan pushed her plate back, no longer hungry. She felt emboldened, and this time she leaned over and reached for the lock of hair by his eye and pushed it back, needing to see those sexy green eyes. "With you? Yes, I think I do," she said, her voice a little thicker, a little lower, and her eyes never leaving his.

It was time sweet sheltered Megan had some fun.

Chapter 4

Megan's internal clock was always off. Since she normally worked well into the evenings, she tended to sleep late into the day. Add the hellish night she had last night, it wasn't surprising she woke up midday still shaken up from the break-in. *What would Ryan have done if he found her?* Her body quivered at the thought and she did her best to put it aside.

After rushing through her morning routine, she made the bed in the room Jax had put her up in and headed out to find him.

"Hello?" she yelled into the hallway of his quiet home. Last night it had been late by the time he'd pulled up to his house, and she'd struggled to keep her eyes open. Without much conversation, she'd followed him inside. He showed her to his extra room, placed her bag by the bed, asked her if she needed anything—but she'd been so tired, she just mumbled incoherently and practically face-planted onto the bed. Too tired to exhaust any more brain cells on the fact that she was about to go to sleep at Jax's house, she fell right asleep. She woke up covered in a blanket and assumed Jax had tucked her in.

But now, in the daytime, she was able to take in the large square space. It was very different from the house he'd taken her to years back, a house he'd inherited from his grandparents: quaint, old, and by the ocean. This was obviously some sort of repurposed warehouse. The pipes and tubing were still exposed on the ceiling and the walls looked to be solid concrete. Everything was a dreary gray and the furniture was mostly black. Not one painting or picture hung anywhere. All the electronics and furniture seemed to be brand new and top of the line, including the biggest flat-screen television she'd ever seen. It wasn't necessarily unappealing, just very cold and utilitarian.

"In here," he hollered.

Padding to the kitchen, she saw him sitting in front of a laptop, reading. "Mornin'," she said.

"There's coffee." He closed his laptop and looked up. It reminded her of the first day she met him, how he'd always given her his full attention. "Want some?"

She nodded and pulled out a chair by the enormous island that separated the kitchen from the rest of the room, watching him pour sugar and milk into a cup of coffee—he remembered how she liked it, which made her heart flutter. "Breakfast or lunch?" he asked.

She reached forward and grabbed a banana. "I'm good for now." She unpeeled it and took a bite. "I have a million questions."

He slid the mug to her and stood across from her, his hands resting on the slab of marble. "I do too. You first."

"You're back."

"That's not a question."

"I can't believe I'm here with you. I mean, I didn't think I'd ever see you again."

His face softened and there was the ghost of a smile hidden somewhere in his bushy beard. "Still not a question."

"How long have you been back?"

"Few months."

"What happened to you? Do you leave again?"

"Got blown up, got discharged, came home, not leaving again." It was short, and she needed more information, but knowing he wasn't going to expand, she moved on.

"Okay," she singsonged, "are you married?"

Then she heard the very familiar and very welcome chuckle of Jackson Irons. It hit her right in the chest. It was her first glimpse of the old Jax. "No. Not married."

"Do you want to know if I'm married?" she asked.

"Already know you're not."

His arms were big and bulky and the way that he

leaned into the island made him look impatient. "Can you sit? You're making me nervous."

He pushed off the counter and sat on the chair across from her, the island between them.

"What do you do now?"

"I co-own Iron-Clad Security here in town. We do all types of security work including bodyguard, government ops, cyber-security, securing homes."

She held out her finger and pointed to herself. "I'm pretty sure I'm in the market for some of that."

"Already on it, Meg."

"Really? Don't I have to hire you first, or something? Discuss prices? Sign a contract?"

"You think I'd sit back and wait for a stalker to break in again while we discuss pricing options? Fill out paperwork?"

"Okay, thanks for rushing on that." She blew out a long sigh, relieved that he was already working on it. She hadn't really known where to begin if the cops weren't going to help her. "Of course, I'll pay you."

"Not having that conversation now."

"Jax—"

"We have a history. Whether or not we've seen each other is irrelevant. I didn't come back from that godforsaken desert to see someone else get hurt. I'm not going to let you be unsafe and I'm not going to charge you to protect you. Wouldn't have done it then, won't do it now."

"It was different then."

"Why? Because I wasn't incorporated?"

She smirked and took a drink of her coffee "No. Because this wasn't your business back then, and because I wasn't really in danger."

"You weren't?" He smiled, but it didn't quite reach his eyes. "You were in danger of dying of boredom, Meg."

"Jax—"

"We'll deal with payment and all that bullshit later. I've seen your net worth. If I need to expense something, I know you're good for it, okay?"

"Fine."

It seemed like his patience for chitchat was wearing thin. He stood up straight and finished his coffee. "I need to go to your house today and look at your current system and then I'll send some of my guys to work on it. But you gotta use it. No point in having a state-of-the-art security system if you don't turn it on."

"Trust me, Jax, I'll never forget to turn on my alarm again." A shiver ran down her body.

"Are you done with the Q and A? 'Cause I got some questions of my own."

"Shoot," she said, taking another bite of her banana.

"How is it that you went from law student to pop star

millionaire with a Grammy in five years?"

She'd known this question was coming. "I never made it to law school. After you dropped me off at home that Monday morning, I told my parents I wasn't going."

"And . . . what? You just joined TNT? I know it doesn't exactly work that way."

"No, it doesn't. Short version is, I waitressed at Robbie's for six months before Tamara—one of the Ts from TNT—walked out on them. They asked me to help out for a couple of gigs until they found a replacement. A couple of gigs turned into a permanent position, and at one of those shows, a scout for RLC was there."

"RLC, the record label?"

"Yep. We signed a contract with RLC, recorded a single. Single blew up. And as they say . . . the rest is history."

"Damn." He shook his head. "Damn," he said again, in disbelief. "How about your parents and the douche?"

"After two years he deserved a face-to-face explanation, so I gave him one. He was livid that I'd humiliated him on national television. You know that video of us kissing at the baseball game went viral, right?"

He rolled his eyes. "I heard."

She took her mug to the sink and began to wash it. "Anyway, he was an asshole and I should've broken up with him a long time before. He didn't love me and I didn't love him either. My parents had pushed us together and being with him had just seemed like the thing that was supposed to happen. Afterward, I found out he'd been sleeping with one of the law clerks at the firm."

"Dickhead," he said, and placed a hand on her shoulder, but she didn't turn around, instead she continued to wash the mug as if its cleanliness was imperative to the survival of all humankind.

"Nah. It was fine. Took away some of my guilt for having kissed you. Plus, the fact that I wasn't hurt when I found out really put things into perspective. I mean, finding out that your boyfriend was screwing someone else should be devastating, right? The fact it wasn't says a lot."

"Yeah, guess it does." He reached over her and turned off the water and took the mug out of her hands. Her heart beat so loudly, she was sure he could hear it. *Was he going to kiss her?* "Megan, look at me. You do this. You move around and fidget when things get too heavy."

She swallowed and turned around. She had forgotten how fast he'd been able to read her and how nothing slipped by him. He was still so perceptive.

Squaring her shoulders, she looked at him, grabbing the counter behind her as she spoke. "Sorry. It's been a rough twenty-four hours. I'm jumpy."

"You don't have to apologize. Just relax. It's still me." He pulled her hands away from the counter and then let them go gently. He was standing casually in front of her, leaning his back against the island, his feet crossed. He grabbed the mug again and waited for her to continue. "So you broke up with the douche and then what?"

Trying to mimic his relaxed posture, she continued. "So after that was done, I went home. My mother and father were pissed I had disappeared for four days and for 'embarrassing' them by kissing a stranger in front of everyone. But it's weird now, looking back. I was in a haze when you left. I was more devastated at you leaving than breaking up with Richard or fighting with my parents. I just didn't want to hear it. So I packed a bag and left. Just like that. The same day I said good-bye to you, I said good-bye to my parents and my long-term boyfriend."

"Damn."

"Yep. Big changes. My parents cut me off immediately. They thought I'd come crawling back since I walked out with zero money, a shitload of devastation, and terrified. But I didn't. It was hard. Robbie had a little apartment upstairs he rented me for cheap and I did pretty well with tips. It was hard learning to be on my own, quickly learning how ill-prepared I was, but I made it work. Some days were really hard, I won't lie. Things are still a little strained between me and my parents, but it's not too bad anymore. They give me my space and have had to learn to accept that singing is my passion. I love TNT, and I'm not going to stop."

Running a palm down his face, he looked at her, those big green eyes full of awe. "That's amazing, Megan. Always knew you could do it if you just went for it."

"You really did change my life." She fiddled with the banana peel on the table for a second before looking him straight in the eye. No matter what, she needed Jax to know that those four days had been the best of her life. "Because of you I realized how much I loved performing, not just singing but being in front of a crowd, and being with Nelly and Taylor who've become family. I always wanted to thank you for that. It's something I always thought I'd say to you if I ever had the opportunity. So, thank you."

"I didn't do anything. You don't have to thank me." Now it was him who was squirmy, so she grabbed his forearm and held it. This time, it was him who needed to look at her in the eyes when she said it.

"Jax, thank you," she repeated, her tone stronger, needing him to know how instrumental he had been.

"You're welcome." He was serious, his smile gone, but he wasn't the intimidating man from last night. Just not the carefree dude from five years ago.

"Any other questions?"

He walked around the island and sat back down.

"Yes. Where's Richard now?"

"Last I heard he was married and living in the DC area. He's harmless, if that's what you're thinking."

"And Tamara? What happened with her?"

"She's around. At first she threatened to sue us and made our lives miserable for about three months, and then she sort of just faded away. About a year ago, she moved back to town and contacted Nelly. I think they've had lunch a few times, she's trying to get her act together and mend fences it seems. Nelly, Taylor, and Tamara grew up together, and there's a lot of history there. I hope they work it out. Nelly has always missed her."

"Well, that's good." Jax paused. "I'd like to know more about your parents. Your mom was not happy to meet me last night."

Megan laughed. "No. She blames you for everything. She thinks you put all these *eccentric* ideas in my head. It's bullshit, because I've always loved singing and they knew it. They squashed all my attempts at music lessons my whole life. Once I left their house, they didn't speak to me—not even when I called them to tell them about signing with RLC. I tried for years and nothing. Then one day my mother sent me a text that my father had had a heart attack. I rushed to the hospital and after that, we sort of all just started getting along again. They never apologized and we didn't really discuss things, we just went back to being okay."

"You stuck to your convictions."

"I did."

"Can I hear one of your songs?"

"Don't you listen to the radio?"

"Actually no. Not really."

She reached for her phone pressed some buttons and played "Ruin Me," the newest single and a song he had to have heard of, because it was always on the radio. "I've heard this before," he said. "That's you?"

"That's me."

"You write the songs?"

"Some of them. Not this one, though."

"Can I hear one you've written?"

She turned off the music and put her phone down, feeling her cheeks warm. "Maybe some other time."

Jax finished off his coffee, absorbed in his thoughts, then stood by the sink washing the mug. "Thought about you a lot," he said, with his back to her.

She looked up, afraid she heard wrong. "You did?"

"A lot."

And the butterflies were back. She went to reach for him, just like he'd done to her, but pulled her hand back. She wanted to touch him so badly. But she was hesitant. He was there to help her, not to start things up again.

She started to confess that she thought about him too, but instead she found herself asking, "Why didn't you come find me? You've been here months, you could've called."

"And found you married? Or in a relationship?" He shook his head somberly, the muscles in his neck and shoulders bunched together, and she wanted him to turn around. Force him to have this conversation eye to eye. Except she wasn't sure she could handle it. Maybe he didn't want to see her again. He'd come to her rescue out of some sort of obligation, otherwise she'd never have seen him again. And if the confident man couldn't bring himself to turn around, she couldn't bring herself to make him.

Pondering his words for a moment, she recalled that the thought of him married or in a relationship was something she thought about often, and it always left her feeling depressed and full of regret.

He dried his hands and turned around to look at her.

"You were the most carefree, laid-back person I'd ever met," she said. "I didn't know people like you even existed. How could I *not* have thought of you?" she asked. He ran his palm down his face again, a gesture she remembered. It was what he did when he was unhappy or worried.

And then he changed the subject. The badass Marine was apparently back. She wanted to finish the conversation but her house was a priority right now, not her stupid lovesick heart. "I have to start setting up the security in your house. I also need to read the old police reports and later we need to talk more about Ryan. Also, I read you have a tour coming up, which I'd like to discuss. But first I'm having my team check for prints, I don't trust the cops' work. My guys are waiting for me at your house. It's better if you hang out here today while I go. Is that cool?"

She didn't like this serious version of him, mostly because he was obviously trying to avoid talking about the past. Plus, he needed to realize a lot had changed. She wasn't a pushover or someone who could easily be steamrolled. He needed to consult with her, not make demands. "Please keep me in the loop, don't hide anything from me or make decisions without advising me first. I have a bunch of calls to make and some work on the new album to do anyway. Do your thing. Money's no object, I want the best, Jax."

"Even if you were destitute, I wouldn't do anything but, Meg," he said. "Help yourself to anything. There's food in the fridge." He pulled out a card. "Here's my number. Don't leave the house. If you need anything you call me, okay?"

"Okay, Jax. Thank you," she said, and he turned to

leave. She reached for his forearm and stopped him. "Last night . . . it was a weird night, I didn't get to tell you, but it's really good to see you, Jax. Really good."

He put his big paw over her hand on his forearm and squeezed a little. "It's really good to see you too, Meg." Then he let go and walked to his room but before he slipped inside he turned and added, "and Meg?" She looked back. "I'm so fuckin' proud of you, sweetheart," he said, before closing the door behind him. Her heart flipped and her stomach turned as she felt her lips curl up in a smile.

With those final words, Jax left and Megan tried to immerse herself in writing but being stalked, threatened, and reunited with her ex-hookup meant she wasn't in the mind-set for writing music. Especially when said ex was still devastatingly attractive. After two hours of doodling hearts and musical notes on her notepad and reliving the roller coaster of a night, Megan finally gave up.

I'm so fuckin' proud of you, sweetheart.

Damn. His parting words still sent a shiver of pure warmth through her. The man she'd met last night was certainly complicated. Rough, caring, tender, hard. Just who had Jackson Irons become? Megan looked around the large expanse of space trying to find something that could shed some light on this new Jax. Unfortunately, there was nothing. Everything in his house seemed to serve a purpose, nothing was there just because it was pretty or decorative.

Hesitantly, she opened his bedroom door and walked inside, feeling guilty about invading his privacy. She sat on the edge of his big wooden bed and ran her hand over the navy blue bedspread. He had two pillows, another large television, and a chest of drawers. Not one single knickknack. Not a photo. Nothing about the house said home. She laid her head down and looked up at the wooden ceiling fan spinning around and around.

How incredible it would feel to wake up next to him.

Even if the house wasn't a home, she felt comfortable and safe there. She turned her head and sniffed the pillow. It smelled just like he did.

She felt like a fool.

Laying on his bed. Smelling his pillow.

What the hell was wrong with her?

What if he came in and found her on her bed?

Quickly, she stood up, smoothed the comforter, and gently closed his bedroom door again. Reality set in quickly when her ever-beeping phone lit up with the latest wave of new missed calls, texts, and emails. Everyone was worried—her label, her PR team, her manager Glen, her friends and family. But she put off most of her family and friends by sending them quick texts assuring them that she was fine and she'd call them all tomorrow, not wanting to deal with them just yet. Her parents would ask a relentless stream of questions that would lead to an argument, and her friends would worry and try to coddle her. She didn't want any of that right now. She was still shaken up from last night and didn't want to relive it by having to recount the story. Those sweet words Jax had said just before leaving that morning were what she preferred to relive.

As for her label and PR, she declined any interviews until she was safe and back at home. In response they spoke in detail about the upcoming tour, which took her mind away from the hellish events of the previous night.

By eight that evening she was tired and hungry and eager to see Jax. Funny how she hadn't seen him for five years and now, after twenty-four hours, her anxiety over not seeing him was so high.

Would he just disappear again?

That thought made her restless and annoyed at herself. She didn't need him. She'd done very well for herself without him. But just because she didn't need him, didn't mean she didn't want him.

She spent most of the day snacking on chips and cookies and now she was in the kitchen getting ready to make a sandwich when she heard the front door open and close. Her heart picked up, but she closed her eyes and counted to ten.

Control yourself, Cruz!

"I brought a pizza," Jax said, dumping the box on the counter.

"Oh, yummy. That beats the grilled cheese sandwich I was about to make."

"I remember your cooking, that's why I brought the pizza."

"Ha. Ha. Living on my own and being broke . . . you learn a few things. Especially how to make a kickass grilled cheese." She put the bread back where she found it while Jax pulled out a slice of pizza and set it on a plate for her, then took one for himself. "Tomorrow you can wow me with your grilled cheese. Today, pizza."

"Sounds good to me," she agreed. "So, how'd it go today?"

Jax motioned toward a chair. Once she sat and he'd eaten most of a slice, he said, "So, you got a fuck ton of trees. That's a problem. Your house is massive, that's another problem. You have the ocean in the back—"

"Let me guess: that's another problem."

He nodded. "A big fucking huge one. And your current security system is shit. How you have a multimillion-dollar mansion and shit security is beyond me. A shit security system you don't even use," he added, taking another bite of pizza.

"But you can fix it, right? You can make it safe?"

"Of course. Made all the calls and work starts tomorrow. Will take a few days. Got a bunch of prints, too. Hope to get some answers tomorrow."

"Oh, good." She sighed in relief. "Thank God. Just make my house safe."

"Not your house, Meg. You. We're making *you* safe." He did the thing where he made her look at him as he said it. No fumbling around, no fidgeting, just his full attention on her. And his eyes were so honest as he said it, she knew he was sincere. She would be safe, so long as she was with him.

With her mouth open and a pizza hovering, she just stared at him. All the emotions she'd felt for him back then hadn't gone anywhere. There was no denying it. It was as if he'd never left and she wasn't sure what to do with it, especially since he wasn't the same Jax she once knew. Spending all day trying not to think about him, trying not to miss him, pretending she was being overly sentimental about her memories and desires for him . . . it was all bullshit. She was deluding herself. Nothing had changed on her part. The problem was, was he feeling the same way about her? Or was he just being a good friend? A good security guard?

Lost in thought, she barely noticed when he stood up. "Going to shower and sleep. Have to be at your house early. You got everything you need? You good?"

She felt the lump form in her throat. "Yep. All good."

She lied. She wasn't good. Not at all. And she wasn't even sure if it was because of Ryan or if it was from having Jax back in her life.

———————

The next morning, Megan saw that there was coffee already brewed and a note stuck to the coffee maker.

At your house. It was signed with his name and, as if he was trying not to be a barbarian, he added, as an afterthought, *Hope you slept well.*

She had slept well. Even though her thoughts kept wandering to the man a room away, the fact he was there made her feel safe and secure. As soon as she laid her head on the pillow she fell right asleep.

Now, making herself comfortable on one of his black leather recliners in the living room, she pulled out her cell phone and called him.

"Hello," Jax yelled into the phone.

"Hi."

"One sec," he said, obviously moving to a quieter area since she could hear the background noise die down. "Hi," he said breathlessly, and she felt a smile form on her face.

"Hi," she repeated, feeling stupid for sounding like a

teenager with a crush. She cleared her throat. "Any news?"

"Nothing. Put in a call this morning to Chief Martinez and nothing's come back from forensics on their end either."

"I'd like to go home. I need clothes, and my notebook, and stuff," she said.

"Not safe yet, Meg."

She looked around his house, which didn't look all that secure either. "And this is safe? I'm alone in here."

"There are cameras all along the perimeter of my house, the alarm's on, and I have my team nearby. Plus, no one would think to look for you there."

Oh God, he'd tell her if the cameras were around more than just the perimeter, right? Like in the interior of the house as well? She looked around as he spoke.

"Megan? You there? Megan?"

"Uh ... yeah, sorry. Um," she said distractedly, "I have some Skype meetings this afternoon and my stuff is in my office. I thought I'd go with you this morning, but you left before I woke up."

This time the silence was on his end of the phone. "I can have Joey bring you over, okay? But you stay inside the house the whole time."

Megan ignored his he-man commands, as if she would want to take a meandering stroll through her garden days after being threatened. "Joey? I remember him." This reunion just kept getting better. She hadn't known Joey more than a few hours, but she'd liked him immediately.

"He has a key. Otherwise don't open the door for anyone. He'll be there soon."

"Hey, Jax?" she began, still looking around the house, her thumbnail by her teeth. She was happy he hadn't given her a hard time about going home but something was still bothering her. "I . . . um . . . do you have cameras inside the house too?"

He chuckled loudly into the phone. "Why? Did you do something you weren't supposed to? Did you snoop? Nothing weird in my medicine cabinet, as far as I can remember."

"I'd never invade your privacy." She scrunched her face and then started to look around again. Was he watching her lie right this very second? "Maybe I'm just worried you're some sort of pervert, looking at me naked or something?"

"Interesting idea you just gave me. Maybe I'll have to install cameras inside the house tomorrow. Or better yet, in your room here in your house."

Was he flirting?

Gah!

She couldn't tell through the phone and with his deep voice, but it definitely seemed like he was flirting.

"I knew you were a pervert!"

He laughed loudly again. "See you in a few, Meg."

"Bye, Jax."

When he said Joey'd be there soon, Megan didn't realize he meant ten minutes. Luckily she was already dressed and was washing the mug she'd used when the front door opened and closed.

"Megan Cruz, as I live and breathe," Joey drawled, with that infectious grin she remembered vividly. He stood by the kitchen door with his arms open looking the embodiment of calm, cool, and collected, much like he had back then. Except now, his once smooth twentysomething-year-old skin was tanner and the lines around his mouth and eyes were more pronounced. His eyes, so brown they were almost black, still held that kindness they had back then. His head had been shaved when she met him before, so she hadn't realized how black his hair actually was.

Where Jax was the all-American boy next door who'd turned into an all-American hairy badass, Joey had gone from Mr. Congeniality to Mr. Tall, Dark, and Dangerous. The humor was still there, but there was something in his eyes that told a tale of things he'd rather forget.

With a smile on her face she went right into his arms. "Joey Clad." When they parted she looked him over. "What do they feed you Marines? You guys are huge."

"You're good for the ego, Megan." He winked and led

her to the front door. "Jax said you wanted to go home. Ready to go?"

"Yep."

He led her to his low-to-the-ground black sports car. She didn't know anything about cars but it looked expensive and fast, so she immediately buckled up. "So how have you been?" he asked.

"Well, except for the stalker thing, I've been pretty good. You?"

"Well, except for the war thing, I've been pretty good, too." She laughed loudly. He was just as playful as she remembered him, and just as quick-witted. Joey and Jax had been two peas in a pod, laughing, finishing each other's sentences, always up for an adventure. She'd only met him once before, and for only a short period of time, but he'd been very friendly and immediately made her feel like part of their group.

"You made it big, Megan. You must be proud of yourself."

Looking out the window, she said, "It feels pretty good, not going to lie. And you? Other than all those new muscles you got, you don't look like you've changed much. Not that I knew you that well before."

He shrugged. "I was lucky. I didn't get hurt, came back and we started ICS, which is doing well."

Didn't get hurt? Did Jax get hurt? She wanted to ask

him, but at the same time she didn't want to pry. But . . .

"Jax, though . . ."

"I know what you're going to say, but give him some slack. He's had it rough."

"What do you mean? What happened?" She turned her body to face Joey, wanting to absorb any information he had to give her about Jax.

"Nothing that doesn't happen to a shit ton of servicemen. The short of it is, lots of men died and he was hurt; lucky to have survived. He doesn't like to talk about it."

She needed more. "He looks sad, Joey. So hardened."

They pulled up to the house and he turned to her. "During the last year, Jax has been . . . not himself. After a few drinks when he would loosen up, he did talk about you, though."

"He did?" She perked up, wanting to know, grabbing any morsel of information he was willing to share. She'd talked about him to Nelly and Taylor too, especially that first year. She always wondered if he regretted those days they spent together. Or the way they parted ways. Did he like her music? Did he know what *Promise Me* was about? "He really had no idea about TNT?"

"Yes. 'I wonder what Megan is doing,' or, 'You think Meg ended up a lawyer?' Shit like that. We didn't really watch a lot of TV in the desert or hear pop music, so no, he really didn't know. Neither did I."

"Oh, well, wow," she said, feeling a little better about things. It would've been exponentially worse if he'd known about her, known where to find her, and had chosen to stay away. She looked down at her purse, zipping and unzipping it repeatedly. "I thought about him too. I wasn't sure I'd ever see him again. It was very surpr—Oh my god!"

Megan screamed when she looked up to her house. "Oh. My. God!" She opened the car door and slammed it shut. "Jackson Iron!" Megan yelled at the top of her lungs. "Where are all my trees?"

No! No! No! This was not happening.

It had to be a dream. Her months of dedication to her yard hadn't been ripped out in a matter of hours. The peace it had given her to map out where every single tree, flower, and topiary would go, and then, with her own bare hands, help plant them, tend to them, and watch them grow. All her planning and hard work . . . no no no.

Joey stood by his car laughing his ass off. "Do you find this funny?" She narrowed her eyes at Joey, pointing at the construction crew on her front lawn.

"A little," Joey admitted as he walked past her to the full crew of men ripping a huge palm trees out of the earth.

"Is that . . ." she sputtered the words in disbelief, "a . . . is that a bulldozer?'

"I believe it's called a backhoe, babe." Joey looked like

he wanted to laugh again, but the glare she gave him was enough to effectively shut him up and send him off to look for Jax.

The man had lost his damn mind! How could he have thought this would be okay? Just moments ago they'd spoken and he'd promised to run things by her first.

Stomping to the front of her house, Megan climbed the grand keystone stairway, taking two steps at a time. She turned to the crew, fists clenched. "Stop! Stop it!" Some of them stopped immediately. Some ignored her, and others didn't hear her over the noise of all the heavy equipment. "Stop immediately!" she yelled again, stomping her foot, at the very moment that Jax came through the front door.

"What are you doing?" he asked, clueless.

"What am *I* doing?" She looked around and swept her arm to the crew of workers destroying her property. "What the hell are *you* doing?"

He had his arms crossed over his chest like some sort of impenetrable statue. Well, she wasn't scared of him. Right now he should be scared of her! "I'm ensuring your safety," he said. "You told me to make you safe."

"By destroying all my landscaping? Setting aside the fortune it cost, it took years to get it this way. Years! I loved it! I picked out every single goddamn frangipani and bougainvillea. Oh my god, my mango tree—" She stomped down the stairs toward the big hole that used to house a mango tree.

"Calm down."

Calm down? Was he crazy?

She whipped her head around and poked him with her index finger. "Do not tell me to calm down!" All the workers were looking at them, awaiting instructions, but she couldn't care less. She was furious and distraught. "You're all fired!" Then she turned to Jax, fighting back tears. "Especially you."

"Why don't you guys take a break?" Jax said. He followed her inside the house seeming equally angry. Why was *he* mad?

"Now, babe, you need security. The shit with Ryan is serious."

Megan bristled. "Don't you think I know that? And don't call me babe," she hissed, her hands clenched by her sides. He was being condescending now, and she didn't appreciate it. He wanted to call her babe when he saw her in the morning or when she brought him a glass of water? Okay, those were all babe-worthy moments. "Good morning, babe." Or, "Thank you for the water, babe." Fine. But babeing when he was pissed . . . no way. That got right under her skin. "This is messed up, Jax. You destroyed my yard." She shoved him out of the way and started into the house but he grabbed her forearm and stopped her.

"Maybe I went overboard, but it came from a good place. I want you to be safe, Meg." When he called her Meg and spoke in that soft tone, she could see the guy from all those years back shining through. She looked over her shoulder and then back at him, her lips quivered. She was trying her hardest to contain her tears. Being angry was easier than feeling nostalgic, which is what happened when he called her Meg and said nice things to her. She closed her eyes and took a deep breath before opening them again.

"I loved my yard. It brought me peace. It was the one thing that I enjoyed doing just for me, without anyone around to film me or critique. Everything I do is always under a microscope and involves a crew of people," she said, her shoulder sagging low and her lips turned down.

She needed space from him, from the disarray around her house, from all the feelings she had when she was around him. "I have a meeting. I'll be in my office."

———————

Jax couldn't remember when he'd felt like a bigger asshole. Obviously, he hadn't torn down her yard with the intent to hurt her or piss her off. But hurting her was exactly what he'd accomplished. This was not the way he'd treat a normal client, acting without consulting with them. But nothing with Megan was normal.

She was Megan.

His Megan.

At least that's how it felt at one time. And thinking of all the shit that Ryan could've done just made him go overboard. Where Megan was concerned, he wasn't thinking clearly.

Standing outside next to Joey, he looked around the barren yard.

"Well, there definitely won't be any place to hide now." Joey teased.

"Fuck you, very much."

"She'll come around, don't worry about it." Joey said, patting him on the back, hard. "She's pretty fucking famous, you know? How did we not know she was famous?"

"When's the last time you saw an MTV video?"

"Pretty sure that's not a thing anymore, Irons."

"Didn't really have time to keep up with the top forty in the desert, did you?"

Leaning his arms on the veranda, Joey said, "You know I didn't, brother."

After a few quiet moments, Joey asked. "You never looked her up? Googled her?"

Jax reluctantly shook his head. "Didn't really want to know," he admitted. "Seeing her happily married with a family, or miserable as an attorney? Neither was anything I wanted to see. Even after I came back last year, I still couldn't bring myself to look her up."

"She's pretty hot. I don't remember her being that hot before."

A deep guttural growl vibrated through Jax's body and Joey laughed. "Relax, man. You should pick up where you guys left off."

"I'm doing a job. She's my client. Not gonna happen."

"Who the fuck cares? She's Megan."

Exactly: She's Megan. How could he not understand? Joey had been there with him when he moped around drinking and waxing poetic about Megan for months. At one point, the men in his squad held an intervention and ruled that the subject of Megan was prohibited.

Starting something back up with her . . . no, it couldn't happen. First, she was his client and he couldn't get distracted—not again. Last time he'd mixed business with pleasure he'd lost his entire team. He should have had his guard up and been ready for combat at any given moment. He had been in war, after all. And second, if it didn't work out, he would be crushed. And not crushed like he had been years back when he lost his friends, but a not-able-to-breathe kind of despair. It wasn't worth the pain.

Except deep down he knew she *was* worth it.

She was worth everything.

"I don't want to lose focus on the objective. Maybe we should call Dawson, he's the best security guy money can buy." Dawson installed the most sophisticated security systems in the market but the prices were astronomical and the wait list was long. ICS only used him on special cases with very high-risk clients.

"Don't do this to yourself, brother. This isn't Iraq. The stalker isn't an IED. What happened then wasn't your fault and whatever happens now won't be either. And you know everything we're installing here is top-grade equipment. Dawson will go crazy and it'll be weeks of construction, installing panic rooms and exit plans and whatever other Inspector Gadget shit he's invented."

"I'm not doing anything to myself, Jo. I'm just doing my job. I know this isn't Iraq but the threat is real. That wacko was here, man. Not just in her house, in her goddamn room. She had a fucking butcher knife in her hand. What the hell was she going to do? He could've killed her." Jax paused. "We were all sitting around laughing and drinking when our entire goddamn unit was blown up. We should've been fucking vigilant. Luis, Estevez . . ." He shook his head thinking about his men. "I think about that moment all the fucking time. They're gone and we're here. Wives lost husbands. Kids lost fathers. It fucking hurts." He pressed his fingers against his chest. "Their friendship got in the way. We got too comfortable. We lost sight of why we were there. And I'm not going to risk her safety because I want to get my dick wet."

He cringed at his own crude words. But he needed Joey to understand that this was work. He'd made the decision about the trees because the fucking lawn was a hazard and impossible to keep safe. Not because Megan was already twisting him into knots or clouding his judgment.

"You're implying I dropped the ball too, Jax. We were all friends. And I know you know that it's not my fault." It's true. He didn't blame Joey. Yet he couldn't stop blaming himself. "Who do you think you're talking to? She's not just some chick to you. You know it and I know it. But if that's the kind of asshole shit you need to say to yourself to make you feel better, go ahead. I'm just saying you don't have to keep her at arm's length. You can have a relationship with her *and* keep her safe. But if you feel that strongly about it, then get someone else from the team to detail her and that way you can be with her." They were both looking out to the yard but that statement made Jax stand up straighter and grip the banister he'd been leaning against. Right now, he hated that Joey knew him so well. It was hard to lie to himself when his brother was laying it down for him.

"No. It's gotta be me. I keep her safe." He felt the vibration from his voice from deep in his chest. His decision was final. He wasn't going to let anyone protect his woman. And yes, he might not ever admit it out loud, but she was his. She'd always been his, and after they parted ways, she would still be his. And there was no way in fucking hell he'd let anyone hurt what was his.

Joey rolled his eyes and shook his head. "You have a hard fucking head, man. I have to go. Got a new client coming in."

"Keep me posted," Jax said, not looking at his friend. He was lost in his thoughts.

Someone else protecting Megan? Fuck no.

He'd sacrifice a possible relationship with her if it meant he was the one keeping her safe. He would never be able to sleep at night knowing someone was doing a half-assed job.

"Will do. And try to keep the heavy machinery rental at a minimum while I'm gone," Joey yelled over his shoulder. Jax didn't bother to turn around when he gave Joey the finger.

Chapter 5

When Megan finally emerged from her office four hours later, she looked calmer, but Jax couldn't gauge her mood.

"I didn't want to disturb you." Jax shrugged, meeting her eyes from the chair he'd placed strategically in sight of her office door.

He'd spent the last hours warring with himself. Should he go apologize? Should he give her some space? Personally, when he was upset, he needed space to think things through, so he decided to go that route with her. Space.

But shit, it was hard not to go comfort her, explain himself, apologize. . . .

Especially since this Megan was so different from the one from years back. She was more confident and feisty now, even though today she'd looked like she was fighting back tears, as if the damn yard had been more devastating than the break-in. Obviously he'd fucked up, not realizing how much the landscaping had meant to her. Now she just looked . . . closed off.

When Megan didn't say anything, he nodded towards the kitchen. "I saved you a sandwich, you must be hungry."

"I am. Thanks." Her voice was cool and polite, completely distant. And in that second, Jax wished he was facing the angry, passionate Megan from the yard. Yelling was better than the tense silence as she walked past him to the kitchen.

He followed her in, and her somber expression when she looked through the window over the sink at the barren front yard gutted him. If he could kick his own ass, he would.

The Marines had taught him a lot. One thing it taught him was how to be a man, how to put his feelings on lockdown and power through any situation. What it had *not* taught him was how to deal with a sad woman. This was a skill set he hadn't acquired.

"I sent the crew home while the installers finish the cabling for the security system outside," he said awkwardly. He pulled the chair out for her and then went around the table to sit too, sliding the sandwich toward her.

"Thanks for the sandwich."

Fuck.

He wanted to yell.

He wanted *her* to yell.

Instead he took a deep calming breath and slid his chair over next to her and turned her chair to face him. He needed eye contact. He needed her to look at him when he spoke as confirmation that she was listening and processing, and also so he could gauge her mood. "Megan? I'm sorry. Really, I didn't think. I feel like an asshole. I was so focused on my mission that I lost sight of things."

With downturned lips, but without tears—thank God—she spoke softly. "I'm not a mission, Jax. I'm a person, and once this is all over, I have to come back home and live my life—and in my life, there's a lot of gardening. My life is hectic and loud and gardening helps me relax so that I can have a clear head when I write my music." She let out a puff of air. "I guess I understand why you did it, but now when I look outside all I'll see is that I'm scared and that this stalker guy can be out there watching me."

"I asked the guys to save as many trees as possible and the ones that were salvageable are all being stored at a nursery. Some were already cut, destroyed, and thrown into the eighteen wheeler before you got here, though. As soon as this is all over, I'll call the crew back and make sure you have all your plants and trees back exactly the way they were. I'll even plant them myself if it makes you feel better."

Jax was desperate for her to understand. Desperate to

make it better. And for a few tense seconds after his frantic explanation, he was sure it wouldn't make a difference.

With a long sigh, Megan's posture eased, just a little.

It was one thing for her to be scared or even angry at the situation she was in with the stalker, but another thing altogether that Jax's stupid overprotectiveness was the cause of her anger, or worse . . . her sadness. He couldn't deal with that. He needed her to trust him. Forgive him. Know that it all came from a good place.

"I know. It's just . . . I'm not used to anyone just coming in and taking over. My life may seem chaotic, but when I'm home, it's sane and orderly and I've made it to where I know exactly what I want and how I want it. Like my gardening, for example. I know it doesn't make sense to you, but it does to me. It unclutters my mind. You swooping in and not only destroying my yard but making decisions on my behalf, without even so much as talking it through first, it's a very big deal for me. At it's core, it's the reason I'm always arguing with my parents."

Jax remembered all about her controlling parents. Hell, he'd witnessed it firsthand the other day when he'd had the misfortune of meeting Rose. He didn't want to be lumped in with them.

Absolutely not.

"I understand. I'll consult with you first. You're the client." She was a lot more than a client, but still. . . .

"I'm going to hold you to that, Jackson. And not only because I'm your client, but because you know me and you know this is important to me. And the fact that you saved some of my trees does make me feel a little better."

"I'm glad, sweetheart," he said, letting out his own small sigh of relief. She even smiled a little when he called her sweetheart. He inched closer to her, tucking a stray strand of hair behind her ear. "I need you to understand that I go overboard because I'm worried. I want to make sure everything is perfectly safe."

"I know. Why do you think I'm letting you off the hook so easily?" She picked up the sandwich and took a huge bite. "I'm also so hungry, I don't have the energy to be mad," she said with her mouth full of food.

"So I'm forgiven?"

"Forgiven is a big statement. More like, I'm not firing you or clubbing you with one of the palm tree stumps you removed."

He chuckled. "Fair enough."

She took another bite, her mouth opening wide—not at all ladylike, but damn if her confidence wasn't a turn-on. The woman was hungry, so she fucking ate. And Jax couldn't take his eyes off her. Especially when she licked some crumbs off of her lips with her tongue. Unable to contain himself, he reached forward and wiped her lip with his thumb, his palm lingering close to her face.

She closed her eyes and gasped softly, then whispered, "déjà vu."

He crinkled his forehead questioningly.

"At that hole-in-the-wall café where you first took me? You did that same thing." She averted her eyes and went back to the sandwich. He wanted to say so many things, but what could he possibly say? He needed to keep this professional. He needed to stop the sly touches. Needed to stop caring whether she was sad, as long as she was safe. Luckily, she changed the subject after the next bite. "This is so good." She moaned and opened up the sandwich to look inside. "Roast beef? Mayo? I know for a fact, that this did not come from my fridge."

"Hell no," he chuckled. "You only had healthy shit. My crew would pass out if I brought out a salad for them. Who the hell eats that much kale? I had one of the guys go to the deli and pick up sandwiches."

"Nancy's going to kill me."

"Who's Nancy?"

"She's the PR chick from the label. She's always on our asses to keep in shape. Thus the reason the food in the fridge sucks," she mumbled with a full mouth.

"That's some bullshit. You look great, Meg. If I haven't said it yet, you do. I had a memory of what you looked like five years ago, but seeing you now again?" He shook his head. "My memory was off. You're gorgeous." Damn it, not two seconds ago he was vowing to keep things professional. Well, this was friendly and they did, after all have a past. So friendly professional would be okay, he thought, knowing full well he was full of shit.

"Thanks." Apparently the table was fascinating, because she was looking down, avoiding eye contact, her face hot. He leaned over and with his index finger he lifted her chin. "Stop hiding your eyes from me."

"I'm not."

"Yeah, baby, you are." His gruff voice and the endearment surprised him as much as it surprised her. The way her brown eyes widened and her lips parted . . .

Fuck. He needed a change of conversation before he leaned over and licked those plump lips. "So anyway, we can stay here tonight. The inside alarms should be done. There's a few things I want to fix, but you should be good. They'll finish the outside shit tomorrow."

She looked up, confused. "We?"

Was that a hopeful *we*? It sounded like it and his pulse spiked. "Until this is all resolved, I'm staying close."

She looked at him questioningly.

"I won't cramp your space, this house is huge, you won't even notice I'm here."

"You're like seventeen feet tall."

"Six-two."

"Same thing. You're kinda a hard guy to blend in."

"I'll do my best."

"Will you keep bringing food like this?"

"Would it make you happy?"

She nodded wildly.

"Then I'll bring sandwiches every day."

It was later that night and everything had finally calmed down. The installers had left and Jax had been debriefed on all the goings-on with ICS and the various new clients. Megan had a few more calls and meetings to tend to. Sitting outside, with his feet on the banister, his arms behind his head, looking out at the ocean, Jax had to admit that her house, although ridiculously huge, was a respite from the noise and crowds of the city. He was enjoying the quiet when the door opened and closed behind him and he dropped his legs and stood.

"No, stay. Mind if I join you?" she said, a hand on his shoulder guiding him back down. Pulling out the chair beside him, she sat, propped her feet up, and handed him a beer. He glanced to the side to watch her as she got comfortable and twisted open the other beer she held. The flowy yellow skirt that went to her calves hung down, almost touching the floor. Her feet were in some kind of fancy flip-flop-looking thing that showcased her pretty toes. The toes were painted white, and her brown hair was tied in a crazy-looking knot on her head.

One of the best things about Megan was that she was beautiful without trying. No makeup, no extravagant hairdo, no fancy skintight clothes. And that's exactly what made his fingers twitch at the moment. He wanted to pull the rubber band out of her hair and run his fingers through it, see if she'd moan his name when he pulled a little on her scalp.

And what was she wearing underneath that skirt?

She used to be a plain white cotton panties kind of girl. Was she now a sexy lingerie kind of woman?

"Any update?" she asked, but he couldn't tear his eyes away from the white tank top that made the swell of her breasts look mouthwatering.

"You're . . ." he ran a finger along her bare shoulder, " . . . glittery?"

She looked down at her chest and then her shoulder. "It's probably just the moisturizer I use after I shower. We call it shimmer, not glitter."

He tried to suppress a chuckle. "Well, excuse me, Ms. Rock Star. I'll have to read up on the correct protocol."

She winked at him, cheekily. "Next thing I know you'll be calling my lip stain ChapStick. I don't know if I could forgive that, Jackson."

When she puckered her lips, he had trouble concentrating on anything else. He loved playful Megan. Except playful Megan was also sexy-as-fuck Megan, and he couldn't tear his eyes away.

"Let me know when you're done staring at my mouth, so we can talk."

He licked his lips unintentionally, and was moments away from pushing her top down, taking her tits out and biting on one of those nipples. Were they still that light pink shade? Did she still taste the same? Hesitantly, his eyes moved back to her face. Her cheeks were flushed but her eyes were locked on his and her breathing seemed a little labored. Fuck. If she looked down, there was no way he would be able to hide the way his cock was straining against his gym shorts.

Sighing heavily, he closed his eyes and turned his face back to the ocean. Why even bother to pretend he wasn't staring? He was. It was obvious. It's not like she looked upset about it. "Okay, I'm done staring. What was the question again?"

She laughed and took a sip from the bottle of beer in her hand. "Any updates?"

She used to hate beer. Even these little changes surprised him. Made him realize how many things he didn't know about her. How much he'd missed.

"Nothing on the prints. He's not in any database."

"So what does that mean?"

"Means we keep our eyes and ears open. Meanwhile, I have my team digging." He turned to her, taking a swig of beer. "I read the police reports earlier today. The original two based on your previous complaints. The first was about a letter you received when you got back from a tour?"

She let out a breath and looked out into the ocean. The concern she'd been hiding was back on her face, and it bothered him that he'd been the one to break that peaceful looking expression. But, this was why he was here, right? For her safety. And it was time to talk more about that.

"We had a show in Amsterdam a year and a half ago. It was the first stop on our European tour. After the concert, we went out to celebrate at a nearby pub and there was a guy lurking around. He introduced himself as Ryan. Very nice, asked for my autograph. The only unusual thing about him was that he didn't want Nelly or Taylor's autographs, just mine, and he hovered a little too long. We hadn't really blown up yet, we were still relatively unknown. But like I said, he was nice."

"Taylor? Your guitarist, right?"

"Yeah. She's in Japan doing some promo for her clothing line right now. I miss her like crazy. Haven't seen her in two months. This skirt is from her line, not that you needed that information." She reached for her skirt and swayed it a little and smiled.

"It's pretty." He took another gulp of beer. "But most things look pretty on you."

Her smile widened and she was about to turn her eyes away, but with his index finger he gently guided her face back to his. It was impossible not to compliment her; she was just that beautiful to him. So she just needed to get used to it. "You have millions of adoring fans. I can't imagine you don't get compliments all the damn time. But with me, you get shy."

"Well, yeah," she said, matter-of-factly. "You're you."

He furrowed his eyebrows. "I don't know what that means."

"I don't know. I guess . . . you're special to me and it means something when you say those things." She waved her hands around, dismissing the comment almost as quickly as she started. "I don't know, I'm just being silly, I guess. What were we talking about?"

He wanted to know more about the "you're special" part of her comment. Special as in a friend or special as in she wanted more? His pulse quickened—he wasn't sure what he'd say if she wanted more, or worse, how he'd feel if she just thought of him as a friend.

He cleared his throat. "You were telling me about Ryan."

"Oh yeah. So anyway, every time I'd move around the pub, he seemed to be there, trying to get my attention somehow. As I told you earlier, he had the most unusual eyes and I told him so. I called him Ryan the Cat." She scrunched her face as if she'd eaten something sour. "He said he'd never been told that before but that he loved cats and liked the comparison. Then he offered to buy me a drink. I politely declined. He asked me to dance, even though there was no music. Again, I politely declined. He even asked if he could walk me back to the hotel. I didn't want to cause a big scene, so I didn't have him thrown out when his presence got a little overwhelming." She shrugged. "Instead, when I realized he wouldn't be leaving anytime soon, I snuck out with one of the security guys back to the hotel. We had a lot of tour dates and I completely forgot about the incident until I got back home three months later and there was a letter waiting for me."

"Tell me about the letter. The report referenced it but I haven't gotten my hand on a copy yet. Should have it tomorrow. "

"One second, I'll show you. I made a copy before I handed it over to the police." She stood up and jogged inside. A few minutes later she returned with a photocopy of the letter.

My little mouse,

I waited for you while you were in the bathroom. But

*when you didn't come back I realized you wanted
to be chased, that is why you teased me all night, so
chase I will my Meggy. I've been watching you, following your tour. When you sing, my cock gets so
hard. I know if you just gave me a chance you'd realize we were meant to be together.*

Can't wait to play again. I love games.
—Your cat.

"Jesus."

"Exactly, right? I wasn't playing games. And honestly,
I just thought he was an excited fan. I didn't really feel
threatened at the time so much as uncomfortable or
maybe even annoyed. Until I got back and saw the letter,
of course. Then I was freaked out."

He shook the letter in his hand. "And this was where?"

"It was mailed here but it didn't have a return address."

"Don't you have a PO Box or some other place where
you get fan mail?"

"Of course I do. That's what's weird. It came here. To
my house. I have everything in different corporations,
including this house. It's not like you can just type in
Megan Cruz in Google and my address pops up."

"And nothing happened with that case."

"They said that without more information, there
wasn't much they could do. All I knew was that his name

was Ryan. Plus, months had passed and I hadn't heard anything else, so I let it go."

Jax took out his phone, flattened the paper on the nearby table, and took a series of photos.

"What're you doing?"

"Sending it to Joey. We have some forensic handwriting software in the office. It works like fingerprints. If this guy's never been in the database, it wouldn't turn anything up, but it's still worth a shot. I'm also going to try and get the original letter and try to run it for prints. I want to make sure the cops didn't miss anything."

"You want me to call the officer who's handling—"

"No, I got it."

"You can check out fingerprints too?"

"Our equipment and software is military grade. The cops are involved because you called them and because it's the right thing to do. But you're crazy if you think I'm leaving this to them and all their red tape. I'm doing my own investigation alongside of them."

"Okaaaay. . . ."

Placing the letter aside, he turned back to her. "So, you got this letter. What next?"

"Nothing until six months ago, which was about nine months after getting the letter. I got a creepy drawing in an email."

"I read about that too. Show me?"

Fumbling around with her phone she found what she was looking for and held it up for him to see. The screen glowed in the dim light. "Is that a mouse?"

"Yep."

"What else?"

Handing him her phone, she said, "Scroll down."

"A cat?"

"A deranged looking cat," she added, and he saw her shiver slightly. Anger took hold of him. He didn't like to see her frightened, and damn, how many months had she been dealing with this. Alone. He turned his attention back to the photo.

It was a hand-drawn cat, missing big patches of fur, its eyes bulging out, its teeth razor sharp. It was salivating.

Jax pulled Megan's chair closer to him and held the phone out so that they could both see as he went back and forth between the two photos. "It's running. Look," he finally said, pointing to the little legs and hair of the hand-drawn mouse. "It's a mouse being chased."

Pulling the screen closer to her face, she shifted her head side to side. "Damn, you're right. That's even creepier. Since I'm the mouse in the scenario, it seems."

"And this email address is bogus, I read that in the second police report," he said.

"Yes. And again the cops said there wasn't much they could do. Ryan didn't use his name. But it's obviously him."

"I want access to your emails. Joey's specialty is anything to do with computers. Maybe he can trace that back."

"Okay, yeah sure."

"Anything else?" he asked.

She shook her head.

"That's it?" He took her hands in his and squeezed. "Even the smallest thing could mean something. Think, Megan."

She looked down at their joined hand and then back up at him and swallowed. "Well, this New Year's Eve we performed at Bayfront Park just a few miles away from here and I could have sworn I saw him backstage. I was in the middle of a song, and when I looked to the side I thought I saw him. When I looked again, he was gone. But it's been so long since that first time, the day I met him, that I may not even remember how he looks anymore. I think it was just my eyes playing tricks on me."

"I need the information of whoever put that event together. I want to see if security cameras caught anything during the setup. And can you get me any videos made during the performance, by RLC or your PR people."

"I'll get Glen, my manager, on it. It was probably nothing, though."

"Or it was something."

She pulled her hands away and sat back, her eyes trained on the ocean as she rubbed her arms, her left leg bobbing up and down.

Damn it.

"I'm sorry I scared you, but you need to be a little scared, Meg. You can't make light of this. If you see anything, even if you think it's nothing, you have to tell me, okay?"

"Yeah. Okay." But she wasn't looking at him.

"You're cold. Let's go inside."

"No, not cold. Just nervous, I guess. I—"

"Tell me."

"I was taught to be strong. My parents may have controlled me when I was younger, but for the most part I had principles and beliefs and I held strong to them." She turned her head and her eyes were full of unshed tears, and all he wanted to do was lift her up and carry her away, never let anything happen to her again, even if it meant he'd have to stand vigil in front of her safe little bubble for the rest of his life. "My mother is the most notorious cutthroat attorney in Florida. Articles have been written about her. And my father, well, he's a shark. I've never seen my mother lose it, not even when I didn't speak with them for almost two years, not when my father suffered a massive heart attack. But, God Jax, I was so scared in that closet. I thought . . ." Her voice cracked. "I thought I was going to die the other night, and now, telling you all this . . ."

That was it, he couldn't keep his hands off her one more second. Fuck, it wasn't even about her right now. It was about him. *He* needed to hold her. Taking hold of her wrist, he brought her onto his lap and into his arms. "There's nothing weak about being scared, sweetheart. You did everything right. You called the police and hid. Anyone who sees you as anything less than brave is a fuckin' idiot."

They were so close, and if he moved forward just a little or if she tipped her head up . . .

It would be easy to get lost in this woman, he thought. But after seeing her admit how scared she actually was, he needed to focus. He could comfort her, but to cross the line into something further—this wasn't the time or place to rekindle something that might have been. Maybe once this Ryan fucker was caught, Jax could see if things were still as explosive as they were five years ago.

Fuck it. That was bullshit—of course it would be explosive.

And right now he couldn't be five minutes without touching her. He stroked her cheek with his thumb. "I should go, Meg."

She twined her fingers with his and brought his knuckles to her lips. "No you shouldn't." Her voice was low and sultry and she said it while kissing each knuckle.

"I'm here to make you safe."

"When you're close, like this, I feel safe." Her hands snaked into his beard and he moaned at the way her nails gently scratched his skin. He pulled her closer, her tits pressed against his chest. His hand snuck under her shirt and he rubbed her back.

"You're making it impossible to stay away, baby." His face hovered so close to her neck. "I'm trying to be good."

"Don't try so hard."

"You're scared," he whispered into her neck. "You have a stalker."

She sat across his lap and there was no way in hell she couldn't feel his cock. The way her ass wiggled in his arms . . . his self-control was waning.

"Right now, I'm not thinking about the stalker," she whispered, bringing her face up to his, her lips a whisper away.

At that moment, her phone rang, shattering the moment with the sound of a popular song he'd heard on the radio countless times. He wondered if it was one of hers.

"Ignore it," she said, her big eyes glazed with lust, and he was about to do just that when it rang again. From the corner of his eye he saw the caller ID light up.

Unknown Caller

Reality hit Jax like a bucket of cold water. To the balls.

Reaching over her to fetch the phone from the table, he showed her the screen, his own mind sifting through various scenarios. Was it Ryan? Were they being watched right now? How quickly could he shield Megan and reach for his gun if shit went down? Two targets in the middle of acres of land where no one would hear a thing . . .

Megan sat stiff against him, while he slid his finger over the phone's answer screen. She spoke into the phone. "Hello?" There was breathing on the other end of the line.

"Who is this? Hello?" Her voice was shaky. Jax's grip on Megan tightened. Was she thinking the same things he was?

He grabbed the phone from her hand. "Hello?" The person was still on the line, he could hear breathing and movement. "Don't hide behind a phone. Who is this? Man the hell up and talk."

Jax stood, Megan in his arm, and gently placed her back on her chair. He looked around the backyard, but all that was visible was her large yard and then the dark ocean. This is the kind of shit that would make him regret starting things up again—being distracted. She had the ability to thoroughly distract him.

Everything around them intensified as they waited for the caller to say something.

Where they had been enjoying the quiet lull of the

ocean and a calm breeze just a moment ago, now every crash of waves or ruffle of leaves in the night air made his skin prick and put his defenses on guard. He wanted to yell and demand that the person speak up, though he knew provoking the caller was reckless. "I'll give you one last chance before I hang up. *Who is this?*" His voice was strong and commanding but it wasn't hostile, even if hostility was the emotion he was currently feeling. The person on the other line didn't speak, but the sound of his heavy breathing grew louder. As if he was exerting himself on the other end. And then, a few seconds later, the call ended. Jax's hand was on the weapon by his side as he continued to look around. Her mansion was so massive it was difficult to secure it by himself.

"It could've been anyone, Jax. A telemarketer, a wrong number." Her voice gave her away. She didn't believe for one second it was a wrong number. Not for one damn second.

Unless the caller was jogging when he called, it wasn't too difficult to figure out what the heavy breathing was all about.

"Bullshit." Jax pulled out his weapon.

"You had that on you all this time?"

"This is always on me." He opened the door to her house. "Ass inside, babe."

She looked around the backyard as if she too was trying to figure out if the caller was watching them. "Now," he barked.

She walked inside and he locked the door behind her. "I'll lock up," he said. He needed to do a parameter sweep before bed and make sure everything was copacetic, then he needed to call Joey about tracing the call. "Good night, Megan."

"Good night?" She looked crestfallen. "But, I . . . I mean—"

This wasn't the time and he shouldn't have even let what had just happened get that far. He couldn't have done anything about the guy calling, but he could've been more prepared to deal with it, if his head hadn't been on the way Megan smelled or felt. She was a far too tempting a distraction that would make his job of protecting her impossible. "Good night, Megan," he repeated, his tone final.

———————

Annoyed at the quick change in Jax from *something finally happening* to *closed-off Marine*, Megan didn't even bother wishing him a goodnight when she walked up the stairs to her room. It's not as if he would've listened anyway—he was already back outside in security mode. Jax was overreacting, there was a big possibility that it had just been a wrong number. That happened all the time, and not just to her ... to everyone. Even though the breathing, almost panting, had sent shivers down her spine.

Quickly changing into pajamas, she grabbed her notebook, sat on the bed, and tried to write. Lately, lyrics hadn't been coming easily, but tonight the words were flowing as she pushed down thoughts about the call and focused on what had almost happened with Jax. Talking about Ryan had been tough, but the second Jax had pulled her into his arms, her emotions had gone from scared to ... something else. Her pulse had raised, her heart had fluttered and damn ... her nipples had gotten uncomfortably hard. It had always been that way with Jax. When he was around, everything else faded into the background.

Megan had only ever begged a man to kiss her once—that horrible kiss cam moment five years ago—but she wasn't above doing just that when it came to Jax. Everything between them was complicated, but even as he had wavered between pushing her away and pulling her closer, Megan had found her mind drifting to how his beard would feel when they kissed. It was soft under her hands. But on the sensitive skin on her face, or between her thighs, would it tickle or would it feel rough? For some reason the thought of it feeling a little rough was alluring. Something about the thought of having the redness, the proof he'd been *there* long after he'd finished, was arousing. But the ringing of her phone had shattered the delicious tension, and then the mood had shifted once again.

With all the confusing feelings pouring through her veins, it was easy to make it all into music. After all Jax had always been her best source of inspiration. The words flew from her pen: lust, loss, rediscovery, the pang of reuniting. At some point—two minutes or two hours later—emotionally and physically exhausted, she fell asleep.

Startling abruptly, the paper of her notebook sticking to her face, Megan sat up, disoriented, in the dark. A noise—something like a whimper—sounded in the hallway outside her bedroom.

Her mind whirled. Was it an intruder? Thoughts and images were racing through her head when she heard another whimper, louder this time—almost like an injured animal—coming from just outside the room. She started to walk to the door uncertainly, hopping from one foot to the next, unsure of what to do. Should she investigate? Where was Jax? The quiet cry came again and Megan didn't stop to think. Whatever the noise was, hiding behind her bedroom door wasn't going to help anything. With a shaking hand, she quietly turned the knob and cracked the door open a sliver.

Right by her bedroom door, on the floor, sat Jax, his legs outstretched, his arms crossed over his chest, his head thrashing from side to side. His eyes were shut tight and there was a muscle spasming on his cheek. His features were distorted, full of anguish and pain. Throwing the door the rest of the way open, Megan kneeled down next to him.

"Jax!" She shook him carefully but he just continued to grumble and move around. "Jackson!"

He threw his head back, banging it against the wall, and impulsively grabbed her wrists. So tightly she winced. "Jax, it's me. It's just me, Megan. You're having a nightmare."

She didn't pull away, afraid of what his reaction would be to the sudden action in this confused state. Instead she continued to whisper to him, nonsense words, sounds, phrases, about how it was just a nightmare and to come back to her until his thrashing settled and his muscles tensed with awareness.

"Hey," she whispered softly when his eyes finally opened. "It's just me, Megan." From the way he looked at her—through her—it was obvious he was still disoriented. "It's okay, you were just dreaming."

Sharply, he released her hands and stood up, heaving for air. "Hey, you're okay. It's okay," she soothed, rubbing her hands over his arms.

"Fuck." His voice was rough, gritty with sleep and the shadow of nightmares. The cloudy look was gone from Jax's eyes, and Megan could see him assessing the hallway, his position, her. Those sharp eyes lingered over her sleep-rumpled shirt, her hair, before setting on where her hands still rested on his forearms and her wrists. Realization set in when he saw his grip. Quickly, he grabbed her hands in his own, his grip now firm but infinitely gentle, while he moved her wrists side to side in the dim hallway light. "Goddamn it!" his voice whispered in a breath. "Megan, did I hurt you?"

"No," she said, still kneeling, her hands out—defensively, or maybe cautiously? "Not at all. Are you okay? Why were you on the floor?"

"Guess I dozed off."

"On the floor?"

He brushed her question aside. "Sometimes I have nightmares." He ran his hands through his hair distractedly. Now he was looking anywhere but at Megan. And didn't that just piss her off a little. His posture seemed defeated somehow, vulnerable in a way she'd never seen him before, and as he stood and walked away she was left crouched on the floor feeling like she'd been hit by a truck.

What the hell had just happened?

With a sense of unease, she followed him into her

guest bedroom. She found him sitting on the foot of the bed, his elbows on his knees and his head resting on his palms. Careful not to touch him, since he seemed completely detached and unapproachable, she sat right beside him.

"Can you tell me what you were dreaming about?"

He seemed so distraught, her heart broke for him. "No." His tone left no room for further questions, and she didn't want to pry and make him feel any worse, either.

"At least tell me if there's anything I can do to help. You say it happens sometimes. What helps?"

"I was prescribed some meds but they make me drowsy and I can't take them while I'm here supposed to be protecting you." He growled out the words. Who was he mad at? Her? Himself?

She decided to change the subject since it was obviously a touchy one. And because it made her feel guilty that the poor man couldn't sleep because he was helping her. "Okay. How about you tell me why you were sleeping by my door."

He didn't say a word, he just kept his face down. Slowly, he turned to her, pain marring those beautiful emerald eyes. She couldn't *not* comfort him, she had to do something.

She grabbed one of his hands and held it. "Tell me . . . please."

"I don't sleep a lot and the house isn't totally secure just yet. Not the way I want it to be, at least. And your room is so goddamn far from all the other rooms. . . ."

"It's just next door to yours."

"Bullshit, it's on the other side of the hall," he said. She wanted to correct him and explain that it was on the other side of the hall, but it was still the next room over. Her room just so happened to be huge and took up a lot of the hall.

Not the time, Megan, she reminded herself as he began to speak again, his voice heavy with stress and exhaustion. "Anyway after checking the windows and doors five times, I was too worked up to sleep, so I just sat down in front of your door."

"For what?"

He shrugged but it was obvious to her why he'd done it. "To keep an eye on me? To keep me safe?"

He fisted his hands in his hair. "I just . . . God, Megan, I just feel like I have to put myself between you and any possible danger. It's crazy, but I can't fucking help it." He practically hissed the words as if he was mad at her for bringing up these feelings in him. Then he stood up and walked into the en suite bathroom, leaving Megan a jumbled mess on the bed.

There are nightmares and there are nightmares. The strangled noises and the thrashing that had come from

Jax put things into perspective. This man—this fearless man—had demons. Scary demons. Whatever he'd endured overseas still weighed heavily on him, and there were no words Megan could say to console him.

Clearly embarrassed, Jax had yet to come back from the bathroom. Seeing such a strong man fight his demons did something to Megan. Maybe he was all about protecting her, but she was all about comforting him. Showing him he wasn't alone. After everything that had happened, she found herself focusing on whether he needed anything. A hug, a towel, enough soap, a cup for water. It was silly, but while she couldn't chase his demons away, she could make sure he was comfortable. So after ten more frustrated minutes of wondering, she snuck her head into the en suite with the intention of checking in on him and leaving. He'd left the bathroom door partly open, and like a moth to a flame she couldn't look away. His bare back muscles were bunched up with tension and his shoulders strained against his neck. Five years ago, he hadn't had any tattoos. Now, there was a piece on his shoulder blade that was so realistic, it looked almost three dimensional. From where she stood, it looked like a compass with a rope around the top that wrapped around an anchor, a tattered American flag peeking from behind, all in different shades of black and gray. It was beautiful, but also sad.

Jax was the sexiest man she'd ever seen, bar none. But the man in front of her was also the most intense and complicated. Unsure how to navigate this Jax made her question every move she made. But screw it. She needed to touch him, at least so he'd know she was there for him in any capacity. She was beginning to hope it would be in a deeper role than just friendship, because she wanted him—and it wasn't just sex. It was the undeniable connection they'd always shared. But if all he wanted was a friendship, she'd accept that too. Because she couldn't just see him this way and walk back to her room and go to sleep. It hurt her to see him hurt.

Carefully she walked into the bathroom. His head was still bowed down, and the thick corded veins on his arms, which looked like they were about to burst from the grip he had on the sink, made him look completely defeated.

Slowly and quietly she moved in close, cautiously pressing her palms against his shoulder blades, which tensed further underneath her touch. But he didn't pull away. Taking this as an invitation to continue, she rubbed her hands up and down his back, eventually bringing them around his waist and together against his abdomen, her face resting against his back. A few hours ago, he'd comforted her when she'd felt weak and needy, swooping in and holding her on his lap. Now, she was going to try to do the same for him.

Years before, when she felt complete and utter defeat, a hug from a friend had all but saved her. She wanted to save him now, to be his friend. Sometimes a hug, a moment of affection, could mean everything. It meant *you're not alone.*

After a moment, the tension loosened and he turned around in her arms.

Glassy and hooded eyes pierced through her, her pulse beating frantically against her chest. It wasn't lost on her that she was wearing just a long T-shirt or that he was in just boxer shorts—or that they were pressed so close together. "I can't lose sight of why I'm here," he said, with a roughness in his voice she'd never heard before. She wasn't sure whether he was saying it to her or trying to convince himself. But it didn't matter.

She had already let it be known that she wanted him when they were outside. He had been hard underneath her, and hadn't exactly been pulling away from her touches. If it hadn't been for the prank call, they would have at least kissed. Taking the plunge now and making the first move, she nodded and kissed his pec muscle, where there was a second tattoo—this one just the words "Semper Fi" in a simple font.

"I need to keep you safe," he said, and she kissed the other pec muscle, her palms moving softly up his shoulders. He was warring with himself, so she kept fighting. It was obvious that he wanted her as much as she wanted him. She reached up, running her hands through his beard and tucking her face in his neck.

"You smell good," she breathed into his ear, nipping his ear lobe.

"Fuuuck..." he moaned, his erection hardening against her stomach with each touch, with each kiss. "You were crying a few hours ago. You're vulnerable. You're scared. This is a bad idea."

Who was he trying to convince?

Getting on the tips of her toes, she placed a small kiss on the corner of his lips, and said, "I'm not scared of you. Never of you. This is a good idea. Let me help you forget your bad dream, Jackson." She kissed the other side of his lip. "I can help you forget."

Jax released a long breath. His shoulders finally relaxed. He grabbed her face in his big hands and pressed his lips against hers. And God, did he taste good. His beard felt soft against her face, and even though the kiss felt different, those full lips felt the same. She pressed her body closer to his and he picked her up, turned around, and set her on the vanity, her legs wrapping around him and her mouth opening to give his delicious tongue access. The way her heart sped up and her senses erupted wasn't just because his mouth was wonderful. It was more than that. She'd never felt this passion before. This inherent need to connect physically with another person. Her entire body was on edge and every touch of his palm against her back, her thigh, her face . . . she just wanted him to feel the same way, the same crazed need she was feeling.

"Meg," he mumbled into her mouth. "Sweetheart, wait. Stop." Pushing slightly away, he pressed his forehead to hers, his chest heaving up and down much like hers. Her palms were on his pecs, rubbing up and down, feeling the small splay of hair on his chest. "We can't. Not yet. Not right now."

"Why not?"

"Because I can't get distracted."

"But—"

He gave her a quick peck on the lips and helped her down. "Please don't make it harder than it is."

"It shouldn't be hard. This should be easy. You're here, I'm here. We obviously want each other. What's the problem?" She gently clawed on his chest wanting to grip him, hold him, force him to take her right there in the bathroom. Her heart was beating so rapidly she didn't think it would ever return to its normal pulse.

"Two days ago was the first day I saw you in years. We hardly knew each other even back then. We can't just start fucking. I'm here to take care of you, not to take advantage of you. It wouldn't be right."

Start fucking? Is that all it would've been?

She grumbled frustratedly. "God, how the tables have turned. All these years, I've thought about the fun, free-spirited guy who showed me how to loosen up and live wild, and made me feel sexy and valued." She blew out a breath and moved her hands from his chest. "Thinking about you took me back to the best time of my life. I understand you're trying to protect me, but damn it, this isn't you. Where's the guy that turned my world upside down and caused me to forget all my worries with one kiss?"

He didn't respond.

Confused, turned on, and annoyed, she hopped off the vanity and stomped out of the room, slamming the door behind her.

Running out of the stadium with Jax, hand in hand, had been the most liberating thing she'd ever done. Even to this day, it was the most exhilarating moment of her life.

She wanted *that* Jax back.

Chapter 6

Todo:

- Haircut
- Lawn
- Dad
- Bike
- Mom
- Fridge
- Water
- Mail

"I have to admit, I'm surprised there's an actual list. I thought you had things in your head you wanted to get done," Megan said, reading through a list written on a napkin in black chicken scratch. He'd pulled it out of his pocket in the middle of the café, where they'd been sitting for the last hour, and handed it to her. "Other than haircut, I have no idea what these things mean."

He ran his hands through his hair and looked at her with a smirk. "Can we do something fun between items? Or are you hell bent on doing all the boring things first and then getting to the fun?"

She snorted and then covered her mouth, humiliated but he ignored her and laughed. "I am not hell bent on anything. We can definitely have fun while we work." Unable to ignore the elephant in the room any longer, she said, "But I have to make a call first."

"I thought you were avoiding your family at least for today. Do you have to call them?"

"I am. But I've been with Richard for two years. Kissing you in front of him . . . it was wrong. I need to make a quick call, or else I'll feel guilty the entire day." She slid out of the booth. "Be right back."

Megan pulled the phone out of her pocket and turned it on while she walked out of the cafe. She had a dozen new voice mails and texts but she ignored them all and dialed Richard.

"Where the hell are you?" Richard yelled after the first ring.

"Richard, we need to talk."

"You kissed another man!"

"Rich—"

"In front of an entire stadium! You humiliated me."

She didn't want to yell back in front of the café, where

she paced back and forth, so she kept her voice as low as she could. But with every word she uttered, her voice got louder and louder. "I humiliated you? You ignored me the entire time we were there. You refused to kiss me on the kiss cam. You ignore me all the time, now that I come to think about it."

"Grow up, Megan. It's a stupid baseball game. Who gives a shit about the kiss cam?"

"I do! I care. And you seemed to care when another guy kissed me!" It was a low blow, but she was upset. "And don't tell me to grow up. What I need is not to be so grown up. What I need is some fun."

"No. What you need is to stop thinking you're a teenager and start thinking about law school next week. I'm busy with the case I'm working on and with the firm, and you—"

She stomped her foot on the sidewalk and looked up to the sky.

Argh!

She wanted to yell out in frustration. "Stop it. I can't remember a time in the last two years we did something that was just fun."

"What the hell are you talking about? We just went to Phillip's party."

"That was his wedding and we went with my parents," she replied, incredulously.

"He works with them. What, you don't want to spend time with your parents now? What the hell has gotten into you?"

"A better question is, why do you want to spend so much time with my parents? You know what . . . don't even answer that. I know why. You want to make partner. I get it. They're the key to that. But I don't want to be your ticket. I want someone who wants me just for me."

"Seriously, Megan, I don't have time for this now. And neither do you. I have depositions Monday morning that I need to prepare for. I'm almost home, I looked for you everywhere. I'll explain things to your parents. Come over to my house, and when I finish the brief I have to work on, we'll have dinner or something."

"No."

"Stop being petulant, Megan. Where are you?"

"You are un-fuckin-believable!" A man who'd been walking by gave her a nasty glance, which she ignored.

"You're cursing now? Nice, Megan. Very nice."

She groaned into the phone, throwing her free hand up into the air. "It's not working, Richard. Hasn't been working for a while. I'm sorry to have to do this over the phone."

"Calm down and come home, Megan. We'll have dinner. I'll forget about what you did."

"What I did? You know what, I grew up with lawyers. I

know all about twisting words around to get me to think I'm wrong about something, when the truth is you're in the wrong here, not me. But it doesn't matter, Richard. I don't want to be with you anymore. Nothing you say will change my mind. In fact, the more you talk, the more I realize how over we really are."

With those final words she turned off her phone, not wanting to hear one more word from him. Her hands shook with how angry he'd made her: *I'll forget what you did.* Who did he think he was?

Breaking up with Richard and then hanging up on him was so out of character, she didn't even know how to feel about it.

"You okay?" She looked over her shoulder to see Jax walking out of the café. "There was a lot of foot-stomping and hand movements. And did you say 'fuck'? Didn't take you for someone with a dirty mouth."

She furrowed her eyebrows and he pointed to the window behind her as an explanation.

Great. The entire café had gotten a show.

"I don't normally curse. Unless . . . you know, the situation warrants it. And this one warranted it."

"And you're okay?" he asked, holding her foam finger in one hand, the other tucked in his pocket.

"Yeah, fine." She let out a big sigh. She was done with Richard and she wasn't going to let him ruin today.

"Shoot, let me give you money for lunch." She started to reach for her purse, but he took her hand.

"No. It's all good. You sure you're okay?"

"No. Not really." She admitted. "But I will be. It's something I should've done a long time ago." She exhaled loudly and then rubbed her hands together. "Okay, first up . . . haircut."

He laughed. "All right, let's do this. But first, give me your phone. No phones today, that's at the top of my list for you." She hesitated for a moment, but he pressed on. "If there's one thing I know for sure, it's that the problems will be there tomorrow; they always are. There's nothing you can do now to fix things, so don't let anyone darken your day. Can you do that for me, Megan? Can you try to relax?"

"I'll try."

"Good." He laced his fingers with hers, which surprised her, but then . . . it felt good.

New.

Different.

Richard wasn't a hand-holder, and she couldn't believe she'd been missing this all these years. "Come on, I'm over there." He pointed to his motorcycle.

Laughing out loud, mostly to herself, she muttered, "A motorcycle, of course."

"Never ridden a bike?"

"Nope."

"My plan's off to a great start. This is going to be fun."

She had no doubt.

He held out his palm. "Baseball cap."

She handed it to him and fluffed her hair while he put the cap away on a saddle attached to his bike, then put a black helmet on her head. "Where's yours?"

"I only brought one, but no worries. You wear it."

His fingers grazed her chin and neck as he secured the helmet on her head, lingering on her skin longer than necessary. They were so close, his green eyes looked so intense as he worked the strap, and his tongue slid out to wet his lips. Then he looked up to meet her eyes and when their eyes locked, he winked.

Winked!

And the damn dimple came out.

She definitely swooned, and he must've noticed the way her pulse spiked, judging from the smirk he sent her way.

"You hop on first. Then once I sit, you hold on tightly and you put your feet on those metal bars. Got it?"

She nodded, unable to speak, her thoughts still on his dimples and the way his tongue came out to wet his lips.

Once they were both on and he kicked the stand up, she hesitantly wrapped her arms around him. He put the kickstand back down, took both her arms, and tightened them around him, roughly. "Tight," he said, over his shoulder. "If you let go, you'll get hurt, you understand?"

"I understand."

"Lean into the turns and just . . . enjoy the ride."

She shook her head and laughed, but when he revved up the engine and took off, all laughter disappeared and she yelped and hung on for all she was worth, trying to ignore the rippling of his abs under her palms and the way his shirt smelled like fabric softener against her cheek.

It was the best ride of her life.

———————

"Dude, where'd you pick up the chick? I've never heard you talk about a Megan before," Joey said later that night at the barbeque. After the haircut, which had taken a total of ten minutes since they had basically shaved it all off, Jax had driven her around South Beach on his bike until finally heading to Joey's house. She held on so tightly at first he thought she'd break a rib, but then as time went on, she loosened her grip, leaned into the turns, and even let go enough to point at some of the yachts parked by the bay.

It felt nice having her wrapped around him. She wasn't the first girl that he'd had on his bike, but it was the first time it felt noteworthy. She felt . . . right. As if she belonged wrapped around him. And when she pressed her cheek on his back and relaxed, something inside of him shifted. It was fast, it was instant, and even though they'd just met, he didn't want today to be the only day he had with her.

Jax ran his hand over his freshly shaven head and looked out to the backyard where Megan was reaching into a cooler. "I met her early this afternoon at the game."

"At the baseball game? You always want to go alone."

How many times had Joey offered to go with him? He didn't want the memory of the game with his dad tainted by anything, and always declined the offers. Normally, Jax was in good spirits. Hell, he was known for it. But on that one day a year, he always felt melancholic and just wanted to be left alone. Funny how he ended up meeting Megan on what was normally a shit day. And meeting her, having her intrude—even if unintentionally—on his day, didn't feel wrong. Actually, it felt kind of perfect. "I do. I did," he said, his eyes moving over to where his friend Mark was talking to Megan. "Long story. Catch you in a minute," he distractedly said to Joey, walking to save Megan from the fucking dog, Mark.

"Mark," Jax said, with a chin nod.

"Hey, man, nice of you to come by. You leaving Monday too?"

"Sure am."

"Too?" Megan asked.

"Joey is also going."

"Oh, wow. That's pretty cool. He's your best friend right? The blond guy we just met?"

"Yep. The tall one. Known Joey pretty much my entire life," he said. "Did you guys meet?" Jax turned to Mark and pointed to Megan.

"Not formally, no," Mark said. "I was horrified she was grabbing a soda at a barbeque. Beer is the only way to go. I came to rescue her."

Jax's eyes narrowed in on Mark, not liking that the other guy wanted to rescue *his* girl, even though he was only teasing.

"I don't really like beer," Megan admitted a little sheepishly.

"'S'cool." Jax ignored Mark and slid his hand around Megan's waist. He knew it was a jerk possessive move, but he didn't want any doubt in Mark's mind, or anyone else's, what the nature of his relationship with Megan was. Plus, she looked so cute confessing she didn't like beer, as if it was something he would judge her for. "Get your soda and come on, let me introduce you to some other people."

Grabbing a towel he kept in the saddlebag of his bike, he set it by Joey and a few other people huddled by the old wooden dock in Joey's backyard.

"Fishing? Here?" she asked, as they watched Joey cast a small rod into the water.

Jax motioned to the towel, and they sat down next to each other. "We like to fish and it'll be a while before we can do it again."

"You like it too?"

"Yep," he said, taking a swig of his beer.

"Is that what you'd be doing if I wasn't here?"

"Probably."

"Don't stop on my account."

"Nah, I'm good." Smelling like fish on their first pseudo-first date was a no-no.

"I thought you'd want to do something more exciting on one of your last few nights in town, like go to a strip club or something. Isn't that what guys do?"

He chuckled. "I suppose some do. Not me, though. I'd rather lay back and relax, drink a beer, fish, hang at the beach."

"I don't think I've done any of those things."

He leaned over and nudged her shoulder with his. "That's kind of sad."

"Tell me about it." She looked up at him and then back out to the sea. "Maybe you can help me with that."

He could feel his smile widen and he rubbed his newly bald head. "Sweetheart, I can help you with whatever you need."

―――――――

"Hey, Megan babe, do you fish?" Joey's holler interrupted the intimate way Jax was looking at her. They were still on the floor on an old towel, sitting next to one another, arms brushing together.

"Um . . . no, not really." Megan wasn't used to being the center of attention. But sitting so close to Jax made her feel relaxed and in control of an unfamiliar situation.

"So, what do you do? You in school? You got a job?" It was a lot of questions but he had a cigar in his mouth, a beer in one hand, and a fishing rod in the other and an easy demeanor to him.

"Nothing much to tell. I start school Monday. And no, I don't have a job."

"Whatcha studying?"

"I start law school."

"A lawyer. Nice. Way to date up, Jax." Jax shot the middle finger at Joey, and Joey blew out smoke and winked at her. "You meet everyone, babe?"

"Yep. I think I did," she said, looking around at the small group all hanging out, talking, drinking beer—not a worry in the world. She'd never met people like this. Her parents didn't fish. Didn't "hang out." They were *proper* and schooled their emotions, and that's what she'd been taught her whole life. This, however, this was refreshing and it felt nice and freeing.

And Jax? Jax was unusually quiet sitting on the towel next to her. Maybe he wanted to know the answers to some of Joey's questions or maybe he was just challenging her to break out of her shell a little and make some new friends. Whatever the reason, he was right there, their eyes meeting every time she looked over at him and their thighs brushing against one another every time she made the slightest move.

As the day wound down, they stayed outside, Jax laughing with his friends, animatedly telling stories of their last tour, all of them in stitches because the stories mostly involved making fun of Joey who was apparently a computer whiz but not the most athletic of the bunch. " ... I had to carry him twice during basic training. I thought he had stopped breathing at one point."

"True fucking story. I'm not ashamed. I wasn't built for that shit. Now, give me a code to break, I'm your man. This guy right here," he pointed his thumb over to Jax, "can't fucking spell the word *code*."

With tears in his eyes from laughing so hard, Jax added, "Captain said that together we'd make one," he held out one finger, "helluva Marine. But separately? We'd be fucked."

Obviously, it was a joke because even though Joey wasn't as built as Jax, the man was still tall and lanky, at least six feet tall, all lean muscles and long limbs. And Jax wasn't a dummy. Just his appreciation for life, Megan figured, made him by far one of the smartest men she'd ever met.

"Who's gonna help me clean these bad boys?" Joey asked, picking up a bucket of fish.

"We're going to hang back here for a little bit," Jax said. His thumb had snuck into the space between the bottom of her shirt and the top of her shorts, and every time he moved it across her skin, she erupted into goose bumps and butterflies flooded her belly.

"Don't do anything I wouldn't do, kids," Joey teased as most of the group followed him back to the house.

"Sun's setting," Jax pointed out.

"So pretty," she said, looking out to the ocean, her palms rubbing her arms and her thoughts focused on the way he was touching her back, softly.

"Cold?"

"I'm okay," she said, still looking out, her arms wrapped around her shins, her chin on her knees.

Jax shifted so he was behind her, wrapped his arms around hers, his thighs snugged on her sides, and held her as the sun set. She didn't push him away. Hell, she didn't even move. Her heart beat so hard against her chest she thought it would escape.

"Meg, baby, breathe," he whispered in her ear, his warm breath caressing her, and instead of breathing like he instructed, she held her breath, waiting for his next move.

Megan was cocooned in his arm and the beauty of the sunset was nothing compared to being held by Jackson. She would remember this one moment until her dying breath. It was perfection and she didn't want to take any of it for granted.

"You smell like the ocean and flowers," he said, his voice gravelly as he brushed her hair aside and buried his face in her neck.

They were both quiet for a while, lost in thought and basking in their budding feelings.

After the sun had set and they'd been quiet for a while, Jax asked, "What now? Where do you want to go?"

"Today was the best day," she admitted. "I think this may be the single most peaceful moment of my life." Maybe it was the sound of the ocean or the wind or maybe it was the fact that they didn't need to fill the silence with words. Even though they'd just met, it felt right to be close to this man.

"I know what you mean," he said, his voice low. "But

that doesn't answer my question. What happens now?"

Slowly she rolled her head to the side where he was mere inches away. "I don't really want to go home yet."

"I don't really want you to go home yet, either." He brushed some hair off her face and leaned in, just a little, and kissed her lips softly. Her heart stopped beating for a moment. It was nothing of note, yet it felt like everything. "If I'm being honest, and without intending to scare you off . . . I kind of want to keep you," he whispered.

Her heart was coming out of her chest. Being kept by Jax sounded blissful. She could picture them happy together, which was disconcerting since they'd just met. But there was something about him—something that felt right and familiar.

"Come home with me. I can sleep on the couch. Nothing has to happen. I still have a bunch of things to tackle on my list you can help me with tomorrow."

Megan rolled her head back to the darkness, unable to see the ocean any longer. Go back to Jax's house? Someone she'd just met?

Why not? Everyone was already pissed off at her. She could bury her head in the sand a few more days, couldn't she?

She looked back at him again. "Yes. I'd like that."

His smile was so brilliant. That alone was worth saying yes to.

Chapter 7

Sitting at the dining room table with two laptops open in front of him and papers scattered everywhere, Jax was completely immersed in his work when Megan finally strolled downstairs at eleven thirty the next morning. He was trying to forget the night before.

What a clusterfuck.

First he'd almost kissed her silly while they'd been sitting outside, then he'd lost his shit when she'd gotten the phone call, and then he'd tossed and turned half the night until giving up and camping by the door of her room. It made absolutely no sense, he was well aware of that, but for some reason being close to her made him feel better. If there was a threat, he'd be right there. Then he'd had another nightmare. When he was particularly stressed, it always happened.

His thoughts drifted to the nightmare that haunted him every single time he dreamed....

Blood everywhere. His ears rang and he couldn't see any-

thing but smoke. Estevez's lifeless eyes stared back at him. He tried to reach for him, but he couldn't move. There was too much pain, too much blood, too much smoke. . . .

"Five things," she said, startling him out of his morbid thoughts.

He looked up and shook his head, trying to shake off the demons.

"What'd you say?"

"Five things. Remember? You made me do five things that I wouldn't ordinarily do."

He sat back lazily and crossed his arms over his chest. Slowly he smiled, big. She had a way of making him feel light again. He, of course, had also spent all morning thinking about what had happened after the nightmare. Her hands on him, her pleading eyes . . .

"Of course I remember. And you made me do five things on my to-do list."

"Yeah the to-do list that never got done."

"I can still picture your look of sheer panic when I told you I hadn't called about shutting off my water or that I hadn't cleaned out my fridge. You were horrified. You said, 'it's time to start adulting.'" He laughed. "I recall thinking, 'God, how old is this chick and why is she so responsible?'"

"And boring," she added. "You thought me too responsible and boring."

Remembering all the ways she lit up every time she experienced something new or how she melted in his arms—boring would not be one of the words he'd use to describe her.

"Responsible, maybe. But boring? No, definitely not boring. And definitely beautiful. I remember that clearly. So fucking beautiful."

She smiled wide, pulled the chair close to him, and sat down. "I think you're just being sweet. I was a nervous wreck those four days, with all the things you made me do."

"Not sweet, just honest. We packed a lot of shit into four days, didn't we?"

She stood and walked to the kitchen, touching him lightly on the shoulder as she walked by. "Not everything, though. Left some things undone."

They'd parted ways knowing that falling in love would have been too easy. Their plans were already set in motion and a clean break was the only way. They hadn't even exchanged phone numbers. He didn't know if she regretted that decision, but it was something he'd always wondered.

Returning a moment later with a mug of coffee, she sat down again.

"You were so scared of everything back then," he continued.

"I wasn't so much scared as sheltered. You made me see that things outside the walls of my parents' house and their rules were possible."

"And you put a little order in my life."

"Well, there is such a thing as being *too* laid back," she said with a smile.

"Not something anyone would accuse me of being now," he said, busying himself picking up the papers scattered on the table and stacking them up into a neat pile.

He looked up at her when her phone dinged with an incoming text, her smile quickly fading as she checked the screen.

"What is it?" he asked, immediately alarmed by her reaction.

"Oh my god," she mouthed, and with a trembling hand she showed him her phone.

`See you in Atlanta, Meggy.`

Attached to the text was a photo of her and her bandmates, the others' faces rubbed out with a black marker.

"What the hell?" she cried.

"Atlanta?"

"That's the first stop on our tour."

He took the phone and tried to send out a reply text but it bounced back as undeliverable.

"Fuck," he muttered under his breath. "Can you tell where this was taken?" Catching her tense shoulders and the way she swayed, he nudged her gently down into a chair.

She shook her head side to side, squinting closer at the screen. "We wear more or less the same thing every time we perform. It's our stage clothes. It's hard to say when that was taken. Oh my god, Jax. Is he going to hurt Nelly and Taylor? Oh God."

"Deep breaths." He slid his glass of water to her but she pushed it away and stood up.

"I'm cancelling the tour. I can't risk this nut hurting them." She began pacing around the room. "They're my family. It's one thing for him to come after me, but to come after them... no, I won't allow them to get involved."

Jax pulled her back down into the chair. "Calm down, Meg. He's probably just pinpointing you, not saying he wants them out of the picture." Though it did look rather damning, he didn't want to add fuel to the fire when they didn't know this psycho's motives yet.

"You can't know that. He literally took them out of the picture!"

Jax took out his phone and dialed Joey.

"Yo."

"Joey, Megan got a text. I'm going to send it to you now. Later I'll bring you her phone."

"What kind of text?"

"The bad kind. Call me if you can get something from this. See if it's traceable, at least to an area. Anything." He chanced a glance her way and her leg was going up and down like it did when she was nervous. She was gnawing on her thumbnail.

"I'll see what I can do, brother. She okay?"

"Not really. Talk to you later." Jax hung up and forwarded the text to Joey.

"I know you're scared—"

"I'm not scared for me, I'm scared for them. I'm not going to let them get hurt because I'm too proud to admit we have a big problem. He's going to Atlanta, Jax. He's going, he's not even hiding it." She sounded hysterical.

Taking her shaky hands in his, he tried his best to calm her. "I don't think he's after them, Meg. He hasn't contacted them once. It's all about you. Don't cancel the tour. Don't let him win. Remember when we met, you were this sheltered girl, did what everyone told her to do? You're not that person anymore. You've grown up, you're independent, you have fans, and you have a career you love. Are you going to let this asshole fuck up everything you've worked so hard for?"

"But—"

"I was going to finish up the security in the house, and then help MBPD with the investigation—whether they wanted my help or not. Now I'll secure the tour instead.

I'll make sure everything is safe. I'll go with you."

"Like my bodyguard?"

"Among other things. My people will secure all the venues and tour buses and I'll be close by at all times too. You'll be safe."

"Jax..." she exhaled. "Nelly and—"

"Talk to them. Tell them what's going on. If they want to cancel, we'll cancel. But if not, let's be brave. Let's not let him scare you off. What are you going to do, hide in here forever?"

"And you'll come with me? On tour?" Her leg had slowed but her eyes were still wild.

Jax had a security firm to run and clients to take care of. Leaving on a three-month tour with Megan was the last thing he should be doing, especially when he knew the truth. Yes, he wanted her safe—needed her to be safe—but his motives weren't completely altruistic. The thought of being away from her for three months, after not having her in his life for five years, was what drove him to say, "absolutely."

And then her leg stopped completely.

———

Megan slept terribly that night. Jax had spent most of the day on the phone and the computer dealing with the security of the house and beginning to put together the team for the tour. She'd barely had a moment alone with him. All the flirting and occasional touches had ceased—both of them focused on trying to figure out what exactly was going on with Ryan. The threat of mortal danger wasn't exactly an aphrodisiac.

The text had shaken Megan more than she wanted to admit. The call had been easy to brush off as a simple prank or wrong number, but even knowing that Jax was in the room right next to hers, she couldn't shake the feeling that someone was watching her. She made sure all the window shades were down and kept the covers over her head the entire night. But she still felt a tingle at the base of her spine that said someone was out there. It made sleep impossible.

"Morning," she mumbled crabbily the next day.

"Up at the crack of eleven this morning," he chuckled. She scowled as she poured herself a cup of coffee.

"I couldn't sleep."

"Didn't sleep much either."

Her eyes widened. "You're worried." Shit, if *he* was worried, where did that leave her? He was the one who'd pushed her not to cancel the tour. Her thoughts were spiraling.

"Calm down. It's not because I'm worried. I don't sleep much normally. So I spent all night trying to figure out where the photo was taken. I narrowed it down by your clothes and the way you were wearing your hair—it's either at Rio de Janeiro or Caracas."

"That was two and a half years ago. How'd you narrow it down?" She stood behind him and leaned into the computer screen. Close like this, she just wanted to touch him. He smelled like fresh soap and Jax and it was so tempting to put aside all her trouble and get lost in this man.

"Surfed the internet for photos of your concerts looking for the combination of your clothes and your hair, and also Nelly's and Taylor's—what I can see through the black marks." His voice sounded gruff, and it made her wonder if his thoughts had also drifted to the growing sexual tension between them that intensified when they were close like this.

"If you're right, that means that the first time I met him wasn't the first time he'd seen me."

"Exactly."

"Oh God, I'm never leaving this house again." She thumped her forehead on his shoulder.

He chuckled and patted her head. "Don't go off on your own, or anything. But you don't have to stay imprisoned in here either. There's still a month before the tour is supposed to start, and by then we'll have a handle on things."

She lifted her head and sat down next to him. "You sound very sure of that."

"I have a good team."

"Good. Looks like we're going to need it."

He shook his head and closed his laptop, turning towards her. "What would you have done today if things were different?"

"I would've gone to Pilates or worked on my yard, but now that's shot—since, well . . ." He winced, following her line of vision to the now barren yard. "Oh, with everything going on, I forgot all about the fittings I have today with my stylist. What am I supposed to do about that?"

Jax winced in sympathy. "I have the guys coming in to finish some things around the house. I don't want you feel penned in, babe, but I don't think I can go with you today. You're going to need to postpone it."

She groaned and narrowed her eyes at him. "One minute you're all for me living my life, and the next you're asking me to postpone something that I have to do. For my career. For the tour that is just a month away. The tour that you convinced me not to cancel, remember?" Megan hated the bite to her voice, hated that she knew Jax was right, hated feeling so uncertain and out of control in a way she hadn't felt in years. When Jax opened his mouth—probably to start a fight, she thought snidely—she held up her hand. "I'll figure it out."

Jax wisely just nodded and left the room. Well, if she couldn't come to the fitting . . . grabbing her phone, she decided she'd just have to make the fitting come to her.

Megan was pushing her couches toward the far wall of the living room when Jax walked back inside the house a few hours later.

"I hope you're ready. The estrogen level in the house is about to climb to dangerously high levels," she said, breathlessly.

"What are you doing?" He gently moved her aside, gesturing toward one of the couches. "Where do you want this?"

"Just push it against the wall."

"You have a shitload of rooms in this house, why are you moving furniture around?"

"My stylist is on her way and so is Nelly. We need space and good lighting. I have a bunch of things to try on and pick out for the tour."

He reached out, and wrapped a finger around a strand of hair that had fallen out of the bun on top of her head. "Are you still mad at me?"

"No, it's not your fault. It's Ryan. I'm just frustrated. Are you mad at me? I can be a little cranky in the mornings."

He was standing close, his hand hovering by her face,

enthralled by the hair on his finger. "I don't remember that about you. I remember you being . . ."—he let go of her hair and looked at her—" . . . rather sweet in the mornings."

She gulped. He was so close, and smelled and looked so good.

"Should I make myself scarce?"

"Up to you."

"Will I have to turn in my man card if I stay?"

She chuckled and kissed his cheek. "Probably." And then she went to open the front door. Once the women began organizing racks of clothes, Jax got back to work.

————————

Megan was standing behind an ornate room divider she'd brought down from her room, trying on a too-tight royal blue bandage dress her stylist had insisted she try on.

"It's Jax. He eats unhealthily," she said, wiggling herself into the dress that barely went past her ass.

"Yeah? He brought you Nutella?" Nelly laughed. "And it's only been like three or four days since he's been around."

"Shut it, sister. The Nutella is for emergencies. The pizza and sandwiches are the problem." She grunted, finally able to slide the dress all the way on. "As well as the chips and cookies I spent all day eating at his house."

"If it makes you feel any better, that one didn't look good on me, either." Nelly noted. "I vote on the white pants and top for the first half. It's from Taylor's line, so she'll love it." Nelly poured herself some more wine as she spoke. "Oh, did I tell you I had lunch with Tamara again?"

"Tamara?" Becca, the stylist, asked as she pinned the hem of some pants.

"The other T from TNT," Megan said distractedly as she turned from one side to the other in front of the mirror, thinking her ass looked way too big in this dress.

"I ran into her at the mall."

"I didn't know her that well, but I know you've kept in touch with her," Megan said, taking Nelly's wineglass from her hand and taking a sip. Life had been good to her, putting Nelly and Taylor in her life. They were the sisters she never had, and if something ever happened to them she'd never—*never*—forgive herself. That made her take a second, bigger, sip before handing the wineglass back to Nelly.

"Yeah, she calmed down the last year and isn't so bad, really. I know she was kind of a bitch back then, but now she's turning back into the Tamara I grew up with again. She went to rehab and everything."

From what Megan had heard, Tamara had been a

world-class diva, always late to gigs, missing some, drugs, drinking. She lived up to the rock star title, even though she wasn't a rock star then. TNT didn't make it big until after she left the band. "But she's really changed. Seriously. It was almost weird to see her acting like a normal human being."

"What's she up to these days?" Megan asked.

"Doing makeup at the mall. She asked about you and Taylor. Said she was happy to see Taylor's clothing line had taken off. She saw you on the news and was concerned."

"Well, that's good that she's doing well. Maybe we can all do dinner when Taylor gets back. I know she used to be like family to you two. I'd love to get to know her."

"That'd be awesome. She was very important to me at one time. She *was* practically family, and you know I'd love everyone to get along."

Jax walked into the room.

"Great! Of all the times for you to come in," Megan whined. Nelly scrunched up her nose and pointed to the screen, shaking her head side to side at the ill-fitting dress.

Rolling her eyes, Megan looked down at herself. "Told you. It barely fits." She pulled the hem down to cover herself more and then pointed a finger at an amused Jax. "I blame you and your crappy eating habits."

"Is that supposed to look bad?" he asked, taking a seat on the couch that was off to the side, making himself comfortable with his feet on the coffee table. "Because from here, it looks fucking great."

"Oh, I like him," Becca said.

"I can't even breathe in this," Megan pointed out.

Jax reached forward and, with his index finger, lifted three pairs of lace thongs that had been tossed on top of a suitcase full of clothes. "I think I'll stick around for the trying on of these."

This playful side of Jax was exactly how Megan remembered him and it completely made her heart melt. She chuckled, grabbed one of her fluffy throw pillows, and threw it at him. "Outta here."

Jax caught the pillow in midair with a smile, then tossed it aside. "I actually didn't come here to stare, although the view *is* rather spectacular." She stood there awkwardly holding the bottom of the dress, feeling like the prettiest woman in the world, the way he looked at her. "I think I'm going for a quick jog around the island. Are you good here without me?"

"I'm good."

"You have my number, right?" he asked.

"Relax, Jax. The island's small, there's still light outside. Go. Don't worry about me. I have my girls here with me and your guys are still in the backyard working."

He was looking into her eyes, his jaw twitching. She boldly cupped his face and moved close. "Jax. It's fine. Really."

He exhaled loudly, searching her eyes for something. "Okay, I won't be long."

"Take your time. Have a good run."

He nodded, leaned in, and kissed her cheek as if it was the most normal thing in the world. "Be good while I'm gone."

Once he was out of the room, Megan turned back to the screen and noticed, for the first time, how quiet her girls had suddenly become. "What?"

Becca was still sitting on the floor with the needle in her hand, but her eyes were swooning. "I love him. I want to have his babies."

Nelly bent over, laughing. "Seriously, that was . . ." She shook her head and wiped tears from her eyes. "Did you even remember we were in the room? It was pretty adorable, Megan. You two were totally googly-eyeing one another. Are you guys back together?"

Becca's mouth opened even wider. "Back together?"

Megan began to wiggle out of her dress, speaking from behind the screen now. "We had a . . . thing five years ago."

"A thing?" Becca asked.

"They were in love," Nelly clarified.

"No we weren't. It was just an intense few days together. And now it's complicated."

She felt Nelly from the other side of the screen. "How is it complicated? There's obviously chemistry."

Megan flicked Nelly's forehead as she came out from behind the screen, going straight for the wine and then plopping down on the couch. Maybe if she talked it out, it would make sense. Because honestly, it was weighing heavily on her. "I'm being stalked, my house has been broken into, I'm getting prank calls, and all I can think about is jumping Jax! What is wrong with me?" she asked, covering her face with a pillow. "I need help. The psychological kind."

Becca sat beside Megan and plucked the pillow from her face. "Why, because you have a crush on that delicious man? I'd send you to the loony farm if you *didn't* feel something for him. He's hot—and he looks at you like you hung the moon."

"But there's so many things going on right now. It's not a good time . . . well, that's what he says."

"And what do you say?" Nelly asked from her other side.

Exasperated by her mix of emotions, Megan stood. "I think he should multitask. He can be with me *and* protect me! What the hell, right? Why can't we be together if we're both feeling it?"

"Exactly." Both women cheered as Becca pressed the newly hemmed pants into her hands so she could go try them on.

"Ms. Cruz," one of Jax's employees yelled from the other side of the house, "there's someone here for you. He says his name is Pete."

"Okay, one second. I'll be right there," Megan yelled back, quickly dressing. "I'll be just a second, ladies."

"We'll be right here. Still have a pile of clothes to dig through," Nelly noted.

Megan hurried to the front door, thinking about what Nelly and Becca had said. Maybe she should go after this thing with Jax, show him that some things were worth fighting for.

"Hey, Pete. Come on in," she called when she saw the older man standing with one of Jax's men by the open front door, waving the security guy off to let him know it was fine.

"Hi, Ms. Cruz, heard you had a scare," he answered, stepping into the house while Megan shut and locked the heavy wooden door behind him.

"Yeah it—"

"Stop right where you are." A gruff voice startled her from behind. "Identification." Megan whirled around to see Jax standing in the doorway to the living room. His green eyes were shining with intensity, and he already had his hand on his weapon.

"Jax don't worry. This is just Pete."

"ID. Now." His voice was harsh and brooked no questions. He was drenched in sweat, his hair slicked back in a messy ponytail and away from his face, his cheeks a little pinker than usual.

"'S'okay, Ms. Cruz," Pete assured her, carefully taking out his ID and showing it to Jax who took it and inspected it.

"Sorry," Megan whispered, embarrassed. Pete, who reminded her of her grandfather, had been bringing her packages since she moved in and his sweet wife baked her cookies all the time.

"No worries, Ms. Cruz." He still called her Ms. Cruz even after years of her asking him to call her Megan.

"I'll take the package," Jax barked.

"Oh, Pete, I'm sorry."

Pete sent Megan a reassuring smile and handed the padded envelope to Jax, who signed for it. "Really, don't worry about it, Ms. Cruz. It's good to see someone looking after you." And before she could make another excuse or hit Jax for being such a jerk, Pete turned and left.

As soon as she closed the door, she ripped the envelope from Jax's hand. "Oh my god, you're crazy, you know that? Pete works for the homeowners' association on the island and brings us our deliveries."

"Everyone's a suspect until we can figure out what's going on." His face was hard and unforgiving. "And where the fuck are my guys?"

"They're out back, calm down. They didn't just let Pete in and give him free rein. I told them he's a friend. You forget that I've seen Ryan. I know how he looks. Pete is not Ryan."

"What if you're wrong and it's not Ryan? What if it's someone else, Megan?" He snatched the package back out of her hands.

"Well, it's not Pete!" How could one person go from hot to cold so quickly? Right before the run he was warm and playful, and forty-five minutes later, he's a world-class jackass with zero regard for her opinion.

"Would you stop?" he said, as she tried to take the package back. "I'm not taking any chances with your safety, goddamn it."

"It's a contract I've been waiting for, for Christ's sake."

Carefully, Jax pulled the tab on the top of the envelope. He inspected the contents before pulling out the papers. Standing with her arms crossed, annoyed as hell, Megan looked down at the document he was holding and extended her hand. "It's a contract," he said.

Snatching it from his hand, she rolled her eyes. "You think?" And with a huff, walked back to her living room, furious, leaving him standing in the doorway.

"That was kind of hot."

"Shut it, Nelly," Megan said, slamming the papers down on the coffee table and going back to try on clothes.

"Okay so maybe he can't multitask. . . ." Becca teased, from the other side of the screen.

―――――――――

Jax wasn't the type to stay indoors or inactive for pro-longed periods of time. Since he was old enough to walk, his parents had instilled in him a love of nature and being outdoors. Jogging, hiking, fishing, camping . . . those were things he did often. If he was forced indoors, he hit the gym whenever he could. But for the last few days he'd either been online or on the phone, and the walls were beginning to close in on him.

Seeing Megan busy with her girls, and his men outside working on security, he had thought he could go for a quick tension-releasing run around the island. But it took far too long for him to stop thinking of the way she kissed his cheek. So open and confident and sweet. Nothing overtly sexy, yet he had wanted more from her at that mo-ment. So much more.

As he ran, he took stock of the palatial mansions that lined Star Island, all of them with the ocean as their backyard. The cruise ships, which were docked on the other side of the bay, were beginning to take off for their voyages full of vacationers. There were seagulls flying by and the sun was directly above him, sweltering his skin while his mind cleared and the endorphins kicked in.

Feeling much better—loose, yet in control—his mind feeling reset, he entered Megan's house by a side door. He was turning a corner into the living room when he saw a man handing her a package.

A package.

Explosion.

Memories of a year back propelled him across the room and caused him to act like an ass. Sure, they should be cautious, but Joey had run a background check on every employee of the Star Island community. Jax knew there was no way Pete was the stalker—not with the knowledge they had about the globe-trotting that Megan's shadow had done over the past two years. And yet, he couldn't have helped his reaction if he'd tried.

He couldn't continue this back and forth with Megan. One second they were affectionate and soft to one another, and the next moment they were at it like cats and dogs. Mostly from something he'd done. But still, it continued to happen and it was getting out of control. He couldn't focus on security or on building a relationship with her because he was too busy constantly switching emotional gears. He was too busy reacting. Just like before.

He didn't follow her into the living room to talk to her, not with her friends still there, and not when he didn't even know how to explain his reaction to Pete. Plus, he'd noticed that she was the kind of woman who needed her space. Difficult as it was, he'd let her have her time to calm down while he took a shower and regrouped, and then they'd talk and he'd try to explain things to her.

———————

Later that evening, after everyone had left, Jax found Megan doing sit-ups on a mat in her home gym. "I brought you a peace offering," he said. "Spaghetti with homemade meat sauce."

She wiped her face with a small towel and jumped up. "You're forgiven."

"So all it takes is food, huh?"

"Depends on the offense," she said, picking up her stuff. "And I know you meant well . . . again." She rolled her eyes.

"Talk to me. I know you can't possibly forgive me just because I made food."

She chuckled loudly. "You've tasted my cooking. I really can forgive you for food." But then her tone changed, as if she was trying to figure something out. "How long are you staying here, Jax? It looks like your guys are done with the install, and the tour's not for another month."

"Am I bothering you?"

"No. I like having you here." Then she turned her head and drawled, "Sometimes."

He smiled, pulled her over to the bench, and sat down next to her. "I know. I know. I'm being overbearing."

She put her thumb and finger together. "Just a tiny bit."

He nudged her shoulder with his while she struggled for words.

"I just . . . it . . . thank you for all you've done, but I feel like it's causing you so much stress. That nightmare the other night, and then losing your temper. I just . . . please don't take this the wrong way, but maybe it's best that it's not you who helps me."

He leaned forward, his forearms resting on his thighs. He couldn't even get upset at what she was saying, since it was obviously causing her a great deal of pain to say it. And really, it was true. All of it. He wasn't handling this well.

Pulling on a thread from her towel, she continued. "I missed you, Jackson. And now you're back and I don't know what to do with that, especially when you're living in my house barking orders and commands. I have all these feelings rushing through me—I'm so scared about

Ryan but at the same time I'm happy and still shocked that you're here. I'd rather have you here in a different role. . . ." She winced as she said it.

He ran his palm down his face, gripping the end of his beard. How must he look to her: wild hair, wild beard, perpetual crankiness? How did she even want him "in a different role"?

"I wish things were different, Meg. I really do. I just found you again, and now . . ." He shook his head, he needed to focus his thoughts. "I'm not going to let anyone else protect you. I'm just not. I have to focus on keeping you safe, and you can kick and scream about it all you want, but it won't change the fact that I feel . . ." He ran a hand down his beard. "It's my job to keep you safe, Meg. *You.* I know I don't have any business feeling that way, but I do." He leaned close, wanting to touch her so bad it physically pained him. "I'll ease up. I promise. But you're stuck with me, for now at least. Once things settle down, we can figure things out."

She exhaled loudly, maybe out of frustration. Maybe she understood. It didn't matter, though, because it didn't change anything. He was here to stay until she was absolutely safe. After that? Well, they'd have to figure it out when the timing wasn't a huge clusterfuck.

"Meet you in the kitchen?"

"Yeah, meet you there," she said somberly. "Give me

ten minutes. I want to take a quick shower."

Feeling domestic, he set the table outside. The smell of the ocean had been the reason he'd never moved away from his hometown. He loved Miami and the fact that at any given time he could be at the beach. "Do you do this with all your clients? Make them spaghetti as an apology?" Megan asked, her hair still wet.

He pulled out a chair for her and then sat down. "Woman? What do you think?"

"I think you'd have a lot of repeat clients if you did."

Her phone rang as she was about to dig into the meal. "Oh no . . . unknown caller." She showed him the screen.

He moved over to her side of the table. "Answer it. Put it on speaker."

"Hello?" Silence. She looked at Jax and lifted her shoulder. "Hello? Ryan, is that you?" And then the call dropped.

"Tomorrow I'm getting you a new number. I don't want you to share it with anyone except your immediate circle. No one else."

"Okay."

He went back to his chair and texted Joey to let him know what had just happened and then looked up. "Don't let him scare you. Eat. Ignore it. We're getting to the bottom of this." But even as he said it, he looked around, feeling as if they were being watched.

She was quiet, placing the napkin on her lap—her legs were bare thanks to the small cotton shorts she was wearing. He reached for her hand and squeezed. "Please eat. I feel terrible about earlier today. I just want to have a normal meal."

"Yeah . . . okay. You're right." She twirled spaghetti onto her fork and took a bite. "This is delicious, Jax."

"Glad you like it."

"I never sit out here. I need to find the time. It really is beautiful." Her eyes were focused on the ocean. It wasn't as late as it had been when they were out yesterday, and the ships were more visible as the sun began to disappear on the horizon.

He turned his head to her. "It really is." She smiled, and when she turned to see he was looking at her and not out to the ocean, she averted her eyes. He wasn't trying to keep his attraction to her a secret, it was blatantly obvious. Acting on it, that was what he couldn't do.

He decided to voice some of his concerns. She needed to know where his thoughts were. It was unfair that he was being so complicated when she'd been so open with him. "Have you ever thought that we just didn't get to know each other enough? That maybe we were caught up in the moment. Do we really know one another?"

She furrowed her eyebrows and cocked her head, utterly surprised he would ask this question. "I don't think anyone has ever gotten to know me the way you did. I'd like to think it was the same for you. Maybe it was a short time, but you saw me. Like really *saw* me, in a way no one had ever seen me before." She shook her head and continued. "No. I refuse to believe that you forget how you used to be. How fun and carefree you were. Don't try to skew that memory for me."

"No, you're right. I was young and didn't have any responsibilities. Things have changed. That's where I'm at, Meg. I just . . . things have changed."

She narrowed her eyes at him. "I've been thinking about it all day. Within an hour of meeting me, you were already working your magic to help me get out of my comfort zone and try new things. Things, incidentally, that I loved doing, and still do." She held up a beer and winked. "I want to do that for you. Remind you. You lost your way but we can find it again. Together. Things have changed, but not that much and not where it counts."

"Meg . . ."

She stood and patted his shoulder. "You said I'm stuck with you. Well, that means that you're stuck with me too. If you're going to stay with me, then I'm making some rules because I want some of the Jax I've been stupidly daydreaming about for all these years back. I like this new

Jax too, and I'm not trying to change you, I just want to remind you of what you seem to have forgotten. Maybe some of that can come back so you can be less growly all the time." She exhaled loudly. "You're fighting it. You're fighting us. But I'm not going to argue with you anymore. I'm going to be as supportive as you were with me back then."

He cringed, unsure where this was going. "What does that mean?"

"It means I'm going to make you remember what we had. It means that if you're going to insist on making me wait until this thing with Ryan is over so we can see if that old chemistry is still there between us, then game on, because I'm going to make it hard for you to resist me."

"Megan, it's already hard to res—"

"Five things, Jax, but this time the tables are turned." She winked and headed to the kitchen. "Game on," she yelled over her shoulder, sounding absolute in her resolve.

Jax stood there dumbfounded, watching her go. If she thought he'd forgotten about the chemistry they had . . . she was out of her ever-loving mind. It wasn't just a spark, it was a fire.

Chapter 8

He'd finally dozed off after spending all night by the floor of her bedroom, and now someone was shaking the bed and squeaking in his ear. "Wake up, wake up, wake up, sleepy head."

He cracked one eye open and Megan was tapping the bed. He groaned and turned his back to her. She ran to the other side, kneeled down, and pushed up one of his eyelids. "I was going to pull the blanket off, but what if you sleep naked? So I'm just going to stand here being annoying until you get up."

"What time is it?" It felt like just minutes ago he'd laid his head on the pillow. He'd been staying with her for a week now, a week that had mostly involved working from his computer while she'd been holding meetings on Skype. Even though they were in the same house and had dinner together every night, they didn't see much of each other during the day. But then the little minx would "accidentally" brush against him when they did see each other, and it almost seemed as she was dressing for the sole purpose of enticing him, with those yoga pants and tight shorts she wore all the fucking time. As the days wore on, his attraction to her intensified—but so did his resolve to keep things professional.

"Six."

"I thought you were allergic to waking up before noon," he teased, his eyes closed.

"Ha ha. Come on. Let's go. Five things, remember. It starts in an hour. Get dressed, wear a bathing suit. We have to be out of here in ten minutes. I'm tired of being inside this house."

With a groan, he finally opened his eyes. "I have a bunch of things to do, Megan."

"Nine minutes!" she sang. She closed the door behind her, ignoring his protest. "Bathing suit!"

On autopilot he jumped out of bed and took a quick shower, wondering where the hell they were going. He didn't feel like surprises or games, but if it made her happy and kept her agreeable to his overbearing-ness, he'd play along. Plus, she was right. They both needed to get out of the house.

Nine minutes later she was shoving a power bar into his mouth and travel mug of coffee into his hand. "For the road."

"A wig?" He reached up and pulled the tip of her short blond hair.

"Don't want to draw any attention."

"Megan . . ." he warned. Yes, he was going to play along, but only so long as it passed protocol and didn't put her in danger. Anything that required a wig didn't sound safe.

"Come on. I've been cooped up in here for days. I can't go anywhere in town because everything "leaves me vulnerable," she said in a deep voice, impersonating him. "So I came up with an alternative. Plus, I'm with you so I'll be okay." The trust she had in him made his heart do weird things. "Make sure you set the alarm to the house," she directed as he followed her into the garage and plucked the keys out of her hand.

She rolled her eyes. "Fine. I'll let you drive."

He laughed and opened the passenger door for her and then hopped in on the driver side. "This car is not made for a man."

She loved her Porsche. "No, it's not made for a giant. Take us to the airport."

"What?" Now he was really concerned.

She threw her head back, laughing nefariously. "Just drive." He groaned but decided to do what she asked. Things had been quiet the last week and this was so last minute, no one would know.

"I thought you were afraid of flying? Did you conquer that?"

She directed him to a private parking area specifically for private jets and they got out of the car.

"No. I still hate it, but it's part of my everyday life now, so I've had no other choice but to deal. And leaving town without letting anyone know where we were going was the best plan I could come up with so that no crazy person could follow us. Genius, right?"

"Megan . . ."

"Just trust me," she said, lacing her hands through his and leading him inside a hangar and then into a private jet. When she touched him, he couldn't deny her—and even if he could, he didn't want to.

"This is very different than the last time, isn't it?"

"Yeah, it is, but it's still an adventure. Plus, this is a plane not a helicopter."

"Where are we going?" he asked.

She winked, her smile huge. "It's a surprise."

They sat across from each other in the jet. She wore a white cover-up thing that was a little sheer, her white bikini peeking through the fabric, along with cutoff shorts and flip-flops that exposed her baby blue nails. When she ordered a Bloody Mary, he took the opportunity to text Joey and let him know what was going on, just in case he was needed. Also, he wanted her house monitored while they were out.

"I'd have liked to have spoken with the pilot and seen the flight plans. Check out that there's no—"

"This is safe, Jax. Don't worry. If I'm with you," she shrugged, "I'm safe."

He liked that she thought being with him was safe even if he wasn't so sure how safe things were at the moment. With a crazy stalker on the loose?

Resting his head back, he watched her reach into an oversized purse and rummage through it until she found earbuds. She popped them into her ears and closed her eyes while holding on to the armrest with a death grip. He wanted to reach for her hands and hold them, but he schooled his desire and focused on the Miami skyline as they took flight.

He hadn't been lying, he couldn't start something up with her while she was in danger. He needed to focus on her safety not her beautiful thick hair, or soft skin, or delicious thighs in those shorts. . . .

Judging by the twenty-minute duration of the flight, Jax deduced they were likely in Nassau or Freeport. When they landed he unbuckled his seat belt and then reached over and plucked the earbuds from her ears, startling her.

"W-what?"

"We're here."

She shook her head. "Oh, uh, okay. I fell asleep."

"Picked up on that. Come on."

Taking her hand, he helped her to her feet. As soon as they stepped out of the plane the sun and heat enveloped them and he was momentarily blinded from the sudden light. He looked over to see Megan adjusting her wig and putting on her sunglasses. "Ready?"

"Yep."

"Welcome to the Bahamas. Freeport, more specifically." She pulled him to the end of the tarmac. "Come on."

After the surprisingly quick trip through customs, she hailed them a cab outside the small airport. "Private plane but we're getting a cab?"

"Yep. I didn't want to make too many plans, you know, just in case."

His grip on her hand tightened. "Just in case someone would find out and come after you?"

She shivered and shook her head, then composed herself. "Nope, not today," she said, pasting a fake smile on her face. "No crazy stalker conversation today. Let's go. Chop chop. We have a captain waiting for us."

"A captain? So where exactly are we going?"

"Deep-sea fishing. I chartered a boat for a few hours." When his brow creased she quickly added, "You still love fishing, right? That was like your thing. I thought that would be one of the five things you don't ordinarily do, and if you *do* do it ordinarily, I figured you didn't ordinarily do it in Freeport." She inhaled. "That was a tongue twister. I'm nervous."

"I see that." He smiled. "I haven't gone fishing in years. And, yes, I still love it. And why are you nervous?"

"I want it to be fun for you."

"It will be."

An hour and fifteen minutes later, they were sitting in the middle of the ocean in a big fishing boat, nothing around them but the clear blue ocean. He looked over his shoulder and found Megan laying on her stomach, listening to music, her wig long gone. She looked relaxed and fresh, so different from a few days ago when he'd found her hiding in her closet, and light-years away from the sheltered, unhappy girl he'd originally met. This was the Meg he'd fallen so fast and hard for all those years ago.

He tugged out her earbuds, startling her, and pulled her up. "Come on."

Shaking her head, she waved him away. "I'm not fishing."

"Why not?" He held out a rod and took some bait. She took a step back. "Gross. No thanks."

He laughed and dangled the bait closer to her face. "Are you afraid of a little bait?"

She squealed and moved back. "No!" She giggled

harder. "Jax! Stay away." He put the rod down, stepping slowly toward her with the bait in his hand as she continued moving back. "Stay away!" And when he took another step forward, she took off running. Luckily they had the boat to themselves except for the captain and a crewman, and they were both in the control room upstairs. With his free arm, he swept her by the waist and lifted her up, her feet dangling underneath her, her back to his front. "You better not get fish guts on me, Jackson," she threatened, but she was laughing so hard he could barely understand her, causing him to break out in a fit of laughter too.

When was the last time he'd laughed like that?

It had been a long time. Years, likely.

Then there was the fact she was wiggling her bikini-clad ass on his cock. His palm was splayed against her flat stomach, his pinky finger too low, too close to her pussy. How would it feel if he were to slide his hand into her white little bikini bottom? Would she be bare? Would she be wet? A small gasp escaped her throat when he realized how tightly and intimately he was holding her, and he quickly released her.

They were just too close and she was too naked and warm.

This wasn't part of the plan.

Reluctantly, he pulled back from temptation and put

her down before stepping back. Distraction was his enemy. Last time he'd lost focus on a mission, most of his platoon was killed. Not wanting to ruin the effort and expense it had taken her to plan this for him, he said, "Tell you what, I'll put the bait on and you just hold the rod."

"I can do that," she said in a hoarse voice, and he cocked his head to the side.

She can do what? What was the question?

"The rod. I can hold the rod," she continued.

The rod? What?

It began slowly but within moments she was shaking from laughter. "You are making me freakin' crazy! Listen to me, I sound like a lunatic." She shook her head and wiped tears from her eyes. "You asked me if I wanted to hold the *fishing* rod, I said I can do that."

"You're going to drive *me* crazy." Jax was not surprised to hear the strain in her voice. Not after the images flashing through his mind of her holding a different rod.

She shook her head and yanked the fishing pole from his hand.

He sighed. "Come on, woman." He sat on one of the fishing chairs that faced the ocean toward the back of the boat and hooked the bait on. "Have you ever fished before?"

"Not really."

"Okay let me show you how to cast."

For the next ten minutes he showed her how to hold the rod and the fishing line, when and how to release the line, and what to click on the expensive reel.

"Now what?" She asked once her line was in the water and she was sitting on the chair beside him. The Bahamian sun shone brightly over them, and there wasn't even a light breeze. The boat barely rocked, and the only noise that could be heard was the commotion they were making.

Once both lines were in the water, he sat back in his chair. "Now we just wait."

"Just wait?"

"That's the beauty of fishing. You just wait for the fish to do all the work."

"How will I know when I catch something?"

"You'll know. There will be a tug on the line."

She sat back and held the pole. "If you say so."

Megan was in the middle of the ocean alone with Jax. It felt surreal, especially since she could physically see his hard shell melting away and the gooey center slowly revealing itself. He had put on a baseball cap and it was tilted down, covering his eyes. He was the picture of relaxation. There was no flirtation going on, just two people who felt comfortable enough with each other not to have to fill the time with awkward conversation.

Maybe he'd dozed off, she thought.

"You okay, baby?" His voice was raspy and growly, and he wasn't even looking at her as he said it, yet she felt it everywhere.

Baby? Oh God, her heart.

"Y-yeah, why?"

"You're quiet and you're staring."

"I am not staring."

"You were."

She huffed, a smile on her face and pretended to twiddle with the reel. He yawned loudly and sat up a little straighter. After a while, his leg began to bob up and down, his hands fiddling with the rod, his drink, the extra line. "You don't know how to just do nothing, do you?" she wondered, fighting back a smile.

"I did, until you woke me up with all your staring."

"Har har har. I thought you liked fishing." She pointed to his leg.

"I do like fishing and I am relaxed. The leg thing is a bad habit. I'll try to stop."

"Are you thinking of all the things you have to do back at my house?"

"Maybe?"

"Well, there's nowhere to go." She looked around the

eeriness and quiet of the vast ocean. "So you might as well follow your own advice and wait for the fish. You're rocking the boat with all that bobbing and I'm bound to get seasick."

"Aren't you hilarious today?" He smiled and reached over to grab two beers, snapping off the top of one and handing her the bottle before sitting back. "Tell me about all the places you've travelled."

She took a pull of the beer. "I feel like I've been everywhere. France, Italy, China twice, Japan, Turkey, pretty much everywhere in the United States. Just too many to name."

"Which was your favorite?"

"Just 'cause I've been everywhere doesn't mean I've actually seen anything. I'm usually there for a few hours and then I'm off to another place."

"Then let me rephrase the question, any place you'd like to see for more than a few hours?"

"We performed in a little town on the outskirts of London. It was so green and the air felt so clean. I'd like to go back there. See England, explore the northern part of the UK. But, I also love it here in the islands. If I had the time, I think I'd stay here for a few weeks. Not in the resorts, maybe rent a house by the beach and never leave."

"Sounds nice."

"And you? I'm sure you did quite a bit of traveling yourself."

He shifted around, reeling a bit and then releasing more of the line. "Less than you'd think. I was mostly stationed in Baghdad."

"Can I ask you something? You don't have to answer if you don't want to." When he didn't respond she continued. "Your leg. What happened? That wasn't there before you left."

He looked down at the horribly jagged scar that ran from the top of his thigh straight to his calf. It was a raised mess of scar tissue. She'd tried not to look at it but she couldn't help it. Not because it was ugly, but because it hurt her heart to think of how it had gotten there. "Ambush. We were attacked at our base by someone delivering a package. I had just been with all of them talking and laughing when I was called out of the room by my captain. The next thing I heard was explosions and I ran back to the guys. That's when a second bomb struck and its shrapnel hit me."

"Does it hurt?"

"Sometimes. Most of the leg is plastic and steel now." He tapped on his thigh, at the angriest part of the scar. "Had two knee reconstruction surgeries and five plastic surgeries to fix the deformity, and I have a steel plate here," He pointed to a dip from where flesh had been ripped off. "My femur snapped in half."

"Oh my god, Jax. You could've died," she gasped, and he looked away uncomfortably.

"Don't look at me like that. I don't want pity or sadness. I don't deserve that. My platoon, my brothers who didn't make it, they're the ones who deserve tears. Not me."

"Jax, I—"

The moment was immediately broken from a loud *zip* noise and her rod bowing forward. "Oh my god!" She gripped the rod and motioned to him. "Here. Take it."

"No," he yelled over the noise from her screeching and the sound of the rod. "Hold on to it as tight as you can. You can do this, Meg," he said, standing close to her—ready to help her if she needed it, but giving her the space to do it herself. "Reel it in a little and pull the rod back. Use your body, not just your arms."

She was trying to spin the reel but her bicep trembled and it wasn't budging. "I can't, Jax. It's too heavy." The rod was now bent so far it looked like it would snap in half. Whatever was on the line, it was big. If the rod hadn't been clipped into the chair, it probably would've flown out of her grip by now. He scooted in behind her, planting his ass on the chair and her ass on his groin, holding on to the rod together with her, effectively caging her in. "Jax!" She continued to yelp and laugh. She wanted to relish the fact she was cocooned in Jax's arms, but the pulling of the rod didn't allow for any thought but gripping the damn pole.

"Don't let go! Reel it in and I'll pull." They continued working in unison, using both of their bodies to reel in the fish. Kenneth, the captain, and Lefty, the crewman, ran down and stood close by watching. Splashes in the water signaled that they were close. "A blue marlin," the captain yelled. "Nice catch, honey. That beauty's about 250 pounds." He opened the side door in order to assist in getting the huge fish on board.

"Holy shit, sweetheart," Jax said breathlessly, trying to help pick up the slack. Her arms burned and the fish was fighting back, splashing and jumping in the water. "Hold on," he instructed her, and he let out some of the line and began to pull it in again. It took another twenty minutes, but finally the beautiful marlin was flapping around on the deck.

Kenneth and Lefty helped Jax unhook the fish while Megan took a hundred photos on her cell from the other end of the boat. "You're going to put it back in the water, right?" she yelled, looking at the way Jax's biceps and forearms worked while unhooking the heavy, thrashing fish. God, he was gorgeous. It didn't get old watching him. Would her heart ever stop skipping a beat every time he walked into a room or said something to her?

"C'mere," he said with a big grin, motioning to her. From this angle she could faintly see a dimple behind the bushy beard. How had she missed that dimple? She took a tentative foot forward and he grabbed her wrist and pulled her down by the fish, causing her to yelp. And right there, in the middle of the ocean in the Bahamas, Jackson took her phone from her hand and snapped his first-ever selfie—Megan, Jax, and a 250-pound blue marlin.

And Megan wanted to get on her knees and thank God for bringing Jackson Irons back into her life again.

God, she was beautiful. It was all Jax could think about as she rubbed her bicep and opened and closed her fingers. "That was intense," she said.

They'd just tossed the marlin back into the water and they were still trying to catch their breaths from all the energy they'd spent pulling it in. His throat tightened as he stared at her. It wasn't the first time he'd been unable to look away from her in the last week, but it felt significant this time. She'd been beautiful before, but now it was a different kind of beauty and he couldn't stop staring.

"Why are you looking at me like that?"

He stood and kissed the top of her head. "Thank you for bringing me here, Megan."

"You're welcome, Jax."

She'd done this for him. Not because she wanted to fish. Not because she was in the mood for a quick trip to the Bahamas. Because he had been stressed and she wanted to do something for *him*. It had been a long time since anyone had cared enough about him to want to see him happy. On more than one occasion, Joey had slapped him upside the head, handed him a beer and said: "Get your shit together, Irons." One particularly depressing time, he'd bought him a case of beer and they sat on his couch watching movies until they passed out. Words hadn't been spoken but once the hangover had subsided the next day he'd felt a little better.

But this was different. So different.

"Be right back," he said, jogging up to speak with the captain, wanting to do something nice for her too.

When he returned he handed her another beer.

"What's happening?" she asked, looking around as the boat began to move.

"You'll see."

Forty-five minutes later, with Freeport a mere dot to their south, the boat stopped and the captain dropped anchor while Lefty handed them fins and masks supplies.

"Snorkeling? What about fishing? That's why we're here."

"Aren't you tired of fishing?"

"I'm fine, Jax and so are you. Let's fish some more."

"Nah, I'm good. How can I possibly compete with that marlin, anyway?"

Her face softened and she looked around at the transparent water, colorful fish, and reef that surrounded them. "This is beautiful." She reached for the strap of her top to adjust it and winced. Gah, I'm burning up," she said, looking at her sunburned arms. Reaching for the sunblock she squirted lotion into her hands and began to rub it on her chest and neck.

"Turn around, I'll get your back."

Quickly complying, she moved her hair out of the way as he slathered lotion all over her back and shoulders. Obviously, it wasn't altruistic—this was the perfect excuse to get his calloused palms on her smooth skin. He slowly rubbed up and down, his fingers moving underneath the straps of her bikini. God, how he wanted to slide those straps down and cup her tits with his hands, pinch her nipples. . . .

His lips were by her neck and she erupted in goose bumps when he exhaled.

But they weren't alone.

She still wasn't safe.

This was just a mirage.

Tomorrow they'd be back home and Ryan would still be fucking with her.

Jax stepped back, handed her the bottle, and grabbed the masks.

She turned her eyes, which were narrowing on him. He went to work adjusting the straps of the masks, trying not to stare at the way her nipples were straining against the white bikini.

He knew he was an asshole: one minute hot, the next cold. She looked like she was going to push him into the ocean.

"Your turn," she hissed, putting lotion on her hand. His eyebrows furrowed as she rubbed her palms on his chest. She started on his pecs and instead of moving up to his shoulders, she moved down to his abs, which tensed underneath her touch. She kept her eyes on his, something she didn't normally do. But she was being brave and brazen as she unabashedly explored his body. He swallowed, trying to seem unmoved by her exploration; his hard cock told a different tale.

But, he didn't move, standing still and letting her touch him.

After it was obvious that all the lotion had been rubbed in and there was no excuse to continue, he stepped away. "Hold your hair back," he ordered her. Lifting the mask to her face, he carefully adjusted the straps. "Okay, that's good," he said in a thick voice, then dove right into the ocean. Maybe the cold water would help regulate his beating heart—and throbbing dick.

The rest of the afternoon was spent exploring all the different colorful fish that circled them around an artificial reef, staying close together and pointing as things swam by them.

"If I don't get out of the water soon, I'll turn into a fish," she finally said.

He smiled and headed back to the anchored boat. "Is that a smile I just saw?" she teased, winded, swimming behind him. "It only took a private plane to the Bahamas, a chartered boat, three hours of fishing, a blue marlin, and a day of snorkeling."

He chuckled again. "I'm not a cheap date, what can I say?" He hoisted himself up onto the small platform at the back of the boat. "Grab that step and take my hand," he directed, reaching for her and pulling her up. They were wet, half naked, and pressed close together, enjoying one of the best days he'd had in as long as he could remember. "It didn't take all of that to make me smile," he said, his voice thick with emotion as he wrapped her up in a towel. "You, sweetheart, you make me smile."

———————

Her heart hammered into her chest. This was the Jax she remembered. The one with a smile that could melt her heart. The one who didn't speak often, but when he did, it was meaningful and perfect. The one who could have her walking out of a stadium full of people, leaving her boyfriend behind. Leaving her entire life behind to start a new one. A better one.

"You ready? There's a storm coming," Kenneth hollered from behind the glass. He pointed westward to where the sky was darkening.

The moment was broken. "Yeah. We're ready."

In an effort to avoid the storm, the captain charged forward so fast that they both sat on their seats holding on. Thirty minutes later they were docking when the downpour began.

"Oh my god, Jax!" She yelled over the thunder and pelting rain. "Hurry!"

"What's the rush? You're already wet."

He was right. She stopped panicking and calmly looked around. She found a little shelter by a shed and waited for Jax to help Kenneth and Lefty tie the boat up and disembark.

While waiting, she found her phone and turned it on. She had ten messages and countless texts, but the only one that concerned her was the one from her manager.

"What's going on?" Jax asked.

"Oh, man. Glen's been trying to get in touch with me. Look." She showed him the phone. It said there was a bad storm heading their way and the planes were grounded. "He checked us into the nearest hotel that had vacancy. Let's find a cab."

"Come on, guys, I'll take you," Lefty said, hopping into a small clunker with the captain. Jax and Megan scooted into the back seat and asked Lefty to take them to the Ocean Breeze Inn. The thoughts running through her mind at being alone all night in a hotel with Jax were more thunderous than the actual storm crashing down on them.

With the rain and wind coming in hard, it took them twenty minutes to get to their hotel and it turned out that Glen had only been able to secure one room. And because of a festival happening on the island that week, rooms were scarce, so the hotel was really more like a very old motel. Megan couldn't help but stare at the comfortable-looking king-size bed, thinking about what the night would bring, while Jax insisted on doing a routine security check of the room. As if Ryan would be able to predict a freak storm and an impromptu overnight stay.

After checking the room, Jax let Megan have the first shower while he called Joey. She needed a moment away from him to regroup, anyway. Tonight would be the night. There was no way he could deny the attraction, it was just too much already. If he didn't do something about it, they could not continue their current living arrangement because she would surely go crazy.

In the little bathroom with the cheap soap and tiny bottle of shampoo, she scrubbed herself clean, thanking God she shaved that morning. She could hear him talking with Joey from the bathroom as she rinsed off and wrapped herself in a towel.

She walked out of the bathroom as he was tossing his phone on the bed. "You think there's a gift shop here where I can get some clothes?"

"Maybe." His voice sounded distracted. "Why don't you call the front desk and ask while I take a quick shower?"

"Okay," she said, sitting on the bed, noting how his eyes slowly perused her body. She had felt him get hard against her while he'd been rubbing lotion on her, and remembered the way his hands lingered on her all day. His green eyes were glowing with heat and she felt the pulse on her neck strumming against her skin.

With one hand clutching the towel, she called the front desk not exactly sad to discover that all the clothing stores were closed. She didn't exactly want clothes right now. Food, yes. Clothes? No.

It had been a great day. The best, actually. Jax brought out something within her that made her forget all her problems and focus on the moment. Maybe it was naïve of her, but with him around, she didn't need to feel scared because he was always there—at the ready to protect her.

It made her defenses drop and her thoughts linger on other things. Other . . . deliciously sexy things.

When he got out of the shower, she was sitting on the bed with her legs crossed, still wrapped in a towel, trying to watch a rerun of an old sitcom on the ancient television. "Gift shop's already closed for the day. I hung my clothes by the AC. They'll dry by morning."

He hung his wet clothes next to hers and sat on the unoccupied corner of the bed, a towel wrapped around his lower half. A zing of awareness shot through her: of the flimsy towels barely covering them and the bed they'd have to share.

I'm basically naked in bed with Jax, she thought wildly.

His abs rippled, his thighs strained out of the towel. She had to adjust her own and look away—he was so damn sexy it was unnerving.

"Maybe there's a vending machine," he said, his heated eyes looking at her. It didn't look like his hunger would be satisfied with food.

Fuuuck.

He wasn't going to be able to stay away. Not with that ridiculously tiny towel, or the way she was looking at him, or the way that one drop of water she hadn't dried off was trailing down her collarbone, or the way her nipples were . . .

"So." Megan's voice was breathy. "Looks like we're stuck here for a while."

"Looks that way." He tried to turn his attention to the grainy television, but his eyes kept finding her—her shiny flawless skin, the swell of her breasts, her long legs tucked underneath her. Being trapped in this small hotel room—a small hotel room with one bed—was playing havoc with his concentration.

"Um, tell me more about the last five years. You still go to the baseball games? How's your mom?"

Huh? Baseball? Baseball . . . it took him a moment to remember what the term meant, he was so out of it. "I've only been able to go to one of the openers since and it was in the new stadium. Wasn't the same. Not at all."

"Yeah, it's pretty huge, isn't it?"

"So you've gone?"

"A few times." Megan said absently, digging through her purse before looking up triumphantly with a few snacks clutched in her hand. "Nourishment!"

Jax caught the bar she tossed with a small smile and a lazy flick of his wrist.

"What else has happened in the last five years?"

"Not much. Well, Mom died a few years ago."

"What?" she shrieked.

"Yeah, it was bad. Car accident."

"Jax, I'm so sorry."

"Yeah, I don't really talk about it much. I wasn't here when it happened." He shrugged, uncomfortable with the conversation. "Let's talk about something else."

"Uh . . . okay. Um, any girlfriends?"

"A few. Nothing that stuck."

"Why's that?" she asked, playing with the end of the tattered white towel.

"Hard to have a relationship when you're not in town."

"Right. Makes sense."

"I saw you dated Tim Trammel." Tim was an A-list actor who was always on magazine covers, and when Jax had looked Megan up a week ago, there were dozens of photos of the couple together. It had stung.

"Yes, for almost a year. He's a good guy but we kind of had your problem. Hard to date someone who's never in town. He was away filming more often than not. And I was on tour a lot too. So we just sort of fizzled out."

They were sitting across from each other, Megan on one side of the bed and Jax on the other. Both in just towels, talking about past lovers.

He was beyond jealous that anyone had seen her naked, touched her skin, smelled her scent, kissed her lips. Somewhere deep inside, he'd pictured her married in a content life. Preferably a platonic, sexless life. Even

that had driven him a little nuts, but never had he pictured her still out there—dating. Sleeping with different
men. Suddenly, the idea of Megan with anyone but him
made him want to pound his chest and demand she
never be touched by anyone else ever again. Because
even if he couldn't be the man for her, no one else would
be good enough for her.

And wasn't that fucked up?

Another drop of water slid down her neck and over
the curve of her chest. He wanted to follow its trail with
his tongue before pulling the coarse cloth of the towel
aside and exploring even further. Jesus, his balls were
heavy with need and his cock was painfully hard. How
the hell was he supposed to get through the night without touching, tasting?

"What's next on your list of crazy shit you're going to
make me do?" he asked, his eyes following the trail left by
the droplets.

"Haven't thought about it. Doing the planning mostly
off the cuff."

He nodded. The conversation was stilted, mostly because he could see the tendrils from her hair falling out
of the bun on her head. More drops of water still lingered
around her long neck, and the valley between her breasts
moved up and down with each shallow breath she took.
The room was too small and too hot for the two of them

to be alone together. He needed her so fucking bad. So fucking bad.

"Had you been to the Bahamas before?" she asked, her voice hoarse. She was obviously trying to make small talk, but the air was so thick it was obvious her thoughts were also on the tension in the room. Her cheeks were flushed and he could see her neck bob when she swallowed and her eyes drift to his bare chest. Through the towel, her nipples peeked out, hardened, and he knew it had absolutely nothing to do with the air. She was turned on.

Jax almost groaned when she inconspicuously pressed her legs together. It was a clear sign that she needed some relief. *God, how he wanted to be that relief. . . .*

She continued anxiously playing with the thread at the end of the towel as her eyes roamed his body, making his cock harden with each second that ticked by. He couldn't even pretend to cover it up if he wanted to.

"Meg," he said, his voice thick. His eyes were on her pink plump lips. Her tongue peeked out to wet her bottom lip and a deep guttural groan escaped his mouth.

"Yes," she whispered, or maybe even whimpered. It was that low and his concentration was lacking.

"I don't want to talk about the Bahamas. In fact, I don't give a fuck about the Bahamas."

She swallowed, her breathing shallow, her eyes glazed.

"You don't?"

He shook his head.

"What do you give a fuck about, Jackson?"

"How fast I can get from this side of the bed to that one and have my tongue in your mouth and my cock inside of you."

The time for thought and sensibility was over. She dropped her grip on her towel at the same time Jax pounced, pushing her onto her back, slamming his lips against hers. Naked, she wrapped herself around him. His heart was beating so profoundly he wanted to consume her, love her so hard and fiercely they would never know where one started and one ended.

And fuck him, he didn't think he'd ever let her go.

Chapter 9

FIVE YEARS EARLIER

Megan's cell phone was burning a hole in her pocket. It was all she could think of. He'd given it back to her a few minutes ago with the promise she wouldn't use it. Turning it on meant facing her problems, so she put it on the counter as she took a quick shower and tried to stop thinking about the fact that she was in Jax's house—the house of a man she had just met while breaking up with her boyfriend in the middle of some sort of life-changing epiphany at a baseball game.

She barely recognized herself.

Once she was out of the bathroom, wearing a too-big gray US Marines T-shirt and some way-too-big gym shorts, she padded to the living room. Jax sat on his big brown couch with a beer in his hand, his bare feet on a wooden coffee table, looking relaxed and at home in his space. "I took a quick shower too," he said when she walked in.

She should've gone straight to bed, since it was so late, but instead she sat next to him.

"You don't drink beer, but I might have wine, not sure if I have soda. I do have milk, which I need to use since it'll go bad and I hate throwing away a good gallon of milk."

"I'm okay, thanks," she said, facing the television. She pointed to the screen. "I love *Jaws*. Scares me every time, but I love it."

"You're a scary movie kind of girl?"

"Yes. Love scary movies."

They settled in to watch, sitting on opposite ends of the sofa. She glanced over at him a few times as the silence stretched between them, becoming awkward in a way it hadn't been all day. Suddenly, Megan wasn't sure what to talk about. Luckily he started talking first, the movie fading into the background

"So, tell me more about Dick."

"Nothing more to tell. I mean, he's my first real boyfriend. My parents love him. I was pretty sure we were going to get married and have kids eventually."

He shifted, turning his full attention on her. "Seems like that's something your folks and Dick want. What do you want?"

She shrugged, never having analyzed her life. Maybe she should have. She never realized how naïve she'd been. "Being a lawyer has always been mapped out. It's what I have to do."

Why?

Why did she have to do it, exactly?

And why hadn't she ever stopped and questioned her decisions—or lack thereof?

"Says who?" he asked, as if reading her mind.

She bit the side of her lip and shifted her weight on the couch, getting more comfortable—physically, though definitely not emotionally. "I mean, if I'm not a lawyer what else am I? My parents paid for the best private schools, I've always gotten straight As, I . . ."

He looked utterly confused by her answer, and frankly, she was feeling confused by it too. Because damn . . . she didn't know the answers to all the whys! She was just doing what was mapped out for her.

"What do you, Megan, like to do? Like, for fun?"

She sat back and thought about it. There was only one thing she loved to do. One thing that brought her joy and passion. The rest of her life was all mundane routine crap she had to do.

"Can I have a sip of that beer?" He looked at the bottle in his hand and then handed it over. She took a big gulp and made a disgusted face before handing it back. "Okay, so, there's this thing I do and no one knows. Not anyone. My parents would have a fit and Richard—I don't even know what Richard would think."

He leaned forward, "Now I have to know what it is."

"You smile a lot. It's nice," she said, veering off topic. "Tell me more about yourself."

"Like I said, I grew up in Miami. My parents—they were always great. When my dad died, that was the hardest thing I've ever had to go through but he always taught me to have fun and live your life doing what you love."

"You have such a great outlook, Jax."

He shrugged. "Dad wouldn't want me moping around thinking of all the what-ifs or sad times. I miss him so much, but I try to think of all the good things. My parents always did a bunch of things with me—camping, fishing, movie nights when I was younger. All they ever wanted was for me to be happy. That was all they ever talked about."

"God, I wish I had that. I don't think my parents have ever asked me if I was happy." That was a tough pill to swallow.

"That sucks, Megan. Really. Your parents should be your biggest supporters and it sucks that they aren't. How about your friends?"

"Most of them went away to college and we sort of drifted apart. I have some friends through Richard, but not many. You?"

"I have great friends. I guess life is good to me, Megan. For me—well, there's nothing for me not to smile about. But what I want to know is what makes you smile."

"God." She threw her head back on the couch. "I always thought my life was pretty great too. My parents gave me everything I ever needed, my boyfriend was faithful, I got a full scholarship to law school at UM."

"Don't take this the wrong way, Megan, but that all sounds boring and cold. Your parents always gave you what you needed? How about what you wanted? Your standards in men are super low if the fact he's faithful is his good quality. A man should just *be* faithful, he doesn't get rewarded for that. He just is." Her ideas of the world were titling with each passing hour.

How can someone so wealthy, so worldly, so educated, be so closed-minded, sheltered, and wrong? All of these thoughts were flying around in her mind as he continued to talk. "How did you even hook up with Dick? Did your parents pick him out for you?"

She bit her lip.

"Jesus, Megan."

"What am I supposed to do, Jax? I mean, the few times I ever tried to rebel, and trust me, it's not a juicy story, like at all, my parents cut me off. I don't have a job or any real skills. Richard wasn't that bad. I just kind of... go with the flow."

"You need to live a little. Paint outside the lines," he said. She took the beer from his hand again and finished it off.

"Thought you didn't like beer."

"Ack," she said, shaking her head. "I don't. Can I have another one?"

He chuckled, got up and brought back two bottles. "So what's your big secret?"

"I sing."

"You sing?"

"I sing."

"Expand, please."

"I've always loved singing and music. I love it. My parents think it's a waste of time. Richard doesn't even know. There's this band I follow on Facebook called TNT, and we've become friends. Mostly because I'm such a huge fan and I interact a lot with them on Facebook and never miss them when they have live shows at Robbie's. You know Robbie's?"

"The little hole in the wall on 57th Avenue?"

"Yeah, that one. Anyway, every time they have a gig there, I sneak out and go listen to them."

"And then what?"

"And that's it."

"You're a twenty-two-year-old woman. What do you do, sneak out the window?"

"No." She rolled her eyes and took a drink of her beer. "I say I'm studying or something and I just go and sit right up front. One day they're going to be huge, I just know it."

Jax shifted his body to face her, his knee touching hers. "Sing for me."

"No way, dude!" she laughed.

"I don't get it. You have this deep dark secret where you hide out in a bar to hear a band?"

"It's not something people I know do." She quickly added, "I know that sounds bad, and I agree that it's bullshit, but it is what it is."

"So change it. It shouldn't be that way. You like to sing, then fuckin' sing."

Shaking her head, she turned back around. "It's not that easy."

"It is. It's *that* easy."

"Just drop everything I've worked so hard to do, and what? Live under a bridge while I sing for quarters?"

"You don't have to be that dramatic about it. You can get a job somewhere and see where the singing takes you. Get a small apartment, break away from Mommy and Daddy."

"You make it sound easy."

"It is easy, Megan. It's just something you have to be brave enough to do."

She turned around to watch the movie, thinking about those words.

You just have to be brave.

"Oh my god!" Megan squealed, early the next morning. "I'm not getting in there!"

"You are." Jax laughed, his fingers laced with hers as the sound of the helicopter blades tore through the air. She looked so cute, wearing the same outfit as yesterday but without the hat. Her hair was in some kind of messy knot on her head, her face pink from the sun—and maybe from nerves.

"I hate heights."

"You got this, Megan," he said, pulling her gently toward the chopper.

If she hadn't had a big huge grin on her face, Jax wouldn't have pushed her to come on a helicopter ride of Miami. Last night she'd fallen asleep watching movies on the couch with him. They'd woken up with her pressed against his side and his arm around her. Oddly, neither was embarrassed. It felt strangely natural. But they didn't talk about it either.

During breakfast she had confessed to never having done any of those touristy Miami things, so Jax made arrangements to spend the day showing her the city she'd never really gotten to know as part of the game they were playing: Five Things.

Hesitant, she stepped into the chopper. Jax followed right behind her and handed her a pair of headphones. The pilot climbed inside shortly after and went through instructions—since Jax had been on helicopters a dozen times, he tuned out the pilot, concentrating on Megan's trembling fingers. Taking one of her hands in his, he smiled and said—loudly, over the noise and into the small mic—"We're good, Meg. You'll love it. Promise."

She looked down at their joined hands and then back up at him and nodded. It took all of five minutes for Megan to go from terrified to pointing out the window with a huge smile on her face, but during the hour-long ride, she never—not once—let go of his hand. And it felt unfamiliar yet wonderful.

There was something about his woman.

The attraction was instant—but not just because she was gorgeous.

She was different.

She was wealthy, but she had not once complained about wearing the same outfit from the night before. He'd been with lots of women, none of them as well-off as Megan, and they all would've thrown a fit. They'd also all insisted on dolling up before stepping one foot outside, unlike Megan who had her thick brown hair piled up messily, her face free of any makeup. No frills, no pretenses, just vulnerable and sincere.

She also always tried to pay her share, but he wouldn't allow it. And the thing he liked most, even in this short time of knowing her, was the way she looked at him.

It was as if he could do no wrong. She listened to him—really listened—and then absorbed what he said. She put on a brave face and powered through whatever fear she had, putting all her trust in him. And extending that trust was the most humbling thing anyone had ever done for him.

As soon as they landed and climbed down, she jumped on him, wrapping all her limbs around him. "That was the coolest thing I've ever done. Thank you, Jax. Thank you, thank you, thank you!" She kissed his forehead and then his cheeks, his hands were busy holding her up but he wanted to grab hold of her face and plant those lips on his.

Slowly she slid down his body. As soon as her feet were planted back on the concrete, he pulled her back to him. Time was suspended for a moment. There was no noise but her beating heart. She swallowed and her face became serious. Last time, their kiss had been spontaneous and she hadn't really had the opportunity to push him away. This time—this time—he was going to make sure she wanted it too.

"I'm going to kiss you."

Wide-eyed, she nodded. "Words," he said, his nose moving softly down her cheeks to her jaw. "Need words."

"Yes, kiss me. Please," she croaked.

He palmed her face and touched his lips to hers, then

searched her eyes. When he saw nothing but the same dazed lust in her eyes as he had in his, he moved forward, harder this time, and she opened her lips to him. Her hands tightened around his neck, and he wrapped his arms around her waist, pulling her as close as she could get. Forgetting they were in the landing pad, tuning out the noise from other helicopters around them, ignoring the tourists watching, he licked the seam of her lips while her tongue touched his, both battling for control.

"Jackson," she whispered into his mouth, an erotic moan that made his cock harder than it had ever been. With closed eyes she turned her head, giving him access to her long elegant neck. He was about to palm her tits—those tits he'd been trying not to eye, obviously, for the last two days—when he pushed softly back, remembering where they were, not able to ignore the noise or the voyeurs any longer.

"Not here," he said, barely recognizing his own voice. Quickly, he took her hand in his and led her to his bike. Getting back to his house—with Megan and her hard nipples pressed against his back while he fought back the most painful hard-on he'd ever had—was a true test of his self-control. She didn't say a single word as he drove, instead holding him tightly, her cheeks pressed against his back.

When they arrived at Jax's house, the heat of the moment hadn't died down—a desire that hummed in the background all the time, a crazed need that happened when they kissed. He pulled her down to the couch, his hands roaming her body, his knee between her legs, her limbs wrapped around him as he kissed her lips, behind her ear, her neck, his hands staying over her clothes at all times.

———————

"I should feed you," he suggested at some point mid-day, when he felt her stomach rumble from underneath him. He looked down at her: she had a loopy smile, her lips swollen and pink from making out for the last couple of hours.

"That would mean that we'd have to move. That we'd need to stop kissing," she pouted.

Without moving off of her, he pulled out his cell phone, dialed, and went back to kissing her, only stopping when someone answered on the other end of the line. "I want to order a large cheese—"

She put her hand over his mouth and took the phone from his hand, laughing. "Pepperoni," she corrected, "and a dozen garlic rolls, please."

Then she handed him the phone again, kissing his neck and his collarbone as he finished ordering and tossed his phone aside and went back to work.

Him palming her breasts while she sucked on his lower lip and gyrated against his knee, they continued to make out feeling crazed and needy. "Oh . . . Jax," she moaned into his mouth when he pressed his knee harder against her core.

"You're so fucking delicious, Meg. I can't get enough of you."

When the doorbell rang half an hour later, she begged him to ignore it, though her stomach grumbled in protest and her lips looked dry and sore. Laughing, he pushed off the couch and went to the door as she righted herself.

―――――――

Making herself at home, Megan took out some plates and two beers and set them on the coffee table where they ate. She tried to tame her stupid grin, but it was impossible. Today was the best day of her life, and kissing Jax made her feel like she'd been missing out on so much. She'd never spent hours just kissing before.

"Eat. Your stomach grumbling is killing the mood." He winked and handed her a slice.

"I was hungry."

"You should've said something earlier."

"I was busy earlier."

Jax took a slice for himself. "You're a good kisser."

"So are you," she said with a mouthful.

"If they gave kissing awards, you'd get it."

She smiled, taking another bite of her pizza. "I've never kissed someone like that or for so long." And it was true, Richard wasn't passionate or intense like Jax was. Jax kissed with fervor, as if his next breath depended on it.

"If we stay here any longer, I'm not going to want to stop, so I think we need to finish eating and get the hell out of here, unless you want to keep going."

She looked down, embarrassed.

"What's wrong?" he asked.

"I feel like I need to be up front with you. I've only been with Richard. He's the only man I've ever slept with, and I don't know if I'm ready to . . ."

"I understand, Meg. I don't want you to feel pressured to do anything you don't want to do." He took a final bite of his pizza. "Are you okay with kissing? Is it too much? I'll stop if it's too much."

"No!" she yelled, her face heating with a blush when he smirked at her emphatic response. "Definitely not too much. It feels . . . amazing," she admitted. "Are *you* okay with just kissing?"

"I'll take whatever I can get, sweetheart. If you're willing to kiss me, I'm taking it."

Sweetheart.

Her heart faltered.

"Thanks for being patient, Jax."

He smiled sincerely at her before grabbing another slice.

Everything with Jax was just so easy, it was unnerving waiting for the other shoe to drop.

Chapter 10

"I want to finish what we started five years ago," Jax said into her neck. His voice was thick and there was a tick in his jaw. "Tonight, I want to finally be inside of you."

Without a second thought, Megan pushed him back and pulled his towel aside so that they were both naked on the old squeaky motel bed. "I've been waiting five years."

He cupped her face with his hands, kissing her like it was their first kiss ever. He took full ownership of the kiss, forcing his tongue into her mouth as she ran her fingers through his beard, needing to get closer to him. Lowering her onto the bed, he licked down her jaw to her neck, her back arching to give him better access.

"So fucking beautiful," he said, running his palm down the valley between her breasts and past her stomach, right to where she needed it most.

It felt familiar, yet different.

He slid a finger up and down, slick with her need, stopping at her swollen clit.

"Fuck."

It came out in a strangled moan, as he sucked a nipple into his mouth and bit down, softly.

"Oh!"

"I missed you, Meg." He moved up her body, whispering into her ear, his beard tickling her neck while his finger trailed lower until he was pushing a finger into her, hitting the perfect spot. Megan could barely breathe as he worked her over, rubbing her clit and moving his fingers in just the right rhythm.

"Oh God! Oh God!" she yelled, arching her back and gripping her own hair, completely lost in sensations.

"Get there, baby," he demanded, crooking his finger in a way that made her almost jump off the bed. She felt her body tighten around his fingers. "There it is, babe. Just let go."

Her head tossed back and forth on the pillow. So close, she was so close.

"I want you inside, Jax. I want to come together." She needed to feel him, to feel possessed by him.

"I don't have protection." His voice was guttural, muffled where it rested against the skin of her neck, his wicked fingers driving her wild.

"I'm clean. I'm on birth control," she panted, pushing against his hand, needing more than just his fingers.

"Thank God," he said, taking his finger away and using his knees to spread her thighs further apart. "I'm clean too, and I'm not waiting another second. Later, I might want you for dinner, but tonight, I need to be inside you. I need to feel you, completely." He positioned himself by her wet and very ready entrance and in one swift thrust he was in.

––––––––––

Neither moved for what felt like an eternity, both savoring the moment they'd been waiting for, for so long. When he lowered his chest onto hers and began to move she wrapped her legs around him and dug her fingers into his hair.

It felt unlike anything he'd ever felt before. It was almost too much, the way her pussy felt, the way her body felt around his. . . .

"Fuck, Megan," he grunted into her neck, as the old bed squeaked underneath them.

"Harder, Jackson." She clawed his back as he thrust into her hard, her nails digging into his skin, urging him on.

He unwrapped her legs from behind him, lifted them straight up in the air, and held them as he moved inside of her. "Oh my god, Jax. Oh . . . oh . . ."

"Don't you fucking come yet," he demanded, slowing his pace, even though he was at the precipice and slowing down actually caused him pain. But he wanted to savor this moment, make it last as long as possible. "I've been thinking about this for years, Meg. Fucking years. In the desert, I jacked off to the memory of your tongue in my mouth and what I imagined this moment would feel like."

Her pussy tightened around his cock like a vise. "I said not to come yet." He stilled his thrusts and pinched her nipple.

"Jackson..." she moaned, almost pained, her eyes rolled to the back of her head, her thighs shaking.

"How do you taste, baby? Sweet? Like honey? When I dream of your pussy, it's sweet honey dripping down my chin while my tongue fucks you."

"Oh God." She arched up, but he held her hips down.

"Did you think of me?" he asked, fucking her slowly. Painfully slow.

"All the time," she croaked.

"Did you touch yourself thinking of me?"

"All the time," she repeated. "But my imagination wasn't as good as this. Jax, I can't hold it anymore." Her body began to tremble, her pussy tightened even harder, and he couldn't hold back any longer when he felt her coming over and over against his cock. He grunted a slew of incoherent words as he let go of her legs and pumped into her two more times before collapsing on top of her.

"Wow. Should've done that five years ago," she said, blissfully and breathlessly.

"No, baby." He kissed her forehead and forced himself to roll over next to her. He'd get up in a second, he promised himself, once he had feeling back in his legs and his brain. "I wouldn't have let you go if we had."

Megan just grunted in response.

When his heart stopped feeling like it was going to beat out of his chest, he kissed her lips and climbed out of bed. "And you needed to go on your own and do your thing," he added from the bathroom, the sound of the storm brewing outside sounding loud inside the small motel room.

"But now you're back and I'm here." She smiled as he walked back into the room a moment later with a hand towel. "And we need to do this again, and often."

"Open your legs for me, Meg." He gestured, tenderly.

He had never had sex without a condom, and thinking of how a part of him was still inside of her began to stir his dick again. Gently wiping her clean was perhaps the most intimate thing he'd ever done, which was weird because he'd just fucked her senseless and now planned on kissing every square inch of her body.

"That spark we had," she said, settling back on the bed, her front to his side, one leg tossed over him as she played with his beard, lazily. "It's still there, isn't it?"

"Fuck yeah, it's still there," he said, holding her closely as the exhaustion from the day and the sound of the storm lulled them both to sleep.

"I never doubted it, Jax."

"Neither did I, baby. Neither did I."

———————

"If you don't hurry up and get dressed soon, I'm fucking you against that shitty old dresser." It was early the next morning and the jet was already waiting for them, but Megan was procrastinating. Right now, they were in a perfect bubble that did not include stalkers, letters, or prank calls, but did involve delicious orgasms by Jax. Jax who was playful, but also demanding. She didn't mind, though, not when it came to sex. In fact, his dirty demanding words turned her on in a big way.

Naked, she watched Jax, who was already dressed and focused on something on his phone, waiting on her to finish. Wanting at least one more round, she bent over, her forearms on the "shitty old dresser." "Maybe I don't want to hurry up," she said, wiggling her ass and gazing at him over her shoulder.

He looked up, his green eyes becoming heated. "Woman . . ." he warned, a smirk on his face, and tossed his phone on the bed. Pushing down his bathing suit, the only clothes he had, and releasing his cock, he stalked toward her. "You play dirty."

She lowered her chest and pushed her ass up in the air, wanting him inside her immediately. Needing the stretch of him. His body pressed against hers. His fingers digging into her skin, reminding her that this was—they were—finally happening. She could feel her wetness dripping down her thigh.

"This won't be slow."

"I don't want slow." She could see him from the mirror right in front of her. The way he confidently gripped his cock made her whimper and her clit throb. "I want it, Jax. Please."

Pushing her down on the dresser, he guided his thick cock inside her. In this position he felt bigger and more consuming, his entire body enveloping her. And, just like he'd warned, it was not slow. Not only was it fast, it was hard. Hard and perfect.

"Hang on," he grunted as she planted her palms on the mirror, pushing back as he pushed forward. Their bodies slapped against each other, but he didn't ease up, not one bit. With one hand he reached underneath her to find her clit. "I'm not waiting," he grunted. "I'm getting you there."

She was unsure what he meant until she felt him pinch her clit. "Holy shit!" she screamed, faintly thinking the neighbors were hearing everything, but not caring enough to stop.

Again he pinched and rubbed as she felt his cock swelling inside her. It was like a detonation switch—all sensation converged in the bundle of nerves in her pussy and she needed to grab hold of something as she came, but the mirror gave her no purchase and she felt herself slipping, her arms Jell-O as the orgasm took hold of her. He placed his hands over hers, interlacing their fingers, his palm to the back of her hand against the mirror. He bit her not-so-gently on the shoulder as she felt him explode inside of her.

Both sweaty and breathless, they slid down to the floor. "You, woman, are trouble," he said, lifting her up and dumping her in the middle of the shower.

They were an hour late and it cost her a small fortune, but it was well worth it.

It was still early when they arrived back in Miami. While Jax met with some of his crew at Megan's house to discuss some new business ICS had contracted, Megan sat on her bed to write. She was worried that now that they were back, things would be different. She wasn't sure where they stood, and they hadn't talked about it. But he'd seemed lighter and genuinely happy on the plane ride back, and she hoped this was a change that would stick.

"I've scoped out your house top to bottom. I know you have a music room," he said, walking in and sitting next to her later that day. His hair was slicked back, his beard long and unkempt, and he wore a T-shirt and gym shorts with steel toe boots. The combination was messy but he looked hot.

She sat up and put her pen and notebook aside. "I do. I hired a designer to create the best space to help me write. To feel creative and comfortable. It was supposed to help the words just flow right out."

"So why are you writing in this room? Hunched over on the bed looking uncomfortable," he asked, twirling her pencil with his thumb and forefinger.

"It's the only place I can write. It's where I feel most inspired. Never been able to write a single word in the music room," she laughed and shook her head. "Kind of a waste of space, that room."

He pushed her down on her back and crawled over her. She wanted to do a girly little squeal of happiness that what had happened in the Bahamas wasn't just a twenty-four-hour fluke. "I'm taking it over, then. That's going to be ICS while I'm here, planning for the tour and working on some other things that are going on."

"Have at it." She wrapped her arms around his neck and her legs around his waist and kissed him. "I have plans for this afternoon, by the way."

"What kind of plans?" he asked, pushing up a little and tenderly swiping some hair off of her face.

"The kind that involves fun."

"Still with the five things game?" he asked, kissing her softly on the cheek and then the lips.

"It's not a game, it's my way of helping you."

"I don't need help."

"You had fun yesterday, right? It's been a while, we can't stop now. I will loosen you up, Jackson." She sat up and slipped out of his grip, kissing him on the cheek and then slapping his tight, muscular ass. "Now get out. I'm feeling inspired."

He chuckled, kissed her one last time, and left to make some calls.

Megan was in her bedroom writing when she heard a sound outside her window. Like pebbles tapping against glass. It was still daylight, and her house was full of people, but she couldn't think of a reason for any of Jax's men to be outside her bedroom on the terrace or even in this part of the big estate. Cautiously, she eased out of bed and opened the sheer curtains of the French doors that led to the balcony.

There was nothing on the other side, so she unlocked

the door and stepped out to overlook the property. Looking around there was nothing. From her balcony she had an unrestricted view of the ocean and the usual boats passing, but nothing unusual, though the hairs on the back of her neck were standing up. Her phone chirped at that moment and she ran inside and plucked it from the bed without looking at the screen.

"Hello?" she said, padding back to her balcony. "Hello?"

She looked down at the screen.

Unknown Caller

She gasped and her eyes roamed all over the property. Was it a coincidence, the way she felt as if someone was watching her, the phone call happening at the same time? "Hello? Who is this?" There was heavy breathing on the other side, and her hands trembled. "Ryan? Is this you?"

She kept the phone on her ear, waiting. When the caller didn't say anything and she didn't see anything she locked the door to her balcony and went in search of Jax.

———————

Annie, Joey's sister and an employee of ICS, came by the house with boxes of equipment. Like her brother, Annie was an ex-Marine and a computer genius. "Thanks for helping me set up these computers," Jax grumbled from underneath the desk as he plugged in a PC, three monitors, a printer, and a scanner.

"No problem. Although you didn't give me much of a choice," Annie huffed, but she had a smile on her face as she waited for Jax to finish the grunt work.

An hour ago, when Megan had ran downstairs with trembling hands and the phone in her hand, Jax had gone insane wanting security amped and the computers up and running with a top-of-the-line firewall. Joey was out on another job and Jax had barked at Annie to get her ass moving. She'd bitched for a solid minute until he told her who the client was.

"I can't believe I'm in Megan Cruz's house. Breathing Megan Cruz's air. Oh my god, I just sat in Megan Cruz's chair. I bet she wrote "Great Day" right on this very chair," Annie said, making herself comfortable in it.

"I really doubt that. She doesn't write in this room. And please stop referring to her as 'Megan Cruz,' it's weird as shit."

"Huge fan."

"I see that." Jax stuck his head out of the room. "Baby!" he yelled. "Can you come here for a sec?"

"Baby?" Annie said. "Oh my god, that is so cute!"

A moment later, a tired and worried but beautiful and sweet Megan staggered into the room. "We have a top-of-the-line intercom system, we both have cell phones, plus you have legs. Why are you yelling like a lunatic?"

Ignoring her complaint, Jax took her hand and pulled her forward. "Someone I want you to meet."

Annie stood up excitedly and walked around the desk. "Meg, this is Annie Clad, Joey's sister. She works with us and helped me set up the computer. I've known her forever."

Annie cocked an eyebrow and elbowed Jax. "Helped you? You didn't even know what a USB plug was." She rolled her eyes and waved him off, extending her hand to Megan. "Hi, it's so nice to meet you. I'm a huge fan."

"Hi, it's nice to meet you too. I didn't know Joey had a sister."

"Yep. They keep me holed up in the office." Annie glared at Jax. "I should be out in the field like the rest of the guys."

"Annie . . ." Jax warned.

"Looks like I have not one but two overprotective brothers. Anyway, I guess I should be heading out, I have a date tonight. It was really great to meet you, Megan. Jax, everything is programmed and ready, call me if you need me."

"Please come by for dinner," Megan said, "or better yet, when Nelly and Taylor come over to hang out, I'll call you so you can meet them too."

Annie, who was normally a serious, hard-assed, kick-ass woman, squealed. Annie was the opposite of a squealer. Jax had never heard a noise that girly come out of her mouth.

A moment later he was alone with Megan in his new makeshift office, tossing out the boxes and cleaning up the mess he'd made. "I'm going to start searching through the cameras."

Megan hopped on the desk, her legs swinging up and down. "I was on my way to find you when you called me." She handed him her phone. "Another call."

Stopping his movement, he looked up. "What?"

"I had a weird feeling a minute or so before the call. First I heard something coming from the balcony, then I sort of felt like someone was watching me."

"Jesus, Megan, why didn't you say something immediately?"

"I'm telling you now," she huffed, full of sass. "Anyway, I really don't think it was anything. I'm just being paranoid, you know, jumping at shadows, and I didn't actually see anything when I went outside."

"What exactly did you hear?"

"Something, maybe pebbles, hitting the glass doors. But they're mowing the lawn outside, it was probably nothing. And the phone was just more of the same. Breathing and then hanging up."

"Next time, you don't go out to look for the danger. You call me."

"Who's going to scale twenty feet? And the maintenance guys would've noticed something unusual. I knew it wasn't anything. Just a feeling. But since you've set all this up," she pointed to the computer system, "I figured it was worth a check. Put your equipment to good use." She grinned, tapping the top of the monitor.

Shaking his head, irritated that she was being careless, he sat down and clicked on the appropriate application, and then scrolled through her phone for the time-stamp of the call "So the call happened at one eighteen, and the noise was from your room, so it would be the east side," he said. He clicked on the correct camera and pressed play. They watched for a few minutes, forwarding and slowing down from between noon and two, just in case. When nothing appeared, he did the same thing with the other cameras nearby.

"I guess I'm just jittery. It was nothing," she said, relieved.

He eyed her carefully, she was still scared, obviously. "Talk to me. What's going on?"

She shook her head. "Nothing, just glad it was nothing," she said, plastering a fake smile on her face.

"Megan, come on. Tell me."

Blowing out a breath she leaned against the table. "I

keep thinking of that moment when I heard the window break, and then his feet as he walked into the closet. I was sure I was dead. I was bracing myself. I can't get that out of my head."

"It was a scary thing, Megan. Nothing wrong with feeling scared and jumpy from it. Until we catch this guy, you're going to be looking over your shoulder constantly, that's normal. I wish I could make it go away for you." He pulled her by the waist onto his lap. "I wish I could take that fear and make it disappear."

"I'll be fine. I'm sorry to make you worry and go through all this."

"It's my job and it's your safety. So never be sorry."

"I think I'm going to go shower. Maybe we can order dinner or something?"

"I thought you had something planned for tonight."

Looking distracted, she stared at him in confusion, then remembered. "Oh yeah, I did. But another time, maybe." She started to walk away, but he took her forearm.

"I don't like whatever is happening right now. We're going out. Either I'm taking you to dinner or we're going to go wherever it was you wanted to go."

"It's not safe, Jax."

"I thought you said that as long as you were with me you would be safe. Did something change?"

"No, nothing changed. But in the Bahamas we were far away from the crazy stalker. Anywhere we go here in town, he could be following us or eating right next to us. Watching us."

Jax didn't like this. She should let him do the worrying. Yes, she needed to be vigilant, but she didn't have to stay holed up inside her house, terrified.

"Go shower. When you're done, we're going out."

"But Jax—"

"No buts. We're going out." He needed her to trust him, know that even with all that was going on, she'd be safe. And even more important, that he wanted to make her happy.

———

Megan did want to go out, and she had planned a fun evening, but now? She felt like it was irresponsible and dumb to go out when her life could possibly be at risk. But she was with Jax and he was so imposing and controlled. If he said they'd be all right, she knew they would be.

It was later that evening as he walked out of her bathroom, a towel around his lower body and his hair all wet, that she stopped him. In jeans with strategically placed rips, and a worn out Pink Floyd T-shirt, she was ready to go. "How long until you're ready? If you're adamant about going out, let's go to where I had planned."

"Which is where?" He'd trimmed his beard and tied his hair back, and damn, he looked good. Less bushy caveman and more trendy bearded badass. He crossed his arms over his chest, waiting for her to answer.

"It's a surprise. Chop chop," she said, clapping.

"Feeling better, I see." He grabbed a hand towel and used it to dry his beard.

"A little. Dress comfortably." She took a step closer. "Have I mentioned that I really, really like this beard?"

"Guess we're done talking about the stalker?"

She ran her hand through his beard, not speaking.

"You have not mentioned it, no. I'm glad you like it, because I'm not shaving it off."

"Well, let me mention it now. I really, really like this beard." She took the towel from his hand and helped him dry it off. "Do you blow-dry it?"

"Sometimes. If I don't want it to drip and get my shirt wet."

"I like your longish hair too. Why'd you let everything grow?"

"Grew it in Iraq. It helped me fit in a little more when I was on missions."

"I thought the Marines didn't approve of long hair or beards. I thought you had to get that standard good-boy crew cut."

"That's for recruit training; once I was in special ops it's different. Then when I got back to the States, I didn't feel like going through the hassle of cutting it."

"It looks good on you. All of it: the hair, the beard, the muscles, the tattoos."

He took the towel from her hand and threw it over his shoulder. "You like the muscles, do you?"

"Oh yeah." She reached up and kissed him, slowly undoing the towel he had around his waist until it dropped to the floor. "I do have a favorite muscle, though."

"Thought you said we were in a hurry," he smirked, watching her eye trail down.

"We are. You have ten minutes. You think you can perform under those conditions, Marine?"

He chuckled, instantly pushing her down on the bed. "You'll be screaming my name and your eyes will be rolling to the back of your head by minute five."

"Cocky."

"Confident," he corrected her, unzipping her jeans and pulling them off, slowly. As if he had all the time in the world.

"I said ten minutes, not ten hours."

"Quiet. I'm trying to work here. I'm deciding how to best utilize my time. I'm thinking that I'm going to use my cock. You know, since you called me cocky."

She followed his eyes down to where his dick jutted out impressively. Looking at her parted legs, her center completely exposed and very wet, he stroked himself a few times, her eyes watching, her weight on her elbows.

"Flip over. Ass up, tits down."

"You're so romantic," she said with a laugh as she did what he asked. Using his fingers, he rubbed her clit until she was completely wet and writhing against the bed. Using his knees to part her legs further, he roughly pulled her ass higher and pushed inside her without giving her a moment to adjust. "I think I want it fast and hard."

"Yes," she mumbled into the bed, pushing back onto him. "Fast and hard."

"Hold on, Meg." And then he was thrusting in earnest, one palm flat against her back pushing her down, forcing her ass up higher, the other hand on her hip pulling her in as he thrust forward.

"Jackson!" She yelled loudly. "Do not stop."

"Wasn't planning to." Then he reached one hand around and began to strum her clit, causing all sensation to converge into a sudden intense orgasm that left her breathless and overwhelmed.

The sex itself may have taken less than ten minutes, but she lost track of the time it took to recover. Laying on top of her, her face still buried on her bedspread, he finally spoke. "I'm smothering you."

"It's okay. Feels good, your weight on me."

He pushed up and she turned over, watching him move off the bed. Reaching forward, she ran a finger down the raised scar on this thigh. "Does it hurt?"

"Not as much anymore. Sometimes, when it rains, or if I'm on it for too many hours, it acts up." He pulled his jeans from his bag by her closet and slid them on.

"Good to know. I won't take you mountain climbing in the rain as part of the five things, then."

He laughed. "I can out-climb you any day, woman. I'm fine. Don't start coddling me."

"I was teasing you, Jax. I wasn't going to coddle you and I absolutely wasn't going to climb anything. That's too much exertion for a girl who sneaks Nutella. I know you're in great shape. I never doubted it."

Pulling down his shirt, he held a hand out for her. "This conversation is too heavy for someone who has my come dripping down her leg."

"You are so gross!" she shrieked, and pushed him back, laughing loudly. "I can't believe you just said that to me."

He winked as she gathered her clothes and went to dress for the second time that night.

"Ready to go? I'm driving," she said, slipping on a long red wig.

He ran his palm down his face. "That should count as

one of the five things, since you driving is an adventure in and of itself."

"Har har. Fine. It's a nice evening. Let's take your bike. I'll give you directions as you drive. Keep you surprised."

She clicked the garage door open and Jax climbed on. "Up you go. Remember, hold on tight. Don't let go for any reason."

"This feels as good as I remember," she said, pressing her cheek to his back.

"You liked it before? You never said anything."

"Are you kidding? I'd just met you. What kinda girl says lovey-dovey shit like that on a first date? You would've run for the hills."

He squeezed her knee and tilted his head back. "The same kind of girl who agrees to have lunch with a stranger and stays for four days and rocks my world so deeply I've done nothing but think about her for five years." Then he turned back around, cranked up his bike and took off, leaving her completely disconcerted.

. . . *Rock my world so deeply* . . . She didn't know hearts could actually skip a beat.

———————

Jax parked in front of a familiar large dome as per Megan's instructions, doing a quick surveillance of the area before getting off the bike. "The planetarium? That's where you brought me?"

"Tonight's the light show. Didn't you do this when you were a teenager? Everyone in Miami came here to make out or get stoned. It's a rite of passage."

"Oh, I know exactly where we are. I'm just surprised you know it's a rite of passage."

"Fine. I've never been here. But I've always wanted to, and it's Pink Floyd night. I wanted to come."

"It's almost like five things *you* haven't done before."

"What can I say, you give me the courage and motivation to try new things, even all these years later," she said, taking his hand in hers and smiling up at him.

"Fine, but no getting stoned."

"Deal."

He paid for the two of them and they walked in, the lights still on. He looked around, making sure nothing seemed off, and then sent Joey a quick text. Checking in when he was with a client was something they did as part of protocol. There were about two dozen teenagers and young twentysomethings loitering around, waiting for the show to begin. Jax pulled Megan over to a corner, close to one of the emergency exits he had clocked. They sat with their backs against the wall, listening to the rock music and watching the laser light show on the ceiling of the dome. She lost the wig the moment the dome darkened and soon his mouth was on hers and his hand was under her shirt. There was an air of privacy with the thrill of being in public and it was exhilarating. Her nipple was just as pert and responsive as he'd remembered.

An hour later, the music stopped and they had to pull apart before the lights came back up. Instinctively, Megan reached for the wig while the room was still dark.

"I can't believe I just made out with you in the planetarium," Jax whispered, righting his clothes, surely looking as disheveled as she did.

"I know. Wasn't it fun?"

He shook his head and snorted, then helped her up, unable to look away from her flushed face and swollen lips. "I feel like I'm back in high school. And with that red hair, it's like I just kissed a stranger."

"It's the smell of weed that's making you feel that way."

He laughed. "No, it's the fact I got to first base with the prettiest girl in eleventh grade."

She shoved his shoulder playfully. "That's sweet."

"Come on, let's get out of here before someone recognizes you."

Once on the bike she carefully secured the helmet over the wig, and wrapped her arms around him.

"You hungry, sweetheart?"

"Starving," she replied.

"I'm going to take you somewhere I think you're going

to like."

"Okay," she said with giddy enthusiasm as he revved up his bike.

They wound through street after street, making their way to a part of town she wasn't familiar with. Finally, he parked his car in what looked like a quiet warehouse district. It was probably booming with people during working hours, but now it was quiet and eerie.

"Where are we?"

"It's called the Skewed Skewer. They make gourmet shish kebabs. Rabbit, alligator, duck—or plain ol' steak or chicken—topped off with their famous sauces. There's no place to sit because he's out back in a food truck and he changes locations every day. But they're delicious."

"If you say so," she said, scrunching her nose. "I don't want weird, just steak for me, please."

"Okay, come on," he said, grabbing her hand and leading them to the line to order.

A few minutes later, they were leaning against the bike, eating their food. "So good." She patted her stomach. "Ugh. My head itches." She pointed to the red hair. "And I'm stuffed." She groaned and yawned. "I hate your bike a little right now."

"You gotta hold on. No falling asleep."

"I don't know if I can. I'm so full and sleepy all of a sudden. Was that a turkey skewer? Why am I so tired?"

"Because you ate both of yours and most of mine. I can call you a cab and follow behind on my bike."

"No," she said. "I'll be fine. It's just a long way back to the island."

"Not that long, maybe thirty minutes."

Her eyes opened wide, excitedly. "Oh! I know. I have an idea. We can add it to the list of five things," she said, jumping up and down before taking out her phone and scrolling for something. The look of exhaustion was gone.

She held out her phone to him. "Take us to this address."

He looked at the screen, his brows furrowing. "Nothing good comes out of that area."

"Yes! Trust me. Taylor told me about this place once."

"That area is just fuck motels, sweetheart."

She waggled her eyebrows. "I know. But they're themed. This one has a space theme. I want to try. Come on, ride an astronaut. Isn't that like a thing?"

He started laughing. "I'm pretty sure it's ride a cowboy. But I'm not judging if you're into astronauts."

"Come on, please," she pouted. "It's been such a fun night, let's do some role play. I'm the sexy alien you found when you were astronauting. Please."

"Astronauting? You make a billion dollars a minute.

You have a house the size of a small island. Hell, you live on a small island! And you want me to take you to a fuck motel, that's probably not sanitary, in a shitty neighborhood?"

"As astronauts!" she added, as if that was the most obvious reply. "You can be the alien if you want. I'm open," she winked.

"You've gotten weird," he said, straddling the bike and motioning for her to hop on. "Funny and weird."

How could he deny her anything, not after it was his idea to get out of the house, and the woman wanted to role play in a fuck motel?

"Come on, abduct me, honey," she goaded him.

Oh, yeah, it was on.

———————

The ringing from his phone woke him up in the middle of the night.

"Hello?" he said, pushing her hair aside. It was a tangled mess around his face, and he had to sputter some out of his mouth while unraveling her naked body from around his.

From the handful of times they'd now had sex, and the way she'd gotten really into character during the role playing last night, it was clear the woman had no issues with her sexuality. He'd never had so much fun with sex before. She was wild, uninhibited, and vocal. He loved it. Maybe because it was Megan, maybe because he was used to sex being mostly about getting off, but whatever it was, it was the best sex of his life. He wondered if this was what it would have been like five years ago. Exhausted and satisfied, he was not looking forward to whoever was calling.

"It's me," Joey said.

"Time is it?"

"Four in the morning." Joey said, which caused Jax to sit upright. Middle-of-the-night calls always came with bad news.

"Jackson, honey?" Megan asked, sleepily.

"Go back to bed, baby," he whispered, then turned his attention back to Joey as he walked to the bathroom and shut the door. "Tell me."

"There was a breach in security at Megan's house. It happened in E1."

"Her bedroom?"

"Yes."

"Fuck! Did you get anything?"

"There's some video but it's not good. It stormed last night and the feed wasn't great. I'm sending it to you now. See if there's anything she can make out."

Jax's heart hammered in his chest, rage taking over, but

he had a job to do and he needed to focus. "Send a crew to see about the connection. I want it airtight. Anyone comes into the area, I want to be notified immediately. He shouldn't have bypassed the front fucking gates. How the fuck did this even happen?"

"There's more." The tone of his friend sent chills down his spine. Jax sat on the edge of the tub and braced himself.

"What's the 'more'?" He looked around the space-themed bathroom glowing from the glow-in-the-dark green body paint they'd used. The huge asteroid-looking mirror showed him that he was a disheveled mess. How it was that sweet, unpolluted Megan had slept with him, an unkempt yeti, was a mystery.

He threw water on his face waiting for the bad news to come.

"I'm calling you from her house. We already did an entire sweep. There was a box on her bed."

Clinging tight-knuckled to the vanity, he asked the necessary question. "What was in the box, Josef?"

A beat of silence passed by before Joey finally spoke. "A dead mouse."

"Fuck."

"Its head was chopped off."

Without hesitation he punched the asteroid mirror. "Jesus fucking Christ."

Chapter 11

Megan didn't say anything during the short drive back to her house. She'd tried to convince Jax to stop at a drugstore to get something for his bleeding knuckles, but he refused. In fact he refused to talk about anything, stewing in his anger.

"I'm sorry," she said, climbing off his bike.

"You're sorry?" he asked gruffly. "For what? None of this is your fault." He said it softly, but by the way his jaw ticked and his fists clenched, it was clear there was nothing soft about him. "Don't apologize again, I don't like it. Come on, let's go inside and see what we're dealing with."

"I should have let you do your job. I feel ridiculous for dragging you to a silly motel when everything is falling apart."

"Ridiculous? Don't, Megan. If you start regretting what we did, I'm just going to be even more pissed off."

"I mean, he was able to get inside. He killed a freakin' mouse. He wants to kill me. I'm not sure how to react right now and to top it off you're furious."

"It's okay to be scared. But you didn't do anything wrong and I'm in no way mad at you. I'm mad at this fucker who's messing with you, I'm mad at my team for not securing your house, but mostly I'm angry at myself for dropping the fucking ball."

She turned her face to him, her lip quivering and her eyes wide and troubled. "He's making my orderly life a mess, Jax."

"We'll fix it, sweetheart."

"I want to be able to enjoy the fact that you're back, and we can't even have twenty four hours of peace. You're going to revert back to that cold stressed-out guy who walked back into my life a week ago."

He pulled her to him. "Last night was perfect, Meg. I know you're doing this five things game because you're worried about me. I get it. But really, I'm fine, you can stop it now. Sometimes I may be that stressed-out guy and I'll probably be an ass, but it's not directed at you. I'll never be cold with you. Worry about you, not about me. Never about me."

"Of course I'm going to worry about you. I finally get you back and it's you, but it's not really you, but I know you're in there and then boom—a dead mouse!"

He had an eyebrow cocked high up; obviously she wasn't making much sense.

Taking a deep breath, she tried again. "I'm just frustrated, is all."

"And I'm fucking pissed. How the hell did he get inside?" he said, mostly to himself.

"He's sneaky," she said, then she mumbled under her breath, "like a fucking cat."

He growled deep in his chest. "My job is to secure against sneaky and I screwed up."

"It's not your—"

"Don't say it, Megan. It *is* my fault, I'm security and your house wasn't secured. But it's going to be okay, Meg. I'll fix this as soon as I figure out what the hell happened."

She nodded and followed him inside, finding Joey and some other people she didn't recognize working on something.

"What the fuck happened?" Jax bellowed when he walked into the house. "I said fortress, and that's what I want this place to be. A goddamn fortress. How the hell was there a breach?"

The crew had worried looks as their boss yelled at all of them. But Jax wasn't done.

———

He needed answers and no one was giving them. How in the ever-loving fuck did a civilian get into a fucking mansion with a gate, cameras all around the perimeter, a state-of-the-art alarm system and damn security constantly conducting surveillance?

"I want fucking answers," he roared, and slammed his fist on the table, scattering the blueprints they had laid out.

"Jax . . ." Megan whispered, but Joey cut her off.

"Megan, Jax," he said, with a chin nod. "Let's go talk outside."

"Not until I get answers," Jax said with heated eyes.

"I said outside, now." Joey, who was by no means a small man, immediately got Jax's attention with his no-nonsense tone. Megan was visibly shaken and Jax was worried that whatever Joey would say was going to freak her out more. He was trying and failing to control his anger over the fuckup. "Sweetheart, why don't you stay inside? I'll go talk to Joey."

"No. I want to know what's going on. I need to know."

"Let me worry about it," he said, tucking a wisp of hair behind her ear.

She pushed his hand away, "No, Jax. You're being condescending, I'm a grown-ass woman and this is my house. I need to know." She followed Joey outside, and so did Jax.

"What's going on, Joey?" she asked, impatiently.

"Cops just left. Filed a report, they took the mouse and

the box but we had already checked for prints. We think Ryan jumped the front gate because the motion sensors didn't go off by the water out back, and we tested them and they're working just fine. That only leaves the front gate."

"What's the plan?" Jax asked.

"We're pulling the tapes from the cameras and we're going to tighten shit up out front and out back." Joey said.

"Call Dawson. I want the latest shit he has on the market. I told you that when we first got here and you vetoed it. Now I'm saying it's gotta be done. I should've done that from day one." Dawson was a genius on state-of-the-art security systems. Sure, Dawson would be overkill, but they needed overkill—they needed panic rooms, bullet-proof windows, iris recognition scanners in all the major entryways, and whatever the hell else he had up his sleeve. "In fact, I'll call him myself. I want him as consultant on this. Why did I listen to you? Security is my gig. You're IT."

Joey glared at Jax, who stood there completely unfazed like he did when they argued.

Fight back, motherfucker.

A good brawl would help him release some of his rage, even though he didn't necessarily want to direct it toward Joey.

"Stop it, guys," Megan began, but Joey cut her off.

"Fuck you very much, Jackson! I may be better at IT than you but that doesn't mean I don't know security. And just because you're a fucking meathead who thinks the answer to everything is running your fist through someone's face, doesn't mean you know security more than I do. You're off, Jax, and you know it. You're not thinking straight. Dawson is overkill. You'll have to endure a month of construction."

"There's a decapitated mouse on her fucking bed. I *want* overkill!" he barked.

"Fine. I don't agree, but if that's what you want, I'll call him." He turned to Megan. "Megan, honey, this is your house and you're the client, is this what you want?"

She looked back and forth between the two men. "If Jax thinks it's necessary . . ."

"Okay, I'll call him," Joey said.

Noise from inside the house had them all turning around in confusion. One of his employees came out. "Hey boss, there's a Ms. Sloan here for Ms. Cruz."

"Taylor?" Megan jumped up and down happily, apparently forgetting her problems for the moment. "It's Taylor! Let her in! Oh my god, Taylor's here."

"I take it Taylor is an approved visitor?" Joey asked.

"She's one of the Ts in TNT," Jax said, following Megan inside the house, feeling a little bit less furious—and more just plain irritated.

"Nelly is the 'N,' I already know about her. Who's the other T?" Joey asked.

"Some chick named Tamara who's outta the picture. Works at the mall. Checked her out and ruled her out already," Jax said, just as Megan was about to answer.

"Well, fuck me!" the woman in a pinup-style dress said, setting three bags on the floor. "This is the way you should always welcome me back to the States, Megan. What's with all the hot men?" She looked from Jax to Joey. "Rambo and Tarzan. Nice."

Megan jumped up and almost tackled Taylor who followed suit, both women hopping up and down, yapping excitedly and incoherently.

"Tee, this is Jax and Joey. Rambo and Tarzan, respectively," she said, pointing behind her, "and the group of men over there with the floor plan of my house, those are some of the guys that work for Jax and Joey's security firm, Iron-Clad Security."

"Security firm?" Taylor eyed Megan, then bent down and picked up a bag that upon proper inspection was a carrying case for a pet. "I brought you security. Cute security. I didn't realize you were going all out. Maybe I need to be briefed," she said, unzipping the bag whose contents were whimpering.

"Oh my god, did you get me a dog?"

"He's a golden retriever puppy. Isn't he the cutest?" Taylor cooed as the shy puppy stumbled out of the carrying case. Megan fell to the floor and began to call to it.

"A puppy? You got Meg a puppy as protection?" Jax said, unamused.

"He's not going to be a puppy forever, Rambo. I did research and I asked professionals, and this is a good guard dog. Plus, Megan shouldn't be all alone in this big house all the time."

"Tee is an animal lover," Megan clarified. "She has like ten dogs and five cats."

"Three dogs and one cat," Taylor corrected her.

"C'mere, puppy," Megan called the dog, who had crawled back into the carry-on.

All this was too much excitement for Jax, whose thoughts were still on trying to figure out what the hell had happened with the lapse in security. He needed to really understand where they'd failed. Everything in him screamed that Ryan was the key. If he could just figure out why he was doing this, he was sure the "how" would fall into place. The obsessed fan angle felt only partly right; there was something else to the picture, and goddamn it, he just wasn't seeing it.

He also needed to figure out what Ryan wanted from

Megan. Was he just being overzealous, or did he want to physically hurt her? A chill ran down his spine as he thought of what would have happened if they'd been here instead of in the motel the previous night. Worse, what if she'd been alone?

"So, I want to hear what's been happening while I've been away." Taylor's voice shook Jax out of his thoughts. "You already told me about the break-in when we Skyped last week, but that's about it. Did they catch the dude?"

"Not yet." Joey said.

"And there's been other problems." Megan scooped the puppy up and walked over to the couch where she sat with her legs under her ass and the puppy in her arms. Jax sat next to her, and Joey stayed standing while Taylor sat down in one of the love seats. "He sent a creepy text the next day, and then he's been prank calling me."

"Creepy?" Taylor asked.

Joey reached for his phone and pulled up the copy that Jax had sent him, then turned it over to Taylor for her to see. "Oh, damn."

"Yep," Megan agreed. "And then we stayed at Fantasies—you know, the motel you told me about—and then Joey called in the middle of the night about a break-in, and there was a box with a dead mouse in it on my bed." It all came out in one long frantic breath.

"Whoa! Back up, sister. You went to Fantasies? With Rambo?"

"You told me about it," Megan clarified. "And yes, with Jax. That's his name, not Rambo, although it does seem rather fitting."

"I'm missing something, aren't I?" Taylor began then it hit her. "Wait! Is this *the* Jax? The one from all those years back?"

"Same," Jax said.

"What the hell? How did this happen? How was I not notified about this? Why didn't you tell me Jax looked like that? And what is this situation right here?" Taylor used a finger to circle the area between Jax and Megan, or lack of area, since Jax had his arm lazily over the top of the couch, Megan tucked in close, one of his fingers wrapped around some of her hair. "And which theme did you pick?"

Joey and Jax smirked and Megan rolled her eyes. "Astronaut."

"Nice." Taylor winked and then leaned in to give Megan a little fist-bump. Jax had to hand it to her, Taylor was something else.

"Jax heard on the news about the break-in and came right over. I'll explain more about that later. Maybe when we're not with said hot guy." She winked at Jax. "And I must've forgotten to tell you about him being here when we spoke, because first, we spoke for like three seconds, and second, we spoke after a crazy lunatic had broken into my house and I thought I was going to be killed. Guess impending death makes me forget to mention Jax. And Jax owns a security firm with Joey, like I said before, and they are working on getting things safe."

"Wow. Left for a few months and things went to shit," Taylor said. "Well, except for Jax being back, of course."

"Which brings me to something you and I have to talk about," Megan said, her body language completely shifting. She leaned forward, her forearms on her thighs and her lips downturned. "I want to cancel the tour, Tee."

"What!?" Taylor shrieked. "Why?"

"The photo has you and Nell blacked out. It freaks me out. If something happened to either of you two . . ." Her eyes watered, and her voice came out like a croak. Jax pulled her in close and rubbed small circles down her back. Nothing would happen. He and his team had been working out a plan to deal with the tour over the last few days, but she needed to have this conversation with her girls. She had made it clear to him she didn't like to be told what to do, so he sat back and let her do her thing. But he stayed just close enough so she understood he was there for her. " . . . I don't know what I'd do."

Joey piped in: "I don't think the photo was intended to suggest he wants to hurt you two. I think he just wants

Megan to know he's all about her."

"Honey, don't you worry about me or Nell. We're big girls. We can handle ourselves and the truth is, nothing weird has been happening to us. We're both just worried about you, since it's all been about you. I think Tarzan's right about that. Plus, you can't just stay holed up in here."

"Meg, sweetheart—" he began.

"I know you're here and I know I'm safe, but there's a crazy guy that wants me for God knows what."

"You think there's a big safety issue, Rambo? Can you keep our girl safe so we can go on tour?"

"I think we're fine. We've got it covered," Jax said, his lips on Megan's temple as he ran his palm soothingly down her back.

"Then we move forward as planned. We can do any rehearsal or PR here in the house. And how about the Fionas concert?" Taylor asked.

"Shit, I completely forgot about that."

"The Fionas?" Jax asked Megan. "You can't go to a concert," he said. "It's one thing to go out to dinner, it's another one to go out to a concert."

"I know." She ran her hand through her hair, a sad look on her face. "My friends Elle and Ro from The Fionas are in town. I always go catch their show when they're here."

"We *always* see them when they're in town," Taylor whined.

"I don't think it'll be possible this time," Megan said sadly. God, Jax hated this. He frowned thinking about the nightmare protecting Megan in a crowd of a thousand people would be. Planning for her own tour was going to be hard enough. "We can't secure a concert in this short notice," he said, talking mostly to himself.

"I know . . ." She blew out a deep breath.

"I'm sorry, Meg. I can't risk you getting hurt." His throat constricted, and he had an overpowering surge of emotions. Not caring who was around to hear, he admitted, "You're too important to me."

"Jax," she sighed, closing her eyes at the feel of his palm against her cheekbone.

The world faded to just the two of them until Taylor spoke.

"Oh . . . I'm loving this." She had a big loopy smile on her face as she twirled her finger at them. "Anyway, how about dinner? You skip the concert and just meet us for dinner? If I can convince them to go to a quiet place, one you can check out beforehand?"

"That sounds reasonable," Joey said. "We'll check it out, it'll be okay, man. Give her some slack. Sitting alone in this house with you for weeks must be a pain in the ass for the poor girl."

Her big brown eyes were begging him to make it work even if she was hesitant. Even if at her core she was afraid, she was putting her trust in his ability to protect her.

How could he deny her? They were being reasonable.

"It's that important to you, babe?"

"My friends are important to me."

"Then, we'll make it happen. Just tell me where by Thursday, okay?"

"Thank you, Jax." Megan said brightly. "And about our tour, if you and Nells don't want to cancel, then Jax is going to go with us and he's going to make sure everything is secure. Is that cool with you?"

"I've added security that I can assign to you and to Nelly," Jax added.

Taylor nodded in agreement. "Of course that's cool with me, Megan. Plus, you have Paisley to protect you." Taylor said, patting the puppy's head.

"Paisley?" Joey snorted.

"I've been in Japan launching my new clothing line. Paisley's the hot thing over there and I've seen every pattern of paisley known to man. Everything's starting to look like paisley."

"You can't name him Paisley," Jax snorted. "It's a male dog."

"What would you name him, Rambo?" Taylor crossed her arms and arched a brow.

"Stop calling me Rambo."

"Rambo!" Megan shrieked. "Let's call him, Rambo."

That night after everyone had gone home, Jax did a sweep of the entire house and grounds, Rambo trailing close by, before he finally joined a tired Megan in bed. After sleeping together in the Bahamas and then again at the motel, they hadn't had the opportunity to discuss what was going on with them or their living arrangements, but spending the night with her was never a question for him. He watched Rambo get comfortable on the small bed in the corner of the room before settling in himself. Megan snuggled closer, and he felt her smooth bare skin against his. "I take it you're okay with me sleeping here with you."

"Very much so," she said as she inched closer and kissed his shoulder. "Did I tell you how much I loved the last two nights?" Her voice was groggy. "Excluding the middle of the night wake-up call."

"You always sleep naked, Meg baby?"

"No. I was waiting for you."

"You know, I had planned to wake up this morning and show you all the things I missed before we were interrupted. I was too worked up to worship your body appropriately while we played space invaders last night."

She had one leg over his thigh and was kissing his collarbone, his cock stirring. "Worship it?"

He pushed her flat on her back and slid his palms down her throat and into the valley between her breasts.

"Oh yeah . . ." He replaced his hands with his lips and began kissing down her chest. "Worship . . ."

He traced his tongue in a straight line between her tits down to her belly button, unintentionally tickling her with his soft beard, her body arching up in response. Using his shoulder to part her legs, he made himself comfortable between her legs. "You remember the first time I licked your pussy?" he asked, looking up at her from between her thighs.

Chapter 12

FIVE YEARS EARLIER

Spending most of the day making out with Jax had made her lust-drunk. But Jax, being the reasonable one, the responsible one, the—was it possible?—less horny of the two, convinced her to get out of the house for a few hours.

After pizza, they went for a walk along the beach and to a small strip mall where she bought some clothes and toiletries. Then they watched the sunset on the beach before walking back to his house. The pull between them was so strong that as soon as he closed the door behind him, she was on him, kissing him furiously, unable to maintain her resolve... again. It was as if he had unleashed something inside of her that could never be undone.

"Baby," he groaned into her mouth. "Sweetheart, you're killing me."

"I'm sorry," she whispered.

"Don't ever be sorry for wanting to kiss." He kissed her

quickly on the nose before stepping back. "I'm going to go to take a cold shower. Make yourself at home."

"I think I'll take a shower in your other bathroom, if that's okay."

"Of course," he said as he closed the door behind him. He looked so frustrated, which made her feel terrible, but she just wasn't ready for sex. At least not yet. And he was so sweet for not making her feel guilty about it.

The cold shower did not assuage her need to be with him and she wasn't sure if she should even go find him in the living room or if she should just go call it a night in his room, which he had told her she could use. But like a magnet, she walked to him, finding him flipping through channels in the living room, freshly bathed.

When he turned his face to see her he did a double take before running his palm down his face. "That's my shirt."

"I didn't buy pajamas. I borrowed this, thought it would be okay."

He groaned, reached forward, and pulled her to him. With a shriek and a giggle she was on him, a thigh on either side of his.

"I think this is what I'm going to think about every day while I'm in the desert. You straddling me, my favorite tee riding up your ass, and those boring, yet sexy as fuck, white panties."

"I want to kiss some more," she admitted. "Maybe other stuff too."

He leaned back a little, his brows furrowed.

"Not all the stuff but some stuff."

"Under the clothes stuff or over the clothes stuff?"

She bit her bottom lip and hesitantly said, "Both?"

"Fuck, Megan." He pressed his lips against hers, smothering his groan. "You're so sexy."

His hand skimmed up her thighs and to her sides and under her shirt to her bare breast.

———————

This was not his first time, not by far, but this was the first time his hand had shaken and his heart pounded in his chest. His thumb rubbed the space right under her breast, feeling its weight, and then up to her nipple. "Oh . . ." she moaned, as he pinched and squeezed.

"Is this okay?" he asked, hoping—praying—it was okay because he wanted to do it again . . . over and over. Her reactions were some of the most erotic images he'd ever seen.

She nodded into his neck. Over her shirt, he brought his mouth to her nipple, his eyes moving up to meet hers. She was riding him, the only thing between them was white cotton and his thin gym shorts, and when his teeth bit gently down her eyes closed and she couldn't have looked more beautiful. Thick long brown hair falling over her shoulder, wildly, her cheeks pink with heat. He had a hard time looking away.

His hand started moving lower and lower, his mouth still sucking and nipping her nipple through the shirt. When he found the waistband of her panties he looked up at her for a moment, her eyes now wide open watching him. Silently she gave him the okay to continue, and he went for it. Slowly, passing a small patch of hair and then finding bare smooth skin. "Is this okay?"

She nodded.

He cupped her pussy before rubbing up and down but in this position he couldn't do all the things he wanted so he stood, holding her up before flipping her around so she was on her back and he was above her. Then his hand went back to what he was doing, slipping under her panties and into her soft wet folds.

Using his thumb to rub her clit, he returned to fondling her nipples over her shirt. Her arm clung to his shoulder and he went a little lower until he slid a finger inside. If he hadn't been on top she'd have fallen off the couch with the way she thrashed underneath him. With his fingers inside and his thumb rubbing her clit, he stared down at her closed eyes, enjoying the way she moved and wiggled, begged and panted. Eyes shut tight and knitted together, her puffy pink lips parted, he couldn't stop staring at how sexy she looked. It made him feel ten feet tall knowing *he* was making her frenzied. *He* was giving her pleasure, causing her walls to contract, her pussy to become wetter, and her whole body to shudder as she came undone with a loud scream, all with just a finger and a flick of his thumb.

Almost immediately she reached down for him, her eyes still shut, but he stopped her. He was in pain—almost dire—but she looked so sated. Today would be about her, as uncomfortable as he was. He shifted, turning her to her side, and squished together on the sofa they fell asleep.

It was early the next morning when Megan woke. The light was peeking in from the sliding doors that led to the back of the house. Jax had been holding her tightly against his chest and snoring lightly by her ear. Last night had been . . . earth-shattering, but in the light of day, Megan felt guilty for not reciprocating at all. Who knew she could be so selfish with her orgasms? Careful not to wake him, she reluctantly left the warmth of Jax's arms and went to the bathroom before starting a pot of coffee.

"Good morning," Jax said, walking in, stretching, his

hand up in the air, causing his shorts to drop a little. Her curious eyes dropped low, honing in on the way his muscles formed that delicious vee on his hips. She shook her head and handed him a cup of coffee. "So, I think we should tackle *lawn* and *bike* today. And what exactly is *bike*?"

Pulling her close and kissing her temple, Jax sat on the counter. "*Bike* just means I need to remember to store my motorcycle in Joey's parents' garage. But I made plans last night while you were in the shower, so those things will have to wait."

"The whole point of why I'm here is to help you."

"Not the whole point, and you know that," he said. "Let's go to the Pit for lunch. It's by the Everglades, and then I have another surprise."

"I don't know if I can handle any more surprises," she said, leaning against the kitchen counter.

He kissed her quickly on the lips. "I'm sure you'll handle it just fine." He winked and then headed for the bathroom.

Thirty minutes later Megan was straddling his bike, her arms wrapped around him, and twenty minutes after that they were parked by a small barbecue shack in the middle of nowhere. "Can't believe you've never been to the Pit."

Megan looked around and it was packed full of people.

"Never even heard of it," she admitted, handing him the helmet and not even bothering to tame her crazy hair. There was an eighties ballad playing in the background, and as they waited for the food, she hummed.

"I want to hear you sing."

"Nope."

He shook his head. "I'm going to get you to sing at some point." He leaned in. "In fact, your whole body sang for me last night."

Her cheeks flushed red and he chuckled.

"About last night," she began. "I fell asleep before . . ."

"No worries."

"I'm not worried." She smiled. "But I kind of want to . . . you know."

Looking amused, he put his elbows on the table, his chin on his palm and said, "Nope. I don't know. Why don't you tell me?"

Taking a sip of her soda, she chuckled. "Stop. You know what I'm trying to say."

"No, I really don't. You kind of want to go on a picnic? You want to hang out some more? You want to go home? What is it you kind of want to do, Meg?"

She leaned forward, her ass lifting off the chair, and she whispered into his ear. "Touch you." She began to sit back down but then came forward again, and whispered, "your dick. I want to touch it."

He groaned, and now it was her turn to laugh.

After a lunch that included gator bites, corn on the cob, sips of his beer—which she stole from him, often—and fried biscuits, they took off again. Thirty minutes later they stood in front of a ten-foot stuffed alligator and a wooden sign advertising airboat rides. "Oh, I've always wanted to do this!"

"Good, because that's what we're doing next."

Pulling him by the arm, she practically skipped to the kiosk, but he stopped her before she reached for her wallet.

"I can pay, you know?"

"I know. But I want to," he said, kissing her nose. "We have twenty minutes to kill before the next boat ride, you want to go for a walk?"

"It's one thing to be on a boat, it's another thing to come face to face with an alligator."

"Don't worry so much, come on." He grabbed her hand and together they walked along the swampy trail, where there wasn't much to see.

"So you like baseball, huh?"

He chuckled at her random small talk. "My dad was a huge Yankees fan. For as long as I could remember, we would take one trip every year and it was to the home opening game of the Yankees. Then in 1993 when we got the Florida Marlins he got season tickets and we would try to catch at least one Yankee game a year and we never missed a Marlins opening game. He never got to see when they changed to the Miami Marlins, though."

"So you going is tradition?"

"Yeah. It's bittersweet, but unless I'm deployed, I try to hit at least one game. I've missed a few openers, though. I have season tickets, always seat L214. L214 isn't as good in the new stadium, but it's cool, that's the seat I've had since 1993."

"That's really nice, Jax. Tell me more about your parents."

They walked through the humid mangrove trail hand in hand. "My mom was a third grade teacher. She retired when my dad was diagnosed with pancreatic cancer. It was a tough two years and I was overseas for most of it. My parents were very close—they'd take trips away, just the two of them. They would fall asleep cuddled together on the couch. They'd hold hands all the time and kiss openly. Neither of them missed any of my baseball or football games. Not one. We weren't wealthy, my dad was also in the Marines until he retired, then he became a postal worker. Joey was around a lot too. He was my neighbor for a little while, but we stayed close even when he moved to the other side of town."

"Sounds like you've had a lot of love in your life."

"Yes. I can't say otherwise. When Dad died, Mom became very depressed. With Dad gone and me far off, it's been hard on her. She doesn't say it, but I know it has been."

"You feel guilty," she said. It wasn't a question.

"I reenlisted. Maybe I shouldn't have. Maybe she needs me here with her."

"It's what you love, isn't it? With what you're telling me, I don't think your parents would want you to do something you didn't like."

He shrugged. He'd never voiced this insecurity out loud. In fact, this guilt had been laying heavily on his shoulders and he didn't even know how to vocalize it. But talking to Megan was easy. She wasn't judgmental or opinionated. She listened and gave him a different—a better—perspective on things.

"Where does she live?"

"With my aunt down in Key Largo."

"So she's not alone."

"Nah, she's not. Maybe you'll meet her?"

"Shit, Jax. It's Saturday and we haven't done a single thing on your list except your haircut and your mom's an hour away."

"Relax. We'll get to it. There's still Sunday." He looked at his watch. "Come on, time to walk back. There's an airboat with our name on it, waiting."

"Are you sure you know what you're doing?" Jax sat on his kitchen counter watching Megan fuck up spaghetti later that evening.

"Hush," she said, reading the instructions from the box with absolute concentration. "I watch cooking shows all the time."

"Meg, the water's boiling. You gotta dump the pasta in there," he said pointing to the colander. "Not rocket science, sweetheart."

She stuck her tongue out at him before opening the box and dumping the spaghetti inside the water and then turning to the other pot that was already spilling over with red sauce from a can. "Ah . . . I'm making a mess."

"You sure you don't want help?"

"I'm good, I'm good," she said, turning the temperature down.

"I've never seen a worse cook in my life," he said. "You are actually the best worst cook I've ever seen."

"Ha ha. We have a cook. No one ever let me do this for myself."

"Thank God. You'd poison your family." She turned around and scowled at him. Still perched on the counter, he reached forward and grabbed her arm, pulling her toward him. "You got a little sauce right here." He pointed to her cheek.

"I do?" She reached for the dishrag but he stopped her, using his mouth to lick it off.

"Oh . . ."

"And a little here too." He trailed his tongue down her cheek to her jaw, followed by her neck.

She pressed closer to him, his legs wrapping around her to pull her close, her head lifting to give him more access to her neck.

"You know what I said earlier? I want to do that now." Her hand drifted down his body and she pressed a hand against his bulge.

"Won't say no to that," he said gruffly.

He unhooked his legs and spread them wider. She snuck her hand into his pants and took out his cock. He'd been expecting a hand job, like what he'd done for her last night. What he did not in any way expect was for Megan to stroke his cock once and then twice before moving down, opening her mouth, and sliding him in.

His head hit the cabinet behind him. "Oh, fuck! Don't stop."

She hummed her response, which he didn't hear because all his blood had rushed to his cock with the vibration of her mouth. He couldn't do a single thing except feel. Firmly and confidently, she gripped the base of his dick, moving it up and down as she swirled her tongue on the head, over and over, sucking and licking. Unrushed, she made it feel as if she was savoring the feel of him in her mouth, not like a task or a job, which made it all that much hotter.

When he couldn't take it anymore she moved down the shaft, going as deep as she could without gagging. He wanted to warn her, stop her, but instead his hip bucked forward. He was unable to stop himself from coming deep in her throat, and, with the strong grip she had on him, he was certain she wouldn't have stopped anyway.

"Jesus, Megan," he said running a palm down his face. "I'm not even sure what to think about how good you are at that."

She used the back of her hand to wipe her mouth clean. "Glad it was good."

"Good?" He shook his head. Good wasn't nearly adequate. "If we're going for oral, then it's my turn, baby." With his pants hanging around his ankles he hopped down, turned her around, and set her on the counter. "Quid pro quo. You'll learn that in law school," he said, causing her to giggle. "Let's see if I'm 'good' too."

She yelped when he pushed her thighs apart and slid her shorts and panties down her legs. "You don't have to. I didn't do it for you to . . . Oh! Oh God . . ."

He loved that she was so vocal. She might have been shy about initiating, but once she got lost in the moment she was uninhibited, loud, and fun.

He didn't give her a chance to talk as he parted her with his fingers and traced his tongue along her pussy, slowly, up and down. She raked her nails along his scalp, trying to grab hold of his hair but failing. Pressing his head forward, she bucked against him, moaning and yelling as he flicked his tongue on her clit, asserting as much pressure as he could. "I'm going to come, Jax. Oh God..."

He sucked hard, pushing a finger inside of her, which caused her to squeeze her legs tightly around his head. It was the most amazing sexual experience of his life, the way she came uninhibited and undone on his face.

Chapter 13

God! The man certainly knew how to work his tongue.

"Of course I remember the first time you went down on me," she moaned, arching her pussy against his face. "It was my first time."

Stopping completely, he wiped his mouth on her thigh and moved back up her body. "What?"

"What are you doing? Don't stop," she said, pushing him back down.

"Dick had never eaten your pussy?"

"Nope. He didn't like doing it." She nudged him with her heel. Why the hell was he talking about Richard? She didn't want to think about Richard. Hell, she didn't want to think of anything other than the way his tongue felt against her clit.

"Damn, I wish I'd known that before."

"Why?"

"Don't know... I would've paid more attention, or done it again, or... I don't know."

"Well, you can shut your mouth now and go back to what you were just doing."

He chuckled before sliding back down and without hesitation latching on to her clit. "Ah . . ."

He hummed in response and held her thighs open with his hands. "Dick missed out," he said, as he sucked, licked, nipped. "I can do this all day. It's sweet like honey, just like you."

"Less talking."

His grip on her thighs was unrelenting and she tried to squirm but he just pushed them further up and apart until her legs were by her shoulders and he wasn't laying down anymore, he was bent down, on his knees, completely engrossed. His saliva slid down her ass and when she was close—so close she could feel her thighs shake—he slid two fingers inside of her, working them in and out in sync with his tongue until she fisted his hair and pushed his head against her, coming hard and intensely on his face and tongue.

"Jesus," he said. When he pulled back, his beard was wet and sticking out all over the place. But he didn't hesitate or let her recover, because he slid his cock right inside of her, still holding her thighs apart. "How am I ever going to stop fucking you when you feel so good?" he said, breathlessly. "I can't stop, Meg."

Was he talking about now or the future?

She never wanted him to stop, she almost said.

———————

I never want to stop, he almost said. He wanted this to be something they did all the time, whenever the mood struck. She was so perfect for him, in every single way. "Come with me. Again. Come, baby," he said, thrusting in and out until he had one arm on the mattress by her head to get purchase, the other arm holding her thigh, her knee by her ear. She was twisted like a pretzel but the look of pure ecstasy on her face was enough to tip him over the edge. She followed seconds behind before he collapsed on top of her. Wiping his beard with a towel, he threw it aside and slid into bed with her.

"That was pretty fantastic," she sighed. "Can we do it again tomorrow?"

Sliding strands of hair off of her face, he leaned in for a kiss. "I hope so. And the day after that and the day after that . . ."

"Mmmm," she said lazily. "I like the sound of that."

He settled into the bed and, in spite of all the shit going on around them, with Megan resting her head on the crook of his shoulder he fell asleep sated and content—a feeling he hadn't known in far too long.

Nausea, sweat, and a pounding heart startled him

awake in the middle of the night.

It was the same dream he often had. He was in the middle of the desert when there was a sudden explosion from somewhere behind him. Leaving his platoon behind, he ran around aimlessly trying to figure out the source of the explosion. But he couldn't find anything, even as he chased the smell of fire and the screaming of his buddies burning. And the more he ran the more alone he felt. When he finally stopped running, he looked around and it was just miles and miles of sand. His skin was hot and dry, and the air he breathed was arid. There was nowhere for him to go. No water, no buildings, no people . . . just more desert. But his friends were screaming for him over and over, needing help—and he couldn't find them.

But this time, for some reason, the dream was different. In previous dreams, he'd just given up . . . too thirsty, too tired, and too hopeless to keep going, eventually waking up feeling that hopelessness in the pit of his stomach for the rest of the day. In this dream, he never stopped. He had a determination to continue moving forward no matter what. In this dream he didn't feel hopeless. But he did feel fear. A deep-seated fear of failure. What if he never found the end? What if he was stuck in the desert forever?

Careful not to wake Megan, he slowly peeled her arms

off of him and slid out of bed, the clock on her nightstand reading 3:30. Immediately, Rambo went on alert and ran to the bedroom door. Fumbling around, Jax found his shorts, slipped them on, tucked his gun into his waistband, and went to the kitchen. Having the gun on him was second nature. Rarely was he unarmed.

He took a detour on his way to the kitchen, deciding to go check the gate for the hundredth time that day. When Dawson arrived later that week for a consultation that would be priority number one. By the time they were done there was no way Ryan would be able to get through it again.

"Stay," he whispered to Rambo at the house's threshold. The dog continued wagging its tail, immune to any command, so Jax shrugged and allowed the puppy to follow him out.

From the front door to the gate was a trail; a long walk that used to be lined with palm trees. It was now a bare expanse of space, without a single place to hide. "Come on, Rambo."

Exploring the darkness, the puppy ran ahead of Jax toward the enormous ornate metal fence and the ten-foot-tall thick hedges that ran along the entirety of the property and hid the house from prying eyes. They were the only trees he'd left standing, in order to give the house some privacy.

Jax followed behind the puppy. It was hard to see anything more than a few feet ahead of where he walked, but he could just make out the energetic wagging of Rambo's tail as he sniffed everything in the yard. Maybe the dog had been a good idea, if only to provide Megan with comfort.

Rambo's sharp, high bark suddenly broke through the darkness. "What is it, boy?" Jax whispered, feeling suddenly exposed in the middle of the yard with nothing to shield him.

Jax looked around, feeling the hairs behind his neck stand up. Reaching behind his back, he took his Sig Sauer from the waistband of his shorts, keeping it shielded behind him, thankful he'd had the foresight to grab the weapon before walking out the door. Rambo continued to bark at the gate, but it was too dark to see what was on the other side.

Standing aside, hidden by the hedges, Jax knelt down in an effort to see further. Rambo continued to bark and then the bark changed to a growl. Fuck, someone was there. Bringing his gun in front of him and removing the safety, Jax crouched, ready to defend himself if necessary.

A noise came from the other side of the hedges, and then a light, like a flashlight. But still it wasn't possible to make anything out. His heart beat faster, and adrenaline was kicking in. The sound came closer, almost like a motor, and the lights brighter. Then the noise stopped and the light shone toward the house. He was a mere foot away, just the width of the hedges separating him from whomever was there.

Rambo growled louder.

This would be his only chance to see the perp, since catching him wouldn't be possible, as there was a gate he couldn't scale between them.

"Hiya boy. How are ya?" the person on the other side chirped.

Creeping closer to where the hedges met the iron gate, Jax risked a look.

He felt his muscles sag with relief. Shit, it was just the security guard from the island, a man he'd met before. He locked his gun and put it away, then stood up and moved forward. "Carl."

Startled, Carl dropped his flashlight. The older gentleman stood with shaky hands, looking around.

"It's me, Jackson."

A hand clutching his chest, the man said, "Jackson. Christ, you almost gave me a heart attack. What are you doing hiding back there?"

"I was just doing a sweep. What are you doing?"

"My nightly rounds. I was instructed to pay particular care with this house. So I brought a flashlight and was going to look around. See if anything was amiss."

As if the old man would be able to do much.

"You carry a gun, Carl?"

"Sure do. May look old, son, but you'd be surprised."

"I'm sure you're capable, Carl. Wouldn't want to cross you, that's for sure," Jax said, trying not to glance down at the flashlight still on the ground. Carl was a good man, trying to do his job, and Jax sincerely appreciated it. "Leave you to it, then. 'Night."

"'Night, son.'"

"Let's go, Rambo."

After the adrenaline rush there was no way he'd be able to go back to sleep. Next week they had that goddamn dinner with her friends and in two weeks they'd be leaving on tour. His anxiety levels were at an all-time high, and if he went to sleep now, he'd be tossing and turning for the rest of the night. And if sleep somehow did find him, he'd surely have a nightmare and wake Megan up. So instead of going to bed, Jax booted up his laptop on her dining room table, and got to work.

By the time the sun rose, he'd gone through the footage from the break-in a dozen times. Not one clue. Nothing. Yawning loudly, he closed the laptop and started up the coffee.

"Hey."

He turned around to see Megan in just her white lace

panties and nothing else, her hair wild and her eyes still sleepy. "Hi," he said, hoarsely, unable to look away.

Would he ever not want her?

Would he ever not find her beautiful?

He knew the answer to each question was a resounding no.

"You're not in bed," she said with a yawn.

Her tits, perfect full globes . . .

She looked down at her chest where his eyes were fixed.

"You want to come back to bed?" She smiled, sleepily . . . coyly.

"No." He was wide awake now, even more so as he took the steps to close the distance. He slid two fingers down the elastic of her panties and pulled her to him, his lips crashing against hers. Without words, he lifted her up, her legs wrapping around his waist, and pushed her against the wall. Her hands fisted in his hair, his beard rubbing against her face, nails digging into skin. It was a frenzied need to be near her, close to her—inside of her. Using one hand she pushed his gym shorts down just enough to free his cock, and he pushed her panties to the side. "Need in," he grunted into her neck.

"Hurry," she gasped as he hoisted her higher, holding her by the ass with one hand, guiding himself in with the other. Using the wall as leverage, he pumped into her as she held on tightly and he feverishly took what he needed.

"Don't stop!" she yelled, her head tucked into his neck, nails pulling on his hair, sweat gathering on their torsos. "Oh God . . ." Her pussy tightened like a vise around his cock, the two of them coming together in an intense orgasm that left them breathless.

Every moment he spent with her was the best moment. Even with the shit happening around them, he wanted her near him. She was a balm to his ever-present anxiety.

"Well, that was unexpected," she said as she unwrapped her legs from around him and slid down his body. He missed the contact immediately. For so long, he'd been alone: as an only child, as a Marine, then as a man who'd lost so many in his life. He'd never thought himself lonely, he had friends and family, but he'd never had a connection like he had with Megan. Like his parents shared. Like he always wanted. Now, having that connection with someone, he wanted to grip it tight and never let go—keep her safe, keep her happy, just keep her.

But there was that underlying fear that he would fail in keeping her safe precisely because of their connection—because by having his heart on the line, his focus would falter. And that's why he couldn't sleep. That's why he couldn't keep still. He needed to catch Ryan and end their constant worry. Only then could he fully commit his heart.

———————

"Please try to relax," Megan said as she placed her hand over his, which was bobbing restlessly on the armrest of his seat while they drove to the restaurant where they were meeting the Fionas and Taylor. It had been almost three weeks since Ryan had broken into her house, and they still had nothing. Megan had received two more breathy hang-ups that week, which they'd traced to burner phones, so even those had been dead ends.

Jax was growing more and more anxious and she was growing more and more scared. It felt as if they were constantly looking over their shoulders. It had gotten so bad, that even with Jax's assurance the house was protected, Megan stayed inside, not even stepping onto her balcony. On top of everything, he was feeling like a failure, not having caught the sonofabitch terrorizing his woman.

"My job is to be vigilant and on my A game, not to relax," he said.

"Are you here as my date or my bodyguard?"

"Megan, there's a crazy man on the loose, sending you dead fucking rodents and prank calling you every few days. You leave in a week on tour, which is going to be mayhem. I need to be both your date and your bodyguard. Just accept it. We should have caught him already."

She blew out a frustrated breath.

"Please. I want you to have fun, but I also need you to be safe. For me. I need you to be safe."

She leaned over and kissed him on the lips. "Fine. I understand. You ready for the paps?" They'd chosen a pretty secluded restaurant that was as low-key as possible. Still, the paparazzi buzzed nearby. Not a ton, but enough to be wary.

"I've detailed celebrities and politicians. The paps don't scare me, but stay close."

He went around and opened the door for her before the valet could arrive and held her close as they made their way into the restaurant. Once inside, he looked around, clocking everything and everyone.

"Come on, they're in the back," she said, walking in front of him.

Despite the strain of the last week, Megan looked stunning. Her hair was in a braid that started on one side of her head and finished at the other, falling down one shoulder. She wore a white dress that was loose but short, and very high heels. Suddenly, Jax realized that despite promising her he'd be both, so far he'd just been her bodyguard and it was time to step up as her date.

Taking hold of her delicate wrist, he stopped her before they reached their party. "If I didn't say it earlier, you look beautiful, Meg. Me being on edge is just something I can't control. It makes me crazy to know you're scared. But I'll try to be on my best behavior, okay?"

She smiled brightly at him, leaned in, and kissed him on the lips before weaving through the tables to their party.

They were the last to arrive, and while quick introductions were made, Jax studied the people at their table. He knew Nell and Taylor, and Elle and Ro—the Fionas—were obviously close friends of Megan's, but what about their manager, Glen, and the rest of the band? Joey had run a basic background check on everyone attending, but sometimes the people closest to you had the deepest secrets. Megan was convinced her stalker was Ryan, but Jax wasn't leaving anything to chance.

While the five friends chatted and caught up on music industry gossip and touring stories, Jax tried to loosen up. It was hard, though; his eyes kept drifting to the other guests in the restaurant and the servers. Megan squeezed his hand. "Relax," she whispered, and he slung his arm over her chair and kissed her temple. He had two men working, one by the back door and one by the front. Everything was safe.

He cleared his throat and tried to calm the feeling of

impending doom that had befallen him. "So, how'd you all meet?" he asked.

"At a music festival in Oregon about three years ago. It was our first big concert," Taylor said.

"Ours too," Elle added.

"We were all so nervous and afterwards we went out for drinks. Been friends ever since," Ro said.

"Yes, and we heard all about you." Elle pointed at Jax. "Mostly when she was sappy and drunk."

He looked down at Megan, who scowled playfully at Elle.

"You talked about me, babe?" he whispered into her ear.

"Shut it, Jackson." She narrowed her eyes up at him and kissed his cheek. "Anyway, we try to catch a show whenever they're playing where we are. They do the same."

The server came out to take their food order and since Jax and Megan had come in after everyone else, Megan ordered a cocktail. Jax ordered a water.

"Going to the bathroom. Be right back." She gave him a peck on the cheek as she placed her napkin on the table, pushed back her chair, and walked to the restroom. He had to remind himself that there was no exit from the restrooms without passing his table first. His eyes still stayed on her until she disappeared into the bathroom.

The group talked and laughed all around him, but he couldn't relax or join the conversation. These were her people, he should be trying to make a good impression, but he couldn't muster the strength to even try. His priority was Megan's safety, not making friends. It was an asshole thought, something he'd likely regret later, once everything was over, but what choice did he really have?

He looked around. Maybe he was overreacting. He'd scoped out the restaurant beforehand, and so had his team. No stalker would dare fuck with Megan with so many eyes on him. There were paparazzi nearby as well as security.

What was the saying? Count your blessings and don't go looking for trouble?

He finally had Megan back by his side and tonight he wanted to enjoy her company. They would have enough to worry about once the tour began. In fact, since he was going to be working nonstop for the next two weeks finalizing the preparations for the tour, this might very well be their last night of fun for a while. Megan's soft kiss on his lips when she returned reminded him that this was what was important, and he promised himself that during dinner, he'd make an effort to get to know her friends and her life and trust that his team had his back.

A lot of food and laughter later he felt a bit more relaxed. Being with Megan, even with the threat of danger hovering over their head, was soothing. It made him remember that there was a life after the military. He hadn't died that ill-fated night in Baghdad, and it wasn't his fault that his friends had.

Ro and Taylor were still there laughing and drinking, but the rest had already left for the night. There was a second concert tomorrow and they had an early morning.

Which seemed like the perfect cue for Jax to lean over and whisper in Megan's ear. "I want to get you home and naked so bad. . . ."

Without missing a beat, Megan pushed her chair back. "We're gonna get going, guys. It was great to see you." She rounded the table and hugged her friends while Jax texted his team a heads-up so they could check the car and cover the area. "It was nice finally putting a face to the man who brought Megan to tears every time she drank too much," Ro said, with a hug.

Jax looked down at Megan, his eyes furrowed. "Tears?"

"I'm a sappy drunk, what can I tell you?"

"It was great meeting you all too."

Holding hands, they walked to the door of the restaurant, but he stopped her before they walked out. From the glass door he looked around the area, his eyes on all the pedestrians and cars. Everything was in order.

He dialed Robbins, one of the two men he'd had detailed to the area, and the one charged with the front.

"Leaving. Anything going on?"

The man, whom he could see from the corner of his eye though he was trained to blend in, replied, "Nothing, boss. It's been quiet."

"And her car?"

"Nothing to report. Just swept the valet parking myself. No one unusual in or out, just the valets."

"Good job. We're on our way. Once we're in the car, you're off the clock," Jax said, tucking the phone back into his pocket and taking Megan's hand in his. "Ready?"

"Seems like a lot of hoopla, for nothing, no?"

"No. I'd rather be safe than sorry," he said, looking around as they stepped out. There were a few clicks from cameras nearby and one in particular was almost blinding. "Damn it," he grumbled, holding her hand to the valet station, where he handed the ticket and paid the guy.

"Thank you for tonight," she whispered into his ear. Her arms were around his neck and his around her waist as they waited by the restaurant door for the valet to bring the car around. "It was fun. I'm glad we did it. I'm happy I got to meet your crew."

"I am too." She smiled brightly and as she kissed him two men came by and took photos of her, blinding them both.

"Jesus," Jax said, rubbing his eyes. "Get the fuck outta

here before I take those cameras."

"One more photo, Megan! Come on, where's TNT?" they asked, just as he saw, between the irritating blindness from the flashes, the car pull up.

"Sorry, guys. Next time," Megan politely declined.

Robbins was a few feet away, opening the door for Megan. "Get in the car," Jax gestured to Megan as he rubbed his eyes one more time and ran around to the passenger side, vigilantly scanning his surroundings.

As he reached for the Porsche's door, the tires of the sports car spun out. If he hadn't taken a step back, it would have run over his foot.

What the fuck!

Before he had a chance to process what was going on, he looked around. Was Megan in the car already? He looked at Robbins' horrified face and without another thought, he took off on foot. Not able to look down and risk losing sight of the car, he took the phone out of his pocket and hit #1.

"Yo."

"He's got her. He's fucking got her!" he yelled breathlessly, as he sprinted as fast as he could. "He's in her car. You have the tag. Call 911." Jax continued to run, pushing people out of the way. "Just crossed Collins Avenue, heading west!"

"Cops have been notified; I have the tracker up just in case you lose 'em."

"Ain't fuckin' losing 'em!" Jax yelled, putting the phone back in his pocket so that he could use both arms to sprint, slipping out of his suit jacket as he ran, tossing it aside somewhere on Ocean Drive. "Move!" he yelled to a bunch of tourists, taking pictures of God only knew what. "Get the fuck out of my way!"

Turning left, he hopped over a roadblock and almost slammed into a moped as the Porsche turned abruptly left. Ignoring the burn on his injured leg and hip, he continued to move, honing in on them, since the Saturday night traffic in Miami was horrific. The light was green but there was bumper-to-bumper traffic. Thankfully, the police sirens were getting louder and because of the congestion he was only a few cars behind the Porsche.

He prayed to God Ryan didn't have a gun, and that the police presence wouldn't further risk Megan. The police were coming in from the opposite direction and he could see them ahead and to the right just as he made his way to the Porsche, barely moving now. Oblivious drivers, some with their windows down photographing the art deco architecture or the eccentric people enjoying the nightlife. Others with low tires and big bass blasting around.

———————

"Please," Megan cried, her hands shaking uncontrollably. "Just let me out. I'll give you anything you want, just let me go."

Ignoring her pleas, Ryan hummed one of Megan's songs as he focused on driving. She tried to press the seat belt button, but he had altered it and it wouldn't let her unbuckle.

"What is it that you want?"

"I like games." Ryan said, with a nefarious giggle that sent fear pulsing up her spine.

"O-okay . . . what kind of games? I can p-play a game," she cried. Anything to relax him so he'd drop his guard.

"I saw you. When he was fondling you in public just now. Saw it. Made me so hard, Meggy. So hard."

She shook her head from side to side. Whatever fucked up game he wanted to play . . . it was going to be bad. She could feel it in her bones. "I'm going to keep you safe. You shouldn't be in the public. You're for my eyes only. Mine. You can sing to me all the time. Doesn't that sound nice, Meggy?"

"Y-yes."

"We can play games too. Singing and games. So much fun," he said, sounding juvenile. "Fuck Marry Kill," he said, his tone now severe. Scaring the shit out of her.

"W-what?" she asked.

"Fuck Marry Kill. Tell me what celebrity you'd fuck, marry, or kill."

"Uh . . ." She couldn't think. She looked through the side mirror and from a distance she could see Jax running toward the slow-moving car. The traffic was horrible, thank God, and if she could just get the goddamn seat belt off, she could open the door and jump out. She began to hyperventilate. "Please, Ryan. Just please let me get out. How am I going to sing if you have me in here?"

"Don't want to share you. I can keep you safe. Strange, dangerous people are everywhere, Meggy. Everywhere. You need someone to keep you safe. Out of the spotlight. Safe," he said, tapping a finger against the steering wheel. One of many tics. He was also cracking his neck from side to side and his voice was fast. Too fast. The man had clearly snapped. "I want to play a game, I said." He slammed his fists into the steering wheel and turned his catlike gray eyes on her, causing her to almost throw up. He pressed the back of a knife to her head, and poked her with it. "Game game. I want to play a game. Game game."

"Help!" she yelled loudly. "Help!"

He thumped the butt of the knife against her head again before closing his eyes and covering his ears. "Be quiet!" he yelled back. He was losing it. She stopped yelling, scared that he was too erratic and out of control.

"Fuck Marry Kill," he repeated, prompting her for an answer.

"Uh—uh." She could not think of one goddamn celebrity at the moment.

She could see Jax getting closer, his gun already drawn. "Your boyfriend's here," Ryan said, oddly calm, looking through the rearview mirror. He went from calm to tightening his grip so forcefully on the steering wheel that it looked like he would rip it off. His jaw pulsed and his shoulder twitched frantically. He looked possessed, which made her fear spike to utter panic.

Then, gunshots exploded and the car, which hadn't been moving because of the traffic, slumped down when the tires popped. Screaming loudly from the sudden noise, Megan tried to open the door but it was locked and the seat belt was still not budging.

"Shut up. Shut up, shut up, shut up!" Ryan yelled at her, his ears covered and his eyes closed. When she stopped moving and screaming, he reached over, fiddled with the seat belt latch, and unbuckled her. Simultaneously he grabbed her hair, sending pain shooting up her scalp as he dragged her over the center console and out of the car.

"You want to know my celebrities, my little mouse? Who I'd fuck, marry, kill?"

She was shaking and tears flowed down her face. He

pulled out his knife and pressed it against her throat. "You," he said. "You. You. You." He whispered the words against her ear, spittle shooting out of his mouth. "I'd fuck, marry, and kill you, after we played all the games and sang all the songs."

She gasped as she felt the pain from the knife tearing at her flesh.

———————

"Calm down, Ryan," Jax said, just a car's length away, watching the knife pressed to Megan's throat. Ryan looked all around, his eyes unfocused, dragging Megan around as he scanned the area. All the police officers had their weapons drawn, and Jax was terrified one of them would shoot and hit Megan while aiming at Ryan. "Hold fire!" he commanded. "Do not fucking shoot!"

"Get your guns down!" Ryan yelled in a shaky voice, hands trembling, and maybe it was purposely or maybe it was due to those shaky hands but the knife dug deeper into Megan's skin and Jax heard her whimper as a drop of blood slid down her throat.

"Don't hurt her. Just calm down, Ryan. Look, no gun!" Jax slowly placed his weapon on the floor and kicked it aside. "Josef!" He yelled at Joey. "Gun fuckin' down!" Joey looked at Jax, then at Ryan, and then followed orders. "Now, Ryan, tell me what you want. Ease up, buddy."

His eyes bounced around the area where spectators were taking videos and pictures from cell phones and where cops were pointing guns at him. It was a volatile situation. "Hey, look at me. Just at me," Jax said, his palms up as he took very small and cautious steps forward. "She can't sing for you if you hurt her, buddy. That's what you want, right?"

Ryan kept looking around, confused or possibly planning his next step. "Listen, Ryan, there's no scenario where you just walk away. The difference will be whether you serve a few months or a couple of life sentences. It's still okay right now. Right now, you let Megan go, and you'll be out before you know it." It was bullshit: kidnapping, assault, battery, the shit went on and on.

As Jax was formulating a plan, his eyes slid to Megan and he saw it in her eyes. She was going to do something. Something stupid and careless. Just as he was about to yell "no" at her, Megan kicked her leg back, her heel slamming against Ryan's groin. Jax and Joey both took off running as Ryan bowled over in pain, letting Megan go in the process.

Stabilize the enemy.

Jax ripped the knife from Ryan's hand and folded his arm high up behind his body, causing Ryan to yelp in pain. The police moved in. The urge to hurt Ryan, to kill him for taking Megan, for hurting her, was overpowering.

"We got it from here, Irons," someone said from behind him. "Irons! Let him go!" Yelling and talking was happening all around him but all he could do was tighten his grip, cause Ryan more pain.

"Jax! Jackson!" Joey's voice snapped him out of his adrenaline-fueled haze. He turned to see Joey on the street, Megan in his arms sobbing. "S'okay, Megan, babe. You're okay." Joey looked up at Jax again and Jax let go of Ryan and rushed to Megan, lifting her off the floor into his arms and away from the crush of people. There was an ambulance waiting nearby, and he headed there. "Stay," Jax said to Joey. "Get all the info. I want to know who he talks to and where they are taking him and what they are booking him for."

"Got it."

Megan was trembling, her arms around his neck. "It's okay, Meg, baby. I've got you. You're okay, sweetheart." She nodded into his neck. "It's all over now."

.

Chapter 14

·

Everything had happened so fast, her brain hadn't caught up.

One minute Jax was kissing her, and the next, Ryan was driving her car. Her first reaction had been to jump out, but he'd attached something to the seat belt clip, making it impossible to unbuckle herself. The look of crazy that Ryan had on his face was not something she'd soon forget. Neither would she forget the look of fear and determination on Jax's face, from the reflection in her side mirror, as he ran toward them.

"We need to ask you some questions." Megan wasn't even sure who was speaking. There was chaos and noise all around her, and she had the sudden urge to cover her ears and ball up in a corner. She heard the officer's read out some of the information from Ryan's license: "Ryan Milano. Local. Thirty-four years old . . ."

"Give her a moment to be checked out by the paramedics," Jax barked to the police officer. *Ryan Milano.*

Now she knew his full name. It wasn't an intimidating sounding name or anything of note. Yet, it was a name she'd not soon forget. He lifted her chin and there was a look of self-loathing on his face as he found the spot where the knife had been pressed. He let go, gently, and left Megan to be attended to by the paramedics. After a short time, some ointment and light bandaging, the cops began to question her.

As she spoke to the police, detailing the twenty horrible minutes in the car with Ryan, Jax's face turned so cold she had to look away.

"Did he have a gun?"

"I-I don't know. He had some contraption thing on the seat belt and I couldn't unbuckle," she said to the police officer, rubbing her scalp where it hurt from where he pulled it.

"You okay?" Jax asked.

"My head hurts." She cleared her throat. "I'm okay, though. Keep going."

The cops asked her more questions. Jax insisted she be checked out again for her headache. Somewhere in the haziness she noticed her friends had gathered around and they were talking to the police as well. Joey had come by too and asked how she was holding up. The paramedics had given her a blanket, and even though it was over eighty degrees, she couldn't stop shivering. She curled up in the back of the ambulance, putting her head against something hard—a gurney, maybe—and closed her eyes.

The next thing she remembered was being lifted from her spot and being in a car, and finally the soft covers of her bed.

At some point Megan woke up, not surprised to find herself alone in bed, since Jax didn't sleep much. It could've been hours. It could've been days. Everything hurt. The skin around her neck, her scalp, her jaw—just everything ached. Taking a hot shower and washing her hair did nothing to alleviate the soreness in her body. She took three Advils and finally went downstairs. She was half-expecting to find all her friends and her parents, so it was a welcome surprise to only find Jax there. She didn't want visitors, mostly because she wasn't in the mood to talk.

"Hey," Jax said from the kitchen table, a laptop in front of him. He closed the computer and went to her. His hair and beard were a mess and there was purpling under his eyes. He looked wrecked. "How do you feel?"

"Like shit."

He led her to the couch. "Your mother had food delivered."

"She did?"

He walked to the kitchen. "She did," he said, bringing her a plate of Mediterranean food, her favorite. "And all those are from friends, publicists, the label . . .”

She looked over her shoulder and noticed for the first time a bunch of flowers and balloons. “Oh wow. Guess it was on television, huh?”

“With the crowd at the beach, everyone with phones, yeah—pretty much every television station is covering the story,” he said, and she sat back and closed her eyes. “I fielded everyone. Thought you’d like to have some time alone before you had company.”

“Yeah, thanks.” Her eyes stayed closed.

“Why don’t you try to eat something?”

She opened her eyes and sat forward, taking a stuffed grape leaf. “Good,” she said with a mouthful. Jax, who was normally very touchy, sat on the other side of the sofa eyeing her with concern.

“Ryan?” she asked.

“In jail. Hopefully for a long time.”

“Thank God. It’s all over.”

He nodded, somberly.

“Are you okay?” she asked, noticing the distance between them. Something was off.

He nodded again and stood, coming back with a glass of water, placing it next to her.

“I have to go into the office this afternoon.”

“What?” she said, louder than she intended. He hadn’t left her side in over three weeks, and he was going to just leave her now, after everything that had happened yester-day?

"The office? Iron-Clad Security? I have new clients I've been neglecting and a big mission that I need to over-see."

"Oh yeah. Sure, of course."

"I have guys still close by. Your security is all set in here, so you'll be okay. I called Nelly and Taylor and asked them to swing by later when you're up to it."

"Jax? Are you . . . are you leaving?"

He stood, running a hand through his hair. "I just told you I have to go to the off—"

"No, I mean . . . for good. Why do I feel as if this is good-bye?"

"It's not good-bye," he said, taking a hesitant step toward her but then stopping before getting too close. "Of course it's not, we still have the tour. I'll keep on for that. Even if the threat is gone, good security is still impor-tant."

"No. Wait. You're running away from me, I can tell. Don't do this, Jax."

"I'm not, I just told you—"

"You told me you'd work for me. I don't need an em-ployee. I need you."

He didn't answer, which confirmed her suspicion. He was leaving.

"A lot has happened so fast. Let's get our heads together. Take a beat to think things through."

Tears welled in her eyes. "I don't need a beat."

"Well," he said, swiping his hand down his face. "I do."

"I can't believe this." Tears fell down her face. "You know what, Jackson?" She spit his name out. "Five years ago, I was stupid and naïve and I followed your stupid plan to part ways. Not even getting your damn phone number. Now, thinking back on it, you were scared. You were running away. When shit gets real, when emotions are on the line, you fucking run away."

"You don't know what you're talking about, Megan. I'm not running away."

"Then stay."

He didn't answer right away. He moved forward and wiped her tears, his face a mirror of hers—full of anguish. Except he was the cause of both of their heartache. "I gotta go, Megan."

"Don't bother with the tour."

"Meg—" He looked down. "I'll call you later. Make sure you're okay."

She shook her head, and turned away. "Just go. It's what you're good at."

———————

Later never happened. He didn't call her.

At nine that evening, she curled on her couch with Rambo and fell asleep with fresh tears running down her face.

The next morning as she was getting out of the shower her doorbell rang at the same time as her phone. She picked up the phone first.

"Ms. Cruz. This is Santino from ICS, there's a woman at your front gate."

"One second, Santino." Megan jogged to the nearest intercom unit and pressed a button, "Yes?"

"Hi, Megan. It's Tamara. I was in the neighborhood. . . ."

"Tamara? Uh yeah, sure, let me buzz you in." Why would Tamara visit? They weren't friends. They barely knew each other. In fact, the only thing she knew about Tamara was that she was the ex-member of TNT and she grew up with Taylor and Nelly.

Megan hit the button and then put the cell phone back to her ear. "It's okay. It's just Tamara. I know her."

"Boss says to keep your cell phone handy and to close the gate once she's through."

"Gotcha," she said. Boss said. That meant that Jax was watching, hearing, observing. But he couldn't be bothered to talk to her himself. As soon as Tamara left, she was going to call Jax and get to the bottom of things.

"Hi, Tamara. Come in."

"Hi, Megan." Tamara said, walking into the house. "I was on my way to work and thought I'd stop by, see how you were doing."

Megan let her in and then closed the door behind her, escorting her to the living room. "Guess you saw it on the news?"

"I did. Nelly told me you were okay. I called, I hope that's fine," she said, nervously playing with the strap of her purse. She had on black-and-white leggings and a black tunic top with black heels and a black belt. She looked very chic and put together, her hair in a severe ponytail, not one single hair out of place. She was a very beautiful woman, Megan noted. She looked nothing like she had when they'd first met five years ago.

And this visit must have taken a lot of strength on Tamara's part.

"There's no hard feelings from my end, so yeah, that's cool."

"I know it's weird, me coming here, but I saw what happened on the news and then . . ." her eyes watered, which surprised the crap out of Megan. "Life is too short. What if I never had the opportunity to apologize for everything that went down back then? It's part of my healing, you know? To apologize. And I owe you a big one."

"Tamara . . ." Megan waved her hand. "No, it's fine."

"No, it's not. I was in a bad place when you came into the picture. I know I caused you guys unnecessary drama with my threats to sue. I want to apologize for that. I've been meaning to apologize for that for a long time. I guess hearing you were almost kidnapped gave me the motivation to move things along."

"No worries, Tamara. Really, it's okay. But thank you for apologizing." Megan said, unsure how else to respond. She really didn't hold any grudge against the woman. But if Tamara needed to do this for herself, it was fine with her. "Oh, goodness. I didn't even offer you anything to drink," she said, standing up.

"Water would be great."

"Be right back." Megan went to the kitchen and when she came back with a water bottle, Tamara was on the far end of the living room where all her awards were kept, including her Grammy.

"Here you go," Megan said, and Tamara looked over her shoulder.

"Oh, thanks." She took the bottle. "Wow, look at all these. You three have made it so big."

"Yep," Megan said just as Rambo ran into the room and started to pull on the laces of Tamara's sneakers. "No, Rambo! Bad dog."

"You have a puppy."

"Yes. It's from Taylor."

"She always was an animal lover."

"Yes. He was supposed to be a guard dog," Megan said, swooping up the dog, which tried to lick her face. "Aren't ya, Rambo? A big cuddly guard dog."

"I love dogs," Tamara said, reaching down and playing with the pup.

"Me too. Isn't he the cutest?"

"Sure is." She stood up and fidgeted with the strap of her purse again. "So, tell me, are you okay? That was an intense scene."

"Yes, I'm fine. A little shaken up, but all's well that ends well, right?" She motioned for Tamara to sit, and Megan sat on the opposite love seat.

"Sure is," Tamara said, sweetly. "And the guy? He's in jail?"

"Yeah. Thank God."

"And you're still going on tour?"

"Yes, of course. I'm not going to let him stop me. Plus, he's in jail, so . . . it's all good now," she said, knowing that her life felt as if it was falling apart with Jax seemingly out of the picture. She had a lump in her throat the size of a watermelon and a Jackson-size hole in her heart.

"You're made from stronger stuff than me, that's for sure."

"I have fans and people depending on me," Megan

hedged. She wasn't strong. . . . She wanted to drop to the floor and cry her eyes out. But instead she sucked it up and made an effort to move forward even if she was dying a little at a time.

"Yes, of course. You're pretty brave, Megan." Tamara's eyes roamed the expanse of the house.

"Thank you." Megan didn't know what else to say. She was tired, heartbroken, and achy, and she didn't really want to make small talk with Tamara, and that thought made Megan feel like a bitch for thinking it when the woman had come to apologize.

The silence stretched out. "Oh, well, I have to run to work." Tamara abruptly stood. "I'm glad you're okay, Megan. And I hope that we can be friends one day. I grew up with Nell and Taylor, it was very hard being disconnected with them for so long." Her eyes got watery and Megan's heart hurt for her. "And now that I have my life together, I'm trying really hard to mend fences and if you and Nell can be forgiving, maybe Taylor will too, eventually."

"Nothing to forgive." Megan said. "It was a long time ago."

Tamara leaned in and gave Megan a big hug. "Thanks and I'm glad you came out all right. I just wanted to come by and extend an olive branch. It was long overdue. I hope I didn't intrude."

"No. It was no intrusion at all. I'm glad you did it. It *was* long overdue."

———————

Jax sat back on a chair in the Situation Room at ICS. It felt like months since he'd been there watching two of his men being ambushed. An hour ago, he'd seen an unfamiliar car pull up at Megan's house through his cell phone app. Maybe he needed to get someone else to monitor the feed. Or, maybe he just needed to delete it entirely. She wasn't their client anymore.

But he still cared about her. Well, *care* was an understatement, but he needed to figure his shit out and get his head together. And since talking with her caused him so much pain, like the pussy that he was, he'd tasked Santino with checking in on Megan.

He should be there, he knew that, but every time he looked at her tired face, he saw his own failure. He saw blood dripping down her throat. He saw the fear in her eyes. He saw the burning wreckage of the bombed military base in the desert.

His fault.

By the end of the day, Jax hadn't done a single useful thing at ICS and he knew it. His mind wasn't in the game, but at the same time he didn't want to go back to his cold home. "Dinner?" Jax asked as he left the room.

"With me?" Joey put a hand dramatically over his chest. "My oh my, you want to have dinner with me?" he fluttered his eyelashes.

"Fuck you very much." Jax went to his office to grab his wallet.

"What's up your ass? Why are you having dinner with me and not the hot little piece of ass that you've been holed up with for the last three weeks?"

"Never mind. I'll eat alone."

Joey patted Jax's shoulder roughly. "Don't be a little bitch. Come on, we can go to the Burger Bee around the corner." They walked out and headed to the nearby restaurant.

"Seriously, though. Why are you here with me and not with Megan? How's she doing, by the way?"

"She's fine. Ryan's in jail," he said, as if that was all the explanation needed.

"So . . ."

"So . . . threat's over."

"And she was just a job?"

"Mind your own fucking business," Jax said as the server walked up and took their order.

"You think Brian can handle it? Shoulda gone myself." Jax referenced the mission Joey was prepping for with Annie. It was a charged situation in a potentially dangerous location, and he hadn't planned any of it, too busy playing house with Megan in the last weeks.

"They got it, Jackson. You know they do. I wouldn't send some inexperienced rookies over there if I wasn't sure."

"And the intel? You think it's good?" Jax asked, anxiously. "Last mission was FUBAR."

"Yeah, but that wasn't on us. That was bad intel from the Feds. This was planned carefully and it's the best intel we could've gotten. We're being paid more than our normal rate. The mission will be easy, so long as the mark is amenable to being escorted back to the States."

"They're never amenable."

Joey chuckled. "Of course they're not. He's facing two life sentences for drug trafficking and accomplice to murder and the dude's never even left his apartment until now when he ran the fuck away like the pussy he is to Colombia."

"Just 'cause he's sitting behind a computer all day helping these drug lords behind the screen doesn't mean he's not dangerous. Don't underestimate him." Joey always had a soft spot for the computer dudes, mostly because he was a computer dude too.

"I haven't. I'm dangerous and I sit behind a computer all day."

"That's questionable," Jax teased. "But fine."

Joey nodded. He'd been going twenty-four hours without sleep, much like Jax. "Jesus, this bounty-hunter business is fucking tiring."

Jax chuckled and took a bite of his burger. "Try to get some rest. Tomorrow will be a long day."

"How about the tour? Everything's already in place."

"She told me not to go, but let's stick with the original plan other than that. I'll stay behind. I'll cover the costs."

"Jackson . . ."

"I'm not talking about it. Her security is shit. Even if Ryan's in jail, she needs better security."

"If this is about you feeling guilty about the way things went down with Ryan, or if you're comparing this to the shit that went down in Iraq, I swear to God, brother, I'll kick your ass myself."

The man knew him too damn well. Jax rolled his eyes and decided to ignore Joey as he finished his burger.

Two nights.

Two nights without Jax. He had copied her on emails to the label regarding security, so he was obviously still going on tour, regardless of what she'd told him when he'd walked out. In a week she'd be on a plane heading to the first stop, Atlanta. She had a million things to do, and she wasn't going to sit around and wait for Jax to get his head out of his ass, no matter how hurt she was.

She missed him something fierce, but she also had work to do now that the threat was over. The bad guy had been caught and was behind bars, and she should feel relieved she was still alive.

Last night, Taylor and Nell had come over and distracted her by talking her ear off about the tour while eating greasy food and drinking wine. She'd mentioned that Tamara had come by and Megan had suggested giving her a chance to work with their makeup artist, Lisa, on tour. Tamara, Nelly, and Taylor had grown up together like sisters. Megan had always felt a little guilty for taking Tamara's place in the band and this would be a chance to ease her guilt while doing something nice for Tamara. It had taken a lot to convince Taylor, but with Nelly's help, finally Taylor relented and agreed to give her a shot.

Picking up her cell, Megan called Tamara the next day. "Hey, Tamara, it's Megan."

"Hi, Megan."

"Hey, so I spoke to the girls and what do you think about coming on tour with us? I know it's short notice but Lisa, our makeup artist, could use some help."

Tamara yelled into the phone. "Are you serious?"

"Absolutely. You were part of the original crew. We'd

love to have you back, even if it's doing makeup. I mean, if you're up for it."

"I'll quit work right now."

Megan laughed. "Text me your email address. I'll have Logan send you the info and the contract, and if you're cool with it, we'll see you bright and early on Sunday."

"Thank you, thank you, thank you!" She sounded so excited it made Megan happy to be doing this for her. People made mistakes and Tamara was clearly trying to learn from them and better herself.

The next call was to her parents. She had been avoiding them, communicating mostly through texts. "Hi, Mother."

"Megan Cruz! We've been worried sick."

"I know, Mother. I'm sorry."

"Are you okay?"

"I am now. Ryan's in jail."

"I know. But you—are you okay? You've been dodging our calls."

"I'm sorry. I was sore yesterday. But I'm better today. Getting ready for the tour."

"You're still going?" Her mother, the calm, cool and collected attorney, practically yelped.

"Of course I am."

"But you were almost killed!"

"But I survived, and now he's in jail and I'm safe."

"You'll be safe when you get a different job," Rose said. Megan rolled her eyes and sighed.

"God, Mother. Are we still doing this? It's been five years. I'm twenty-eight years old. I've made millions of dollars. This is not a job, it's my career. It's my dream. I'm living my dream, how many people can say that?"

"Me. I can say that."

"Well, that's great. I'm so happy you guys are doing exactly what you love. You both set out to be attorneys and became the best lawyers in Florida. But I never wanted to do that. Never."

"Before you met that Jackson . . ."

"No, Mother. Never. Maybe I came to the realization after I met him, but I was unhappy way before meeting him and deciding to pursue music."

"Meg—"

"Mom, I'm not doing this. I called to ask you for a favor, but forget it. I'll call you when I'm back from the tour."

Her mother exhaled loudly. "I'm sorry. You've had a hard week. I'll stop. Tell me, what it is you needed."

"I need you to watch Rambo while I'm gone." Megan said. She had told her mother about Rambo during one of their brief phone calls. Originally, she had planned to take him on tour, but it was going to be too hectic and crowded and she felt it wasn't safe.

"Yes, of course."

"Okay. I'll bring him to you this afternoon."

"And stay for dinner?"

"Yes. Sounds good. Say hi to Dad for me."

Megan's creative juices were not flowing. When she was stressed she either wrote music or gardened and right now she wasn't able to do either of those things. Most of her things for the upcoming tour were already packed, so finding herself with nothing to do was rare. She sat outside looking out over the skyline, watching the cruise ships that lined the Port of Miami across the MacArthur Causeway. It occurred to her that although she'd been all over the world, besides the brief trip to the Bahamas with Jax, she'd never really been on a trip just for fun.

And just like that, all her plans to focus on herself and her music were out the window and she was thinking about Jax again. She should have fought harder for him five years ago. She should have fought harder for him two nights ago. This thing between them wasn't just stress and proximity. It wasn't just sex or passion, though they certainly had both of those in spades. No, he was running from her, running from his feelings, and she needed to know she'd done everything she could to salvage the relationship before acknowledging it was really over.

Over before it really started.

Ugh.

She didn't want to be with someone who didn't want to be with her, but before she faded out of his life forever, Megan needed to hear it direct from Jax. She needed him to say flat out that he didn't want to be with her.

She would try one last time.

She picked up the phone and called him, but it went straight to voice mail. "Hi it's me. So, I was thinking . . . we did three of the five things. The Bahamas, the planetarium, and Fantasies. You owe me two more—or should I say, I owe you two more. Anyway, I miss you, Jax, and I know you're pushing me away, and I don't know what to do to make you stop. I can't be the only one feeling this thing between us. This could be the start of something great. Please call me or come over or . . ." a lump formed at the back of her throat, " . . . just stop pushing me away. Come home, please." And with those final words, she hung up. She stared out at the port for a while while finishing her tea, then decided to dress, pack up Rambo's things, and go have an early dinner at her parents' house.

Home.

She'd wanted him to come "home," as if he lived there with her. Truth be told, he liked being at her house, with her. But right now, almost losing her, knowing it had been his fault, his head was a fucking mess.

Had he just checked the fucking driver's seat . . .

Had he been focused . . .

If he hadn't been kissing her . . .

The fucker had a knife to her throat. He could have driven off and taken her to God knows where. All these things were whirling around his head as he sat in his office waiting for news of ICS's latest mission.

"Whatcha doing here this late?" Joey asked, sitting back on the chair in front of Jax's desk.

"Going over the plans from the venues."

"For Megan's tour?" Joey asked. Jax nodded. "The guys already did that. I did that."

"Well, I want to go over it myself."

Joey rolled his eyes. "Still not getting any, I see."

"Shut the fuck up."

"Annie's bitching about wanting to go out in the field again," Joey said, pinching his nose with his thumb and forefinger.

"Why don't you let her? She'd be an asset."

"Are you crazy? No fucking way. Ma would have my head. Plus, it's safer here."

"Behind the desk?" Jax said. "She doesn't want that."

"I'm not talking about it anymore. Just wanted to give you the heads-up in case she comes bitching your way."

"I'm not getting between you and your sister."

"You don't gotta get involved. You just need to *not* give her any fieldwork," Joey said, standing up and leaving the room. At the doorway, he turned.

"So, you're really not going on the tour?"

"No. I'm not needed and the label wanted some of the work we had originally planned scaled back. I'll just be in the way."

As he walked out, Joey shook his head, looking disappointed in him. "You're an idiot, you know that?"

Five years ago, Jax thought, he and Megan had both been at a crossroads in their lives, but now they both had their lives planned out and their chosen paths were so different. Being with her would mean living in fear every time a rabid fan said or did the wrong thing. And he wasn't sure that was something he could handle. Maybe he had been romanticizing the idea of Megan five years ago. Maybe it wasn't as magical as he'd been making it out to be.

And maybe he was just being a coward.

Chapter 15

"I have not slept on your bed yet," she said.

"Since you got here, neither have I." It was the next morning and Jax kissed her nose before moving off the couch. "Tonight, the bed. My neck's killing me." He rolled his head from side to side.

Tonight? They hadn't talked about another day, but no way was she leaving today. "Okay" was her answer as she hopped off the couch. "You want me to make breakfast?"

He pulled her to him by the waist. "No, baby. Never want you in my kitchen again." He kissed her nose with a chuckle and shuffled her into the bathroom. "Eggs, bacon, coffee okay?"

"Yes. I think between breakfast and my failed attempt at dinner last night, we have most of your fridge cleared."

He looked inside and agreed. "Tonight we can eat lots of ice cream."

"Well, at least we're getting another one of the items of your list done."

"And a trip to visit my mom, she's been calling."

"Oh good, so that's another one," she said, fumbling with her shirt.

"You okay?"

"Me? Yeah, fine. Maybe I should go?" she mumbled awkwardly, pointing her thumb over her shoulder.

"Why? No. Stay."

"To meet your mom?"

"Yeah, sure. Why not? She's going to love you."

Love.

Damn.

She was taking it out of context but it made her heart beat a little faster. A little harder. It was way too soon but damn if she didn't feel something completely new and profound in her chest that she'd never felt before. Not even close.

Yes, she definitely wanted to meet his mother.

———————

"Stop fidgeting, Meg."

She whipped her head toward Jax, surprised. "No one calls me Meg."

They were walking up the path to the apartment building where his mother lived. "Sorry. Does it bother you?"

"No. Just realized that I've never had a nickname. I like

it."

As he leaned in and kissed her lips, her eyes opened and something passed through them that made his heart pound. How had this happened? He wished, for the first time, that he didn't have to leave on Monday. Tomorrow. This was their last day. Damn.

She broke eye contact first and when he turned his mother was standing by the door with a big smile on her face. "Hi, ma."

"Jackson, honey, how are you?"

Jax brought his mother in for a hug. "And who's this?"

"Ma, this is Megan Cruz. Megan, this is my mom, Silvia Irons."

"It's lovely to meet you, Ms. Irons."

"Please, call me Silvie. Come on in. I was starting to think you were going to leave without coming to visit."

"Never, ma. You know that."

"Do I? You leave tomorrow, for goodness sake." she said, filling two glasses with iced tea. "Hope you came hungry. I made a roast, your favorite."

"Smells delicious, Silvie." Megan almost groaned. Home cooked in her family meant prepared by a chef, which was no substitute for good food made with love and butter.

"Ma makes the best food."

"You'll eat anything, Jackson," his mother said.

"That is not true. Ask Megan. I wouldn't touch her sandwich the other day, it was disgusting looking." He wrinkled his brow and Megan shoved him playfully.

"It was not. I'm not much of a cook, but ketchup on a sandwich is not weird."

"It is if it's a grilled cheese," Jax said, and his mother and Megan laughed, spending the rest of the afternoon chatting and having a nice and relaxing lunch.

It was still early by the time they had to drive back to Miami. The sun was right above them, the warmth enveloping them as the bike roared back to the city. Megan held on tight, her cheek on his back. She couldn't remember a time she'd felt this way. It was scary, yet peaceful. Watching Jax say good-bye to his mother was emotional. Knowing that there was always the possibility he'd be hurt, or worse . . .

"You okay?" he asked as they walked into his house. "You're quiet."

Without much thought, she threw her arms around him and broke down in a sob. "Hey. What's going on?" he asked, holding her tightly.

"My mind's reeling with all things war . . ." she sobbed.

He moved back in order to look into her eyes. "Don't

think of those things. I'll be fine."

She wiped her face with the back of her hand. "I'm sorry. I can't help it." Her heart felt heavy. She'd never met anyone whose entire way of being was to enjoy life. Nothing more. Nothing less.

"Come on, I don't want to see tears, let's go empty out my fridge," he said, with a smile that didn't quite reach his eyes.

"No, there's one thing left to do that you can't avoid anymore."

"What is it?"

"Your father. The cemetery."

Jax nodded. "But first let's do something fun," he said, an odd expression on his face.

"Stop avoiding."

"I'm not. Come on." He took her by the hand to his room and handed her one of his bathing suit bottoms and a T-shirt. "You didn't happen to buy a bathing suit at the mall, did you?"

She shook her head. "What are you up to?"

"These'll do, then. Meet you in my backyard in ten minutes."

She didn't understand what they were going to do, but she didn't care. So long as it was something they did together, she knew she wouldn't regret it.

Ten minutes later, Megan walked out in clothes she

had to tie a knot in to keep from slipping off and saw Jax picking up two very long boards.

"What's that? Surfing?"

"Nope. Paddleboard."

"Oh, I've always wanted to try. Is it hard?"

"Nah . . ."

———————

It was midday, and Megan had fallen off the paddleboard too many times already. She was completely done with this stupid strenuous activity. Jax, on the other hand, was standing on top of a red board, parallel to her, holding the paddle in one hand and maintaining a conversation as if it wasn't the hardest thing ever.

"Ten more minutes and then we go, okay?" Megan said.

"Fine."

"How long do you normally stay at the cemetery when you visit?"

He shrugged. "Never been."

"Pardon?" she said, almost falling off her board.

"I've never been to the cemetery."

Wide-eyed, open mouthed, she repeated, "pardon?"

Letting out a big huff of air, he carefully dropped down on his board, linking his legs around hers so as to not drift off. "I know, I know," he said, solemnly. "I've never visited my dad's grave. It's just . . . it's hard, Meg, you know?"

"Jackson, he was your dad. You two were super close."

"I don't think it's really necessary to have to go to the gravesite. I mean, I think about him all the time and—"

"You had it on your list, which means it's been weighing on you. It's time you did this. You have to do this, Jackson."

"He's the only person I've known to have ever died. I've never been to a cemetery before."

"Neither have I. But I'll be there. We'll go together, and you can say whatever you want, or not say anything at all. But you've got to go."

He rubbed his palm over his bald head and sighed. "Yeah, I know."

After swimming to the shore, walking back to his house, and quickly changing clothes, they drove to the cemetery, which was surprisingly close to Jax's house.

"Should I . . ." Megan pointed over her shoulder to a bench on the far side of his father's spot.

"No, come with me. I need to get this over with."

Once they found the site, Megan just stood there, unsure what to do. She'd never had anyone close to her pass away. But the tension radiating from him made her heart break, so she decided to take the lead. Without hesitation, she placed the small bunch of wildflowers they'd purchased into the vase by the marble stone with his father's name. Then she sat on the patch of grass right by the site, Jax looking down on her silently.

"Hi, Mr. Irons. I'm Megan Cruz. I'm friends with your son, Jackson," she said, looking up at Jax expectantly. When he still didn't speak she continued. "I haven't known Jax all that long, Mr. Irons, but what I've learned, I like. A whole lot. I think a lot of it has to do with the kind of father you were to him. He's a good person and with what he's told me, you wanted him to be happy. I've never met someone like him before. I can't tell you whether he's happy or not, although by the smile he always has on his face, I would venture to say he is. I can also tell you, Mr. Irons, that he makes other people happy. He's made me very happy these last few days. So, for that, I thank you." Again she looked up at Jax, his eyes watery. He cleared his throat and looked away.

"Hey, Meg, you think . . . maybe I can have a minute with my pop?"

Megan stood, brushing the grass from her pants. "Yes, of course. Take all the time you need." She began to walk away, but he reached for her hand and stopped her. He didn't say anything at first but then whispered, "Thank you," before sitting in the spot she'd just left.

———————

"Where are we going?" she asked later that evening. She was exhausted from waking up early to drive to the Keys to visit his mother, driving back, paddleboarding, and then the cemetery. It had been a long, draining day. All she wanted was sleep, but he was so excited it made her want to play along.

"It's a surprise."

"No, please. No more surprises."

"This is a big one. Hope you're ready," he said, parking his bike at the familiar empty lot.

"Robbie's?" she asked, looking at her favorite dive bar.

"Did some research and TNT is playing tonight."

She squealed, bouncing up and down. "I've been off the grid since Thursday! I totally forgot about TNT being in town." She began to pull him inside, familiar sounds pouring out of the bar.

"One more thing . . ."

"What?" She looked back at him with a big smile on her face, but before he was able to say anything she heard from the stage, "Megan! Megan, you've been holding out on us, girl! Get your cute little tush on the stage."

Her face completely paled. "Please tell me you didn't."

"Oh, but I totally did," he said with a shit-eating grin, hustling her onto the stage.

"You don't even know if I can sing."

"You said you could."

"I could be wrong!" she yelled, panicking.

"Ladies and gentlemen, we have a special fan who's going to join us for a song." The crowd cheered at the lead singer, who he'd learned was named Tamara. She looked strung out and was slurring her words, but the crowd seemed too excited to care.

"This is Megan," the drummer yelled and then thumped her sticks together and they began to play a song. He'd never heard of it, but apparently the entire packed bar knew it—and so did Megan, who shyly took the mic in her hand. Tamara began to sing, nudging Megan with her elbow.

Soft at first, Meg began singing, then once she became more comfortable, the words came out easier until she was belting out loudly and confidently.

Jax tuned out all the noise, his ears seeking her melodic voice, his eyes tracking the way she moved on the stage. She was made to perform.

The bouts of shyness he'd seen disappeared and a confident woman took their place.

He was completely smitten by Megan Cruz at that moment.

When she finished, the crowd roared and she jumped down from the stage.

"Baby! You can fucking sing!" he yelled over the crowd's response. Her voice was sultry and raw and it completely took his breath away. She was made to sing, she glowed up and transformed up on that stage.

"That was . . ." She jumped up and down. "I can't even describe the way it felt."

"You need to do that. Promise me you'll do that. Even if it's just for fun, you have to sing. God, that was phenomenal, Megan. Listen to the crowd. They love you!"

—————

In her simple cotton panties and one of his T-shirts, laying on her stomach, her feet moving up and down one at a time, she looked years younger. He pulled on a pair of gym shorts when he came out of the shower and slid in bed with her. "Did you have fun today?" he asked her as she turned over, resting her head on her palm. Had they really just met a few days ago? It felt as if she'd always been in his life, fitting in perfectly.

"The best time. You?"

"Watching you sing was unbelievable. The best part of the last few days."

"And I think we conquered most of your list."

"Seems like it," he said, running his hand down the side of her body, up the curve of her hip and down her leg. "I want to touch you."

She turned over on her stomach, slightly parting her thighs. "Then touch me."

For the next hour, they made love without intercourse, touching and loving each other's bodies. He memorized each and every contour, hoping to burn the memory of Megan deep into his brain. Afterward, they lay in bed together, eating ice cream out of the carton. "I'm sorry for getting all girly on you earlier today."

He smiled and winked and continued to eat, mostly because he didn't know what to say. He hadn't said anything a few minutes ago either. He wasn't a hearts-and-feelings kind of guy and the thought of never seeing Megan again made him feel too many things.

"I monopolized your last days in town."

"Nothing I'd rather be doing than this, Meg."

"Tomorrow's going to suck." She put the spoon into the carton and pulled up the covers.

It was absolutely going to suck.

He put the empty carton on the nightstand, turned off the light, and settled into bed, pulling her close to him. "Yeah. It is," he admitted.

They didn't speak for some time, lost in their thoughts. "What do you think would happen if you weren't leaving?"

"Don't do that, Meg. Not good to think of what-ifs.

Let's just enjoy tonight, okay?" She turned into his arms, her face pressed against his chest, and a surge of emotions hit him all at once.

"Are you scared?" she asked, looking up at him in the darkness. "Of war? Of leaving home?"

He shifted his body, turning onto his back, her head in the crook of his arm and her arm across his bare chest.

Life was sweet for him. His first deployment had been to Afghanistan and he'd seen his fair share of shit but nothing horrific. He didn't know where'd he'd be going next, but was he scared? No, not really. Maybe it was naïve on his part, but no, he wasn't scared. He'd have his unit with him. Those were his best friends, his brothers.

But the tightness in his chest was certainly new.

He was scared of never seeing this woman again. There was no way of making promises to her. He didn't know where life was going to take him, and worrying about a girl half a world away wasn't something he wanted—even though a woman like Megan did make him rethink things. Plus, her life was so uncertain too. They were two different worlds colliding into each other in a weird twist of fate.

"No. I'm not scared," he began. "Is it weird that I just met you, but I think I'm going to miss you?"

She slid up and kissed his lips. "So much, Jax. I'm going to miss you so much." Rolling over, taking her with him. "I feel like I missed you even before I met you," she admitted.

"It's going to be hard being over there thinking about you over here."

"Do you think it's better to just part ways completely?"

"Like what? Never talk again?"

"Meg, the way I feel for you . . . it's intense. I can't be the only one feeling that way. I also can't be over there missing you, especially when I don't even know what's going on with you. I mean, will you get back together with Dick? We're headed in different directions, Megan."

"I broke up with Richard, whether he believes it or not," she said into his chest. "But I don't think I can do emails and phone calls for years and years with you while I'm trying to concentrate on school."

"So this is it. It'll suck, but it's for the best."

Cupping his face, she pulled him down to her lips. "Doesn't feel like the best."

"No. It absolutely does not feel like the best."

That night they went to bed somberly, holding each other tight, neither actually sleeping.

"Fuck!" Megan yelled as she tried to style her hair.

Jax ran into the bathroom. "What's going on?"

"Nothing. It's nothing." She tossed her brush on the vanity.

Taking her hands in his, he turned her around. "Talk to me. What's going on?"

"Orientation starts at noon, which means I have to leave here at eleven because I can't be late to my first day of law school. I don't think any of the clothes I bought at Walmart work and my hair sucks this morning and . . ." Her eyes watered and her bottom lip quivered.

He pulled her close to him. "I'm going to miss you too, Meg." Because that was the root of the problem. He'd felt it too. She didn't give a shit about her hair or her clothes. In the four days they'd spent together she hadn't worn any makeup, she had done nothing but wash her hair and let it air dry, and she hadn't given a shit what she looked like, as far as he could tell.

And as soon as the words left his mouth she sagged into him and a ragged sob left her throat. "I wish you didn't have to go."

"I know."

"I wish . . ."

He pushed her away slightly and wiped the tears from her face. "Finish up, I'll drive you to your house so that you can get your car, then I have to come back and finish locking up. My plane leaves at six."

She felt like she was going to throw up. The ball that sat in the pit of her stomach was making her nauseous. "Okay, I'm ready."

He nodded, took his keys from his pocket, and led them to his bike after giving him directions to her house.

"You passed it, Jax." She tapped his shoulder when she saw her parents' house on her left, but he kept going and parked his bike at the corner of the dead-end street. It was early in the day, but where he parked, there was no one around. He climbed off his bike and helped her down.

"I just wanted to say that these last days with you were amazing, Megan."

She had a lump in her throat and it was hard to voice all the emotions she was feeling. She didn't want him to leave and the thought of going to law school or going back to her boring unfulfilled life where she was pushed around by her parents was making her head spin. She didn't say any of these things, though, because the ability to talk had left her and she was crying freely now, unable to control the tears streaming down her face.

"Don't stop singing, Megan. Promise me that."

"I promise," she croaked.

"Don't settle for a douche that your parents pick out. Promise me that."

With a whimpering sob, she said, "I promise."

"Don't stop having fun, Megan."

"I promise."

"And promise me that with any decision you make, you'll always ask yourself whether it'll make you happy. It puts things into perspective. Life isn't that hard. If it makes you happy, do it. If not, then don't."

"I promise, Jax."

"It was the best four days of my life, Megan."

Her sobs were louder now and she wrapped her arms around his waist, smelling him, feeling him, wanting to remember this moment for eternity. "Best four days of my life, Jax." She wiped away the tears. "Thank you for giving me that."

They hopped back on the bike and he left her at the gate of her parents' ostentatious Coral Gables home. "I'll see you around, sweetheart."

"Be safe, Jackson."

"Be happy, Megan." He winked, kissed her one last time on the lips, and rode off, leaving her in front of her empty house, sobbing.

Chapter 16

"I can't believe he didn't come," Taylor huffed from the seat behind Megan on the plane.

Nelly shoved Taylor's shoulder. "Stop talking about it, Tee!"

Megan turned her face to the small airplane window and tried not to cry. She chanced a glance across at the two men Jax had sent instead—Ben and Jason, neither of whom were looking at her. They sat there like two soldiers, quietly upright with their guards up. Megan leaned back, closed her eyes and tried to tune out the hurt she felt.

It was over.

Really over.

Somewhere inside she'd thought that once he'd had a few days to himself, once they saw each other again on tour, it would all be okay. In fact, that's why she hadn't fought him or the label in allowing ICS to be the security detail.

But it was all for nothing. He wasn't coming.

She didn't say anything the entire plane ride over and her friends knew her well enough to know she needed space.

A bit more than an hour later they arrived to Atlanta, where they would be staying for two nights. After that they'd be getting on buses for the rest of the tour. Jason and Ben were as methodical as Jax—they wouldn't allow any of them to debark from the plane or walk into the hotel . . . or basically do anything until they "secured the perimeter."

She was sick of it.

All the security.

All the military mumbo jumbo.

All of it.

She had put up with it for three weeks because her life had been in danger, but now the threat was over and Jax was trying to somehow assuage his guilt for dumping her by getting her this overzealous security detail for a tour that was perfectly safe.

It was utter bullshit.

Pissed off, Megan stomped ahead of Jason and Ben and went straight to her hotel room, the men hollering behind her to slow down. But she didn't care and instead opened the door and slammed it shut, leaving her bodyguards huffing and puffing outside.

After assuring Taylor and Nelly via a bunch of texts that she was okay, Megan took a hot bath, skipped dinner, and went to sleep. The way she felt—having been blown off without even the decency of a phone call—made her ache so bad that the hurt had turned into anger. She refused to cry anymore.

With a throbbing headache, she was woken up early the next morning by the sound of her phone ringing. Blindly reaching for the nightstand, she found it. "Hello?" she answered it, half asleep. "Hello?" she said, louder this time and definitely more annoyed. When no one answered she sat up and looked at the screen, trying to clear the cobwebs out of her mind.

Unknown Caller

Her heart started to pound and she pulled up the sheet higher. "Hello?" This time her tone was more subdued.

There was a sound from the other side, like a laugh, maybe . . . and then the call ended.

She looked at the phone, as if it held all the answers.

Ryan was in jail. Maybe it was just a coincidence. People butt-dialed all the time, or called wrong numbers. It could be anything. She would mention it to one of Jax's guys later this morning, she thought. Even with those thoughts, she double-checked the security latch on her door and the lock on the balcony windows. But the weird feeling didn't go away, and when her phone rang again a moment later she hesitated in answering it.

But then she saw it was from her mom.

"Hello?"

"Megan?"

Megan looked at the clock and then became worried. Her mother wouldn't normally call her this early in the morning. "Did you just call by accident?"

"No. Hey, Megan, Rambo's been throwing up all night. Your father wants to take him to the vet."

That wasn't what she expected. She stopped pacing around the room and thinking of the previous call. "Uh, yes, thanks. I'll text you guys the vet's info. Please keep me posted."

"Will do."

"Thanks, Mom, talk to you later."

If the morning was a sign of things to come, today was going to suck.

Jax was in his office back in Miami when Jason called. He was supposed to report back directly twice a day; he'd reported upon arrival yesterday and now again today. Jason explained how Megan had dodged them again that morning as they walked into the venue for sound check. It seemed she wasn't so much evading them as ignoring them. But that didn't surprise Jax. His Megan was feisty when she was mad, or when she was told what to do. It was fine. So long as they had eyes and ears on her and she was safe she could be pissed if she wanted.

God, he missed her.

He was being an idiot.

When Joey walked right into Jax's office without knocking, Jax's love life took a backseat. He knew Joey well enough to know something was going on. The hair on the back of his neck stood as Joey made his way to him, but instead of sitting down in the guest chair, he stood, placing his palms on Jax's desk.

"Got the prints back from the box, the one with the dead rat."

"Yeah, what about it?" He felt his jaw tick.

"You wanted them matched to Ryan."

Jax nodded, his eyes intent on his friend. Yes, he wanted all his t's crossed and his i's dotted. Protocol for ICS made it mandatory, and his feelings for Megan made it urgent. With Ryan in custody, Jax had instructed the team to cross-reference his prints with the ones found on the box. The crime scene lab in Miami was backlogged, and with their suspect in jail, waiting on the prints to go through the official channels would take too much time. With Megan's safety on the line, Jax didn't want to wait for concrete evidence that Ryan was responsible.

ICS didn't have the same bullshit to deal with.

"Get to it, Josef." The conversation had made his stomach drop.

"It's not him. The prints don't match."

Jax stood up so abruptly that the chair fell back. "What?"

"So, I called Chief Martinez, and get this: Ryan admitted to breaking into Megan's house. Admitted sending that one letter after meeting her in Amsterdam—the original one that came by mail. Had no choice but to admit he planned to kidnap Megan, since everyone saw him do it. Swore he wasn't planning on hurting her. Said it got out of control once the police got involved. He just wanted to talk to her, he said, be with her the way she wanted to be with him. He said they were in love. But he played dumb about the texts and about the dead mouse."

"He's crazy. He could be lying. What the hell are we missing, Josef?"

"Martinez thought Ryan was lying too, which is why he didn't call and tell us. Guess he didn't think it was important. Until now that the prints came back."

Jax ran his fingers through his hair. "So what the fuck does this mean? There's two stalkers? Either Ryan has a copycat or he has a partner? What the fuck?" He slammed his palms on the table.

"I don't know yet. I have the guys working on it. Got

Annie trying to crack the code off the phone. Martinez is getting a warrant to search Ryan's house and hopefully there will be something there that can explain what the hell's going on." Joey squeezed his shoulder. "This is one fucked up situation, brother."

Jax almost threw up.

He'd sent her off to Atlanta without him, and there was still someone out there who wanted to hurt her. "She's still in danger." It was said in long exhale.

"Sure looks that way."

He swiped his wallet and keys from the top drawer of his desk. "Book me the first flight to Atlanta. And brief the guys. Tell them to keep a close eye, but not to let Megan know anything yet. I don't want her to panic before I get there," he yelled from the hall, already halfway out of the compound. He needed to grab his emergency bag from his house and get to Atlanta as soon as possible.

Especially since the stubborn woman wasn't listening to Jason or Ben. She probably wouldn't listen to him either, but at least he could pick her up and tie her down if it meant keeping her safe.

As soon as the plane landed in Atlanta, Jax hopped a cab and went straight to the venue. By the time he arrived, TNT was already performing. He was unable to take his eyes off Megan on stage—thank God she was safe. The last few hours he'd been alternating between trying to see the missing piece of the puzzle and fighting off the terrible what-ifs that filled his head.

After the last song was over and they yelled their good-byes to the audience, Megan reached for a towel hidden behind one of the speakers and wiped her brow as she walked offstage, not even looking at her surroundings. Her breasts heaved up and down as she breathed heavily and her cheeks were pink. She barely looked like the Megan he knew in that hair and makeup. She still hadn't seen him and he was standing right there.

She needed to keep her eyes open, watch for danger.

Her carelessness upset him.

Jax stood with his arms crossed over his chest, unmoving, as she barreled right into him.

"Ow!" she yelled, and once she looked up, she took an unsteady step back, her eyes wide. "Jax? Wh-what are you doing here?"

"You didn't see me. I could've been anyone, and you didn't see me. You need to watch where you're going and keep vigilant, Megan."

People were walking past them and the noise was intolerable. "Excuse me? You came back just to be an asshole to me?" She looked pissed the hell off and was about to open her mouth and rip him a new one when the other girls walked offstage—all smiles, until they saw Jax.

Taylor stopped dead in her tracks. "You've got a lot of

nerve—" He completely ignored her because it was time to get back to the hotel and deal with the crazy who was out to get her.

What the hell was Jax doing there? And in complete commando-badass mode.

It was like he had two personalities: sweet carefree funny man or soldier. Never the twain shall meet.

She was finally able to get words out of her mouth. "What are you doing here?"

"I'll explain later. Right now we need to head back to the hotel," he barked. "I want everyone in the limo in two minutes, then we'll use the back elevators as soon as we get to the hotel."

"Yeah yeah yeah. They've already gone over this with us a hundred times, Jax," Taylor said, pointing at Ben and Jason behind them. "What's all the hoopla all of a sudden?"

"We go over it as many times as I think we need to," Jax snapped, shocking everyone with his curt response.

"Jackson!" Megan said as they walked quickly to the limo. She hadn't even had a chance to change clothes or grab her things from the dressing room.

Taylor stalked toward Jax. "Excuse me? How dare

you—" she began, a hand on her waist.

"I don't have the time or the patience, Taylor," Jax said, taking Megan's hand, which surprised the hell out of her, and pulling her into the limo. The sudden touch startled her and she flinched. He looked hurt for a second before going back to being a dickhead. "Just fall in line. You can be pissed off later," he said to Taylor, then turned to Megan. "Seat belt," he barked, and began to type furiously into his phone.

The limo ride was short, not even ten minutes, and no one said anything. She was pumped full of adrenaline from the concert, shocked he was there, and still pissed and hurt.

As soon as the limo parked, he took her hand and pulled her out. "Come on. Let's do this."

"Jackson! Are you crazy?" Megan asked incredulously, glancing over her shoulder to see a scowling Taylor being ushered out, Ben close by her side. Jax didn't answer, he just walked out of the limo quickly, his eyes vigilant to all the goings-on around him. "Eyes and ears open at all times, you got me?"

His hands were on hers and she couldn't even enjoy it.

"Would you slow down?" Megan said. "I can't believe you just talked to Tee that way."

He didn't answer. Instead, as soon as they all got inside the large service elevator, Jax was on his phone typing again. Taylor was still scowling and Nelly seemed worried. Megan wanted to rip the phone from his hands and demand answers.

Without looking up, he began to belt out fresh orders. "The rest of the crew is scattered throughout the hotel as of yesterday. We have dinner being sent up at 2000 hours, then tomorrow at 0800 we meet downstairs at the lobby to head out."

"Yes, boss," Jason said. Ben nodded agreement.

"Can we please talk about the fact that you're being a dick?" Taylor asked, her arms folded over her chest.

"No," Jax replied, not bothering to look up from his phone. "Once we get upstairs, straight to your rooms. Jason and Ben will explain the new plan."

Something was going on.

Shit shit shit.

Now Megan was worried. Big time.

The elevator stopped and he looked up. "We're here. Come on."

She felt nauseous and without much thought grabbed his forearm and squeezed. He stopped what he was doing and looked down at her, then took her hand and pulled her to her room.

Once inside their room, Megan snatched the phone away from Jax's hand. He glared at her. "What the fu—"

"I need you to stop for a moment," she demanded. "At

the very least, you've always looked straight at me when we talk. So stop and look at me." He let out a breath, and with arms over his chest he waited for her to continue. "I get that you've been stressed. I understand that you're looking out for me. But, you need to remember I'm a person. We—me, Nell, and Taylor—are all people. This is going to eventually be resolved, and you're going to be left with three pissed off and unforgiving women. Why are you here? What is going on? Why are you being an asshole?"

"Don't really care if you all are mad at me. Last time I let my guard down, you were fucking abducted," he said, snatching back his phone. It all made sense now. The guilt was obviously getting to him. She was about to tell him it wasn't his fault, when he spoke again. "I'd rather you're all uncomfortable or upset than dead. I drop the ball, you get dead. It doesn't matter whether you're all mad at me."

"Jackson," she exhaled. He was being completely unreasonable and overbearing and not even trying to listen, but it all made sense to her at that moment. He was pushing her away because he was scared. He'd never admit it, but he was scared that if his heart was on the line and she was hurt . . .

"You once told me only to do things that made me happy. You said that would put everything into perspective. And except for the last few days, you make me happy, regardless of all the shit going on around us. So I've chosen happy. I choose to take that risk with you. I've made it clear, I've made my choice. Now you need to stop and decide if I make *you* happy."

He let out a breath and tossed his phone on the bed. "C'mere, Megan." He pulled her to him by the wrist. "I'm going to explain this one time, then I'm going back to work. I have a meeting with the hotel security in five minutes and then when I get back we need to talk and you're going to listen."

"I'm not some soldier you can bark orders at." Megan's voice was calm. "And nothing that happened with Ryan was your fault, if that's why you dumped me. Stop blaming yourself and stop pushing me away and answer my question. Do I make you happy?"

"I'm trying to do my job. Stop being difficult and talking about *us* when what we need to be talking about is your safety."

"I'm not being difficult!" Now she was getting frustrated. He'd put her through hell the last couple of days and she wanted an explanation. "I know what's going through your mind and you need to stop."

He glowered at her, his eyes murderous. It was the first time she actually realized how big and imposing he was. "I don't think you do know. Because if you fucking knew you'd give me some goddamn slack to do my fucking job."

"Ryan is in jail in Miami. There's no threat here. What happened happened. It's all over now."

"You don't know what you're talking about! The reason I'm back is because he isn't acting alone."

She stopped cold and grabbed on to the table next to her. "What?"

"The prints we took, they don't match the one on the box with the dead mouse."

"Oh my god . . ." she exhaled. She closed her eyes and counted to ten and reopened them. "But none of this is your fault. And it's something that Jason and Ben can handle, right? Maybe the fingerprints were wrong. Either way, it's not your problem anymore."

He inched forward, and she took a step back. "Are you fucking outta your goddamn mind? We were kissing and not one damn minute later a crazy fucker abducted you while I was standing right next to you. Right the fuck next to you. That fucker's hand on your neck with a knife—it's ingrained in my brain!" he yelled, poking roughly at his head. "I see it every time I close my eyes, every time I look at you. I see his hand gripping your hair and dragging you out of the car!"

"Jax, it's not . . ."

"Stop it, Megan! I lost my entire platoon in Iraq. Seven

men that I considered brothers. Loved them and I'm still dealing with that loss. Served with them on two tours, hung out while on dwell time, got to know their families. They were my friends, my family. I'm just now, over a year later, coming to terms with their death, which took a lot of fucking therapy, by the way. But if you—if you, Megan, if you were killed . . . I would die. I would not survive that. I won't. I would lose my goddamn mind. So I'm not going to calm down. Every single fucking person is a suspect as far as I'm concerned. I love you, but I love you alive and if that means being a dick, so be it. I have a meeting with the hotel's security. Do not, for the love of God, open the door for anyone. Not anyone." With that he was gone, slamming the door behind him.

He loves me?

Megan paced around the room. She wanted to go after him and kiss him—or punch him, she wasn't sure. She had a lot of things running through her mind and didn't know where to start, so she decided to give him space. He needed to cool down and she needed to process what he'd just told her. And she also needed a shower to get all the gunk off her hair and face.

Megan startled when she heard the front door opening and closing an hour later. Jumping off the bed in her pajamas, she walked out to see Jax tossing his wallet and keycard on the table. His hair was sticking up all over the place and there were dark circles under his eyes. "We have access to the service entrance and exits as well as the service elevators. There's guards all over. Luckily, it wasn't difficult to reinstate the original plan."

"Jackson—"

"I called the office and Joey's sending two other guys we've used before. They only work for us when we need a hand and they weren't busy."

"Jackson—"

"Do not give me shit about adding more people to the team," he said, running his hand through his hair. "I got a bad fucking feeling and I'm not going to explain shit again."

"Would you stop!" she yelled and tugged on his beard. "I'm trying to talk. Stop cutting me off and listen, damn it!"

He had his arms crossed over his chest and an eyebrow arched up. "Sit," she said, pointing to the nearby sofa. Two angry people wouldn't resolve a thing, so she made the decision to soften a little. It didn't mean she wasn't still hurt or upset at the way he handled things, but she needed him to know the way she felt. "Please, honey. Sit."

He let out a breath and followed her to the sofa. She pulled out her phone, swiped to the track she wanted, and held the phone out to him. "Listen to this."

"Megan, I've heard your music before. I don't have ti—"

"Just listen. This is one I wrote. The first one I wrote. Listen to it. Really listen."

Leaning forward, looking as stressed out as anyone could look, he held the phone in his hand, his forearms resting on his thighs.

> *Promise me you'll always sing.*
> *Promise me you'll always laugh.*
> *Promise me you'll always have fun.*
> *Am I happy? I ask myself every day.*
> *You came into my world and made all the gray go away.*
> *You lighted my life and I never want to be dimmed again.*
> *Even if we never meet again, thank you for this weekend.*
> *Thank you for letting me be me.*
> *I wish things were different . . . I wish you'd never left.*
> *But always, I'll promise you, I'll never be the same again.*

Megan chewed on her lower lip while watching him intently. It was by far her favorite song and the most personal.

Would he understand how much he'd always meant to her?

Jax's heart swelled. It had been so long since he'd felt it beat; it took his breath away. "Play it again."

"Jax."

"Again," he said, and again the words poured out. "I don't know if I'll ever be that same guy from all those years ago," he admitted when it finished playing.

"I don't think I'll ever be that girl from all those years ago, either."

"I don't care. You're better."

"You are too," she said without missing a beat. "I'm sorry I got you in this mess. I wish things were different."

He pulled her to him. "It's not your fault. You have nothing to apologize for. But I do need you to just listen to what I tell you to do. It's always going to be for your own good."

"I know."

"And I may get a little abrasive."

"I know that too."

"And maybe a little crazy."

"Got that also. But I'll try to be patient," she said.

"'preciate that, sweetheart."

"You dumped me," she whispered. "You broke my heart." Her eyes welled, but his girl was strong. So she held it back but still gave him shit for leaving her. "You were an asshole. A big one."

God, she was breaking his own heart right this second.

"I'm sorry. So damn sorry. All these emotions . . . I'm not good at dealing with them."

"I can tell. I forgive you. But never do that again. You have to promise to stop pulling away from me."

"I promise," he said. "And I choose happy too. What you asked me earlier? You do make me happy. You always have. I realized I was an idiot for walking away before all this shit went down and I was going to come tell you, but then Ryan . . ."

Now the tears did actually fall, but they seemed like happy tears. "I love you, Jackson. I think I loved you five years ago too."

He pushed her back into the bed and climbed in too, hovering above her. He took her face in his hands. He needed her eyes on his when he told her, correctly this time: "That song . . ." He shook his head, overcome with emotion. He wanted to say so much, but he pushed through the lump in his throat and instead he just chose the words that mattered most. "I love you too, sweetheart."

Her phone began to ring and they both looked at each other, puzzled. It was late.

"I swear to God, we have the worst timing. When this is all over, I'm packing us up and taking us on a vacation where there are no goddamn phones." He looked over at the screen and then to her. Shit, it said "unknown caller."

"Oh, damn," Megan said, pushing him aside and sitting up. "I forgot to tell you and the guys that someone called and hung up this morning."

They'd switched out phones last week and she had a new number. So this was more disconcerting than the original hang-ups. "How could you forget to tell me? Did you give anyone the new number?"

"My parents called right after and I totally forgot," she looked at the screen. "Speaking of . . . give me a second, Rambo's sick and I want to know how he's doing. And no, the only people who have my new number are close family and friends."

Megan reached for her phone. "Hi, Mom." Rolling her eyes, she put her mom on speakerphone when he gestured that he wanted to hear the call. Let her think he was being paranoid, as long as she was safe.

"Megan, I have some bad news." Rose began, but her father took the phone.

"Megan, you there?" For the second time that night, Jax's spine tingled. Whatever her father was going to say, it wasn't going to be good.

"Dad? What's going on?" Megan stood and her hands trembled as she paced.

Jax neared, listening intently.

"We took Rambo to the vet."

"Yes, and?"

"I'm sorry, Megan, but he's not doing well. He lost a lot of blood."

"What? " A sob broke out as she said it. "I-is Rambo going to die? H-how . . . wh-what?" She sat back down. "It was just a bug. All he did was throw up. What do you mean he lost a lot of blood? You took him to the vet, and he—" She couldn't finish the sentence.

Jax came to her and took the phone from her hand, taking it off speaker. "Mr. Cruz, this is Jackson Irons, what's going on? . . . I see. . . . And the vet confirmed that? . . . Someone from my team will need the chart and more info. . . . Yes, sir. Of course. Expect my call tomorrow."

Jax put the phone on the table and slid a palm over his face before squeezing the back of his neck.

"It was rat poison. Someone gave him rat—or mouse—" He emphasized the word so that she would understand the connection. "Poison. He's in critical care. If he makes it through the next few days, he should be okay. But, Megan, it's not looking good."

"Holy shit." Megan trembled before sliding down the floor.

Chapter 17

Feeling light-headed, Megan reached behind her and held on to the nearest wall. "Rambo was poisoned."

"Megan . . ."

"I just . . . how? I mean . . . what?"

"I'm sorry about Rambo, sweetheart." He opened a water bottle and handed it to her. "Fuck. That just confirmed it. There's someone else."

Jax Skyped Joey and told him about Rambo while Megan sat on the floor listening to the conversation and trying to wrap her head around the fact that someone had poisoned her dog. "Joey, I need you talking directly to Martinez."

"On it," Joey replied.

"I want to know what exactly was given to Rambo. I want to know where we are with the search warrant, and I want you there when they search the house. I'd go myself but I'm not leaving Megan. And I want to know every single thing we can about Ryan Milano. Where he grew up, where he went to school, who his friends are . . . everything."

"Already on it," Joey said. "I'll call as soon as I have anything. Be safe. Jax, man, take care and try to keep your head on straight."

When they hung up, Jax went to the huge bathroom and drew Megan a bath. "Come on, Meg. Why don't you go take a nice long soak? Try to relax. I'll order us some food."

Megan was pacing around chewing on her thumbnail. "I can't relax. This isn't funny anymore."

"Was it ever funny? You were abducted."

"I know that, Jackson. But I thought it was over. Now my puppy might die. He was poisoned, he's bleeding out. Do I have to worry about what I eat now too?"

"Go shower, baby. Your job is to leave the worrying to me."

Megan appreciated his concern, but she couldn't relax. She walked to the bathroom, turned off the bath, and unplugged the tub, then stripped naked and took a quick hot shower. When she got out, Jax was speaking to someone on the other side of the door to the room.

"What's that?" she asked after he shut the door, pointing to the large bag in his hand.

Jax went to the table and emptied the bag. "I had them bring up one of every kind of food they sold at the hotel store that was sealed. It's mostly junk, but it'll do for tonight. Tomorrow we'll figure something out. If we go to a restaurant where no one is expecting us, the food should be okay."

She took a bag of pretzels and sat on the couch to eat it. Scrolling through her phone, she saw that the buzz surrounding the previous week's attack was still top news, something she'd been avoiding reading about. Tossing the half-eaten bag of pretzels away, she went to bed.

Curled into a ball on her side of the bed, she felt the mattress dip a few minutes later. Jax had been making calls when she'd gone to sleep, but apparently he was done. She felt his bare chest behind her as he pulled her close.

"Are you finished with work?"

"Not even close."

She turned around and pressed closer to him. "I'm scared."

"I know," he said. "Don't be. I'm here. We're not leaving anything to chance this time. You're going to be okay. We're going to be ten steps ahead of him. I just got you back, Meg, there's no way I'm letting someone take you away from me again."

"Okay, Jax."

"You blew my mind tonight. Your voice on that stage, the crowd . . . everything."

"It was a good show." She yawned into his chest, his hand soothingly caressing her hair until she finally succumbed to all the stress of the past week.

———————

The next morning Megan woke up to an empty bed. She did her morning ritual before putting on a pair of sweatpants and an old T-shirt. In the other room, Jax stood with his bare and muscular back to her, looking out at the Atlanta skyline from the glass doors that led to the balcony. He was on the phone, barking orders at someone when she wrapped her arms around his waist. "I expect a call at 0900 hours," he said, tossing the phone on a nearby table.

"The search warrant came in. They're going into Ryan's home now."

"Good," she said, as his stomach rumbled. "I'm hungry."

"I made arrangements, and we're leaving now instead of at eight." She looked at the digital clock and saw it was only six in the morning.

"Do the girls know?"

"Yes. Ben and Jason have been advised."

"What time did you do that?"

He shrugged. "Doesn't matter. Sometime in the night

while you were sleeping."

She looked at the purple circles under his eyes. "You didn't sleep, did you?"

"I'll sleep later," he said, kissing her head and then patting her ass. "I packed up all your shit. Get your toiletries together and do a final scan of the room. We leave in ten minutes."

Megan quickly packed up what was left and looked around. "Okay. You can call the bellhop dude."

"No. Until we know what's happening, I want all your things handled only by me or someone from my team. No one else," he said, pulling the two bags toward the door. "Let's hit it."

As soon as she stepped onto the bus, she was surprised to see that Nelly and Taylor were already there. They were usually as slow in the morning as she was. "This bites," Taylor yawned, sulking. "Are you going to tell us what's going on, because these two are tight-lipped and it's starting to piss me the hell off. If I wasn't sure it involved your safety, Megan, I'd have told them to fuck off for waking me at this ungodly hour."

Megan looked at Jax, who was talking with Ben and Jason, for permission. She was shocked she'd even thought about asking; she never asked anyone for permission. But everything seemed so grave at the moment that she wasn't sure which way was up. Jax gave her a slight nod so she finally spoke. "Rambo was poisoned."

"What?" Nelly asked, her eyes wide.

"Is he going to be okay?" Taylor asked.

"I don't know," she heard herself croak.

"No," Nelly whispered, and began to sob. Taylor put an arm around her and asked, "But isn't Ryan in jail? How can he poison someone while incarcerated? After the hell you went through last week, I thought everything was over."

"Looks like either there's a second stalker or he was working with someone else," Megan said. "I don't think we know yet."

"Holy fuck." Taylor said.

"So Jax wanted to change the schedule, I guess. I don't even know what the plan is. I do know that I'm starved. He didn't want me to eat room service last night. Just in case."

"Oh God!" Nelly cried louder.

"S'okay, Nells. I'm sure he only wants me. Everything has been about me. Don't worry."

"I'm worried *about* you, you idiot. I don't want to think of anything happening to you."

"Don't worry about me, I'll be fine."

The tour bus was huge, easily accommodating the six of them, with one big bed at the back of the bus on a second floor of sorts, a small bed underneath the big one, and then three more small beds. One pulled out from the right wall; the couch underneath became a bed; and then there was another pullout on the left side. The small beds were—small.

"You guys are going to stay here? With us?" Nelly asked. The men, who were always serious, nodded. Nelly sat on one of the beds, which doubled as a sofa when they were awake. Like per usual, she was tapping the pillow, which she had propped on her lap as if it was a drum.

Taylor, who had a needle and thread in her hand, sat next to Nelly. "I figure you two called dibs on the big bed?" Taylor looked at Jax and then Megan.

"Yes," Jax said, quickly. "Then I call the one on top." Taylor pointed to the one right above where she currently sat.

"And I call the other one." Nelly pointed to other bed on top, across from Taylor's.

"Why do I get a feeling we just got the shit beds?" Jason said to Ben.

"Let's just say, when these two," Taylor pointed to Megan and Jax, "Start bumpin' and grindin', you'll be the first to know."

"I call that bed!" Ben quickly pointed to the bed that was currently being used as a couch, leaving Jason stuck with the bed under Jax and Megan.

"Damn . . ." Jason moaned.

"Oh, relax. We're only going to sleep up there," Megan said, rolling her eyes. No way would she have sex on a tour bus with four other people, and the driver, a few feet away. Plus, she was still sad over the loss of Rambo.

"Yeah, right." Nelly said, still tapping. When she got nervous, the tapping always intensified and by the way she was beating that pillow, her stress level was obviously pretty high.

"So let's talk about the stalker situation." Taylor dove right in. "If Ryan didn't do it, or didn't do everything, who did?"

"No idea," Megan replied. "I've been trying to think and I just don't know. I mean, as far as people that don't like me . . . I'm not sure. It has to be a fan who I don't know, I think."

"Ryan looks so familiar, though," Nelly said, absentmindedly.

"You too?" Taylor added, looking at Nelly. "When I saw his face on the news I thought the same thing."

"Wait? So you've both seen him before?" Jax asked, leaning forward, his forearms on his thighs.

"I don't know. Maybe. I can't place his face, but it's familiar somehow," Nelly said, glancing at Jason. When she noticed he was looking at her hands tapping, she quickly sat on them.

"Maybe you remember him from Amsterdam, where I

first met him," Megan offered.

"Maybe," Taylor said, with a shrug.

———————

Later that night, Megan could feel Jax tense beside her in bed. "You know sleep deprivation isn't going to make you catch this guy any faster."

He huffed a breath out in the dark. "I want answers. The police aren't sharing what they found in Ryan's house yet. Joey and Annie would've gotten in and found whatever needed to be found already." There was quiet frustration in Jax's voice. Megan could tell he didn't want to take out his frustrations on her, but his anxiety was almost stronger than hers. At least she had her music, her band, and even him, to take her mind off of things. He was a man of action. Sitting waiting to be attacked wasn't his MO.

"There's nothing you can do, Jax. Just try to stay in control. We'll be in Baltimore by the time we wake up and then we'll have a few hours before sound check at the hotel to relax."

"I'm not going to relax until I break this fucking puzzle."

She rolled over on top of him on the small bed. "I know something that'll help you relax," she whispered against his lips.

"No. Please don't!" Taylor yelled from somewhere below.

"Mind your own business," Jax yelled back, but Megan could feel his smirk.

"If you two start humping, it'll be all our business." This time the muttered reply was from a decidedly masculine voice from the bed below theirs.

Megan tried to muffle her giggles. *Oh, god.*

"She's right, baby," he whispered in her ear. "You're loud. Always have been."

"Am not," she whispered back.

"Baby ... hate to break it to you, but you're a screamer."

"TMI, guys. T-M-I!" Nelly hollered, making Megan groan and tuck her face into Jax's neck, causing him to chuckle loudly.

God, it felt good to laugh. It had been a long trip to Baltimore. And her nerves were stretched thin. Jax had barely talked to anyone. And while she'd played silly games to pass the time with Nelly, Taylor, and even Jason and Tamara a couple times, he'd stayed on his phone or laptop. Megan was glad to see bridges mending between her best friends and their childhood best friend, but even the insane stories Tamara shared about TNT back in her time didn't draw Jax out. His foot bounced up and down relentlessly. So this easiness, the one they always shared, was a welcome distraction. The only thing better would've been a private room somewhere.

But alas, that would have to wait.

"I said only one entrance!" Jax yelled at the local security at the Royal Farms Arena in Baltimore.

"And I said it's a fire hazard. We keep all doors open."

Jax stood, pushing the table over on his way up. "Cancel it. Cancel the fucking concert," he roared.

Over the ringing in his ears, he heard yelling and shouting but he didn't fucking care. Taking out his phone, he called Ben. "Yeah, boss?"

"Get the girls, pick up our shit. Concert's fucking cancelled. Tell Glen."

"Uh . . . pardon?"

"You fucking deaf? Cancelled. On the bus in ten," he said, stomping toward the stage where he heard the sound of drums and guitars being tuned.

"Jackson!" He heard Megan from the microphone. "Jackson. Come over to the stage, now, please. Honey." It was in an acid tone.

He moved quickly until he was around the back and Megan was walking down. "Why is it that Glen over there has a huge throbbing vein about to pop off his forehead?"

"They don't want to cooperate. We're canceling."

"They?" she asked, her arms around her chest.

"Yeah, they," he snapped, loudly, sweeping an around toward the front of the arena. "The arena people."

"Calm down and talk to me, please," she asked. Her voice was calm, sweet even, but the glint in her eye was anything but polite. "Obviously, you're pissed off about something, but you need to explain. Because I need to explain it to two other women, a record label, my freaking manager, and fourteen thousand fans!" By the time the last word had come out, she was yelling.

He took her by the elbow and led her to her dressing room. "I want every person coming into this arena to come in through just one of the entrances. I don't want this to be a free-for-all. That way I can have some of my men monitoring, as well as cameras. I need to be able to control this crowd."

"Okay, sounds reasonable. What's the problem?"

"The problem is that the dickhead with a badge in charge of the arena is not allowing it. He says it's not efficient and it's a fire hazard, which is bull-fucking-shit because we're not locking the doors. They can use any goddamn door to leave. I just want to control who gets in and how. I also want all bags checked, and the fucker said no to that too."

Megan reached forward and plucked his cell phone from his pocket.

"What are you doing?"

"Making a call," she glared, her quirked eyebrow daring him to question her.

Megan dialed and then, "Larry, it's Megan. . . . Yeah I'm here. Sound check. Hey, listen, there seems to be a problem with security here. Well, you know I don't want to be a prima donna or anything, but you know what's been going on, right? With the stalker . . . Okay, well, the dude's still out there, Larry, or someone is. I don't feel comfortable with the way they're handling security here, or not handling it, for that matter. I want my people to take care of it. I'll pay. Whatever it takes. It needs to get done. Yeah, well, it's going to be more pricey if it gets cancelled and we have to return all those ticket sales, right? Yeah, that's what I thought. Coordinate it with Glen. Thanks, Larry." She swiped the screen and slapped the phone into Jax's palm. "Give him twenty minutes, I'm sure it'll get resolved. And for the record, I appreciate your concern for my safety, I really do, but you can't just cancel a concert. It's millions of dollars plus TNT's reputation. You have to consult with us first."

He snarled.

"I'm serious. This is my career."

"And if you're dead there's no career to be had."

"I get that. But you have to trust me to help you handle things that just might be out of your control, like a call to Larry, the president of the label, for example."

"Fine."

"Fine," she huffed, just as his phone rang.

"What?" he bellowed into his phone. There was a pause.

"I'll be right down." He swiped the phone off. "Matter resolved."

She shook her head and rolled her eyes and was turning to walk back when he hooked his finger through a loop of her jeans and pulled her toward him. "I love you," he barked, almost mad, but he could feel the slight curve up on the corner of his lips giving him away.

"I love you too," she said, with the same upset tone, before he gave her a hard kiss and let her go.

"Everything looks good, boss." Jason said from the other side of the stage.

"All good in the back," Ben confirmed.

Jax adjusted his earpiece, keeping watch on the stage. "Keep an eye out. We'll be out of here within an hour."

Jax scanned the crowd and behind the curtain. Backstage passes had been limited for the show, but even then there were more people than he was comfortable with in the wings. Techies, label people, costuming. Tamara and

Lisa were nearby, as was usually the case. During breaks the girls would sometimes run backstage and change or touch up their hair and makeup, and Lisa and Tamara were usually nearby.

Taylor was in the middle of a guitar solo when Jax happened to glance at the stage. While everyone's attention was on the light spectacle going on around the stage while Taylor strummed, Megan was wetting her bottom lip with her tongue and her eyebrows were furrowed. To anyone watching, it didn't look like anything unusual, but to Jax, who knew her well, it was odd.

As Taylor slowed down, Megan grabbed the mic and began to sing. It was one of Jax's favorite TNT songs, other than "Promise Me," of course. He hadn't even known it was Megan when he'd caught himself singing along to it months ago on the radio. It was called "Junebug" and it was one of their faster tempo songs.

"There's something wrong," Jackson said into his mic.

"Where? What?" came the replies from his men.

"Standby, not sure yet," he responded.

"I don't see anything," Tamara said, looking around as if for impending danger.

"Neither do I," Lisa added.

"She sounds weird," Jax said, getting closer to the stage. Megan cleared her throat and shook her head mid-song before going back to singing. He could see

Taylor and Nelly looking at each other, confused. There were three songs left on the show, and she cleared her throat again and held the microphone out to the crowd, smiling, so that the audience could sing the chorus. She did that often, but this felt off, her smile was off, and that cough . . . it was unusual. The song ended, the crowd cheered, and Megan said something to Taylor, who nodded and went into a solo. Megan stepped over by the drums and gulped some water. This was only the second TNT show he'd seen, but this wasn't something she normally did. She jogged back to center stage, the fake smile still plastered on her face. "Come on, Baltimore! Let me hear you sing." And she did that microphone thing again, where the crowd sang the song. Midway through the song, she turned to the girls and said something Jax couldn't hear and Nelly and Taylor went into a solo.

Megan jogged off stage toward Jax.

"Can't feel my tongue," she mumbled, almost unintelligibly. "Lipth tingle."

He pulled her to where there was more light, Tamara and Lisa following, holding the light from their phones to her face. "Your lips are tingling? Is that what you said?" Jax asked, cupping her face and checking it out. "Open your mouth."

"Can you breathe okay?" Lisa asked.

She nodded. "Yeth but tongue feelth big."

"May be a little swollen," he said. "I'm calling the para-medics."

She nodded as he placed the call to the team on standby as per the requirements of the venue. Tamara pulled her to a nearby chair. "Breathe, honey," she said. "Anything else? Lightheaded? Did you eat anything un-usual?"

Megan shook her head. As he was about to let Nelly and Taylor know, he heard Taylor's voice on the speaker. "Looks like our girl Megan's had herself a little emer-gency." The crowd booed. "But we're not going to let that ruin our night, isn't that right, Baltimore?" The crowd cheered. "Let's see if we can get Nelly to break one of her drumsticks, shall we?" The crowd was hysterical. Nelly was notorious for getting so engrossed in her drums that she'd break a stick or two, and then throw the broken sticks, which had TNT's logo on them, to the crowd. Al-ways the show-woman, she pulled an extra stick out of her cleavage and began to jam out until sweat poured down her face. Taylor joined in as the crowd sang the last song.

Jax held Megan's hand while the paramedics checked her vitals, breathing a sigh of relief when they looked her over and concluded it was nothing urgent. "Looks like some sort of reaction. Maybe you ate something you're allergic to. I'm going to give you a shot of Benadryl, but it's going to make you very sleepy very fast."

"Do it," Jax answered for the unnaturally mute Megan. "Ben and Jason, get the girls back to the hotel as soon as it's over. No hanging around. I'm leaving with Megan," he said into his lapel.

"Anything we can do to help?" Tamara asked.

"No, just stay here. Maybe grab anything she may have left and take it back to the hotel with you."

The paramedics gave her a shot and advised her to go to the doctor or the hospital if it worsened or if she had any trouble breathing.

"Come on," Jax said, shuffling Megan out of the enormous arena through the downstairs corridor which lead to the back entrance.

"You okay?"

"Tired," she said in a muffled voice, her eyes looking heavy and her feet sluggish. "Everything's in slow motion."

The drug was hitting her fast. He lifted her up into his arms before her eyes shut and she was out.

Chapter 19

"Where are we?" Megan asked when she opened her eyes, her mouth dry and her throat burned. "Water?"

"Are you feeling better?" Jax asked, reaching for a water bottle and holding it up to her lips.

"Yes but . . ." She looked around. "This isn't the hotel."

"No, it's not. We're in Newport, Rhode Island."

"Geography was never my strongest subject, but didn't we pass New York?" she asked, sitting up. The last thing she remembered was feeling loopy while holding on to Jax's hand as they walked out of the arena to the car. The next leg of the tour was in New York, not Rhode Island.

"We have a few days before the New York concert and a buddy of mine has this house. Called him last night and he let us borrow it."

"And the girls? The crew?"

"No one knows. Only Joey."

"Jackson! They'll worry."

"They know you're fine but they don't know where you are. I don't want anyone to know."

"Why not? And how'd we get here?" she asked, sitting up higher, moving the hair from her face.

"Drove most of the night. I need to keep you safe. I also need a breather so that I can figure out a plan. This will give me a couple of days where I don't have to be looking over our shoulder and use the time to figure out what our next move will be."

"Okay," she shrugged, taking in the view from the double glass door leading to the water. "I can live with that."

"Good. How do you feel?"

"I'm groggy, mostly. My head feels all cloudy and I'm sleepy but not tired."

"That's the antihistamine. How about your tongue and lips?"

"That's okay. Feels back to normal. Must've been something I ate."

"Ever happened before? Are you allergic to anything?"

"No, never, and not that I know of."

"Didn't think so. By the way, your parents called a few times. They saw the news."

"Damn, does everything have to be plastered on television?"

"Pretty much par for the course when you're the lead singer of TNT."

"I asked your mom about your allergies and she said the same thing. That you're not allergic to anything. Also, it looks like Rambo may pull through. They've been able to stop all the blood loss; now it's just a waiting game. He's still very lethargic."

"Oh, thank goodness." She let out a deep breath, then took the water bottle from his hand and drank down half the bottle.

"It's not an allergy, Meg. Someone tampered with something you ate."

"No." She looked at him. "No," she repeated. "I just felt bad, is all."

"Too many coincidences, sweetheart. Your dog and now you? Someone messed with your food."

"I didn't eat anything unusual. The restaurant we stopped at on the way to Baltimore we went to on the fly. I don't think the cook would be in on it. It just makes no sense."

"I need to put the pieces together."

"I'm going to take a quick shower," she said, distractedly.

———————

"You feeling better?" he asked, when she came back into the room and sat beside him on the bed.

"Yeah, taking a shower and washing all the product out of my hair made me feel a lot better."

"Good," he said, kissing her shoulder, but before he could pull away, she reached for him and kissed his pec where his tattoo was. "I still can't believe someone poisoned Rambo."

"I know, baby. But he's doing better." He brought her in close and kissed her forehead. "We're going to figure this out and make you safe."

"I know. It's just . . . it's all so crazy. All I want to do is sing. Dealing with all this was not part of the plan."

"It never is. Unfortunately it comes with the territory." She laid down, her head on his lap, and he put aside his thoughts for a moment in order to comfort her. "I love you, Megan.

She smiled wide, looking up at him "I love you too, Jax," she said with a smile as her stomach began to rumble.

"That's kind of embarrassing."

"My tongue has been deep inside of you and I've licked every inch of your body; I think we're passed feeling embarrassed about anything, don't you think?"

"Maybe." She shrugged. "Then I'll go ahead and tell you right now, I'd kill for a big juicy steak. Medium. And a baked potato with all the fixin's and corn on the cob. Since you said not to be embarrassed I'll also tell you that I'll probably lick my fingers at some point and have to undo the top button on my jeans."

He laughed. "How 'bout I save you the embarrassment and you wear my gym shorts with the elastic waist."

"Sounds like a plan." She pulled his hair, and he crawled up her body and kissed her fiercely.

"I'll go make us dinner. I didn't buy potatoes, though."

"I can live without the potatoes. I'll help you cook."

"Okay, so there is one thing you should be embarrassed about," he began and her eyes furrowed. "Your complete and total lack of any sort of cooking ability."

She laughed and threw a pillow at him on his way out of the room. "I'm going to go back and scour the internet for any photos of my concerts to see if I can find anything at all."

"Good idea. Anything that seems off, you tell me."

The next day, Megan sat outside on a lawn chair writing in her journal while Jax sat next to her, his laptop on his lap, going through all the notes from Ryan's file his team had scraped together. The previous night they'd both spent hours and hours going through any photo they came across online, checking for anything unusual. Today he was focusing on the staff. Not just TNT's staff but the label, the venues . . . everything he could think of.

"Find anything juicy?" she asked.

"He has a ton of photos of concerts on his hard drive. Most of them zoomed into you."

She closed her notebook and slid in beside him on the lawn chair. "Creepy."

"Yep," he said, scrolling from photo to photo. "And the interesting thing about it is that they all look like they were shot from the side of the arena. Not from the audience."

"As if he had a backstage pass?"

"Or like he worked there," he said, and then he sat up, almost knocking her off the chair. "Hand me my phone, will ya?"

She reached over and picked up his phone from the small side table.

"Joey, I need you to find out if RLC Records ever used Spotlight Lighting and Production on tour. If so, I want to know whether Ryan was put to work on TNT's 2014 tour during that time. . . . Yeah, that's what I'm thinking too. Later."

"What are you thinking?" she asked when he hung up.

"That he worked with you or for you."

"I'd have known, I'd have remembered when I saw him after the tour."

"Maybe he looked different. Maybe you weren't paying attention to the crew."

"I'm not such a diva I wouldn't know who was working with us, Jax."

"Well it's worth a check," he said, kissing her shoulder and placing the laptop on the floor. "And you're kind of a diva, baby."

"Am not."

"Really?" He flipped them both over, Megan on her back and Jax hovering over her. "I'm going to fall!" she yelped.

"Overdramatic too."

"Am not."

He pushed her shirt up and sucked a nipple into his mouth, causing her to arch. "And too talkative."

"Shut up and do that again." She pushed his head down into her chest.

He slid one hand between them and rubbed her over her shorts. "Oh, that feels good."

He turned his attention to her other nipple.

"More. Hand inside." She tugged on his hand and tried to shove it into her shorts.

"And way too bossy."

"Am not."

"Want to make a bet?" He sat up. "You sit and let me do whatever I want to your body and you." He held his fingers up, watching her frustrated scowl. "One, be quiet, two, be still, and three do what I say without questions.

But if you talk, I'll stop."

Her eyes narrowed and he burst out laughing. "You're dying to talk, aren't you?"

She moved two fingers across her lips like a zipper and then opened her arms welcoming the challenge.

Forty-five seconds later she was begging and screaming his name.

He didn't stop.

"Wow. Best sex ever," she said, breathlessly.

"And you didn't follow directions. At. All."

"What? I did everything you asked me to do."

"Sweetheart, you didn't stop talking, yelling, or telling me what to do the entire time. I had to tie your hands to get you to obey."

"I don't like that word. Obey." She made a face. "And you tied me up because you like kink, not because I wasn't following instructions."

He rolled his eyes and kissed her nose just as his phone began to ring. He reached over to press the answer and speaker buttons.

"Talk to me, Josef."

"So, interesting stuff. SLP did not work with RLC Records but they did work with TNT before they were signed with RLC. They helped with the small gigs in 2012."

"2012? Megan wasn't even in the band in 2012."

"I know. But there's gotta be some sort of connection," Joey said.

"Anything else?" Jax asked.

"Not yet."

"Okay. Anything new, you call. Even if it seems like nothing."

"Gotcha."

After he hung up, he stood, slid his gym shorts back on, and paced back and forth. "Gotta think this through."

"What is SLP, anyway?"

"Spotlight Lighting and Production. It's the lighting company where Ryan was employed for a short time. Only about a month."

"What made you think to ask about SLP and not his other employers?"

"It's the only one that could sort of make sense with a band. He worked at some retail stores for different periods of times and then was unemployed and in the middle of that, had a short stint at SLP."

———

It was later that evening, when both of them were lounging around the living room trying to figure out a connection with Ryan, when Jax's phone rang again.

"Jason."

"Hey, boss. Sorry to bother you, but Nelly wants to talk to you. Says it's important."

"Put her on."

Jax hit the speaker and Megan slid in next to him.

"Hi, Jax. How's Megan?"

"I'm good, Nell. I'm here. You're on speaker."

"Hi, Meg. We miss you. It's not the same without you on the bus." Nelly said.

"I miss you too. I can't wait for this nightmare to be over."

"So, I've been going crazy thinking where I knew this Ryan guy from. I've been going over it in my head, looking at photos to see if it jogged my memory, and then it hit me all of a sudden."

"Nell," Jax interrupted, "before you say anything else, where are you? Who's by you?"

"Just Jason. We stopped for dinner. I'm still on the bus. Everyone else, even the driver, is out."

"Okay, go ahead."

"So, before you came along there was this— Oh, wait, Taylor just walked in . . ."

"Left my phone in here. Hey, whatcha guys doing?" Taylor asked, and there was silence, probably because Nell wasn't sure what to say.

"Hi, Taylor. I'm on speaker with Nelly," Megan said, and Jax shot her daggers. "I trust them, Jackson! They're family."

"Wait! What? Are we suspects now too?" Taylor shrieked. "What the hell?"

"No. No! Jax is just being overly cautious, is all. Nelly was just about to tell us she remembers where she's seen Ryan before."

"I don't like this. It's tearing us apart. You know Nelly and I would never hurt you." Taylor continued.

"I know," Meg said, and elbowed Jax.

"Calm down," Jackson said. "Just keep going, Nelly, and shut the door of that damn bus. I don't want everyone knowing what we're talking about. Jason, I want the door secured. No one else walks in until we've hung up. You hear me?"

"Yes, boss."

"Okay so as I was saying—and Taylor may remember better than me. Taylor, remember those gigs we used to play around Florida before Megan came along? We didn't know anything about the lights, and Jeff, our old manager, kept saying that it was important to look professional, so we hired that company to help us."

"Of course, what about it?" Taylor asked. "Oh shit . . ."

"Yes!" Nelly said, excitedly. "You remember, right? That lighting guy, never knew his name."

"Oh yeah, of course. Yes, oh my god, that's him. Oh fuck, wait a second." There was silence.

"Taylor?" Nell asked, concern lacing her voice.

"Fuck. I knew there was something up with that bitch. I knew not to trust her," Taylor said, sounding as if she was talking mostly to herself.

"What?" Jax stood and barked at the phone. "What is it?"

"Tamara. Tamara slept with that guy. Remember that lighting guy who she disappeared with and went on a two-day binge? You took over that night, Megan."

"Oh my god, yes!" Megan covered her mouth. "That's the day I met him. I didn't remember that. I thought I'd met him at the Amsterdam concert. Oh shit, I remember. He was a lot thinner back then and he was wearing glasses."

"When she finally came back our manager fired the guy and Tamara. And maybe that's when the obsession began."

"Are you sure about this?" Jason asked.

"Absolutely," Taylor said. "And don't you find it interesting that the little bitch, who's surely seen Ryan's face plastered all over the television, hasn't mentioned she knows him."

"Damn," Megan said, surprised she'd forgotten about it. It had happened so long ago and it was such a brief and insignificant meeting.

"It can't be," Nelly said.

"She knew you had a dog. She knows where you live, so sending you a letter directly to your house would be easy. The lip thing—"

"She didn't do my makeup, Jax. Lisa always does it."

"Yeah, but she has access to your stuff. To your lipstick, for example," Jax said.

"I knew we couldn't trust her. I knew it," Taylor added.

"The motive's there," Jason added. "Bet you she wants back into TNT. You're in her way."

There was a collective silence.

"I need to think on this," Jax said. "This conversation never happened. You hear me? I want you to pretend nothing happened."

"You're going to let that crazy bitch keep working with us?" Taylor shrieked.

"Right now, this is all speculation. When we arrest her, I want that shit to stick. I want her to rot in jail. Right now, all evidence points to Ryan. There's nothing concrete on her."

"I don't feel comfortable. . . ." Nelly said.

"It's okay," Jason said. "We'll figure it out. I've got a handle on things here, Jax. I'll brief Ben. Let me know when you have orders."

"When everyone's out to lunch, I need you to go to the bus and take something that belongs to her and send it overnight to Joey for prints."

"Got it, boss," Jason said.

"Act normal, ladies. We'll talk later."

———————

Tamara?

"Let's calm down and think about this, Jax."

"I am," he said, pacing the living room. "It fits, Meg. She wants to take you out. She wants TNT. She doesn't want to hurt Nelly or Taylor because she needs them. They're two-thirds of the band. You came in, took over, and now you've got a Grammy, multimillion-dollar contracts, traveling around the world, while she's giving out samples at the mall. She didn't have even a fraction of that when she started the band with Nelly and Taylor."

"But she apologized. She's been so friendly."

"She's not going to walk around with a sign telling you she's your stalker."

"I don't know. It's so . . . extreme."

Ignoring Megan's concerns, Jax called Joey. "It's Tamara. The stalker is Tamara."

"What? Are you sure?"

"Positive. She dated Ryan for a short time. She's in our fold. Fuck, man, how did I miss that?"

"We checked her. You know we checked everyone."

"Slipped through. But the shit is all speculation, speculation I know is fact, but we need proof."

"Hear you loud and clear brother."

Jax paced back and forth, driving Megan crazy. She still couldn't believe it, but it made sense the more she thought about it. "I feel so betrayed. I was nice to her, I gave her a job."

"No, you're a good person. A trusting person."

"What's the plan? What are we going to do?"

"Right now? Just wait on Joey. He knows what we need to make an arrest that sticks."

The rest of the evening was just a waiting game. Megan ate half a tub of Nutella and chewed her fingernails raw.

When they woke up the next day and headed to New York for the concert, Megan was a ball of raw nerves. There was nothing they could do until Joey got more information, and that meant going onstage and performing for a sold-out crowd with a crazy stalker right under their noses. All while looking Tamara straight in the face during prep and pretending she didn't know Tamara was trying to hurt her.

It was going to take major acting on Megan's part.

Chapter 20

"Hey!" Joey said over the phone. "We got her, man. Bitch's going down."

"Wait. I can't hear you." Jax signaled Ben, letting him know he was taking a call. Ben gave him a thumbs-up and Jax moved to a quieter area. "Talk to me, Josef."

"I'm in her house right now, brother. It's beyond fucking disturbing. She has a cage with live mice. Also, a big motherfucking photo of Megan with mice drawn on her . . . eating her face. There're sketches of Megan everywhere. There's also photos everywhere of TNT before Megan became the singer. They have hearts drawn around them and the new ones, the ones with Megan, she's cut out. The cutout pieces are crumbled and in the rat cages. Disturbing as fuck. The chick's clearly mental and obviously has it in for your girl. And not surprisingly, I found a box of rat poison under the sink. There's also a sketch of Megan's house with entrances and windows on it. Looks pretty accurate."

"Damn," Jax grunted, running a hand down his face. "I have Jason keeping an eye on her under the guise that we're trying to keep all the staff safe. I want to bring her in so badly, man, but it's not enough. I want her down for a long fucking time. Plus, I'm assuming you broke in, so, you need to have a hell of a good reason to go begging Martinez for a search warrant to make your findings legit. This is all good shit, at least we know we have to keep an eye on the bitch, but we need more. What is she planning on doing? I'll bet my right nut she's planning something big. I feel it, there's more coming."

"Hold your fucking horses, man. I got more. She's got a basement. You know what the bitch has in her base-ment? TNT. Ironic, isn't it? She has C4 and coke bottles and fucking internet printouts on how to make fucking bombs. Recipes!"

"You telling me she's been on the road with us while carrying bombs?"

"Looks that way. Fingerprints came back from the brush Jason overnighted me—they match the original letter, plus the box with the rat."

"Jesus Christ. We need Ryan to confess. He needs to point us to Tamara so we can get that search warrant," Jax said. "Call Martinez. Ask him to let you talk to Ryan yourself. Get him to talk."

"You can't just sit on this information, though." Joey's

voice was tense. "If she has a bomb with her, a whole bunch of people are in danger right now, not just Megan."

"Go handle Martinez. Get that search warrant. I'll figure things out here."

"Careful, Jackson."

"Always am, Josef. Always am," he said, shutting off the phone. By the song playing in the background he knew there was still four more songs left, which was about thirty minutes of showtime. Tamara wanted her band back, there was no way she'd make a move on Megan while they were on stage. Megan was safe for now; he just had to keep her that way.

Midway through the next song, Jason skidded to a stop a few yards away.

Shit.

"Jason, what are you doing here? Where's Tamara?" Jax asked.

"Slipped out," he panted. "My com is on the fritz. Lost visual on her nine minutes ago."

Jax's mind cleared to just the mission. Throwing Jason an extra communication device, he called Ben from the radio. "Ben, eyes on Megan at all times. Jason, you take the east side, I'll take the west."

Jax reached to his side and felt his Sig Sauer. He couldn't take it out in the middle of Madison Square Garden. He went room to room and there was no sign of

Tamara anywhere. "Anything?" he asked Jason.

"Negative, boss."

"Go up front. Stick to the outer perimeter; she could lose herself in the crowd but remember she doesn't know that we know, so she may not be sneaking."

"Got it, boss."

Meanwhile, Jax went farther down to the bottom where the service entrance was located. He opened the heavy door and was met with a long, winding corridor. He remembered it from the plans he had studied in preparation for this detail. Cement walls lined both sides and old lights flickered above. It was completely empty and so hidden, he couldn't even hear the thumping music or the screaming fans from above. It must've been part of the original structure built in the late sixties; he was even lower than Penn Station.

Since he was alone, he pulled out his weapon and proceeded carefully, but once he hit an old furnace and another set of stairs leading back up, he felt he was off. Tamara wasn't there, and he didn't feel as if she'd been there either. It was too obscure, and most people wouldn't have known it existed.

Instead, he ran back the way he'd come, in complete Marine mode, focused and determined.

At this time there would be a packed lot full of buses and a few limos. His heart raced as the adrenaline kicked in. Pressing the metal bar with his hip, he snuck out. It was dark and there was no sign of anyone around. He moved soundlessly through the buses, looking for Tamara, until he reached Megan's bus, which had the door open.

Stealthily, as on the missions he'd done time and time again, he climbed inside, unable to see much with the darkness. His arms were stretched in front of him, and his fingers were on the trigger of his gun.

Then, bent over by the bed that he and Megan shared, he saw Tamara shuffling around. Her back to him.

"Don't fucking move," he barked, gun drawn. "Turn around. Slowly." She began to turn around. "Hands up!" he demanded, and she did as he said. "What the fuck were you doing, Tamara?"

She didn't respond.

"You have three seconds to tell me, or I'll shoot." Still no answer. "You better think fast because you don't have long to decide how this will play out." Not a single word out of her mouth. "What have you done?"

"I think you know exactly what I've done," she finally said.

"So you want to kill Megan? You're so jealous you want to kill her?"

"She's not here, is she? If I wanted to kill her I would've set the bomb in her dressing room. I would've put poison in her makeup instead of numbing cream in her lipstick. I don't want her dead, I want the bitch to go the fuck away. I just want to scare her," she said, her eyes looking around, and then she grabbed her phone and pressed something.

"I said, don't fucking move!" he said, and she held her hands out again, but he could hear the ringing of an alarm from inside the Garden. And she smirked.

She'd set off the fire alarm.

"The bitch took everything from me. Everything. That Grammy . . . that was supposed to be me. Me! Taylor and Nelly? Those are my friends, not hers. TNT? There's no M. Even Ryan was in love with her. She's trying to take over my life!" Her voice had escalated to the point she was now yelling.

"Let's calm down. Take a breath."

"Do not tell me to calm down!" she shrieked. "We both need to get off this bus."

"No!" He yelled, uncertain as to exactly what he was going to do. "This is a parking lot, you'll kill a bunch of people if that bomb goes off."

"It's your fault!" she yelled. She was talking erratically and it was obvious she was having some sort of meltdown. "I wasn't going to set the alarm yet. I wanted the bomb to go off, then the alarm. Those two things had to send her into hiding indefinitely." She sounded hysterical and nervous, maybe even unsure of what to do, and if there was anything he'd learned it was that there was nothing worse than a hopeless enemy, someone who thought they had nothing to lose.

Jax looked out the window and saw people running out of the building. "Fuck."

"You're going to kill a bunch of people, Tamara. Turn it off. Shut it down," he yelled, pushing her aside and finding the rudimentary bomb. It was an unsophisticated explosive devise tied together with wiring and an old cell phone, but even still, he wasn't sure where to pull or what to cut to stop it.

"I don't know how to turn it off. Let's just get out," she yelled. She headed to the exit, but he grabbed her before she could leave.

––––––––––––

Something was obviously off. Jax was never far away during her show. Normally, she would look over every once and a while and she could see him close by, reassuring her. But tonight he'd been missing almost all of the second half of the show. That wasn't a good sign, not at all. The tension was almost palpable. So much so, the girls noticed, and Megan could see them looking around from time to time.

What the hell was happening?

As soon as the last song ended, Megan practically ran offstage. Her entire body had broken out into goose bumps and her heart was racing. "What's happening? What's going on?" she asked Ben, who was closest.

"Nothing, why?"

"Bullshit!" As soon as the words left her mouth the fire alarm for the entire Garden began to ring, and Taylor and Nell came rushing forward. The noise was deafening and she could barely hear Ben yelling something into the mic on his lapel.

"This way. Hurry," he said, shuffling the three down to the service entrances.

"Where's Jax?" she yelled, but Ben continued moving quickly down the hall.

"Ben!" she yelled again, and then grabbed his forearm. "Where is Jax?"

"Not sure but it doesn't matter, you need to come with me."

She listened and followed him quickly as they wound down a corridor, suddenly flanked by Jason. "Wait here." Ben spoke first, just before they got to the door that led outside. Nelly and Taylor were right behind her, huddled close.

Ben exited the building, gun drawn, and her heart beat faster. The noise from the fire alarm was making her insane and she was nervous for her fans and the chaos that was surely ensuing upstairs. "Are people in danger?" she asked Jason, who was looking around, his gun out.

"Not sure. But priority number one is you, Nell, and Taylor."

"Ben! All those people!"

"Honey, if it makes you feel better, the psycho bitch just wants to kill you, not everyone else, otherwise who'd come to her concert once she offed you and she took over TNT?" Taylor's words were matter-of-fact, but her wide eyes gave away the fact she was scared.

"Thanks. That does *not* make me feel any better."

The door opened and Ben came through. "Okay, looks good, let's go. We're enacting the evacuation protocol. Straight to the limos. They're pulling in."

"I'm not leaving Jax." Megan refused to move.

"You are," Jason said, physically hustling them outside. Megan looked to her right where all the buses were lined up. As she was going to look away she caught movement through a window of her tour bus. A shadow of a man, a Jax-shaped man, passed by the window. Jason and Ben were busy shuffling everyone in and she squinted again. Definitely movement.

She took off running into the night.

Jax could see Megan feet away from the tour bus with Jason and Ben in fast pursuit. In a split-second decision, he shoved Tamara down the steps into Jason's waiting grip.

"Stay with them, Megan. For God's sake, listen to me this once." Then he turned to Ben and the rest of the arena's security that was nearby. "Try to clear this area. There's a bomb on the bus," he said, running back into the bus and locking the door.

Megan pounded against the doors. "What?! No! Get out of there, Jackson!"

The parking lot of the arena was mayhem. The police wouldn't get here in time, and he couldn't stop the bomb. His mind made up, he slid into the driver's seat. He looked one last time out the window to see a confused Megan pounding on the door. Behind her Tamara was kicking and screaming as Ben and Jason subdued her. Jax looked into Megan's eyes, mouthed, "I love you," and pounded his fist against his heart as he turned on the bus and drove off, needing to get away from the crowd.

There were nine minutes remaining, according to the cell phone device attached to the bomb. He pulled out his phone and set it on speaker as he called Joey, quickly explaining everything.

"Fuck man, get out of that bus!" Joey yelled back.

"I need to get it as far away from everyone as possible. Even then, it may not work, how the fuck do I stop it?"

"I can't figure that out without looking at it. I mean, what kind of bomb, the phone, is it the detonator or just a clock. You need off that bus, brother. Now! There's no place you can go with only five minutes. Not with all that traffic and the people in the area. You're fucked. Just get out."

"I need you to tell me how to stop it," he repeated as he drove west trying to get away from Madison Square Garden. The problem was the fucking arena was in the middle of the city. The traffic was unbearable and he was about to make shit a lot worse by driving a bus with a bomb into the middle of Manhattan instead of away from it. Joey was right, there was no place to go.

"I have an idea," he said, stopping the bus. "I need you to do your IT hacking magic and make sure any train running under the Garden stops."

"What are you going to do, man?"

"Just fucking do it. Five minutes!" he said, looking at the clock.

Abandoning the bus, Jax jumped out with the ticking bomb in his hand and ran inside, pushing pedestrians out of the way. "It's a cement dungeon. Lowest number of casualties will be down here. So long as there's no train—I don't know how powerful this homemade shit will be."

"Oh my god, you're fucking crazy," Joey yelled.

"What the hell else am I supposed to do?"

"Okay, fine," Joey said as Jax ran back to where he'd just been a few minutes ago. "Done!" Joey yelled. "All nearby trains halted."

When there were only forty-five seconds on the timer, Jax set the bomb in a corner and then ran back up as fast as he could, saying a prayer on the way up that the bitch's bomb-making skills were subpar.

"No!" Megan yelled from inside a car as the earth shook underneath her. She clawed out of Ben's grip trying to get out of the car, but he wouldn't let her go. "No!" she cried, a heart-wrenching sob escaping her lips. He was dead. He had a bomb in his hands, he had to have been dead, right?

No, it just couldn't be possible.

The police, firefighters, and ambulances started to arrive at the arena and people were forced to leave the area while they investigated the situation. There was some smoke but there hadn't been any great massive explosion as she suspected a bomb would make.

"I need to go see what's going on," Jason said. "But you need to stay here."

He called Nelly and Taylor over. "I promise you, Megan, if anyone can give you answers quickly it will be me, but if you don't stay here with Nelly and Taylor I can't leave. Promise me you'll stay here."

"I need to know wh-what . . ." And she dropped to the floor and began to cry.

"Then promise me you'll stay put."

"Megan, honey, breathe for us," Taylor said, as Megan took in a deep shaky breath and broke out in sobs. "Go. We've got her. Hurry back."

Jason went toward the arena to get answers. Megan felt as if she was going to throw up or faint or . . . she didn't even know. The hole in her heart was too big and she couldn't catch her breath. "In and out, Meg. In and out," Nelly said through her own sobs.

Wiping tears out of her eyes using the top of her shirt, Megan looked up and from afar she could see a figure pushing the paramedics out of the way. "Oh my god!" Megan yelled and set out in a sprint. "Jax! Jackson!" she said, running to him at full speed. Bracing himself for impact he caught her in his arms.

"You fucking crazy man!" she said, raining kisses on his face full of soot. "Are you okay?"

"No," he groaned and she slid down his body, taking a good look at him for the first time. He was full of scrapes and scratches, a deep laceration on his arm, and he was gripping his leg—his damaged leg. "But I'll live."

"Paramedic! Over here!" she yelled over his shoulder and two men came running with a stretcher.

"It's over, sweetheart."

"You saved me again, Jax," she said, helping him onto the gurney, her tears still flowing and her lips quivering. "Let's get you all fixed up so that I can kick your ass for giving me a heart attack. Don't you ever run into a building with a bomb again!"

"I promise I won't," he said, as the paramedics wheeled him to the ambulance. "That could be one of your five things I wouldn't normally do." He tried to laugh but gripped his ribs in discomfort.

Chapter 21

PRESENT DAY

"The Bahamas was the first thing," she said, ticking off with her fingers. "Then the planetarium, followed by our alien abduction sex."

"Three seems like enough, don't you think?" he said, smiling back at her.

"No. I don't think so." She held out five fingers. "Five things you wouldn't normally do. Not three. Five."

"Okay, so what do you have in mind? Because I have two ideas, but you have to be brave. How brave are you feeling, sweetheart?'

"With you by my side? The bravest."

"That's what I like to hear. Grab your purse."

"Where we going?"

"It's a surprise."

"Wait, what about Rambo?" she asked. Rambo, who was fully healed, was wagging his tail and looking up at them expectantly.

"I already told your parents. They'll be by this afternoon to pick him up."

It had been nearly three months since the New York incident, and only one tour date had been postponed as a result. Now that the tour was finished and Jackson was pretty much healed, they'd decided they needed an overdue vacation and proper chance to reconnect. But every time she would ask where he wanted to go, he would give her the runaround.

Now she was on a flight to Vegas, by the look of the images outside her window as the plane landed. "I only know of one reason you go to Vegas," she said cheekily. "To gamble."

"Woman, tonight you're marrying me."

"Is that a proposal?" she asked coyly, her hands on her waist. Her smile was huge and her cheeks pink.

"I'm not proposing." He took her hand and hailed a cab. While on the plane he'd booked a suite. "To the Bellagio, please," he told the driver. "Actually, no. I need a mall. A good mall, one that has a jewelry store."

"Jax," she said with the biggest smile on her face he'd ever seen. "You're nuts."

"I almost lost you, like, three times in the last few months. Hell, I lost you five years ago. I shouldn't have let you go then. I'm never letting you go again, Meg. We can have a big huge wedding once we get home, if that's what you want. But right now, I just want you to be my wife.

Will you do that for me? Will you be my wife, Megan?"

"I thought you weren't going to ask."

By the time the ring was purchased, somehow the paparazzi got wind that Megan was in Vegas, and they had to fend them off at the door to the chapel, and Jax was losing his cool. "Before we do this, you sure you're okay with this? With all of this?" Megan asked, pointing to the crowd of photographers outside.

"This is your dream, sweetheart. You're a fucking rock star. My woman's a rock star, and I couldn't be more proud."

"Thanks to you, I'm living my dream."

"Then I'll deal with the fame and the paparazzi."

Wearing ripped jeans and a red polka-dotted blouse and carrying a small bouquet of white roses, Megan walked down the carpeted aisle to Jax, who also wore jeans (not ripped) and a blue T-shirt that couldn't have been more appropriate had it been planned—with the words *Semper Fi* over his heart.

He held out his hand to her, the preacher said his part, and when it was time for the vows, Jax interrupted the preacher with his own words.

"I shouldn't have let you go five years ago. I was just a stupid kid. But Megan, I promise that I will never ever let you go again. Because you make me happy and I'll only do things that make me happy from now on."

With tears in her eyes she said, "Five years ago you made me promise you that I'd always sing. Because of you, I sing, Jackson. Five years ago, you made me promise to only do things that make happy. I always ask myself whether I'm happy, Jackson, and when I'm with you, I'm always happy. So I know that nothing is more right than becoming your wife."

Just as he was going to kiss his wife, the paparazzi burst through the chapel door and started clicking photos.

"Our first kiss went viral," he teased. "How do you think this will bode?"

She fisted his shirt and pulled him into her. "Honestly, I don't care."

He chuckled. "Then kiss me now, wife."

Epilogue

It was the home opening game of the Miami Marlins, and Jax was excited to be going with Megan. It was where they first met more than five years ago.

She was walking down the steps in shorts that were way too short, sneakers, and a Marlins jersey. He'd asked her to change before they left the house. In response she'd given him the finger and walked away.

His woman did not like to be told what to do.

Which made him smile.

It was a lesson, she told him time and time again, that she'd learned from him, from the four days they spent together, but it was always in her. She was always a lion, it's just that she'd been caged up for far too long and needed to be released. All he did was dangle the key her way during those four days. She walked out and she took charge all on her own. It had nothing to do with him.

Holding two beers and a huge tub of popcorn in his hands, he barely noticed who was sitting next to them.

"Surprise! "Happy birthday!" He put down the food and drinks and looked around. It was Joey, Annie, Nelly, and Taylor, all yelling and cheering.

"I bought the rest of the row," Megan said, getting on the tips of her toes and wrapping her arms around his neck and kissing him. "I never want you coming to this alone. You'll always have one or all of us. Happy birthday, honey."

He had a lump in his throat. She'd given him so much already. "Thank you, Meg," he whispered. Then went about saying hello to everyone. And when the moment of silence was called after the national anthem, he closed his eyes and thanked his mother and father who were clearly watching over him.

"Hey, look!" Nelly pointed at the jumbotron, and they were all front and center. Not hesitating one second, Jax pulled Megan to him, dipped her back, and laid a long inappropriate kiss on her—in front of everyone who was there to watch. He would never hesitate in kissing his wife. Not ever.

She was the reason he slept soundly every night.

During a lull in the game, Joey announced that ICS had an appointment on Monday with a new client, Rocco Monroe.

"Oh. My. God!" Nelly yelped. "The movie star?"

"*People* magazine's Sexiest Man Alive? Please let me come to that meeting!" Taylor clapped excitedly.

Annie shifted to the side. "Why didn't I know about this?"

"Just learned about it this morning," Joey said, and then turned his attention to Jax.

"He needs a bodyguard for an upcoming movie and wants a consult. It's a big deal. The studio's footing the bill."

"Jason could work it," Jax said, thinking of the men they had on payroll. They could always subcontract someone if they needed to.

"Yep. I thought of Jason too. But he's on that other job—"

Annie stood up from her chair with her hands on her waist, looking every shade of pissed off imaginable. "Hello? What about me?"

Joey laughed and turned back to Jax, who threw his hands up in a gesture that clearly said *leave me out of this*. He knew better than to get between the siblings.

"You think I can't secure a pretty boy like Rocco Monroe?" Annie's voice was hard, and Jax had to fight back a wince in sympathy. This was a fight his friend wasn't going to win.

"Annie . . ." Joey grunted.

Annie turned around, said a sudden good-bye to the girls, then grabbed her purse and turned back to Joey, her index finger pointed close to his face. If the jumbotron panned in on them now, they'd get a very different view than earlier. "Joey, you're an asshole. I'll be there Monday and I'm not letting you decide. I'm letting Rocco decide."

"He's not going to pick you, Annie. I'm sorry to be an asshole, but . . . he's just not."

"Wanna make a bet?" she hissed, her eyes glaring, as she stomped out of the ballpark.

Megan turned around and looked at them. "A hundred bucks Rocco picks Annie over any of the men on your team."

And that was the problem. With that body and that attitude, of course he'd pick her.

The problem was, what was he picking her to do?

Acknowledgments

First and foremost, I'd like to thank my betas, who read this book twice. So, thank you Heather, Leisha and my author BFF Scarlet.

Sarah Younger, my agent who really has made my dreams come true. It's unbelievable to me that this is our ninth book together! Nine books, lady! How did that even happen? Thank you for being you! And of course for introducing me to the lovely Lizzie Poteet. This was my first attempt at romantic suspense, your patience and hardcore amount of redlines was exactly what I needed and I feel like I've learned so much with this book. It's been a pleasure working with you and I hope this is the first of many to come. Also, the lovely team from SMP who came up with the beautiful cover.

Last but not least, my family. My parents, who help with the kids so I can spend my time juggling work, writing, and a family. To my kids who have learned to live with mom sitting on the couch and writing at every spare moment of the day. I love you guys so much…you'll never know. And finally, my husband. Who always supports and loves me no matter what crazy idea I have.

Who listens to my yapping about deadlines every single day over and over. Who somehow comes up with good ideas when I'm stuck and who truly takes over home life when I just don't have time to adult or parent. You truly are the best husband, partner, and best friend. I love you. 2016 was especially hard, but I know 2017 will be great. We got through it together and are stronger because of it.

And to all the bloggers and readers out there who read my books and then are wonderful enough to spread the word—without you there'd be no books and I wouldn't be doing what I love. Your support hasn't gone unnoticed. Thank you!! I wish I could hug each and every one of you.

XOXO

About the Author

Author photograph © Gabriel Escudero

USA Today bestselling author Sidney Halston lives her life with one simple rule: "Just Do It"—Nike. And that's exactly what she did. After working hard as an attorney, Sidney picked up a pen for the first time at thirty years old to begin her dream of writing. Having never written anything other than very exciting legal briefs, she found an outlet for her imaginative, romantic side and wrote *Seeing Red*. That first pen stroke sealed the deal, and she fell in love with writing. Sidney lives in South Florida with her husband and children. She loves her family above all else, and reading follows a close second. When she's not writing, you can find her reading and reading and reading. She's a reader first and a writer second.

When she's not writing or reading, her life is complete and utter chaos, trying to balance family life with work and writing (and reading). But she wouldn't have it any other way.